Plague of Equals

J. Oestreicher

&

D.R. Oestreicher

Omega Cat Press ≡ California

Omega Cat Press, independent publishing since 1990

Cover design by Jason P. Schumacher

Cover text by Samantha Oestreicher

Cover photograph by Joy Oestreicher

ISBN: 0-9631755-4-8
ISBN-13: 978-0-9631755-4-0

1 2 3

Dedication

Wednesday People and all the amateur scientists in our family.

But discord, the eternal plague of equals, had fired up a new war …
Justin's History of the World, Book XVI, Chapter III, 4th century C.E.

PRESS RELEASE

2 October

The Assembly has today decided to award

The Prize in Physiology or Medicine

jointly to

Michael Johnson, Angeline Moreno,

Dr. Liam Shaughnessy and Dr. Zaara Yassin

for their discovery of

"Acquired Immunoproficiency Syndrome (AIPS)"

1 ≡ MIKE

Mike closed his eyes, letting the water of the stream flow past his body, seeking balance. Balance the yin, the yang; peace, harmony, rain in balance with action, light, sunfire. The sun warmed his chest and shoulders, the water cooled his legs and feet. Simply by standing in the stream, he was changing the stream. And himself.

At peace, he waded to the shore and used a piece of his old blanket to dry himself off. He dressed and padded up the hill on a narrow winding path through the dense grove of keruing trees toward his tiny home. There was a disturbance in his garden, rustling, grunting, ripping among the vegetables.

"Agh! Bug out!!" he yelled. He switched to Vietnamese, "*Di di!*" When that also failed, he picked up a stick. Panic gripped him. He could feel the adrenaline threatening to take him over. Once again he was reminded: *balance is a gift*, and like life itself, especially the lives of those he loved, temporary and fleeting. He took a deep breath, exhaling slowly.

Then, waving his stick like a fearsome weapon, he chased his pig—and the chickens, they were in there too!—from the small patch of vegetables. *Damn pig smelled the ripe mustard greens, that's what. Knocked down the fence —and the chickens followed. Wish I had a roll of chicken wire.* He stopped

1

running and stood with his hands on his knees, breathing hard. *It would be so cool if I could get some chicken wire*. Villagers didn't use it; vendors didn't sell it. No chicken wire. *Well, there's work to be done.*

He straightened up, rubbing his back. He found the damaged fence section and propped it up in place to seal off the circular plot. *"Di di!"* he shouted as the brave pig peeked around a tall keruing tree and blinked at him. Without even thinking, he grabbed his KA-BAR knife from its calf sheath, and threw it in the direction of the errant pig. Satisfied with the rustling branches as the pig retreated, he retrieved the knife and cut an armful of fern canes to repair the fence.

Forty years. He was still repairing fences and trying to repair the wartime damage to this small patch of earth. Now his small patch of earth. He realized he was standing with an armload of ferns, staring at nothing. Eh. No time for spacing out. Got a fence to fix.

Since his ancient linebacker's body was no longer limber enough to lean over, he sat in the dirt to reweave the fence. He opened a space between two sticks and forced in a new green branch, snaking it behind one thin fence post and in front of the next until the fence was once again a large basket around the garden. His finger bled a bit, and sweat rolled down his cheeks, but he didn't complain. These repairs always took longer than he expected.

He admired his handiwork: vegetable garden finally secure. He leaned against his jeep, scavenged from when the Army left in 1975 and still running. He gave it a pat, tapping the muddy fender, and looked up at the sun.

From high in the sky, heat poured through the canopy hole made by his small clearing. His little house was set a bit apart from the nearest village; he was alone. The yard was a solar oven at midday. The ginger-colored Ha Giang chickens hid under the house, and the potbelly pig retreated into the undergrowth of ferns. He climbed the stairs to his house—a platform with woven walls like the garden fence, with a thatched roof—so different from the stucco and tiles of his childhood home back in Oakland, back in California.

His chair, four intersecting mahogany dragons, hand carved from a single log, owned one corner of his small home. He yawned and lowered his 300 pound body into the dragon's lair. Outside, he could hear the chatter of red-cheeked squirrels, and the dry breeze whispering through the walls. Sunlight seeped through the thin thatch above, forming bright lines that crisscrossed the wooden floor. He napped.

The sun had moved across the sky towards the western horizon, so when the woven door banged open, the room filled with sudden ruddy light. His old body sprang from the dragon chair, rolled across the floor and grabbed his M21. In prone position, shielded by a 50-pound sack of rice, he zeroed in on the door through the rifle scope.

The scope magnified Chi as she entered the hut. The sun made her hair appear longer and blacker. The shadows accentuated her high forehead and prominent cheekbones. *It's only Chi*! Even before he could get up, she clapped her hands and exclaimed in Vietnamese, "The war is over! It was over before my mother was born. You have no more battles to fight. Put away your gun!"

No, your mother was born during the war. She was a baby when the war ended.

He flipped the M21 safety on and cleared the chamber before sinking the butt into the floor and levering himself up. He replied, also in Vietnamese, "Really, the war never ended. Maybe there's no more napalm, but Agent Orange remains. It's in the water, in the food, and your family suffers from a little bit every day."

Chi just smiled with a nineteen-year-old's confidence. "Forget the war."

But he could not. He had also been nineteen when he shipped out to Nam, also full of confidence. Death had taken away too many of his friends, and pretty much all his confidence.

"All that gray in your black hair. You're too old to be jumping around and pointing guns. Someone could get hurt."

He handed her the rifle as a peace offering. She put it under a blanket behind the rice sack. She squatted down near the cold charcoal stove and waited. As if seeing her for the first time, he stared at his daughter. *You've grown into a beautiful young lady. If anything happened to you, I'd—*

She pointed to the open door. "Mai Linh and her family are here. It's time. We've walked here and the hospital is still far away. We want you to drive the rest of the way, okay?"

Mai Linh's baby. That got his attention. He had a mission. Pigs, fences, even war could wait. Agent Orange lingered. A baby was a rare and important event.

He grabbed his keys. "Is her whole family here? Never mind. I don't care. Load as many as you can into the jeep. The rest can wait here."

Chi hugged him. Her small arms barely reached around his waist. He picked her up and pointed her towards the door. "Get going, I'll light some incense and pray that the roads are okay."

In a few minutes, Mai Linh, her mother, brother Duong, and two aunts were in the back of the jeep. Chi jumped into the front next to him as he let the jeep roll downhill and popped the clutch to start the engine.

The old jeep coughed gray smoke. The gears growled as he downshifted to compensate for the worn brakes. He could hear whispered Hail Marys and the clicking of Buddhist prayer beads from the back seat. Prayers to cover all the bases.

With one hand on the wheel and the other on the gear shift, he guided the jeep over the rocks, sometimes driving, sometimes sliding in the dust. Chi's hand rested quietly on her knee as he furiously worked the gearshift lever. They were on their way to Da Lat and the nearest hospital.

Her small hand reminded him of another small hand. As the old jeep bounced down the familiar mountain path, his thoughts drifted back to a time over forty years before when the mountain exploded with unnatural fire and death.

He crouched down to camouflage his large frame in a perpetually dark forest of tall trees and short predators—snakes, spiders, VCs. Above the canopy, C123K propellers overwhelmed the jungle hum. He heard the rear doors clang open overhead. Heavy boxes crashed on the ramp. In a little while each ray of sunshine illuminated sparkling dust and his nose twitched with the sweet smell of Agent Orange as it gently descended from the passing aircraft. He thought to put on his gas mask, but only briefly. The sounds and smells were too close to waste time. Not again. His position had been targeted, accidentally, **again!**

With his machete in one hand and M21 sniper rifle in the other, he fought his way through the undergrowth. He used his football running instincts to weave through the foliage. Up ahead, a clearing, a village, his target appeared. He grabbed his PRC-25 handset, dialed the recon frequency and called, "Robin Hood, Robin Hood, Little John here, come in."

While he waited, he watched. Three children played tag with a frightened red chicken. A woman struggled to lift an iron pot over a fire. A baby cried.

"Robin Hood here; proceed, Little John."

He looked around again, thinking, God I can't bomb another village of women and children. Look at that shack. A pig, fire, a few chickens. They could be Aunt Josa's neighbors in Tracy. This could be my poor Aunt Josa's farm.

The C-123K called again. "Robin Hood here; proceed Little John!"

Why bomb these people? If we don't, who would even know? Who would even care?

Forget the mission. He decided how, then enacted his plan. "Little John here, target in sight."

He looked up the village on his recon map, called in the wrong coordinates.

A troop of monkeys screeched. That's right guys, scream. *"Danger, danger, all jive cats split, exit the scene! Those crazy Americans are going to bomb the trees again."*

Feeling better than he had in a long, long time, he headed back the way he had come. Soon he smelled kerosene and turned to watch the misdirected liquid fire raining harmlessly through the canopy. Satisfied with his subterfuge, he continued back until a scream stabbed his heart, a definitely non-monkey scream. He dropped his pack and sprinted toward the scream. When he reached a small clearing spotted with puddles of flaming jelly, he shouted, "No! No! No!"

A burning child stood frozen in the middle of the clearing, a flaming chicken under each arm. Fire licked around her feet, her arms, her hair. He tackled her, rolling her over and over, trying to put out the flames with his body and his will. Finally the flames subsided. He held her charred body and cried while the chickens flopped and squawked around them, until, finally, they stopped. She still breathed.

She glanced at him, eyes wide, as if trying to imagine what more this demon might have in store for her. He watched her eyes, the only unburned part, white and wet with tears. The eyes moved left and right, never resting. She sobbed some of the few Vietnamese words he knew. "Con tôi, con tôi"–My child, my child.

He was confused, but he held and rocked her, slowly recognizing the curves of a woman, not a child. A woman, a mother. Where was her child? When the sun finally disappeared into the western trees, he held a black corpse. Black, like me. *He slowly got up. He carried her back to the village whispering into her melted hair, "I'm sorry. I'll take care of your child. I promise. I promise I'll protect your child."*

He didn't realize it at that time, but his mission had changed utterly.

2 ≡ ANI

"Great day for a protest march, isn't it?" Constance called. "Even San Francisco has a sunny spring day now and then."

Ani nodded, but her "yes" came out more of a grunt as she struggled to get her bundle of signs down the stairs. SAVE INDIGENOUS CULTURES, and NO DRUG TESTING ON TRIBAL PEOPLES, the signs said in bright red and magenta inks.

She may have made too many signs, but as a poor student, she went wild when she received a small grant from Save Our Native Cultures. She justified this exuberance because she was the sole *rivereño* representing her Amazon family among all these *nortes*.

The SONC insignia, a brown thatched hut, was dutifully placed on the back of each sign. Her backpack, filled with SONC pamphlets and a bottle of water, slipped from her shoulder and tangled with the sign handles.

"Here, let me take some of those," Constance said, grabbing about half the stack that Ani was struggling with.

"Thanks. That's the trouble with a third floor flat: I always try to make just one trip up or down the stairs, and I always realize about halfway that I have tried to carry way too much stuff."

Constance tilted her head as if trying make out the meaning of her accented words, but finally grinned. "Yup. Been there, done that."

She never knew what to say to that bit of old American slang, though it was one of Connie's favorite expressions. So she just smiled as she shoved the entry door wide open, making space for her roommate to pass by out to the street.

The two made their way to what passed for the Quad of their tiny, new University. "Institute for the Study of Mankind," the old-style bronze lettering said on their main classroom building. "San Francisco Academy of Indigenous Studies," the new printed canvas banner said that hung from the portico of the administration building.

"Gregg's meeting us with his truck. I hope," Constance said, eyes scanning the narrow streets—more like driveways—that ran around the Quad.

"He's supposed to be here at 11:30 to pick us up, assuming he found some gas money. We'll meet the other marchers in front of City Hall and pass out signs there."

Ani nodded. She could feel her straight black hair bouncing in the sun. Maybe she should have given Gregg some of the grant money for gas. Too late now. "That should be plenty of time so we're ready to start at noon." She really wanted to obey all the rules with this march; if they could get permission to organize more protests, they'd begin to get some real attention on the issues.

Still holding the stack of signs, Connie gingerly sat down on one of the park benches that encircled the Quad area—a flat piece of grass with one lone bay tree in the center. The benches mostly faced outward, toward the little streets.

Ani leaned her signs against a concrete trash bin and flopped down on the bench beside her *norte* friend. She fished in her colorful native-woven backpack for her water. "They approved the march up Polk, across Golden Gate Park and down Larkin Street," she said, and took a swig of water, "but not that little block we wanted to take on Market to get to Hyde."

Connie's wry smile let her know she had again mangled the pronunciation of something. Her English was still not as perfect as she wanted it to be. Who would take a Peruvian *rivereño* girl seriously if she sounded like an uneducated hick? "Hick" was one word of American slang she felt confident to use.

"What?" she said.

"Larkin eh-Street," Connie said. "I love it."

She grimaced. Between her native Quechua and Spanish, she had acquired practically at birth some pronunciation habits that just weren't going away.

"But I understood you perfectly," Connie went on. "That takes us past City Hall and the U.S. Embassy and Federal offices. Is the piece up Hyde so important?"

Ani slid the elastic hair tie from her wrist, pulled her hair back into a pony tail. She nodded fiercely as she wrapped the band twice around the thick bundle. "Headquarters of Jericho Industries, who own BioTyne, who produce one of the drugs they've been testing on my people."

Connie's pale eyebrows went up. "Okay! That's a good target. I bet we can cut across on Grove and get to Hyde that way."

"It's not approved."

"What are they going to do, when 500 people show up and walk across one measly little block? Arrest us?"

She shrugged.

"Well, they won't. It's too much trouble. Especially if we've been good in every other way, which we have, getting permits, alerting traffic cops and the Academy about our plans. We'll be fine."

"Yah, I hope so." Admiring the flash of blue in Connie's eyes, she once again studied the contrast between the two of them: blonde and pale and fine-boned Connie, dark and dark and sturdy Ani. Connie's face was all soft curves; hers was angles and planes. Connie was considered pretty, but Ani was—the most kindly description she'd heard was that she was striking—a strange American word. She looked more like her ancient Inca ancestors than she did like some of her own brothers.

She thought of her family with a pang. Missing them was the biggest part of the price she had paid to get to the U.S. for her education. SONC had completely paid her way in dollars—tuition, air fares, housing—everything. Everything but a trip home. She had not seen her family once in the three and a half years she had been in North America.

A ratty blue pickup truck pulled up in front of them. "I can't shut it off," Gregg yelled, his long black hair blowing out the window. "The battery's dead."

The girls grabbed their signs, threw them in the back, and squeezed themselves and their gear into the cab.

The beginning of the march went as Connie had suggested it would: around the Civic Center, past the several Federal buildings, and down Larkin to Grove. Even the little connection on Grove over to Hyde that they didn't have permission to protest upon went smooth as silk. They'd split into two rough groups to minimize their numbers; she and Connie led the first group through, then Nero and his friends came through and rejoined them.

Ani wrinkled her nose as they passed a sewer grating and the inevitable stink of human waste rose up. She stepped carefully past soggy newspaper scraps which had stuck to the street like spongy dead leaves, then smiled as they passed a window box full of geraniums that bloomed fluorescent orange, nicely complementing the protest signs.

But things did not go so well as they marched, chanting, up Hyde Street into the shadows of taller buildings, to the Jericho headquarters. There they were met by a wall of counter-protestors, who carried signs and slogans in exact opposition to those that she had made.

"NO CURE, NO BABY," one sign said, with a picture of a limp dead infant in its mother's dark arms. "THIS COULD BE PREVENTED!!" another sign screamed, which carried a hideous picture of deformities caused by cutaneous leishmaniasis. She shuddered. The pictures were effective. But the people and their attitude made her angry, a deep slow-burning rage in her belly.

"Oh, it is so easy for you to say, 'go ahead, test on people far away from here!'" she shouted. "Do you think we are all stupid? Do you think it does not affect my people to have all these experiments done on them?"

"So instead you want them to get ugly and die!?!" a black man, wearing a brightly striped red and gold dashiki, yelled back in her face. "*You* don't care about *my* people! *You* don't care about finding a cure for this..." He thrust at her his sign with a picture of an African leper colony, "because *you* don't have this disease, eh?" He thrust his sign again, clipping her shoulder with the corner of the stiff cardboard.

"Ow!"

"Hey!" Gregg yelled, stepping between dashiki-man and Ani, and using his own "NO EXPERIMENTATION" sign as a sort of shield, he pressed his way on through the pro-drug testing group. "Follow me!" he called, "Go to the front of the building, show the bigwigs not everyone can be bought by their dirty money!"

Ani, Constance, and about a dozen others managed to push through the space Gregg made. More of the anti-testing group surged behind them, pressing back the pro-group until it split into two.

"Divide and conquer," Connie giggled, and waved her sign as Ani raised her voice to lead the chant.

"Leave native peoples alone!" she yelled, and her group picked it up.

"Leave native peoples alone!" It sounded good with 50 voices carrying the words on the air, then swelled even louder as more voices joined in and echoed against the tall buildings.

"Go back to the jungle and rot!" a pro-drug testing demonstrator yelled back, but it wasn't loud enough to carry to the others. There weren't as many of them as she had first thought. She waved the rest of her group forward. Chanting, they blocked the front entrance of the Jericho building.

A few frustrated people in business suits wedged by the protesters on the edges of the crowd, exiting the building. No one attempted to get in. She tapped Connie's wrist, asking for the time. Connie retrieved her phone so Ani could see the time. It was only 12:30! They could stay here for another fifteen minutes according to their permit. They might actually make the news, get their message across. She believed the American people were goodhearted. They would not approve of the use of native peoples as lab-rats, if they only knew how widespread the drug-testing practices were.

They did make the news, but not the way she wished.

In the moment she had looked at Connie's phone, something had changed amongst the pro-drug testing demonstrators. They went silent then began pushing individuals of her group away from the crowded area. They were rough about it. Then she saw a big raw-boned blonde girl punch Nero in the stomach. Nero, a slight Brazilian boy, disappeared from view. A tall curly-haired anglo man whacked Gregg over the head with his SAVE THE CHILDREN sign.

"Hey! No violence!" She screamed, but it was too late. The pro-drug protesters had turned into a mob. More of them boiled out of the Jericho headquarters, carrying more signs which were used as weapons, and fists and feet found unsuspecting targets.

Of course her group fought back in self-defense. In moments, it was a full-blown, bloody melee.

P+P BLOG POST

Pride and Prejudice (apologies to Jane) aka Lies, Damn Lies, and Statistics (apologies to whomever said it first)

A blog dedicated to odd stories about numbers

The Census Quiz

1. Why has a certain southwestern state moved up in the percentage of high school students graduating?

   A. Teacher incentive programs reduced the high school dropout rate
   B. Well-educated retired folks migrated in from snow country
   C. Uneducated youngsters emigrated to overseas construction

2. How did a large western state increase per capita income?

   A. Trade missions to Asia stimulated economic growth
   B. A declining birth rate allowed more adults to work full-time
   C. Uneducated youngsters emigrated to overseas construction

3. Why did a large central state experience an increase in people over 65?

   A. Their health care system delivered superior service to seniors
   B. A declining birthrate decreased the population under 65
   C. Uneducated youngsters emigrated to overseas construction

4. Why did household size decrease in a certain mid-western state?

   A. Increase in the availability of affordable housing units
   B. A declining birthrate
   C. Uneducated youngsters emigrated to overseas construction

5. What explains the decrease in households headed by a single mothers in a large eastern city?

   A. Faith-based programs reduced promiscuity and teen pregnancies
   B. Increases in teen miscarriages
   C. Uneducated youngsters emigrated to overseas construction

Answer A comes from the news and the others are from even less reliable Internet sources. And as usual, you are welcome to imagine for yourself which answer is most likely.

That explains everything, doesn't it? Or maybe not.

3 ≡ ELEANOR

The room was like all these sorts of rooms to Eleanor Powell. They blended together after all the years, neutral walls, neutral carpets, beige or gray cushions on the chairs, or blonde wood and no cushions in a few of them. Tables, podiums of wood or gray-painted metal. Metal water pitchers, too cold to drink, dewed with condensation. No more ashtrays though. Thank God, she thought. That was progress of a sort, as were closed-caption monitors at each podium, and the computers and large projection screens scattered about.

But real progress, cures for the killers, respiratory infections, diarrhoeal diseases, malaria, and tuberculosis, killers of children, were still elusive. She never forgot that.

She reached forward and slid her name card to the right edge of her podium. She wanted to be sure she could see the committee members, and that they could see her. If she could stop things at this preliminary hearing level, there would be no need for further battles with the World Health Organization, which like all U.N. groups really did seem to have the world's best interests at heart. They had just been misled in this instance; it was her job to set them straight.

The chairman of the committee, Monsieur Docteur Mercatur cleared his throat. "*Cette réunion va maintenant venir à l'ordre.*"

The murmur of translators was going to make it more difficult for her to hear, she realized. She turned up her earphone. She wasn't going to be able to read lips to comprehend what she couldn't hear—not if the chairman spoke French, and half the committee spoke Spanish or Portuguese, and the other half differing African dialects. She tapped ON the screen in front of her that provided closed captioning in English. It was always a few paragraphs behind, but at least she could clarify or confirm possible misunderstandings.

The chairman went on in French. The captions eventually caught up, "These meetings are for the purpose of considering proposals to restrict clinical drug trials among indigenous peoples." He set down the paper that he had read the statement from and looked around at each of the participants. "Our purpose here is twofold: to assess the degree to which drug testing and scientific research has been imposed upon indigenous groups against their wishes and perhaps without their knowledge, as well as to determine whether limiting such testing will ultimately have a beneficial or harmful effect upon such peoples." He took a sip of water, setting his glass down with deliberation. "We have invited a panel of physicians, scientists, researchers and other experts to testify, and we hope, clarify what our position on this delicate issue should be. Also to help formulate ethical guidelines or regulations, if any, that will be of the utmost benefit to all of the communities involved."

Only a little bit biased, she thought. *I can work with that.*

The chairman introduced the first speaker, a timid little German physician Eleanor had run into before at these sorts of hearings. The good Herr Doktor quoted reams of studies that demonstrated, in the most irritatingly boring manner possible, that in the long run the benefits of widespread drug testing programs resulted in overall improved health of indigenes—which is exactly what anyone with a gram of common sense knew would be the case.

Next Docteur Mercatur introduced a representative from SONC—Save

Our Native Cultures—one of the groups lobbying in favor of the proposed guideline revisions. This tall elegant black woman, Akinyi Boako, began her presentation by prompting her computer to generate a slide show that displayed on the several screens around the hearing room. Eleanor hid her smile at the incongruity of Boako dressed in tribal robes, jewelry, and headdress running the high-tech equipment that extolled tech-free village life. The colorful presentation featured many high-definition pictures of happy children in traditional costumes. But she stopped smiling when the African woman began to speak.

"Because these tests, and the administration of antibiotics, inoculations and prophylaxes of other sorts contravene—indeed, demolish—the teachings of our shamans, our medicine men and women, our tribal *waganga,* the entire World Health Organization programme of modern medical care is destroying the structure of village life. By usurping the traditional role of native healers, WHO and other well-meaning groups are destroying native cultures around the world!"

Oh, God, she thought, *Another tribal-elders-know-all fool!* "That's an absurd argument," she blurted out, but fortunately only a couple of nearby attendees heard her interruption. The African SONC lady buffaloed on.

Eleanor shook her head. Oh, I know you. You'd rather let your people die from endemic diseases than allow your culture to change one smidgeon. The supreme idiocy of it all was that these groups need only change just a tiny bit. Allow modern medical treatment for modern diseases. The shamans could still help their people within their belief system, with topical ointments, psychological support, communications with the gods. But these were fools and worse-than-fools who wanted to go back to nature, to the *pure* indigenous cultural state. How many of their people wanted to do that, anyway? Had anyone actually *asked* them? Or was it being decided *for* them by their more educated cousins who no longer even lived in those villages?

She believed profoundly that none of them really wanted to die just to live in some primitive state of yore.

At least she would speak next. She leaned forward, ready to make her counterattack.

After a brief break, she was introduced—doctor, philanthropist, ethicist, M.D., Ph.D. Even she was impatient by the time M. Mercatur was done.

She smiled as she spoke, "We must consider the ethical implications of allowing people to die who do not have to. Consider the misery of trying to live with the diseases, including AIDS, that would run rampant among their populations should all medical aid be stopped!" She took another deep breath. "I sympathize with the efforts to maintain a long and lovely cultural history. However..."

She paused and looked around at the entire committee, the groups of scientists poised to testify, the representatives of citizens who would be affected by these proposals. "However, if such idolatrous paganism actually worked to heal your citizens, these diseases would have been eradicated—utterly exterminated—long since. Instead they are still on the increase among your peoples, to the point that your nascent tourism industries are going to die in infancy because even the healthy visitors to your country can no longer avoid infections of all sorts. Unfortunately helminth and hanta are just as fatal to Christians as they are to pagans: of course people are scared to come near you!"

"A blessing," Ms. Boako murmured.

"NOT a blessing!" she shouted. "God above, are you really saying you would rather let your people DIE than admit your shaman cannot save them? *Would* you?" She glared at the young African woman, who did at least have the courage to meet her eyes, though she had no response.

She shook her head. "No shaman has the same skills as a medical doctor with years of training and research behind his or her prescriptions. And please be fair, here. We also have a long historical cultural and scientific background, one that can offer healing to your people." No one spoke.

She tapped the touchpad on her laptop, starting her own slide show. She put up a list of references. "These studies, showing increased life expectancy in villages that have permitted inoculations or clinical trials, are strong indicators of how effective these programs can be. Modern medical science is helping many to live. On the contrary, where such programs are blocked, we have this."

Her photos did not show happy tribal peoples dressed in traditional costumes. Her slides showed dead babies, sick children lying listlessly with flies crawling across their faces, beautiful young black-skinned women with horrid yellow pustules covering their arms and legs and necks, a pile of wasted bodies wearing tattered tee shirts and nothing else. "Is this your glorious shaman's demonstration of ability?" she said, her voice cold, controlled, and murderously angry now. A slide with a young boy, blood running from his ears, belly bulging, and his eyes pleading with the camera. "He could have been helped with a simple series of pills. He's dead now, because the village elders did not permit the drug testing which would have cured him and thousands like him."

A skinny girl wrapped in a filthy tribal robe, carrying a withered naked baby whose eyes seemed ready to pop from its face, its tiny hands just dry black skin over bone claws: "She and the baby would be fat and healthy today, if they had only received two simple inoculations—but they also are dead." She paused the slide show. "Where was the shaman, for them?" she asked. "Why did she not help them?"

She skipped ahead to show the village the way it had been ten years before. She had done her research. She knew those children. The SONC representative knew them too. Ms. Boako grew up in a neighboring village. The patterns of their baskets and fabric were almost identical, their language was the same. The two villages might have even shared the same shaman, at least at one time. The last slide showed abandoned, roofless huts, drifts of dry soil blown against the rocks of empty fire pits, tumbleweeds lodged against the poles of the barren cattle pens.

"This village is now dead," she said. "Where is the shaman? Where is the culture you are trying to save?"

4 ≡ LIAM

Liam scribbled on his datapad deriving the Gaussian distribution from an infinity of binomial distributions, a favorite distraction. Looking up from the orderly limits and integrals, he despaired of any good coming from this meeting. After his own department had turned him down for tenure, he could be certain the university committee was never going to reverse the decision. He should never have joined a liberal arts school in the first place. They weren't capable of understanding his research, so they reduced it to simplistic clichés and post-modern political correctness.

He despised being the nerdy mathematician, like an extra in a B sci-fi movie, but as hard as he analyzed his situation, he couldn't figure out how to fix it. *Something needs to change, but what*?

On his right sat Mei Li from math—the committee chair and the only faculty member who could do arithmetic without moving her fingers or her lips.

At the head of the redwood table, Dr. Lopez from gender studies, off topic as usual, droned on about her personal accomplishments as the first college graduate in her family, the need for diversity, and the importance of academic standards. She had received her Ph.D. from a university he never heard of. He still wondered if it maybe was an internet degree.

The short, bald guy from Chemistry or Physics, he could never remember the name, lost his tenure at a good school back east and wandered from one campus to another until he settled in Boulder. Across the table sat the lady from Dance, habitually dressed in a black leotard with a plunging neckline and the name Nureyev tattooed between her aging boobs. Liam really wasn't more of an oddball than this lot, was he?

He leaned back in his chair, eyes drifting past Lopez to the dark wooden bookcases behind her and finally to the narrow windows squeezed between the shelves of leather-bound books—now obsolete and covered with red dust. Through the windows, the snow-covered peaks of the Rockies reminded him of his grandfather's ranch in the Bitterroot Valley. He never forgave his mother for selling it to developers to divide into ranchettes—vacation homes for rich Californians.

Now here he was in the Faculty Library on the top floor of the Shaughnessy Administration Building, recently renamed in exchange for a sizable donation from his mother, money she received from those developers.

Fractional intellects, *1/n as n approaches infinity*, filled the remainder of the dark leather chairs. If the College of the Rocky Mountains couldn't put together a better a tenure review committee, he didn't want tenure anyway.

He set his datapad on the desk and counted ten shallow breaths. Frustrated from two hours of breaking down his research into simplistic nibbles for an ignorant and antagonistic committee, he tried ending this pointless meeting. He closed his datapad with a snap, signaling he was ready to go. In his most bored and condescending voice, he repeated for the third time, "If you don't require any more math tutoring, I have a plane to catch. You know the United Nations is paying my expenses to attend the WHO conference on population and development in Iquitos. I don't want to disappoint them."

Dr. Lopez, a tall woman with a thick salt and pepper braid—*probably failed high school algebra*—stood up. "You'll never get tenure with that attitude. Multi-culturally sensitive research demands more than just numbers. In your case, your paternalistic Eurocentric bias destroys your work, regardless of any potential value that might be buried in its quantitative foundation…"

He didn't hear the rest. *What a typical liberal arts attitude: more concerned about multi-cultural sensitivity than the reality of data.*

If the Economics department had just approved his tenure, he wouldn't be here. But, like this committee, the department had other priorities.

Dr. Lopez finished her little lecture.

He stared at her, unable to read her face. "I expected you to appreciate the significance of my research, especially the part about the importance of women—"

Dr. Mei Li from Mathematics took a deep breath and interrupted, "Let's not rehash the arguments again. You're an Assistant Professor of Statistics in the Economics department. I can vouch for the brilliance of your statistical work. Your findings on population decline and low birth rates make ground breaking use of cross-linking commercial and government databases. However, your career would be better served if you stuck to the numbers—avoiding speculation on history and sociology."

Forgetting his decision to cut his losses and leave, he stood up. At five foot, five and three-quarter inches, he never argued sitting down. "The five-thousand year population explosion driven by male dominance is coming to an end! Women are refusing to be baby factories and we are on our way to a better—"

The physics or chemistry professor jumped in. "You are totally unprepared to debate these subjects!" He'd hoped for support from the only other scientifically trained person in the room, but instead he heard, "You just epitomize the reclusive, anti-social nerd…"

He leaned towards the misguided science teacher. "Reclusive?! I'm speaking at a U.N. Conference! And my data is available in the cloud, and right now several researchers are confirming and extending my work. I'm far from reclusive!"

Dr. Li shook her head, just as his mother did when she scolded him, "Order please. Can we get back on topic?"

Liam, still standing, snapped back, "Look around you. Most of you are women and most of you have chosen not to have children."

The dance professor interrupted, "That's not what we're discussing!"

Dr. Li hit the table with her gavel. "Do I have a motion to adjourn?"

"So moved."

"Seconded."

"Meeting adjourned. Dr. Shaughnessy, don't you have a plane to catch?"

In a few seconds, as if a fire alarm had rung, the room emptied.

His numbers were good; he knew that without a doubt. He looked up at the recently installed painting of his mother hanging over the fireplace. "Why did I let you talk me into settling at a liberal arts college? At M.I.T. ideas mattered, I didn't need to think about attitudes."

"Are you talking to me?"

He spun around. "Mother? What the hell are you doing here?"

Alexandria Moore Shaughnessy wore a simple brown jersey dress, accented with gold—earrings, necklace, bracelets, and anklet. He was no arbiter of fashion, but he felt she looked ridiculous. She looked younger than the picture over the fireplace—and tougher. Honey blonde hair replaced the dignified silver gray. Her tanned, muscular calves and forearms belied the artist's vision of feminine elegance rendered in gentle curves and soft features.

She took a half-step towards him, placed her hand on her hip, and stopped—posed like a runway model. "I thought you'd be on your way to the airport already, but I'm glad I ran into you."

"My meeting ran late. I really have to run."

She moved into the doorway, blocking his exit. "I've been speaking to Valenzuela, you know—Dr. Lopez, and she tells me you've fucked things up again. You should to learn to get along with people. Don't think I'm going to save you again."

"I didn't ask you—"

"I'm also late." She shook her gold watch in his face, like the rabbit in *Alice*.

Then she was gone. As he shoved the heavy oak doors open, he wondered if he'd just imagined her.

5 ≡ MIKE

When the jeep carrying Chi and the pregnant Mai Linh and her family bounced off the dirt track onto the smooth asphalt highway, Mike's consciousness jerked back to the present world. They were close to Da Lat.

He needed to find his balance again, his peace. He needed to leave the memories behind—of wandering the mountains in a haze, sometimes marching towards the Americans, sometimes toward the village to find the orphan child. Eventually, he found himself alone, the Americans gone, the villagers moved on. Once he finally tracked the baby down, he stayed put, never venturing farther away from her than Da Lat. He knew Da Lat.

He stepped on the gas, silent until the jeep was parked on a slope behind the Da Lat Hospital. He and Duong carried Mai inside and placed her on a waiting gurney. They sat on folding bamboo chairs. Mike took out his knife and a piece of cam lai wood, whittling a pile of purple and white chips in his search for its hidden treasure.

Mai Linh's brother, just a year older than Chi, paced back and forth like a caged leopard. The two aunts waited outside and smoked their pipes. A nurse in a clean white dress with a Red Cross pin on her hat rolled the gurney away with Mai's mother following. When Chi got up, the nurse shook her head and said, "Only one allowed."

Chi frowned and sat back down. Staring straight ahead, she spoke softly, "Mai's been married three years and no children. One died before her belly got fat, and another was born too soon, too small." She sighed a near-silent sound. "We could see the tiny fingers and toes."

Mike leaned over and held her small hand. Duong paused his pacing, to stand next to her on the other side and put his hand on her shoulder. The boy seemed uncertain, touching a girl so close to his own age. Chi's breath caught in a sob, "This time she went to the missionary doctor, instead of the shaman, and she took the big pink pills every day. This is her biggest baby. Please let it be okay." Duong patted again, and Mike leaned forward.

He didn't want to talk about the baby any more. It felt like bad luck. He pointed to a big map of the central highlands that hung on the wall next to a picture of Ho Chi Minh and a Vietnamese flag. "When your grandmother was alive, those hills were filled with villages. Terraced farms grew rice, beans, yams and other vegetables. Now we have old people, dead villages."

Chi squeezed his hand tighter.

While Chi was listening, he wanted to say more. He began, "I remember — " but he could not say it, the whole story of the napalm and his promise. Instead he just cryptically added, "I promised your grandmother."

Silence reigned over the next hours, the aunts trudging inside the room and back out into the night for smokes, Duong sometimes joining them, sometimes Mike or Chi.

Then the nurse opened the door and stood in the most respectful *gassho* position with her palms pressed together at the middle of her chest.

Mike and Chi took shallow breaths, their chests seeming to rise and fall in unison. Duong ran to get the aunts. Outside, the empty road waited in the dawn light, the nearby gardens were still. Inside, the phones, the air-conditioner, and the clocks all waited. For the five people in the waiting room, time stopped.

The nurse bowed. "Baby boy. You can come in now."

Mike hugged Chi, swinging her around in circles until her feet hit the wall. Chi gasped, "Not so much, I can't breathe."

25

Duong and the two aunts only stopped hugging long enough to file through the small door. Once inside, everyone hugged Mai Linh's mother.

The baby coughed, small puffs of air, tiny spasms. Mai held the baby at her breast.

Mike tensed. *Something's wrong.*

Mai squeezed her breast. Milky fluid spilled between the baby's lips and his head jerked back. He coughed again.

Everyone talked at once, laughing, hugging. In the midst of all the noise and commotion, Mike froze. *Can't they see it?*

Mai Linh held the baby so his mouth touched her breast, encouraging him to taste the mother's milk. He coughed louder, loud enough to be heard above the happy commotion in the room.

Then the baby stopped coughing.

Mai Linh screamed. "He's not breathing!"

Mike reached over and gently patted the baby's back. He recognized the stillness, punctuated by brief spasms. The mother was right, her baby had stopped breathing. He withdrew his hand as if he'd touched a hot stove.

Everyone around the bed fell silent. Mai Linh's face was a mask of grief.

The nurse ran to the phone. The hospital PA announced, "Code Pink, third floor, neonatal."

Not yet, Mike vowed. *Not until I try.*

He reached out and took the baby from Mai Linh's trembling arms. His large mouth seemed to swallow the baby's head as he attempted to force air into the tiny lungs.

The body vibrated and jerked, hiccupped and spasmed, then got very quiet again. The mother's eyes filled with tears as she looked at the tiny form in anguish.

The nurse held the door as a doctor ran in immediately followed by a cart of equipment and two more people in hospital scrubs.

The doctor examined the baby. At first, she seemed to be in shock, murmuring, "Such a healthy baby. Such a healthy baby. How did he die like this, so soon? It is not possible."

Quickly she regain her composure and turned to Mai Linh , "I will need to do an autopsy. This does not make any sense."

Mike snapped back, "I goddamn KNOW it doesn't make any sense. DO what you like; I keep telling people it's Agent Orange. Maybe someday someone will listen to me."

Mai Linh just wept, quietly.

The body was cooling in Mike's arms; not knowing why, just feeling that it was right, he wrapped it in a blanket and placed it at Mai Linh's side.

Mai slumped, exhausted, barely breathing herself. The baby looked peaceful.

Another death.

The family stood in silent mourning as the chill of early morning crept into the empty spaces around them.

Finally, boiling inside, Mike threw his keys to Chi. "You take them home." He walked out, out into the shadows of the trees at the edge of the town, fists clenched.

Fuck standing in the stream. He had been standing in it for forty years, and nothing had changed. Nothing.

6 ≡ ANI

The flight on LAN Airlines was direct from San Francisco to Quito, landing in the Ecuadorian capitol airport at 10:00 A.M. But Ani was stuck in the airport until 5:00 P.M., when her flight to Iquitos was scheduled to depart. They were still having to close the Iquitos airport all day because of the vultures flying around the nearby dump and endangering the airplanes.

She grimaced as she lay across three form-fitting seats, trying to nap between echoing loudspeaker announcements about flights departing and arriving. Civilization had not been particularly good for her people. Iquitos, once a sleepy river trading town, had imported the problems of cities everywhere when it had become modern.

While she approved of putting trash into a garbage dump instead of throwing it into the river, town officials had only gotten part of the plan right. Failing to pay the price of a bulldozer meant the trash lay in heaps upon the ground instead of being buried. It was a big vulture dining room. Fortunately the huge birds were only active during the day—or perhaps it would have been better if they swarmed around the dump and the airport, all night as well as all day. Then the town government would have had to do something about it. As it was, they just closed the airport during daylight hours, and travelers had to arrange their schedules accordingly.

She bought an English-language newspaper, but instead of reading it, she tented it over head to make it dark, like the jungle sky. Then she grinned. The closed airport meant the vultures had won, though, didn't it? A victory for a native population! She drifted off to sleep.

She woke hours later when someone thumped the row of seats she was lying on hard enough to shake her backpack onto the floor. She sat up and yawned, glancing at the tall Anglo man who had just sat down three seats away from her. He ignored her, intent on setting up the computer he pulled from his beat-up leather briefcase. She stared at him a moment. He looked familiar, but she couldn't place him. Big guy. Curly light-brown hair, light skin, square jaw. She shook her head. Maybe he'd been on the earlier flight, or she'd seen him here at the Quito airport before she took her nap.

She reached into her backpack, noting that two of the seams were coming unraveled. Maybe she would buy a new one while she was home. She pulled out her water, and an American granola bar, thinking about her dwindling funds. She had used up most of the money she had saved from odd jobs, mostly teaching Spanish, to buy her ticket home. Her scholarship —assuming she still had one after the riot—would only pay for her flight home after her education was complete. Then she thought, *What if they not only stop my scholarship, but also kick me out of school*? That was too depressing to even imagine.

She sighed. She'd paid for this trip herself *and* she had to forgo her two-weeks-between-quarters paid internship when she decided to visit her family—double pain—more money out, less money in.

But it was necessary, she argued with herself. It was for family. But it also meant all the money she'd worked to earn in the past year was now gone. She'd intended to send it home, as she had the previous two years, but that wasn't going to happen now; instead she was sending herself home. She finished the granola bar, licking honey from her fingers.

She'd gotten a letter from her little brother Tomito. It took months to reach her, and had cost him two *soles* to mail. Their eldest brother, Marco, was working on a tourist riverboat. Paco—no she must call him Brother Gabriel now—had joined a Catholic monastery. Mañuel had built his own home next to their father's, and was working the yuca plantation. Carlo— who knew what Carlo was doing. He couldn't seem to stick with anything. But the others had either helped the family by contributing their earnings, or by leaving so they no longer required food and clothes from their parents.

Except little Tomito. His letter was charming, and in decent Spanish with not too many mistakes. His words brought tears to her eyes, even now, even here in this dry deserty air-conditioned building. Tomito learned some handicrafts from their aunt, and sold a few bits of jewelry and baskets to tourists who stopped along the river. The shaman had not been able to help him much with his club foot, so he had been thinking carefully about what he could do with his life. He had decided to become a teacher, since that did not require as much physical ability as farming or fishing or other normal *rivereño* activities, and he was good with little children. She nodded. It was a good plan. He was going to need help to go to the teacher's college, though. The application needed to be just right, and sent to the right people. Especially since Tomito would not be able to pay for his classes.

She wiped the tears from her cheeks. The BioTyne medicine they had given her mother was supposed to *cure* diseases. But it had made Tomito come out wrong when he was born. Carlo and the other boys had treated Tomito badly, as if it was his fault or a curse from the gods, until Angeline explained to them what had caused his problems. She was fierce in his defense, and even more fierce in stopping further drug tests. Or trying to.

She sighed again. Her family was doing well enough, she reasoned. *She* was not. She needed to go home. She needed to be in the jungle, to swim in the river, to breathe the air of her people. She needed to speak to the shaman. She needed to purify herself, reset her goals and her thinking.

That was why she spent the money to fly home now. Things would be better soon. She would be better. She would be better able to sense what to do to help her people.

Finally she boarded the small plane for the short flight over the Andes to Iquitos. She couldn't sleep any more, so she browsed through the newspaper. She was in such a travel stupor that she almost missed the pictures from the previous day's riot, until she recognized a picture of herself. *Good time to be going home.*

7 ≡ ELEANOR

Back home, Eleanor paced around her office that consisted of the entire second floor of her Sands Point, Long Island home. She stopped at each colonial-style, twelve-over-twelve window, and admired an acre of grass with a curved bluestone drive, a clay tennis court, and below the bluff, a rocky beach with a narrow band of white sand. Finally, she settled in her favorite Herman Miller desk chair overlooking the Long Island Sound. On a clear day she could see upstate New York, but not today.

Today her computer offered up an incident report from San Francisco, including photos, from one of the many private investigators she used to do her social research.

"Miss Angeline Moreno, a student at the San Francisco Academy of Indigenous Studies..." *those people*, Eleanor thought, *are already a thorn in my side. What now*? "...appears to be the ringleader of the anti-testing protest group," the report stated. "As directed, the pro-drug-test group had already formed a defensive line around the Jericho headquarters when the anti-group arrived." She nodded. *There's someone who can follow instructions.* "We were able to disrupt the march to the extent that Miss Moreno and several others of her group were arrested, and have since been placed on academic and/or scholarship-funding probation, and may be considered out of the picture for a while."

"Good," she said to her computer. "Mr. Kolnikoff, I believe I owe you an apology; you aren't quite the screw-up I was beginning to think." Not that she'd ever say any of that to his face.

She closed the folder, and was about to move on to the next report, when her brain processed the last line of the report. She clicked it open again.

"Miss Moreno purchased a ticket home to Iquitos, using her limited personal funds. She departs early today."

"Well, dammit, she's not out of the picture then, is she?"

She scrolled down to "Green Beret" in her contacts list. She didn't use real names for sensitive entries.

A rough voice answered, "Ryan here."

"Mr. Kolnikoff?" she checked.

"Of course," the voice at the other end responded.

"So you're answering your own phone again?"

"Oh?" he paused, "Oh yes, Claudia took today off to pick up a cat in Palm Springs." With no further explanation, he continued, "I trust you received my report?"

She had enough chit chat, "I need you to go to Iquitos…immediately."

"But— "

"Mr. Kolnikoff, I intend to pay you a bonus of $10,000 to take care of the inconvenience to your schedule. That should be more than sufficient."

A small silence. "Plus expenses?" a more polite voice asked.

She never worried about such details. "Oh, certainly. The plane ticket, your hotel and meals, ground transport and your daily fee as usual. The $10K is a bonus, Mr. Kolnikoff."

"You know, it's Ryan. Dr. Powell, my name is Ryan."

"Yes, I know, Mr. Kolnikoff." She smiled as she imagined his eye-rolling expression. "You are to keep an eye on this Miss Moreno, and attend a UN-sponsored conference in Iquitos. It's about population and development, not that you could miss something this big in a place that small.

"I particularly want the U.S. attendees kept happy, very happy, and all troublemakers kept far away from them, as behind a brick wall. You are my bricks, Mr. Kolnikoff. The conference begins tomorrow. I hope your passport and inoculations are up to date."

"Should be no problem. Claudia takes care of that stuff. Just email the details to her and she'll take care of everything."

She tried not to let her frustration get the better of her. "I need you to go right away, not after Claudia finishes her latest rescue mission."

"No problem. She's always connected. Her jet has internet and she can let the co-pilot fly while she takes care of this."

She never knew what to say where Claudia was involved. The woman was full of surprises and knew more people than God. *If she wasn't my half-sister, I'd think she was some by-blow of Howard Hughes. Crazy cat lady.*

8 ≡ LIAM

$\mathbf{D}$r. Liam Shaughnessy looked out over the delegates at the WHO Conference. As one of the keynote speakers, he would address everyone in the big tent before the conference broke into smaller working sessions at different hotels in town.

His eyes scanned the delegates seated in folding chairs and fanning themselves with bamboo fans hand-painted with jungle birds. He dug the toes of his shoes into the dirt floor to prevent his legs from swinging back and forth under the speakers' table. He ran his freckled hands though his curly red hair and wiped them on his new suit. He smiled, recalling the ignorant scorn of the tenure review committee. Today, under this tent on the banks of the Amazon, his credibility would be assured. The delegates of this conference would recognize the brilliance of his analysis and not waste their time on people's attitudes.

The Conference organizers took self-congratulatory turns at the podium, while his feet swung back and forth and stopped, and swung again. He imagined his mother sitting in the audience saying, "Yet another birth control failure," as each speaker finished. He protected his note cards from his sweaty palms by holding them with his finger tips. The colorful bird on his bamboo fan swooped back and forth in a futile attempt to fight the humidity and heat. Portable fans blew the air around, but did little to cool it.

He counted the house, twenty-five rows, average twenty seats in a row, more than half occupied, maybe 300 delegates. Most were the products of rape, coercion or birth control failures. Did any woman ever actually *want* to have a baby? Certainly his mother had taught him that she did not, her friends did not.

The first speaker rehashed the connection between economic progress and lowered birthrates. "Over half the world's countries have fertility rates under two." The audience applauded and even a few cheered.

If they like that, they'll love my talk. He checked his cards, neatly numbered one through twenty-three, barely listening to his introduction. "Doctorate from … Post-Doc with … Professor of Economics and Statistics… Please welcome."

Scattered polite applause and international chatter filled the hall as he walked to the podium. "Delegates, I want to thank the U.N. and the city of Iquitos…"

After the traditional opening joke, he jumped into the central thesis of his presentation, "My meta-analyses of population structures combined with longitudinal studies of individual public-health accounts have uncovered birthrates less than half the published numbers. Today I will show you that many northern-hemisphere cities would be on a path to extinction without southern-hemisphere immigration. I predict a significant improvement in living standards and civil rights as the northern-hemisphere indigenous urban populations crash."

He paused a moment to admire his cleverness referring to the populations of major cities as "indigenous," contrasting with the word's usual connotation of primitive and uneducated.

The audience got quiet, only the sound of the electric generators and fans remained, as he turned to the second PowerPoint.

"I am not a sociologist, or a psychologist, and certainly not a politician."

He paused again for the translators catch up, waiting for the gentle, early morning laughter. "The numbers tell part of the story. Decades of declining birth rates have depleted the high-fecundity cohort ages fifteen to thirty-five in cities like Berlin and Tokyo. This is a long-term trend."

He noticed that most delegates were older than his thirty-seven years— that dearth of twenties and thirties provided another validation of his analysis. Waiting again for the translators, he turned to card three, the one with "speak slowly" in large block letters across the top. "Most significantly, thanks to my algorithms to cross-link health accounts with individual financial transactions and government records, I've shown that native fertility rates are significantly below the reported levels."

Now came his most important slide: "Population Decline Fallacies, by Liam Shaughnessy, Ph.D., College of the Rocky Mountains, Boulder, Colorado, U.S.A."

He read each point. "Factors found to contribute to declining birth rates: birth control, contraception, abortion. Factors found not to contribute: marriage delays, financial insecurities, inadequate health care. Only one factor contributes to an *increasing* birth rate: immigration."

He diverged from his prepared notes to emphasize the point for this audience. "Nothing but a woman's right to choose controls birth rates."

Much of the audience cheered at this point. *That's more like it. If only Lopez was here and Mother too.*

He continued talking about meta-analysis, multivariate statistics, control variables, and the miracle of cross-linked databases, until the red light flashed. He flipped to card twenty-three. "Therefore, if there is a population crisis, it is a decline or crash: an implosion, not an explosion. We are heading toward the vision of Margaret Atwood, not Thomas Malthus. However, as the Black Plague demonstrated in the fourteenth century, this is a crisis that will benefit the survivors with improved living standards and civil rights."

After some polite applause, he took questions. A dark gentleman in an orange and black dashiki stepped up to the audience microphone. "Why hasn't this been reported anywhere else?"

In a replay of the meeting in the Shaughnessy Administration Building, he placed his hands on his hips and glanced up at the tent ceiling. He took a deep breath and looked at the audience. "Government bureaucrats take the easy way out and lump different groups together in their statistics, especially when the resulting analysis supports their preconceived conclusions."

He stepped out from behind the podium and spoke softly. "We shouldn't be too harsh with them. Privacy laws, coupled with highly mobile populations, make it difficult to track individuals. But, let me tell you what I discovered when I cross-linked government and commercial databases with individual medical records."

He paused to be sure the translators had caught up. "No one born in Osaka and living there all their life had a baby last December. What a surprise. Over ten million people live in Osaka, but every new mother was an immigrant. A recent immigrant."

Now he whispered. "The other months also revealed low birth rates. Berlin was very similar. So was Minneapolis. As I mentioned, privacy laws prevent me from sharing my raw data, but an anonymized data set is available online. I'm sure other researchers will reach the same conclusions with the data I have provided or with their own data."

"Is that just a fancy way to obfuscate that no one has corroborated your results?"

He was prepared for this comment and put up his last PowerPoint with the link to the data set.

He smiled. "You see? My research is open. But why hasn't everyone seen these trends? I'll tell you."

He assumed his professorial tone. "In some data sets two conflicting trends confound the analysis. Do you remember how the natural global cooling trend made it difficult for scientists to recognize global warming? Similarly, with population studies the rapid increase in life expectancies, almost too fast to be explained by medical science, hid the drop in fecundity or the live birth rate that I have finally uncovered."

A woman with a saffron sari and a red spot on her forehead walked up to the microphone. "What do you think is the cause of this alleged decline?"

He went back behind the podium. "The credit goes to the women. Tired of raising their children in a world of violence and poverty, they have obviously refused to be coerced into child bearing by the traditional means of marriage or rape."

She smiled wryly. "Do you really believe most children are born of coercion?"

He smiled back, "Don't you?"

A tall, thin man with an accent introduced himself, "I'm Dr. Shekhar Bhave, epidemiologist, CDC. Thank you for the interesting paper and also the link to your data set. I will certainly take a look at it."

The fans crackled as the hummingbirds, parrots and kingfishers struggled to cool down the audience. There were no more questions. He touched his fingertips together in front of his chest and bowed to the audience.

Aside from that one mild heckler, the presentation went well. He stopped at the registration table to buy three copies of the DVD—one for Lopez, one for Mother, and an extra.

Outside, he jumped into a waiting taxi like the one he'd grabbed that morning to get from his hostel to the conference—not really a taxi, a tricycle chimera consisting of the front half of a motorcycle and the back half of a rickshaw. This noisy little contraption fit well into the Iquitos street scene. Each driver seemed to embellish his vehicle with unique decorations and his name. Eduardo had wrapped every strut and panel in silver tape. The taxi was named *los sueños argentos*, silver dreams, he thought it meant.

He had a chance to think while the silver dreams bounced through the soccer field where the tent had been erected and out onto the street. It stopped in front of one of the small hostels in town. The U.N. only paid airfare and his budget couldn't afford the newest tourist hotels built for the booming ecotourism trade, so he stayed at the *Hostal Rivereños*.

The building from the colonial period combined Spanish influence and tropical necessity—wrought iron balconies and bamboo shutters. The internet said, "A decent, but basic, place," which evidently meant that the electricity worked most of the time. He stopped at the desk and pulled out his Spanish phrasebook. "Can you get me on a flight to Lima tomorrow morning?"

He had what he wanted from the conference.

With his DVDs in hand, he would have left immediately, except the airport closed after 9:00 AM to allow the vultures to use the airspace for their daily excursions to the town dump.

9 ≡ RYAN

"**R**yan Kolnikoff. Russian, eh?" the Peruvian immigration man at the small Iquitos airport said.

"No," Ryan said. "American." He smiled

At the kiosk behind him, another U.S. citizen who had been on his flight was passed through without questions. Ryan shook his head. Did he have a flag on his passport or something? Why him? He had taken special care to have no weapons or anything that could conceivably be utilized as a weapon on his person or in his carry-on gear. So was it just his name that bothered them? Or—

He scowled. Claudia had assured him that the proper registration procedures were followed and he shouldn't have any problem with his Glock, which was correctly in his checked baggage. In her understated way, Claudia reported that one of her buddies camped at the Peruvian Embassy while she called the Ambassador to check in on the ambassador's two Abyssinian cats and pull some strings to get the permits in record time.

Of course he had packed his weapon and ammo according to TSA rules. Everyone had promised, "In and out *no problemo*."

The official moved on to, "Purpose in Peru?"

"I'm attending a United Nations conference on population and development in Iquitos."

The guy nodded. "You have no return ticket booked."

Ah. That's the problem. Of course he had no idea how long his "purpose in Peru" was going to last, so he hadn't booked a return flight. He covered with the first story that came to mind. "I was hoping to add on a little vacation, some tourism after the conference."

The official's warm brown eyes smiled before his mouth did. "Ah."

"If that's okay," he said, unable to resist the dig.

"Of course. You are most welcome," the guy said, handing back his passport and two extra pieces of white paper. "Keep these forms with your passport until you depart Peru."

"Will do," he said, tugging his documents from the man's firm grip. He slid them into an inner pocket of his vest and Velcroed it shut as he strode to the baggage claim. He wasn't sure what he'd expected, but Iquitos had surprised him so far. Excellent English from the immigration official. And the airport itself—it might be in the middle of nowhere in the Amazon jungle, but it was clean, modern, and air-conditioned. *Guess I thought I was going into the wilds,* he thought, grinning to himself.

He found himself towering over the few native people who clustered around the baggage claim conveyor. The bedraggled American passengers were mostly sitting down or stretching out, since the bags had yet to make an appearance. He nodded at the Sacramento couple he'd sat beside on the flight. He didn't see the protest-march girl from San Francisco, which was good. She might have recognized him during that layover in Quito, but she hadn't said anything. If she saw him again here, she was pretty certain to get the idea he was following her.

Which he was, in a way. Was she going to the Iquitos conference, or would she go on to her home, a tiny village somewhere along the river?

He drifted toward the small vendors' kiosks on the other side of baggage claim, looking longingly at a café booth. He could go for a big cappuccino about now, assuming they offered those here. He grimaced. There was too much he didn't know about this place. He hadn't been able to do his usual careful research because of Eleanor's demand he get here *now*. She was one pushy old lady, but she also was paying his bills, and no private investigator could afford to pass up the bonus plus expenses the pushy old lady offered.

He'd been able to send Reneé enough to pay for braces for their youngest daughter Tina. Tina's complaint that her vast overbite made her look like a giant rabbit had been supplemented by the dentist's opinion that the badly misaligned teeth were going to start causing health problems. That had been enough to get her parents on the same page—about that issue, at least. He was glad he'd been able to do the right thing. Since the divorce, he'd felt constantly in the wrong—even though Reneé was the one who'd filed for divorce after she had found a new love of her life. He sighed.

Reneé was a good woman; he believed that deep in his heart. He also felt he was not the vile, careless s.o.b. she claimed he was. He was gone a lot for his job. She wanted a steady partner who was there to support her constantly. Reneé's new partner was a stay-at-home mom. That freed Reneé to finally finish her law degree. They wouldn't have much income until she finished and got a job.

So Eleanor's fat check was doubly satisfying for him. He now felt like a hero, at least in Tina's eyes.

A bell rang, bringing him back to the present and Iquitos. Bags from the Quito to Iquitos flight came up the ramp, tipping over onto the flat conveyor and swinging around the bay. Passengers pulled them off in twos and threes. He waited patiently for his to appear.

Though he kept his eyes open, he never saw the Moreno girl. Perhaps she had not checked any luggage. *Students travel light,* he remembered his oldest daughter telling him.

His two bags did not come out. Finally there was only one other person still waiting, and no other bags going around the empty conveyor to be claimed. The conveyor stopped.

Was he going to have trouble with his bags now, too?

Then abruptly things started up again, with the bell and beep announcing the arrival of four suitcases, his two, and the two belonging to the other guy, a slender black man dressed in a rumpled gray Nehru suit. He didn't remember seeing the guy on his flight, but there had been 133 passengers, according to the roster he'd managed a peek at when the stewardess had done a seat check to clear up someone's seating misadventure.

He grabbed his own bags with relief, unlocking the gun pouch and checking surreptitiously to be certain the Glock was there. All was as it should be: dark blue heavy-grade nylon, double-stitched pouches that still looked new even after half-dozen of the old lady's round-the-world errands. Another thing he'd been able to afford with Dr. Powell's bonus money: decent luggage, decent gun, decent gear. He was almost as well equipped as he'd been when he was in Special Forces.

He carried them through the customs area, was waved through without a search or second glance. Weird.

Outside, he stopped and got his coffee—no double capp, but a nice dark *café con leche* that tasted great. Still sipping, he made his way past the usual airport crowds to the doorway and open air.

It was 8:30 A.M., and outside it was about 80 degrees, with maybe 90% humidity. He stepped back inside the air-conditioned building to finish his coffee, surrounded by gesturing vendors.

"Taxi, señor?" and, "Es-special tours!" they called.

It looked like a pretty do-it-yourself kind of place; no lines, no special parking areas, just good old market economy tactics. He wasn't comfortable enough with his Spanish to try and negotiate, though. And if his researchers were correct, there were Quechua and Cocama speakers here, too.

"Do you speak English?" he asked one of the taxi people.

"Sí, my good English!" one smiling driver shouted.

"Sir! I speak English," another voice called, and he glanced in that direction. The guy looked like a little brown-skinned elf, with slightly pointed ears, a disheveled mop of thick brown hair, and smiling brown eyes. He was wearing a clean green cotton shirt with a collar, jeans and rubber flip-flops.

"Okay," Ryan said, nodding at him.

"I am called Roberto," the guy said, pushing past the others. "I will help with your bags." He picked one up, and Ryan grabbed the other as they eased their way past the remaining vendors and a sudden clump of citizens trying to get through the door all at once.

"You are going to the conference?" Roberto asked him, loading the suitcases into the back of a very small, very worn-looking miniature Saab. Noticing Ryan's attention to his vehicle, Roberto smiled. "I have automobile, not tricycle. Very nice, very rare!" He was obviously very proud.

Ryan grinned. It was impossible not to like these people. "Very nice," he agreed. "Yeah, I'm going to the conference, but first I need a hotel."

"Yes, my man. Which hotel?"

"Uh, I don't have one booked. Do you know anywhere there's a room available?"

Roberto's smile faltered. "Ah, is very, very, difficult."

Ryan reached into his cash pocket where he kept a small amount of small bills handy. He pulled out a nice ten *soles* note.

"No, no," Roberto waved his hands, refusing the money. "There *is* no rooms," he said.

"Ugh, well I couldn't book one before I left, but I hoped when I got here, there might be something. A cancellation, maybe."

Roberto shook his head. They stood on either side of the small dusty white car and stared at each other.

"What about youth hostels, or like, the Y.M.C.A.?"

Roberto flashed a quick grin, but shook his head again. "All full."

He leaned against the roof of the car. "Okay. What am I going to do. Um. Anyplace to camp out? In a tent?" He could buy one, maybe, if he could find a place to pitch it.

Roberto scratched his nose. "Maybe I can make arrangement. So, the cousin of my sister's husband, she sometimes have guest in room?"

"Okay. Like in her house?"

"Yes, in her house. Yes. In the room for guest." He had a little trouble pronouncing "guest," but in general his English was excellent. This relative's guest room was probably okay.

He nodded. "That could work. How much would she want?"

Roberto tilted his head. "She make cook *desayuno*, breakfast. She make the café," he nodded his chin at Ryan's empty cup.

"Sounds good."

"How long?" Roberto asked, pulling a cell phone out of his jeans pocket. "How many days? I call her."

The conference is scheduled for today, tomorrow and the following day, he thought. Plus a day to figure out if I'm done and book a flight home, or move on to Eleanor's next errand. "Say a week," he said, holding up seven fingers. He braved, "*Una semana, siete días.*"

Roberto nodded, pressing a button, then began a rapid conversation in a language that was not Spanish.

Despite all the delays, he made the conference in time for the end of the first speaker's presentation, and all of Dr. Shaughnessy's talk on population decline. He wanted to ask the little Irish guy if he believed in leprechauns after hearing the seemingly far-fetched conclusions—but Shaughnessy was supposed to be the expert, so Ryan just shrugged and listened.

He sat through one more talk before the break for lunch. The other delegates had signed up sufficiently in advance to be included in the Conference-sponsored luncheon, but Ryan had to find his own meal. He left the stuffy canvas tent for the outdoors. The large meeting space had been set up on a rather ungroomed soccer field—fútbol, here—he remembered, so he had to walk quite a ways to the taxi area. As he had hoped, Roberto was there, leaning against his little Saab, chatting with other taxi drivers, most of whom had the tricycles with lawnmower engines that were much more common than cars.

"Lunch, my man?" Roberto called as soon as he saw Ryan.

"Sounds good. And someplace where this will work for international calls," he held up the calling card he had purchased at the Quito airport. They claimed it was going to work "all over South America," so it was time for him to let Dr. Powell know what was up.

He did his best to explain. "Well...he believes all women are victims of rape, marriage means nothing to him, and babies are all accidents." He wasn't sure what to say next. "Have you ever heard of this guy?"

It sounded like Dr. Powell snorted. "Not all the U.N. Conferences are vetted that carefully, and this one is particularly small," her voice came crackling back. "I imagine his numbers are good, but his conclusions don't sound completely in line with current thinking."

He nodded into the phone. "Is there the slightest chance this guy could be right?"

"What, that men have been impregnating women against their wishes for millennia?"

"Uh— "

"Or that most babies are unwanted?"

He didn't say anything.

"Or that life's going to be better now that there seem to be fewer of us?"

"Yeah, I guess."

"I've always believed that life is better now that there is decent medical care for those of us that accept it, and that most folks haven't a clue what's good for them, no matter how many of them there are."

He stared up at the blue, blue sky. Fluffy clouds scudded by directly overhead, but everywhere else was clear. "No jet contrails," he said. "That's where I am."

The pushy old lady actually laughed out loud. "Yes, it's rather charming down there, isn't it?"

"Definitely not big-city. I'm staying with my taxi driver's sister's husband's cousin, or something like that," he announced, trying to be friendly.

"Oh, I didn't know you knew anyone there."

"I don't."

Dr. Powell laughed again. "Well, I hope you don't get dysentery."

"Thanks."

"Check in again tomorrow. About this time would be good," she said. "Or sooner, if you see any familiar faces."

"Will do," he said, and disconnected.

P+P BLOG POST

Pride and Prejudice (apologies to Jane) aka Lies, Damn Lies, and Statistics (apologies to whomever said it first)—A blog dedicated to odd stories about numbers

AIDS in Africa - Fact and Fancy

This post selects four different statistics from Africa. In each case a government organization or an NGO issued a fancy statement with references to the AIDS Epidemic. Email in your own alternate statement and I'll post the best ones in a few weeks.

1. FACT: In the last decade the number of orphans in a certain country in southern Africa has fallen by 1.2 million.

FANCY: The AIDS Board reported that their successful AIDS prevention program, through education and the distribution of condoms, has conquered the problem of AIDS orphans. Fewer children were orphaned when their parents died of AIDS. Birth control has allowed couples to delay their own children in favor of adoption. The happy result is a shortage of adoptable children.

2. FACT: The number of villages within an east African country's national reserves has declined 57% in the last decade.

FANCY: An international conservation fund has supported an innovative program to educate villagers living within the national reserves. This program encouraged villagers to pursue educational and career opportunities in the wider global community. Many individuals have gone on to university studies at the fine schools locally and internationally. These students have subsequently settled outside the reserves, many bringing their families with them. This has reduced the human population pressures in reserves.

3. FACT: A different south African county's teacher corps, which started in 1998 with a single itinerant teacher assigned to each locality, now has a full-time teacher assigned to each school.

FANCY: The teacher corps was chartered to educate young children about AIDS. The message of prevention through abstinence has reduced the incidence of early pregnancies, increasing the pool of graduates available to teach. Driven by happy memories of their teachers, many high school students sign up to teach when they graduate.

4. FACT: The most recent infrared satellite census of hunter-gatherer bands in

sub-Saharan Africa shows a decline of 61% in the last decade.

FANCY: A well-funded NGO reports that the effort by AIDS groups to contact every person in sub-Saharan Africa has increased contact between remote nomadic tribes and the outside world. Through this exposure to external diseases and cultures, these tribes are being decimated in a way reminiscent of the Spanish conquest of the new world in the sixteenth century. If these well-meaning contacts are not stopped, these tribes will be extinct within the next ten years.

That explains everything, doesn't it? Or maybe not?

10 ≡ ANI

The tiny Rio Nanay *peque peque* headed into the dock below Ani's village at Nanay Libre. The little water taxi cut its motor and drifted the rest of the way in. She could see her own family dock a little further downstream, but the taxi would not stop there. The wood of the Moreno family dock was new, Papa had to remake it almost every flood season. The village stairs were older, covered in moss and slippery. She climbed up the dozen steep stairs above the floating dock, and onto the muddy bank. She breathed deeply as she climbed, her lungs not accustomed to the warm wetness of the air. San Francisco had a small measure of dampness, but it was never warm and damp at the same time.

She smiled, remembering Constance's bemusement when she had first arrived in California. "It's so cold," she had said, when she wasn't complaining about how dry it was.

"Welcome to California," Connie had said. "It's a desert. This is what passes for rain here," she'd waved her hand at the pale fog of the Golden Gate city, "most of the time." She'd smiled her impish smile, and Ani had made her first friend.

"Well, look at me," she said to herself now—in English—as she turned up river along the path. "I'm not even back home yet, and I'm already missing my *norte* friends and weather. *Ay de mí.*"

The path she traveled was barely damp. It was March, the wet season, but the heavy rains and river water hadn't come up as high as it would later. She had to walk west along the bank to get home. It was pleasant, still early in the day and not so hot, yet. A kingfisher swooped over her head on its way to the river and a late breakfast.

She admired the greenery, renewing her enjoyment of all the growing things. Fat pale bananas hung down from one tree; another had no fruit or flowers. A stand of wild cane separated a field of manioc, or yuca, from someone's beans which had been spread out to dry. Wild rice filled in the spaces between a huge breadfruit tree and a row of cornstalks that still had a few late ears waiting to be picked. Chickens scratched in the shade of the corn plants, or roosted among the sheaves of rice.

As she passed the little elementary school, she saw some of the children kicking a *fútbol* across their playing field. The ball went wild, lodging itself amongst the strands of a pink-flowered vine she had never learned the name of. The ball was only visible by virtue of its black and white pattern. A little boy trotted toward the ball. He waved at her, and she waved back. There did not seem to be many children at school today.

She slid the elastic hair tie down off her pony tail and onto her wrist, and finger-combed her hair so it lay across her shoulders, long and shining, the way her mother liked to see it. Soon enough, she was home.

She paused to admire her brother Mañuel's new house, set back from the river another ten or so meters from her parents' house, and up another half-meter on taller stilts to avoid floods like the one that had washed through Papa's house a dozen years ago. Everything on Mamí's floor had been swept away. Extra wood for the fire, piñas, some pots and pans that had been in use, so weren't hung up high on the wall—all of it was washed out by the flood waters, which dropped back to normal within hours.

For days afterwards Ani and Toqui had found things out in the cane field behind Mamí's house—all the way back to Ica's house and the forest beyond they had found her mother's things. They made a game of it, in ten-year-old fashion, finding pots in banana palms, rotten piñas washed back among the plants they had been cut from. Toqui had found a fork stuck into the side of a gourd that was still growing, attached to a piece of torn vine. They never found Mamí's favorite spoon, though. Years later. Tomito had carved another one, she still missed it so.

Before her, she could see Mañuel had put all of his considerable skill into weaving the palm fronds for the roof; it looked very good. He had bought some sawn lumber for the bedroom walls, she noticed. More and more families were getting the nicer flat cut boards, because it was a very great deal of work to find, trim and weave enough of the traditional narrow branches into a wall, though those did let more of a breeze blow through, welcome on hotter nights.

Tipa, Mañuel's wife, apparently noticed her standing there staring, and stepped into the open-sided kitchen area where Ani could see her. She called something Ani couldn't make out.

Ani waved. "It's Angeline from *el norte*," she yelled, and stepped over the pile of cane scraps by the hand cane press to come closer to where Tipa stood.

"Angeline?" Tipa cried. She lifted a towel to wipe her eyes and look again. "Ani?"

They both laughed and ran toward each other, Tipa hopping from the ramp to her kitchen down to the ground, Ani avoiding chickens and ducks that scattered, clucking and quacking. They met and hugged, then stepped back and looked at each other.

"I did not know you were coming!" Tipa cried, laughing, and hugged her again.

"I am here," she said. "Just for a two weeks, then I must go back to finish my school, but I needed to come home, Tipa. I needed to see all of you!"

It was so good to speak Quechua with someone who had no accent. She was teaching a class in the northern Quechua dialect at the Academy, and the few other Quechua speakers attending had been intrigued at how different it sounded than the more widespread southern dialect.

Tipa, of course, spoke the same way she did, and it was a lovely sound in her ears.

53

Midday meal was the biggest among all the *rivereño* families. You ate lightly at breakfast, stuffed yourself at midday, and ate lightly again in the evening or just before going to sleep. She hung up her sandals and backpack and helped cook and serve.

Mamí made one of Ani's old favorites, a river fish doused in sauce and herbs and wrapped in leaves to bake over the charcoal fire. They also had some nice spicy salsa to put over it and on the manioc and fava beans that had been steamed with enough chiles to make her eyes water. Papa got out a bottle of *cachaça*—cane rum. He passed the bottle around the circle of family seated on the floor, and each one took a sip, even Tomito, who was much bigger than the *little brother* she always thought him. Tomi was a child no longer and Mañuel had passed the bottle directly to him, bypassing Tipa who sat between them.

Paco was missing, of course—Brother Gabriel was at the mission learning to be a monk. But Mañuel and Tipa and their little daughter Chaya had joined them, and Carlo and Tomito were there. Marcos was away on another riverboat trip, babysitting tourists on the Amazon, but due to return in a day or so.

"If he doesn't go to Nauta to see his lady," Papa said with a wink.

"He is getting married!" Mamí said, eyes flashing.

"Oh ay, and what fine day will that be?" Carlo said, rolling his eyes. "He is never going to marry her when he can get what he wants for nothing!"

"Carlo!" Mamí said with a scowl.

Mañuel reached across the table and thumped Carlo's knuckles with the wooden serving spoon. "Be nice. This is a celebration!"

Something in his tone made them all look at him. It seemed he meant something more than her visit. Mañuel poked Tipa in the ribs, and she blushed and looked at Chaya instead of at the rest of the family who were all staring at her now.

"Aha!" Papa said. "After so long, a baby brother or sister for Chaya!

Mañuel said, "The *jengibre* worked."

Papa laughed, "Ginger rum always works, but that must be her last rum for a while."

Tipa nodded, and Mañuel raised his chin, a proud look in his eye.

They all laughed and clapped, and Papa sent the bottle of *cachaça* around again. This time everyone watched Tipa to be sure she didn't have any.

Mamí looked very happy surrounded by her family.

The peace lasted through the meal and the clearing of the dishes and food. Tomito went to help at the school. Mañuel went out to his fields to cut some cane. Papa sat in the kitchen breezeway, dangling his feet over the side, and patted the space next to him with an expectant look at her. She handed the dish she had just washed to Tipa to dry, then stepped silently over to her Papa and sat down.

"You know we are proud of you," Papa said. "But we miss our only daughter who is gone so long she is a stranger to her family."

"I know, Papa. I have missed all of you so much."

"So tell me some things you have learned in this far away place."

She was beginning to think of herself as Angeline again, now that she was home where people could pronounce her name without making her wince. She spoke about the politics and academics and languages and economic issues that all seemed to knot-weave native peoples into nets and nooses, even here, so far away from all that First World busy-ness. "Even something so simple as allowing our shaman to practice our kind of medicine, instead of being forced to take their kind of medicine, even that is complicated."

Papa shrugged. "How is it complicated to say, 'No, we will use our shaman's help only'?"

"The *norte* medicine is very strong. They believe it can cure things even the shaman cannot cure, so people want to try it. Should someone stop them? And, you know, Mañuel has bought the sawn boards for his house walls, Papa, and why should he not?"

Papa was nodding. Mamí called from the kitchen. "He bought them with those *soles* you sent last winter, when we got my fine pot!" she laughed and thumped the round cast-iron pot with the flat of her hand, so it rang like a dull bell.

"So, it is quicker to buy the sawn wood, and Mani does not need to fight with the snakes to find nice liana or straight branches to make into walls, and he has time to spend catching more fish for Tipa and Chaya," Papa said.

"Oh, that is a fine and holy goal," Carlo's voice drifted to them from out in the yard, where he had taken off his shirt, and was sprawled in the shade of a ceiba tree. "Catch more fish." His laughter was harsh, like his voice. "He could have used the money to buy a boat, with a motor. He could be getting paid big tips to bring tourists to the Preserve, instead of living in this dump and scratching in the mud."

"Carlo is still bitter that the gods have not handed him a nicer life," Papa said. "He still thinks it is stupid to work hard, or to do anything in the old ways."

"That's right," Carlo said, insensitive to Papa's sarcastic tone. "It *is* stupid."

Or maybe he just doesn't care what Papa thinks, Angeline thought.

"Do you realize how the tourists laugh at us, living in the mud just like our grandfathers and their grandfathers? You've been to Iquitos, Papa, but you haven't been to Lima, like Angeline has. You haven't been to Los Angeles, or San Francisco—real cities, where they have glass in all the windows, and elevators, and soft silky rugs on their floors instead of splinter boards. It's so much cleaner and richer and better you could hardly believe it. Right, Ani?"

"It may be cleaner and richer in some ways, but it is NOT better, Carlo. It's just different."

Her brother sat up. She could see the muscles in his arms move as he tensed up, stretched, and rubbed his face. "So you say. I know better."

"You do not know better, Carlo. How could you? You have not been beyond Iquitos, either, and everything you imagine in your head is not necessarily true."

"Oh, and what is so wrong in the San Francisco *you have* been to, then,

56

little sister?"

"The air stinks from all the engines that run their cars. Their cars are too big, and they jam up all their roads. Every morning, every night. They hate this, and complain, but they do it over and over again, and do nothing to fix it. The buildings are so tall they block the sun, and the streets of the city are dirty and darker than any jungle path you have ever walked even at night in the rain. Their people beg on the streets, because most of them do NOT have the money to live in those fancy places you imagine are so fine. Just a few people do, and even they are not happy.

"And the people are not well! Many are sick, coughing and pale, and the ones who do not have body sickness have the mind sickness so they are crazy. They take guns into their schools and kill little children! You cannot imagine," she said, and felt tears flood her eyes and stream down her cheeks while she grabbed for her father's strong brown hand. "You cannot even imagine."

"You have been visiting the wrong places, then," Carlo said. "That is not how it is in films and photographs. That is not how it is in books and magazines."

"Those are not the truth, Carlo! Those are the best of the places, they do not show the worst!"

"Oh, they have worse things than the floating shantytowns? Than pissing in the same water you take a bath in?"

"Iquitos is washed clean every year by the floods! Nothing washes the slums clean in Richmond. Nothing makes the Mission district smell less like a sewer. I tell you, you cannot imagine, Carlo. You cannot!"

"You know, they feel so sorry for us, they are coming again to give us medicine, and make our schools cleaner, and help our families be clean and healthy and strong!"

"No!" she said, and looked over her shoulder at Mamí.

Her mother nodded. "Even our shaman has agreed. They did this medical thing, giving shots in Libertad village, and saved two babies that were sick, and helped even the shaman to see better, so we want them to do it here, too."

"No, mama. That's what they said before, and Tomito… "

"It was a mistake, with Tomito. No one knew I was pregnant, not even me. If they had known, Angeline, they would never… "

"That's what they always say! If only we had known! And what will it be this time? Will they know Tipa is pregnant? What will they do to *her* baby? They think they know so much, but they make mistakes all the time! And then they don't help fix what they wreck. What the shaman did for Tomito was much more than any of the stupid *norte* doctors could ever do for him. All they did was promise! Now you are going to trust their promises again?"

"It's too late, little Ani," Carlo said. "They have already begun giving the medicine. You are too late to stop it." He laughed, stood up and put on his shirt.

She jumped down to the ground and stalked out to where Carlo stood in the sun.

"I am sorry you think you have been cheated, Carlo. But I am even more sorry that Mamí and the shaman and the elders have agreed to this drug plan."

Carlo eyed her sideways. "It is not even regular medicine," he said in a low voice. "It is more of that testing kind of drugs from those CUI people, where they are not all certain it works. Supposedly it is to cure river-blindness and some other things."

"No! Oh, I can't believe the villagers can be so stupid!"

Carlo quirked his lips into a sort of sneer. "Yes, I know you can't. It is a peculiar kind of blindness you have."

She bit her lip. Maybe she should go back to Iquitos where the CUI offices were. They used to store the medicines there, she had seen them. If she could not convince the health officials at the CUI office to stop the tests on her people, then—well, she would think of something. Dump the stuff into the river, maybe.

"You always did see the worst about modern things, An-jell-EYE-n," he said, giving her name the ugly *norte* twist. "But somehow you don't see the worst about our mud-people culture at all, do you?"

She just shook her head at him. "You don't understand."

"No, I don't. But why would I, when I have not been where you have been, eh? You have a choice. You go off to the fantasy land, and come back and tell us we don't want that, oh, no. That is easy for you to say, little sister. You say, oh, you must stay and rot in the mud because what they have in other places is no better. I say you lie, Angeline! You do not know what is best for us! You do not know what is best for me, at all."

Behind her she could hear Papa growl, a mutter of disgust low in his throat. "*Tukuy suwan, llapanmi suwa nin,*" he said. A thief thinks that everyone else is also a thief.

"Like how you spend your money," Carlo went on. "You make sure Tomito gets more than his share, but Carlo gets none, eh? Because when you sent money, I had a job and you said I didn't need it. And now I have no job and you send no money, just yourself, so I get left out again. Though I have figured out a way to fix that."

"What are you talking about?"

"I am going to make my own money."

Carlo had had grandiose plans before, and yet, here he was back at home and as penniless as ever. Irritated with his persistent selfishness, she made a face at him.

"A lot of money, from your nice *norte* friends."

"Oh, certainly."

"I can steal a person from this conference, and hold him for ransom," he said. He looked at her then rolled his head back and looked at the sky. "I cannot imagine why I would help you. But. I might be able to get the drug tests stopped the same way," Carlo said.

"What?" It felt like her brain was frozen.

"But I will not share any of the money with you, because you have not shared any of your money with me." He nodded, confirming that part of his plan to himself.

"You're kidnapping someone?"

"You got it, chiquita."

"That's crazy talk." She could not believe how twisted Carlo's thinking had gotten.

"Of course you would think so, but you really have no idea how lost these tourists can get. They will pay to get back to civilization. They will pay a lot. And I will keep the money."

"You couldn't kidnap a hungry dog, much less a person who was actually worth money!"

He nodded again, "Oh, I can and I will. And I will not share with Mamí and Papa, because they haven't shared with me, of course," Carlo said. "And none to Tomito, I think, because little Tomi has already gotten plenty. Even Mañuel has, because he's such a fine butt-biter," Carlo said.

"Butt—?" then she realized what Carlo was trying to say. "You can't even *say* that in Quechua, Carlito! Doesn't that tell you something? You have to use English to say: 'ass-kisser!'"

"Fine, then. Save them yourself." Carlo flipped his middle finger up in a very non-Quechua curse and stomped away into the yuca field.

11 ≡ LIAM

Liam skipped down the old wooden stairs two at a time, only slowing when he came in sight of the *Hostal Rivereños* lobby.

When a long-forgotten rubber baron built this elegant home in the late nineteenth century, his wife probably decorated the front parlor with Victorian fashions imported from Europe, but today two wooden benches and a low table sufficed as dining room for breakfast and hotel lobby for the rest of the day.

Before he stepped into the lobby, the *hostal* manager stopped him, "All the airplanes to Lima are booked. This is a busy time with the U.N. conference. Let me recommend Carlo, excellent English-speaking guide, to show you around the area."

He had seen enough of the impoverished city from taxis, and he didn't want to attend any more conference sessions. But what else could he do? Around the breakfast table, the other guests' faces glistened with sweat as they sipped the hot coffee and spread papaya jam on their white toast. The river breezes offered the only respite from the heat and humidity, so he certainly wasn't going to stay inside. "Gracias, that sounds great."

A thin native man stood in the lobby, undoubtedly Carlo, his guide for the afternoon. The man, or boy, since age was difficult to determine, leaned against the wall with his hands clasped behind his head. The scene reminded him of an old sepia photograph. Carlo had light brown skin, dark brown hair, and even darker brown eyes. His tee shirt might have been white or tan once, but today it was brown. Except for his sparkling white, movie-star teeth, Carlo blended into the unpainted wooden walls.

He compared Carlo's tee shirt, faded shorts, and sandals to his own attire. He wore blue convertible travel pants with multiple pockets and zippers, a tropical-patterned shirt, and an explorer vest with mesh vents and more pockets. Everything treated to repel insects, as well as UVA and UVB. His boots went up over his ankles to foil snakes, and of course his socks were treated similarly to his pants, even though the pants were tied so tightly around the boots not even a thread of sock was exposed.

Carlo smiled as he approached. When he got closer, Carlo reached out his hand and greeted him, "G'day mate. Liam, right? Ready for a walkabout?"

He considered saying something like, "I'm no Aussie," but figured it better not to confuse the guide. "Sure let's go."

"I'm Carlo. You are very fortunate to have a true *rivereño* as your guide. I have a great tour and dinner planned for you. You should leave your key at the desk, but be sure to bring your wallet. We're going give you an opportunity to contribute to the local economy—a visit to the famous Iquitos Artisan's Market."

He tapped his back pocket, tightly sealed with Velcro, and a front one that jingled with an assortment of one, two, and five *soles* coins. Carlo laughed and headed for the front door. He followed. Once in the street, Carlo waved to a tricycle-taxi driver.

"*Rimaykullayki, hola,* hello."

"*Napaykullayki, hola.*"

Carlo and the driver shook hands, smacked each other on the back, and exchanged what must have been gossip or jokes, because they both laughed heartily. He hoped they weren't laughing at him. Finally Carlo turned to him. "Let's go," he waved to the seat in the tricycle.

There wasn't much opportunity for tour guiding while the noisy vehicle raced down the main road, which he recognized as the one to the airport. Along with other tricycles, they dodged the large tourist buses until they arrived at an isolated parking lot with a rough wooden sign suspended between two trees by ropes: *Mercado Ferial de San Juan*. The taxi driver let them off and returned in the direction of town without getting paid.

"Best handicraft market in Amazon."

He looked down the two aisles and quickly estimated there couldn't be more than thirty stalls, more likely only twenty. Best handicraft market? The neighbors consisted of two old houses, a building supply store that sold bamboo and bricks, and empty land—jungle creeping up on what passed for civilization. He assumed both Carlo and the taxi driver received commissions for bringing in customers here.

He felt trapped, but resolved to make the best of it. He went to the first stall and examined some carved masks. His mother had African masks displayed in her home in Rancho Santa Fe, a rich San Diego suburb—long wooden faces with elongated noses and almond eyes purchased on safari in Kenya, or maybe Tanzania.

The ones here were made from gourds and had rounder faces and eyes. He picked out the three biggest ones, since his mother would expect a large present. When the woman asked for about twenty dollars in *soles*, he didn't haggle, but he silently apologized to Carlo. *Maybe this is the best market*. He happily walked to the next stall.

"When younger, I make flutes and gourd masks and sell them here. When older, I work on the tourist boats. I learn English there. I speak good English, yes?"

He felt generous. "Your English is great."

The two men were an odd couple walking through the market—lean and dark, short and freckled.

Carlo stopped front of a parrot, "Should I take your picture here?"

He looked up at Carlo and squinted his eyes. Carlo pointed at the bird and pointed at him, "*Pukar y q'umir, rojo y verde*, red and green!"

He looked at the colorful parrot and remembered his own hair and eyes. In a sepia world, he stood out like a tropical flower. He reached into one of his zippered pockets and pulled out a small digital camera and handed it to Carlo. "Sure. Take a picture."

Carlo admired the camera. "Beauty! That's some camera. Once I rescued a camera for a tourist on the boats. He gave me a 1,000 *soles* reward. If you have such a fancy camera, you must be important, rich man too, eh?"

He enjoyed the admiration, especially after the disrespect he received at from tenure review committee. It was salve to his still-stinging ego. He put his hands on his hips and stood up straight, almost five-and-a-half feet tall. "I'm a professor at a university in America. The United Nations paid for me to come down here to talk at the conference." It didn't feel like bragging to say it to Carlo's friendly face.

"Beauty! I hope you find much to buy here, foreign aid from an American professor to my people."

After a half hour, he had spent a couple of hundred *soles*, maybe seventy-five dollars, and had Carlo juggling a vast assortment of masks, carvings, fans, flutes, baskets, and jewelry. They returned to the parking lot to find their taxi driver had returned for them. The driver said something to Carlo in their native language and Carlo replied. "This all belongs to my important American friend. Take us back to the *hostal*."

Carlo pulled a large cord bag from the back of the taxi. The sack kept expanding as Carlo packed everything for the trip back to the hotel. "You need to take these to your room before we continue."

At the *hostal*, he picked up his key and climbed the three flights to his room carrying the large sack like a tropical Santa Claus. As he unpacked and displayed his purchases across the bed, he realized that his wallet was missing. In all the excitement, he had his pocket picked! The joy of being the rich American vanished. He remembered his mother's warnings and again he was the scolded child. He fell down on the bed, wrapping his arms around his cold center, fighting off frustrated tears.

He used his foot to push the souvenirs to the floor and reviewed his sorry life, starting with his mother's unfortunate birth control failure, the tenure committee's rebukes, his wallet gone, and being stuck in Iquitos. He called down to the hotel manager—99 on an old rotary phone, "Did you get me on a plane out of here for tomorrow morning?"

"No, sorry *señor*, the next day, *mañana* after *mañana*."

Everything was going wrong. He was going to just go to bed. Carlo could just wait downstairs until he got tired and left. He looked at all the souvenirs on the floor. "How am I going to get these home? I need another suitcase. That sack is not going to work."

He decided he had to return the sack, so he stomped down the stairs counting each one, "Thirty-three, 34, 35, 36."

Thirty-six steps, he was back in the lobby. Carlo jumped up with a big smile. "I forgot to tell you. Your wallet fell out in the taxi. Put it away. You don't need it any more today and the streets of Iquitos are filled with pick pockets. Lucky for you, you have Carlo for your guide. No one with Carlo ever loses anything. Hurry, we don't want to be late for dinner."

Emotions flip-flopping, he ran back up the stairs. "Well, I did do something right. I was smart enough to get a well-recommended guide." He locked his wallet into his big suitcase and ran down the stairs two at a time. "Thirty-two, 34, 36. *Vamos*!"

Outside the hotel, Carlo flagged down the same taxi and repeated the *"Rimaykullayki; Napaykullayki,"* greeting ritual. The jokes were even funnier this time and then they were off. They headed cross town to a long slope that led down to the river. "This is the Belen Market. Everything is bought and sold in this market—fresh fish, chickens, vegetables, local cigarettes, cooked foods, herbal remedies…an aphrodisiac for your girlfriend maybe…herbs to make you stronger?" Carlo winked. "I know you important *americano* have lots of girlfriends and need your strength. No?"

He looked down the empty streets with deserted stalls and back to Carlo, who laughed, "It's too late today, but you can walk to here from your hotel tomorrow morning when everyone will be here. Don't forget to take your camera, but not your wallet, just a little cash."

The taxi drove past rough huts built on stilts with thatched roofs. Carlo spread his hands out, "The Venice of Iquitos!"

Liam held his hand over his face to ward off the smells of sewage, rotting vegetation, and worse smells that he couldn't identify. "I've been to

Venice. It's nothing like this."

When he was a teenager, his mother couldn't stand for him to be around all summer, so she sent him away. One summer he'd gone to Venice. He'd also been to Paris, London and Madrid. He'd been miserable. His only friends were tour guides. Once again he was stranded with only a tour guide for company.

Carlo put his arm on Liam's shoulder. "Well mate, we pretend is Venice?"

Well, Carlo wasn't to blame for his loneliness. He tried to join the festivities. "Where's our gondola headed next?"

The taxi turned back up the hill. When they reached the high ground, Carlo resumed the guide chatter, "The rich folks and important businesses claimed the best land, above the flood water."

The buildings didn't look any better or more modern than the *Hostal Rivereños*.

"Welcome to the *Plaza de Armas*! That's the Iron House designed by Eiffel. Do you know Eiffel? He designed the Eiffel Tower in Paris and your Statue of Liberty."

He didn't mention his summer in Paris. "Yes, I see the resemblance."

The Iron House looked like nothing he had ever seen—inside-out construction—the iron girders all visible.

"That's the Iquitos cathedral, neo-gothic, completed in 1911, eventually."

Eventually they returned to the Artisan's Market.

In an attempt to match Carlo's ebullient attitude, he waved his arm toward the sign. "The best handicraft market in Amazon."

Carlo reached over and pulled Liam's arm into the taxi just before the taxi dove into the jungle, following a narrow path that led to a river. "This is the Nanay River. My canoe is tied up over there. Let's go catch some piranha and my sister will cook you dinner."

The dugout was made from a single log. Before he could say anything, it floated into the river with him at the front.

Carlo pointed to another paddle behind Liam, "You can paddle if you want." He knelt down and picked up a paddle trying to remember what to do next. The only time he could remember paddling a canoe was Davy Crockett's Explorer Canoes during his senior trip to Disneyland.

At first he just held on tightly to the sides, afraid he would roll over into the water as the boat rocked back and forth with each of Carlo's stokes. When he didn't get dumped into the water, he picked up the roughly-made paddle and after a few awkward strokes, he felt he was contributing to the forward progress. The little canoe moved quickly up the river.

"Over there is the zoo. No time today, but if you stay, I could take you. That bridge is the road to Nauta, paved, almost 100 kilometers. See where the river water turns black? The piranhas live there. Black water feeds piranhas. We fish here."

Carlo took a large snail from a bucket and smashed it against the side of the boat. The boat rocked and Liam grabbed the gunwales again. Carlo cut a piece of snail and placed it on a small hook. A couple of yards of fishing line connected the hook to a stick. He handed the stick to Liam.

He took the stick and looked at it. If this had been a computer or a car or an espresso machine, he would have known what to do, but he just stared at the stick in his hand.

"Stir up the water with the end of your stick, drop the hook in, and jerk it out when you feel something, like a little bump."

Carlo demonstrated and in a few seconds a small silver fish dangled at the end of his line. Liam felt silly, but he dropped the hook with the piece of snail skewered to the end, splashed the water with his stick, and waited. In the meantime, Carlo prepared another stick and immediately caught another fish. "At least we'll have something to eat," he muttered to himself in between stirring up the water and passing the hook to Carlo for more bait. Just then he felt something and pulled the stick up. A silver and red fish hung at the end of his string.

"I got one! I got one!"

He dropped the stick, line, hook and fish into the bottom of the boat, uncertain what to do with the flapping fish. Carlo picked up the fish, unhooked it and threw it into a bucket. "Dinner, yum, yum!"

After about two dozen fish, very few caught by Liam, Carlo declared, "That's enough," and they continued up the river. Liam leaned back and admired the bucket of fish, the lush jungle and the birds between his random strokes of the paddle.

"Black-collared hawk! Take a picture!"

He took this as an excuse to drop his paddle. He took his camera from its water-proof sack, and centered the raptor in the frame.

"Red-necked kingfisher!"

He zoomed in to get this small bird with a long beak and distinctive black and white markings, and of course a red collar, before picking up his paddle again.

"Gray heron! Take a picture!"

He gave up paddling and just kept his camera ready. He wasn't much help with the paddle anyway.

Eventually they stopped at a small dock and a sign that said, "Nanay Libre."

Carlo jumped out and held the canoe steady as Liam crawled off the shaky boat. They climbed the stairs to the muddy bank. They walked to a tiny thatched house on stilts.

Carlo dropped the bucket in the kitchen, actually a fire and a wooden stump in front of the hut. He guided Liam around the village. Most of the women and children ran away as they walked around.

The huts were much like the ones they saw in the swamp beyond the Belen Market, though this village smelled better. Carlo proudly identified the small vegetables plots, the farm animals—chicken, pigs and hunting dogs, the pets—parakeets and monkeys, and the still where the villagers made molasses and rum from a small plot of sugar cane.

The highlight was the soccer field and the school. "We have over thirty students and a teacher from Lima in our school."

He couldn't resist saying, "In my classes at the university, I have 150 to 200 students in each one."

"Beauty! Such a big school, it must be very important."

They stopped in front of two men standing with crossed arms. "These are my brothers, Mañuel and Marco." The brothers nodded and dispersed. "Please excuse them. Their English is not so good as mine."

Carlo pointed to banana leaves on the ground. "Time to eat. Have a seat."

The "table" was already set with yellow corn meal and a blue drink.

Carlo poured the blue drink into gourd cups. "*Chicha*," he said, "Blue corn drink."

They were sipping the sweet liquid when a young woman about the same height as Liam appeared carrying another banana leaf. Carlo proudly pointed to the big stack of small, crispy broiled fish on the leaf. "Those are the fish we caught."

The woman set the huge leaf between Carlo and Liam. She spoke a short burst in their not-Spanish native language. Carlo responded sharply, squinting his eyes.

While they appeared to argue back and forth, Liam examined her face. He realized he was staring and tried to turn away, but something held his attention.

Finally, Carlo turned to him. "This is my sister Ani. She also speaks some English."

She looked at him and before he could avert his eyes, he was falling directly into hers—dark brown eyes, so dark her pupils and irises blended into mysterious deep pools.

She smiled and pointed to the fish. "Primitive culinary delights of the primordial Amazon."

Astonished at her English, he just stared. Before he could respond, she disappeared.

He raised his hand to wave goodbye, but she didn't look back. He wanted to say, "Thanks for cooking the fish," but it was too late. He turned to Carlo thinking he might say, "Your sister is a good cook," or "Is she also a tour guide?"

But Carlo picked a rock and threw it in Ani's direction missing her by a wide margin. Liam decided to mind his own business, not wanting Carlo to get any ideas about him and Ani, remembering Carlo's earlier comment about lots of girlfriends.

They ate in silence using their fingers. He realized he must have been starving; he ate thirteen fish, two helpings of corn meal, and three gourds of the drink which he later discovered was fermented. By the time they finished, it was dark and Carlo took out a big flashlight to guide their walk back to the dock.

He looked back into the dark. "Tell you sister *gracias* for the nice dinner."

Carlo just grunted and kicked a rock into the water.

As they coasted down the river Carlo shined the light into the dark jungle. Every now and then he'd stop. "We look for red eyes…monkey or snake." Most of the time the red eyes were spots on moth wings, but they were lucky enough to find a couple of monkeys and a sleeping kingfisher.

"You met my sister and two of my brothers. What about you? *Hermanos*? *Hermanas*?"

"None, *nada*. My mother did not want children; I was an accident."

"I don't know. Don't understand."

Carlo found two more moths and finally a snake. "Look at that! A sleeping anaconda. Beauty! It must be four meters long. It could eat an entire pig. This is lucky. Too dark to take a picture, but you remember this is your entire life."

Carlo stowed the paddles as they coasted to the dock near the city. "Your mother is a happy woman?"

He thought this was an odd question, but after some thought he answered. "Oh yes. She is very rich and loves to give people presents. In fact, they named one of the buildings at my university after my mother because she helped them so much."

"Very rich, must be nice."

He went to bed happy. He didn't have to get up early for the airplane. This had been one of the best days. The conference was forgotten, tenure forgotten. He looked forward to exploring Iquitos again tomorrow. In the morning, he'd walk to the Belen Market, remembering to leave his wallet at the hotel, and maybe he'd have Carlo show him the zoo tomorrow afternoon, and maybe back to Nanay Libre for another sample of the "primitive culinary delights of the primordial Amazon" and those lovely dark eyes.

12 ≡ MIKE

When Mike left the hospital in Da Lat, it was as if 40 years snapped away. He was back in uniform, M1 helmet emblazoned with MP in large white letters. Back straight, eyes forward, he marched out of town along a familiar road until he reached the meandering path circling Xuan Huong Lake. Couples walked hand-in-hand. On this windless afternoon, the mirror lake surface reflected lovers dressed in white.

He was on patrol, on mission—Military Police. Xuan Huong Lake was a favorite destination for R&R. The war had spared Da Lat. The colonial city greeted all visitors with its European elegance and French romance regardless of their politics or nationality.

He knew all the U.S. soldiers flocked to Da Lat to meet exotic girls with long black hair, almond eyes, tiny waists, and sexy French accents. The Army brass paid for a boat to blast music from the center of the lake—the Rolling Stones, Country Joe and the Fish, the Supremes, the Beatles, and, the big favorite in Da Lat, Patti LaBelle singing, "*Voulez vous coucher avec moi ce soir.*" His job was to make sure everyone stayed friendly. So he was on the alert when he heard sounds of a struggle.

He was snapped back to the present when, off the main path and behind some bushes, he heard a young woman's voice shout, "Non, non!"

followed by a man, "Teasing bitch," and a loud slap. He ran over and found the couple on the ground, her blouse torn and his hands pulling at the waistband of her jeans.

"Stop! Leave her alone," he shouted in Vietnamese.

Moving closer, he saw the young man had a blonde crew cut and square chin. The man pursed his lips when he saw Mike. His muscular arms tensed. He replied in English, "Who the hell are you? This is none of your business old man."

Mike reached down to his calf, took out his knife, spread his legs wide, and crouched in a well-practiced knife-fighting stance. "I've killed men better than you."

The kid's blue eyes reflected the late afternoon sunlight as he stared, unblinking, at the knife. He reached into his jacket and pulled out a gun. Bullets sprayed across the landscape until Mike's knife lodged itself in the gunman's shoulder.

The kid dropped the gun and grabbed his wound. Mike tackled him, pulled the blade from his shoulder and held it against his pale throat. "Enough?"

"To hell with you—she's not worth it."

Mike kicked the gun into the lake, then kicked the kid in the gut. The kid gasped and held his stomach. Mike helped the girl to her feet and then looked back—to be sure the boy was leaving—while she buttoned up as well as she could. The kid struggled to his feet, staunched the bleeding with his jacket, and limped away.

He said, "We also better get out of here."

The two of them walked towards town. He put his knife away, noticing how good it felt to be back in the fight.

As an MP, he'd broken up many similar couples. Some were battle-hardened fighters and had not backed down as easily as this kid. Either way, all regretted going up against him. One unfortunate soldier had ended up with a lethal knife wound. The court of inquiry had declared it "self-defense," and Mike never regretted it as much as he regretted the innocent women and children he felt he'd murdered in the forest.

He left the girl at a dance pavilion. "Go home. You'll have other, better days."

As she faded into the distance, swaying her hips from side to side, he laughed out loud. His knees weren't so stiff and his shoulders weren't so sore. He felt better, energized. First he bounced on his toes, like a boxer, then he jogged.

For a moment, he turned back toward the villages, and Chi and Mai Linh, but his heart raced and he was soon panting. He bent over with his hands on his knees to catch his breath. He turned in another direction. A gentle slope carried him down towards Saigon. Though it was hundreds of kilometers away, farther than he'd traveled in dozens of year, just a few steps in that direction set him thinking of the United States. *Can I return to Oakland, to Aunt Josa's farm in Tracy? Who do I want to see? Who wants to see me?*

He stopped. Saigon was too far. He changed direction again, and walked around the lake in a fog between being a MP and a murderer of villages.

He thought of the young woman he'd "rescued." He could still do this. He could fight.

Every few steps, he picked up the pace. He felt stronger than he had in years. With each lengthening stride he came closer to a decision. Mid-stride, gliding, almost flying, he made up his mind. *Tomorrow I'm going to Saigon, to the American Embassy. I'll force them to deliver real medical assistance to the few remaining villages in the highlands.* He was clear, now. He had his mission.

He woke up, wrapped in his jacket with his arm for a pillow, in a leaf-lined hollow. He didn't recall tucking into the camouflaged nest, but combat training was like that—when you needed it, it was there. After relieving himself in the bushes, he headed toward the train station. The bright sun and clear sky seconded his decision to head for Saigon. He hadn't gone a hundred meters when he noticed a small woman running and shouting, "Mike. Mike!"

He shook his head and rubbed his eyes. "Chi?" He stopped, brushed some dirt off his clothes and ran his hand across his leaf-snagged nappy hair. "What are you doing here?"

She gave her quizzical smile. The morning sun reflected off her white teeth. "You did not come home. I came to find you."

During the war as a sniper, and a medic, and doing recon, he'd always worked alone. His decision to go to Saigon today didn't include anyone else, certainly not a nineteen-year old girl. But her sweet, innocent smile, her soft brown eyes made it difficult for him to send her away.

"How'd you get here? Where's the jeep?"

She shrugged. "Jeep is home, out of fuel. I walked."

He knew Chi would only be in the way as he headed off to battle the American Embassy—*in the way and in danger*. He wanted her back safe in her village. But to send her walking all the way back?

"How did you find me?"

Standing tall, she proudly answered, "You always talked about patrolling around Xuan Huong Lake, so I think that would be a good place to look for you when you did not go home. I waited at your house, and no you. So I came here."

He tried again to work up the grit to send her home, but his pride for her cleverness and determination got in the way. "You're one smart girl."

"Woman. I am a woman. I'm nineteen, old enough to get married."

He didn't want to argue with her. *I never win when I argue with her, not since she turned five or six. Maybe I can scare her.* "Okay. Okay. I'm going to Saigon to get medical help for the villages. By now they must have some cure for Agent Orange. I'm going to force them to give it to us. There might be fighting, shooting. People could be killed, maybe me."

"Killed? Do you have to force them? Maybe they want to help. Have you ever asked them?"

He recognized that look in her eye. This was not going to be a short discussion. He sat down on the nearby bench, took out his knife and worked on the dragon he'd discovered while waiting at the hospital. It had been sleeping in the purple and white cam lai wood, next to a sharp wooden blade—a cam lai knife with a dragon handle. "Your mother must be worried about you." She scowled at him, eyebrow raised. He sighed. "No. I've never written, spoken, anything to them."

Chi sat down and looked deep into him with her dark child-eyes. "Why not?"

He sighed, and after a moment, shoved the dragon carving into his jacket pocket. He examined his fingers and cleaned his thumbnail with the Army knife. "It's complicated. I just didn't. But I'm going now. It's going to be dangerous so you need to go home."

"Uncle Michael Jefferson Johnson, tell me what's going on."

He flinched at the "Jefferson" as much as the "uncle." "Who told you my middle name?"

"My mother."

He threw the knife and it stuck into a sapling, ten meters away and no thicker than Chi's wrist. *I can still do it.*

He stood up and walked slowly to retrieve his knife. "They think I'm a deserter. After I helped bury your grandmother's charred body, I couldn't go back to my unit. I tried, but I couldn't. I didn't tell anybody. I just disappeared."

"Is that still a problem now?"

"Yes. Soldiers are not supposed to just disappear. Not in the middle of a war, not unless they're dead...or captured. If they find me, I could be executed by a firing squad."

"Oh." She stared at her feet a moment, then jumped off the bench and started to walk away.

His energy to go to Saigon had drained away as he told his story, but he judged more energy had drained from Chi. Perhaps she would go home now. Perhaps if she went home, he could still complete the mission.

When she was a few meters away, she spun around. Her hair flew out in a spray of black, then settled again against her small shoulders. "Well it doesn't matter to me, you can go get yourself killed! But mama would never forgive me if I let you go and do that by yourself."

"It's dangerous! It's not your fight. I'll take care of it, it is my problem."

Chi stamped her feet, stalking back to him. She stood on her toes with her nose only centimeters from his and spoke quietly. "It *is* my fight, and my problem. I have a boyfriend, and mother has given me permission to marry him. Soon I will be pregnant and I don't want to end up like Mai Linh. This is *my* battle for *my baby*. It's *more* my fight than yours!"

Damn your mother. She raised a headstrong, outspoken, fierce little woman. Without my help.

But then, he had never been able to refuse Chi anything either, any more than her mother had. He looked at the young woman who stood before him. He tried to be objective. Married? Already? He hadn't realized that there was anyone that serious in Chi's life. He was missing things. He was getting old, indeed.

Mike and Chi entered the train station beneath the three yellow gables that could be seen across the Da Lat valley. The plaque said that the French built it during the 1930's. They sat on a hard wooden bench and discussed their plans.

"You don't have a Vietnamese identification card and they certainly will check before we enter Ho Chi Minh City."

He laughed. "I could kill the person who checks ID cards."

As soon as he said it, he thought of Mai Linh's baby, and Chi's grandmother, and was sorry.

Chi didn't smile, which of course made him feel worse. He had hoped she thought he was joking, but he wasn't sure himself.

He looked around the station. He felt claustrophobic with so many people so close. He didn't remember any problems with crowds when he lived in Oakland before the war. This must have happened over his years of isolated village life.

"Look at those people." He pointed at tourists speaking languages he'd never heard and wearing backpacks like none he'd ever seen. They casually boarded the train. "They certainly don't have Vietnamese identification cards."

"They have passports. Do you have an American passport? Or any passport?"

Now he felt glad that she had come along. The outside world was scarier than he remembered it, and more complicated. "No, of course I don't have a passport. I had a military ID but it disappeared years ago."

Chi smiled. "That's it. We'll tell them you're my uncle, visiting from the States, and you lost your passport. I'm taking you to get a new one."

His internal flinch again at "uncle" was, he hoped, not obvious to her. To cover his confusion, he continued his stupid joke, "Good plan. And if that doesn't work, I can still kill the inspector."

Chi just gave an exasperated sigh, then it was their turn to board.

After a time of quiet, she regained her usual enthusiasm for her surroundings. Together they studied the plaque that retold the glories of the Swedish engineers who built the rail line. Chi and Mike admired the switchbacks built to negotiate the rugged terrain and marveled at the many tunnels. The plaque had said, "Over a kilometer of tunnels."

When they emerged from the darkness of one of those tunnels, a uniformed man stood next to their second-class seats. "Identification please." He said it in Vietnamese and repeated it in French. As they'd earlier agreed, Mike was silent. Chi responded in Vietnamese and told the story about the lost passport.

The official and Chi argued back and forth. During this time, Mike slipped his Army knife from its sheath and surreptitiously held it in his jacket pocket. The official said something to Chi about going to his office to fill out some papers.

Mike recognized this as a slang expression similar to "between the sheets" in English. He gritted his teeth and studied the official. The man's jacket was unbuttoned, so a stab below the rib cage and thrusting up into the heart was inviting. He gripped his knife, slowed his breathing and concentrated on his target.

Chi argued some more and refused to go to the man's office. The official pressed his point, leaning over Chi in an intimidating way and repeating the "between the sheets" phrase until it sounded like a demand.

Mike examined the official's necktie. The loose knot left open an easy path to the soft spot above his Adam's apple and directly into his brain. Mike decided the brain would be quieter, though messier. He could see a tunnel approaching. He could be done and they could disappear before the train exited the dark tunnel. This was his chance.

However, the man abruptly cleared his throat, punched their tickets and moved to the next passengers.

Chi leaned over to him. "All fixed."

"Between the sheets! Who did he think he was?" Chi shrugged. The light dimmed around them as they entered the tunnel. Mike re-sheathed his knife. He whispered, "If he was still here, I would have killed him now."

"Good thing it is fixed, then," Chi said, making a crooked smile.

When they left the tunnel, the man collecting tickets had been replaced by a young woman pushing a food trolley down the narrow aisle. She dressed much the same as Chi and the women in the village—long shirt over trousers, buttoned down the front and at the cuffs of the long sleeves. Buttoned at the short, stand-up collar. The cotton looked finer and the colors brighter than those available in Da Lat, but it was the same women's wear Mike had seen for years. He thought of Chi's mother and smiled. An Ly had always looked good, no matter how poor her clothing was.

The trolley offered pho soups, barbecue pork, bánh xéo, and sweet coffee.

"Oh look! *Bánh xéo!* Let's get some of those," Chi said, bright-eyed as any child. "So good, and so hard to make over a fire in the village."

Worried about his fast-dwindling cash, Mike hesitated, but only for a moment. Chi's joy was too big to quench.

They bought a couple of the savory fried omelets for each of them. He ate his with his fingers, thankful for the warm food, and now that the crisis had passed, grateful that he hadn't killed anyone.

13 ≡ LIAM

Liam sat on one of the wooden benches in the *hostal* with the other early risers, sharing the breakfast of coffee, hopefully boiled long enough to kill whatever lived in the water, freshly baked rolls, and papaya so ripe that it oozed between the fork tines. Two guys from Germany were laughing about the girls they met the night before and discussing their plan to take the bus to Nauta. A couple from California kept saying, "Did you ever see so much water?" as if they were expecting the Amazon dry season to be like a desert. Several U.N. delegates were discussing the day's working groups: "Third World Clinical Trials," "Waterborne Parasites," and "Sustainable Development."

Glad to be missing those, he thought to himself.

He was feeling pretty good as he finished breakfast. Before he walked out he remembered to take his malaria pills, then headed towards the river and the Belen Market. As warned, he'd left his wallet locked in his suitcase. In one zippered pocket he had his small camera and in another about ten dollars in small Peruvian change, mostly one sol coins. He didn't plan on buying much, but he remembered that if he took someone's picture they'd expect a one sol tip.

After a few blocks of colonial buildings much like the *Hostal Rivereños*, he recognized the crowds and excitement of the market. Evidently the natives got up much earlier in the morning than he had, for the streets were jammed and even the small tricycle taxis had difficulty moving forward. He felt proud he'd found the market on his own. Even as the throngs jostled him, he felt confident. This was going to be a great adventure.

He wandered down a narrow alley of stalls crowded with fish mongers. He recognized baskets of piranhas at one stall. *I caught some of those*, he thought with smug satisfaction. Another stall sold snails as big as his feet. He recognized catfish with their whiskers. Some were small like the piranha, while others grew to be two or three feet long. He stopped to take a picture of a table covered with brown fish that looked armor plated, like something from the time of the dinosaurs.

The camera flashed and an old lady stretched out her hand, mouthing words in a language he didn't recognize, not Spanish, probably Quechua.

"Huk a yichu. Hug an yay."

He reached in his pocket and handed her a one sol coin. Whatever she had said, that seemed to be the right response. He stood a little taller and entered an aisle where men and woman were cutting something that looked like tobacco and rolling cigarettes in toilet paper.

He held up one finger and a man with brown teeth handed him a misshapen white tube. He took the man's picture and handed him a silver coin. The man smiled. Liam didn't smoke, but today seemed like one for adventure. He placed his prize between his lips and leaned over the counter. The man lit a match and he puffed, imagining he looked like Bogart on *The African Queen*.

The smoke made him dizzy, but he managed to smile at the vendor as he staggered away. After bumping into several shoppers, he regained his balance. He took one more puff and turned the corner before he dropped the foul smoldering ember on the ground. A brown boy in shorts and a tee shirt with a picture of the Golden Gate Bridge was swift to pick up the butt and disappear into the crowd.

He turned down another alley and stopped at a stall lined with shelves of bottles. Liquids, powders, and plants of every color of the rainbow—a Technicolor explosion in a world of brown people, dirt and water. This was *Pasaje Paquito*, the herbal market touted on all the internet sites. Without a guide, he'd negotiated the Belen Market maze and found the hidden treasure! He smiled at the thought of buying aphrodisiacs for the tenure review committee. It would be a cute joke.

He was feeling magnanimous. When he returned home, he would make amends to the committee, be a little more politic, and maybe even invite his mother for dinner. The academic life was pretty good after all—working nine months a year, writing a few articles, and traveling around the world. He could get used to that. In fact, he had already gotten used to it.

He turned into the first kiosk wondering how to find those aphrodisiacs so many internet bloggers wrote about. Directly in front of him was a table piled high with leaves as big as dinner plates, with white, yellow and orange flowers. The leaves were still attached to their roots—looking like giant dandelions. Smaller leaves tumbled together like a crazy mixed salad of spinach, baby lettuce, watercress and parsley. Some of the plants were tied in bundles, while others were collected in fast-food containers. "McDonald's!" One of the other customers glanced at him and he flushed, realizing he'd said it aloud. The man raised an eyebrow, but turned back to his business, and Liam tried to turn himself invisible.

He looked at the back wall of the shop, where pint and quart bottles with labels advertising vinegar, cooking oil, beer, catsup, mustard, and cough syrup stood on wooden shelves, like some exotic liquor store display. However, by the colors alone, he knew they contained something else and not what their labels said. Maybe they *were* exotic liquors. A young girl, maybe seven or eight years old, came up to him, "Love potion? You want love potion?"

He looked at her round face, her big smile with sparkling white teeth. Her eyes seemed so big for her small face that he reevaluated her age. She couldn't have been older than six. She tugged at his arm. "You want love potion?"

He first reaction was, *she's so cute*, but the idea of buying aphrodisiacs, which had more to do with sex than love, from a six-year old upset his sensibilities. He felt embarrassed, like that first time he tried to buy condoms. He ran out of the booth. He walked down the center of the alley examining each stall, ignoring the exotic wares, just searching for one not containing small children.

At last he entered into a cubicle containing a single old lady sitting in the corner spinning wool. She wore a long brown wool skirt and had a colorful wool blanket wrapped around her shoulders over a plain white shirt. The sun had been up awhile and between the heat and humidity he was sweating in his jungle shirt with mesh vents and built-in protection from the sun and insects. He wondered how she could look so cool dressed in wool from ankle to neck.

He walked right up to her. "Love potion?"

She smiled as if she had guessed that was what he'd want. "For man or for woman?"

He looked right into her narrow eyes, surrounded by wrinkles from her smile and age. "Woman," he said trying to not whisper.

Without stopping her spinning, she shouted something, and in a minute the little girl from the other stand appeared with a cellophane envelope containing a bright red powder. The girl smiled at him. "*Dos soles.*"

He gave her a silver-and-gold two soles coin, pocketed the envelope, then quickly walked away from the shop.

He was at the next corner, turning uphill towards the *hostal* when he realized his camera was missing. Not believing that it was taken, he patted the pockets in his pants and shirt. Not there. Incredulous, he unzipped and unsnapped each one and put his hand in to check. He still had his collection of change and his love potion, but the camera was gone, definitely gone.

He tried to remember if he put it down when he paid the old woman to take the picture of the fish. He frantically zipped and snapped all his empty pockets.

When he looked up, he realized he was in an open space. Everyone had moved away from him while he did his frantic pocket search. The only people within two meters of him were two uniformed security officers. Their jackets said, *"Mercado Seguridad."*

He ran over to them, "Pickpocket! Someone stole my camera. It was an expensive camera and it had all my pictures on it."

The two men looked at each other. "What would you like us to do?"

Even before he finished saying, "Can you get my camera back?" he knew the camera wasn't coming back.

"You want a report for your insurance?"

He recalled something about making a police report. He wasn't sure if that was for auto accidents, hurricanes, or pickpockets, but it sounded like a good idea.

"Did they get your passport too?"

"My passport? Yes I have it—or, no, it's back at my hotel. No, they didn't get my passport."

The men smiled at him. "Good. We always advise tourists to leave their passport in the hotel safe."

He just smiled back, even though he thought he was getting a run-around. The *Hostal Rivereños* didn't have a safe, but this was no time to argue.

"Let's go to the station and make a report."

"Can we do it now?"

"Now? Certainly, follow us."

The three of them marched down one alley after another. The crowd opened up as they passed by. At first he tried to keep track where they are going, but as they continued deeper into the market he gave up. He was sure they'd direct him back to the hotel district after he filed the report.

After he was completely lost, he saw a streetlight, an open square, and colonial buildings. He was out of the market and back to civilization. He relaxed. *I'll fill out some forms and be back to my hotel. The insurance will buy me a new camera; I was ready for one anyway. I think I'll contact Carlo. We can visit the zoo and get his sister to cook dinner again.* He wasn't going to let a little thing like a camera spoil his day.

They turned down the narrow street and he could see the big *Seguridad* sign a few doors down. Just then a bag was thrown over his head, and arms grabbed him roughly around the throat and shoulders. "Rich American professor," he heard, "you cooperate or we slit your throat and leave you dead." He couldn't figure out how to not cooperate or do anything else.

They tied his hands behind his back. The bag over his head was smotheringly thick, he could barely breathe. His feet left the ground as he was lifted and thrown across a vehicle seat—a taxi tricycle, by the noise— and bounced down the street. He heard his coins bouncing out of his pockets on the street and the delighted cries of children picking them up.

Inside the bag, he gasped for air and wished he had gone with Carlo for the day. In exchange for a small adventure, he had lost his camera and probably his chance to enjoy another dinner with Carlo's sister. Maybe forever. He squeezed his eyes tight shut and did his best to simply endure.

P+P BLOG POST

Pride and Prejudice (apologies to Jane) aka Lies, Damn Lies, and Statistics (apologies to whomever said it first)—A blog dedicated to odd stories about numbers

Surprise: Medicare Trustees projected the outlays from the Medicare Hospital Insurance Trust Fund (HI) to fall short of income, However tax income exceeded outlays in recent years, and this trend is projected to continue.

What's Up? Medicare administrators say: The Affordable Care Act, innovative partnerships with private insurers, and free-market forces have driven down the cost of Medicare and reduced fraud.

I'm sure P+P readers want to ask if people are just staying healthier.

Surprise: Social Security Trustees projected the outlays from the combined Old-Age and Survivors Insurance (OASI) and Disability Insurance (DI) Trust Funds (OASDI) to fall short in the near future. Now the Trustees' report this milestone is no closer than it was five years ago.

What's Up? When Internet News Services questioned the Social Security Commissioner, he quipped, "I guess people are living longer."

The astute reporter followed up with, "If people are living longer, why aren't Medicare expenses increasing faster then projected?"

The commissioner reiterated the benefits accrued from the "innovative partnerships with private insurers."

Again, astute P+P readers suggest that healthier seniors are a more credible explanation.

That explains things, doesn't it? Or maybe not.

14 ≡ CARLO

As the lights of Iquitos brightened ahead of them, Carlo lowered the throttle on the outboard motor of Ruiz' aluminum boat, the perfect transport for their "covert operation." The wake behind them dropped as he slowed to turn the bend where the Nanay merged with the mighty Amazon. Tito leaned back in the bow seat and rested his arms along the fancy wooden gunwales that ran all the way around the rim of the boat. He grinned over his shoulder at Carlo. It was nice to travel in style. Much better than a soggy dugout canoe. The motorboat was especially swift downstream.

Carlo thought about that speed and power for a moment. When they finished, they'd head back up the Nanay past his village and several others, to their camp. They'd be pushing upstream against the current on the Nanay. They weren't going to be as fast as this. Well. He nodded. He could take advantage of eddies at the side of the current, that would help their speed. And it was a light streamlined boat.

They were going to be in a rush on the return trip. Absolutely. He grinned. Soon to be an even lighter boat once they dropped off their "cargo."

He puttered along past the Iquitos waterfront, waving a few times as he saw — or thought he saw — people he knew. It was hard to make out faces in the dark. Even with the streetlights, people didn't look the same as in the bright daylight. But that was good, because it meant they wouldn't be sure it was him they had seen…in case there were any questions later. Tito just stared at nothing. He was from Puerto Maldonado, and claimed he knew no one in Iquitos.

Eventually they passed the piers of Port Masusa. They'd come around the third side of the peninsula that was Iquitos City. Now he gave more fuel to the engine as he pressed upstream, but he immediately had to give way before one of the tourist boats, a two-story gleaming jewel against the dark water that was coming in late from a sunset and dinner tour, no doubt.

The tourist boat was docked and unloading as they left it behind them, heading into the darkened market area. Eventually their little boat edged alongside the shore and he noticed the CUI warehouse, letters bright red against the whitewashed adobe walls. It was behind a security fence, but they had some heavy duty wire cutters, courtesy of Tito's toolbox. Carlo stared at the building as they passed, thinking, *CUI would have to wait. First the U.N. Site.*

That was the primary objective. Tito's toolbox also provided the plastic explosives they'd use to blow up the main meeting hall. Carlo checked the heavy canvas bag with the ransom note and the videotape of their kidnap victim. Poor Dr. Liam Shaughnessy. He had certainly been surprised to end up a captive out in the jungle. No — he corrected himself, snickering. Not poor. *Rich* Dr. Liam Shaughnessy.

Pusac and Ruiz were back at the campsite with their prize. He had had to do the videotaping himself, because neither of the others had ever operated a video camera. He shook his head. The only one besides himself who seemed to know what he was doing was Tito. Tito had been in the *Ejército del Perú* — the Army. Tito had experience with small arms and ammunition. And better yet, Tito had a cache of explosives. Tito was going to do the actual blowing up. Carlo chewed his lip. He should probably mention to Tito that he wanted to use the CUI offices as a secondary target.

His ex-military friend took another drag on his cigarette and turned to stare at the Moronacocha Lagoon.

"Tito!" he called, at exactly the same moment Tito turned to him and said something.

"What?" Carlo said.

"I thought we were going up the Lagoon."

"No man. I never go that way. It does not always go through, the lagoon is an oxbow, gets too shallow sometimes."

Tito nodded.

Carlo thrust his chin back the way they'd come. "Hey, what about the CUI warehouse, for a secondary."

"What is that, is it military?"

"No, it's, uh—it's letters mean, like Clinics United or something like that. They go around trying out new drugs on people."

"Oh, them." Tito said. He took a last drag on his black cigarette, then tossed the butt into the river. "You got a thing against them?"

He thought about trying to explain about Ani, but that might make Tito think he was weak for trying to please his sister. Instead, he said, "My little brother, you know? He has a bad foot, because of them, because of their tests."

"Oh, yeah?" Tito said. He nodded ever so slightly. "Yeah, I guess." Tito waved a camo-covered arm. "Assuming the first goes well."

"Yeah," he agreed. "Assuming."

At last they rounded the bend nearest the new high school and its *fútbol* field, where the U.S. Conference had set up its big tent. He aimed the boat at a small floating dock and shut off the motor. He crouched down, dug out an oar, and paddled quietly to the dock. As soon as he had thrown a rope around an upright post, Tito lifted his pack of gear—his toolbox— onto the little dock.

"You want me to come, or stay here?"

"I think maybe you come, to check out for guards and whatever," Tito said. He didn't seem to care much either way. "Unless you think someone is going to steal your boat."

Carlo glanced around. The ground periodically flooded here, so there were no houses, and the floating shanties that used to congest the area had been burned out a few years back, before they built the new school. Locals still claimed the city government had their *Policia* do the deed, but there never had been any proof. *More likely someone's cooking fire got out of control,* he thought with contempt. Shanty people weren't real *Rivereños,* everyone knew that.

But it was a lucky fire for them, because it meant no one was nearby to see them. "It should be fine," he said. He flipped the locking key on the motor, just in case some random *niño* thought he'd try something.

He grabbed his video camera and the ransom package, got out of the boat, and they hiked rapidly across the swampy fields to the higher ground where the playing field was located. The big white U.N. Tent glowed slightly in the distant security lights from the school. He ran into the tent, up to the podium and set down the camera and ransom demand note.

He was amazed how fast Tito got the explosives set, and the detonator rigged to go off in four minutes—enough time for them to get back out into the swamp, but not too long.

He galloped back to the boat, tossed his empty canvas camera sack next to Tito's toolbox. Tito had already sat back down ready to be chauffeured away. They still didn't see anyone, so he just flipped the switch, jerked the cord and started the motor. The boat swooped around in an arc and they headed swiftly back the way they'd come.

The bomb was not very loud, but it succeeded in shredding one end of the tent, exploding chairs through the sky in an interesting black on gray pattern. "Beauty, Tito," he murmured.

That was easy! Boring, he thought. *Good thing we have a secondary target!*

Soon enough the little boat had nudged up against the wharf where the CUI building sat, just waiting for them, it seemed.

Tito was calm as Carlo rolled onto the wharf, crawled up to the chain-link fence and cut a hole big enough for them to fit through. "Not too big," Tito said.

Carlo kept his eyes open for police, since he knew the area was patrolled. He just didn't know how often the guards came by, or if they ever walked this back side by the docks. As soon as he had the hole ready, Tito was through with his toolbox.

He got the charge set, and this time Tito ran a wire connected to the detonator, so he could set off the explosives from the boat, and then they'd make their getaway. Carlo was worming his way back through the hole in the fence when things fell apart.

"Crap!" Tito yelled in Spanish. "Hurry up!"

Carlo pulled his legs through the hole and looked where Tito was looking. A pair of guards had just turned the corner and seen them. One of them shouted something, flashing a big light onto Tito as Carlo grabbed Tito's shoulders to pull him through. Tito had the detonator in his hands, and Carlo saw his thumb move to the firing button at the same time as he heard a ping and a bullet—he thought it was a bullet—burned past his ear.

"*Mierda*!" He put a hand over his ear, and Tito pushed the button, and the devil's building blew up.

Chunks of adobe, boards, glass, pieces of unknown scrap exploded in every direction. Carlo curled up into a ball, with his arms over his head, hoping nothing too big would hit him.

Something hit Tito. The whole top of his head exploded. Carlo stared a moment in disbelief, then realized one of the security guards was just about on top of them, face all bloody, gun now pointed at him. He rolled off the wharf, figuring he'd get lost in the dark water. Instead he landed, hard, in the boat.

The guard fired at him. He heard the bullet hit something, maybe the boat, maybe the water. Somehow in his absolute panic, he managed to yank the starter. The engine roared and the little boat leaped away from the dock. He wrenched the knot loose, threw the tie-up rope into the water where it snaked out behind him. He saw it begin to sink as he flattened himself in the boat, hoping the bow was pointed somewhere, anywhere, away from the docks. It took a minute to realize the guard had stopped shooting.

He risked a peek over the side of the boat. He was looking back at the blazing building. The guard had gone back to help his fellow patrolman, who was down and not moving on the wharf. He could just make out Tito's dead, bloody head. His friend's body seemed absurdly small lying there.

Only when he had gotten into the dark waters of the Nanay, far from the city lights, did he realize that one of the bullets had hit him. His left foot was a bloody mess.

It seemed a little ironic, in that first shocked moment of discovery, that this was the same messed up foot as Tomito's.

He didn't even want to look at it. He pulled off his tee shirt and wrapped it around his foot, tying the hem and a sleeve together to stop the bleeding. Wearing nothing but his bloody shorts, he steered the boat toward home. Half crazy from shock, he said a prayer of thanks that he had left his good jeans at home that morning. At least they weren't all messed up.

Parts of the journey to his home, Carlo did not remember at all. He slid past the dock, and rather than try to move upstream back to it, simply tied up at the dead tree below his family's house. He dragged himself up the embankment by the brute force of his arms and right foot, and collapsed on the ground. He remembered moaning. He woke up to Ani wiping his face with a damp cloth.

"Carlo?" she said softly. "Carlito?"

He lifted his head and looked at her. "Oh, good," he said. "I was looking for you."

"Oh, Gods, Carlo, you are all over blood. Where are you hurt?"

"Just my foot. It's not so bad. I think the blood must be Tito's."

"Tito?"

"Yeah. We blew up the CUI office. For you. For Tomito."

"Oh, Gods. Where is Tito?"

"Dead." he laughed wildly. "Blown up."

Ani gasped. "Oh, no. But you.... You can't stay here.... Mamî, Papa!"

"No, I can't stay here," he agreed. "Help me, Ani. The hostage I took, he needs water, in the boat. Two cases fresh, not refills, for him. But he needs...I need...."

"I will get what you need. Be quiet."

Angeline disappeared for awhile. He dozed. It was nice on the riverbank, starlight shining down.

Then Ani was back, with her backpack and a bag full of things.

"Do you have a boat?"

"Yeah!" He scrambled up to his elbows, looking over the edge, suddenly frightened that Ruiz' nice fast boat had drifted away. But it was there, still tied to the tree, bobbing three meters below them.

"Oh, how am I going to get you down there?"

"Just go down and move the boat," he managed to say. "I'll roll into the water, then climb aboard."

"Are you sure you can?"

"Yes, Ani. Just do it!"

For a wonder, she followed his directions, clambering and sliding down the bank into the boat. She put her things aboard, then climbed in herself, pushing against the embankment so the boat floated out, leaving a nice deep gap in the eddies. He aimed for the open space, rolled off, splashed down. The water felt good, blessedly cool and wet. He came up, swam a couple strokes, grabbed the side of the boat and got his right leg over. Ani helped haul him aboard.

"There's a paddle, till we get far enough away," he said gesturing weakly toward where he'd stowed the oar. Why was he so shaky? He was weak. Tito wold be ashamed.

"Where to?" Ani's voice was almost too soft to hear.

"Remember where Paco was going to homestead over by El Porvenir?"

"Yes," Ani said. "I think I can find it." He heard her gentle strokes with the paddle.

"Up the Nanay, and turn left past Yuto," he giggled.

Then he took a nap.

15 ≡ ELEANOR

Hoping her staff hadn't made a mistake with their suggestion for publicity, Eleanor glanced around the television studio. She knew from other TV shows there would be a green room to wait in—but where? One of the makeup staff saw her and whisked her away to a dressing table.

"Is Ms. Thomas here?"

"Yes, Jacquilin is right over there."

But Eleanor couldn't look. She couldn't do much of anything for a while, except tolerate the attentions of the makeup and hair artists. At last it was time and they were escorted to the set.

She ignored the bright lights. She searched to be sure that Jacquilin Thomas was seated in one of the overstuffed pale green armchairs before taking her own seat beside her and across from the star of the show, Jenna Williams.

Jenna's hundreds of golden brown braids had been caught up in an elaborate clasp and hung down behind her head in straight braided rows. She looked like an Egyptian goddess. Her makeup artists had prepared her eyes to enhance the look—rather like Cleopatra meets Janet Jackson.

In contrast, the Haitian Jacquilin looked almost plain with her dreads and blue chambray shirt and straight black skirt.

That's okay, she thought, giving Jacqui a reassuring smile. *You're a sick person, regaining her health. You're not supposed to look stunning like Jenna!* She nodded as Jenna's crew asked if they were ready, and the cameraman shouted,

"ON FIVE, FOUR," he stopped talking and held up fingers for three, two, one, while one of the crew held up a sign that read, APPLAUSE.

"ON AIR," the cue board said.

The audience duly applauded, and Jenna laughed and said into the mike, "Welcome my friends!" The applause died down on cue, and Jenna went on in mellower tones, "We have a great show for you today, and we're starting off with a medical miracle. I'd like to introduce you to Jacquilin Thomas who recently cheated death!"

The sign said, WOW, and so did the audience, with murmurs of awe and excitement thrown in for good measure.

"And helping with this miracle, and ready to tell us all about thousands of other similar resurrections from the near-dead, we have Dr. Eleanor Powell, of the World Health Organization."

World Health Organization? she wondered. Of all her myriad affiliations, she puzzled why had Jenna's staff chosen that one?

OOHH, APPLAUSE.

She allowed herself a small ironic smile. It was flashy and plastic and ever-so-American, but still, the publicity could help, especially if it helped the average citizen believe in the efficacy of clinical trials. *Not that I'll use the word efficacy*, she remarked to herself, after the camera had moved back to the much more photogenic Jenna.

She was glad the camera was not on her when she felt her phone vibrate in her suit pocket. Who would be calling her now? Everyone on her staff knew better than to interrupt her schedule—and they knew her schedule in fine detail, having created it—so it shouldn't be anything but an emergency, a *real* emergency. At a moment she was certain the audience, the camera and the nation's viewers' attention was focused on the Egyptian queen, she glanced at her phone's screen. *"Green Beret?" Ryan Kolnikoff! That dunderhead.*

Well, perhaps not. She had told him to call her if something important came up, and it was her own fault she hadn't ever specified to him when *not* to call. Whatever it was, he was going to have to wait. She smiled warmly and nodded as Jenna Williams explained in simple words to her audience that Jacqui had been saved from the congestive heart failure that had killed her mother, her two aunts, and one of her sisters.

"Now, you were diagnosed at risk from this disease, is that right?" Jenna asked in her lovely patois-accented sing-song voice. Jacquilin nodded.

"It's a problem that runs in my family," Jacqui said in her creole accented tones, and turned to Eleanor with a beseeching look.

She reached over and patted Jacqui's hand. "Jacqui's doctor noticed Jacqui's growing fatigue, weakness, and shortness of breath. At the age of twenty-six, Jacqui could no longer jog the three miles a day she had been running since she was eight. Given her family history, this was a very bad sign."

There were murmurs from the audience.

"Then came rescue, in the form of clinical drug trials," Jenna said, practically quivering with excitement, "run by the United Nations World Health Organization. Jacqui was saved!"

Jacquilin nodded and smiled warmly. "And my younger sister and brother, too!" She glanced at Eleanor as if to be sure she had said the right thing. Eleanor nodded gravely, then glanced at Jenna and smiled at the audience.

"That's right!" Jenna caroled.

"And all because they were willing to try a new treatment plan that didn't have FDA approval yet," Eleanor said. That was the important point; she needed to make sure they understood.

"They can't use those drugs in the U.S., is that right?" Jenna asked, following the scripted questions.

"Not yet. Not until the clinical trials are complete and the results verified by the Food and Drug Administration. So Jacqui, and Haiti, are lucky because they got to use this treatment five years ahead of anyone in the United States. A lot of people in the U.S. just like Jacqui and her brother and sister actually died because they could not get this medicine yet."

AWW, OOH, the audience said, still following the cue cards like little lambs.

"But now they can," Eleanor said, reassuring them. "The FDA has approved this drug and it is now available. But it would have been too late for Jacqui."

"Except they said YES to these drug tests, right?" Jenna said. She turned to her audience. "They said YES!"

And the audience shouted YES at the same time, on cue, so Jenna's voice was multiplied by 200 times into a resounding YES!

"Now, they would not be testing something that wasn't safe, would they?" Jenna asked.

Eleanor shook her head. "Before real people use these drugs, many, many tests are made in laboratories all over the world, to be certain the medicine does exactly what it's supposed to and nothing else. They've already been tested over and over again before they are given to people. Approval for human clinical trials is a very serious decision. The only reason it is still called a *test* is that we are trying to measure how effective the medicine is—how good it is at doing what it's designed to do. There is no risk that a drug would actually be harmful."

A glance at the audience assured her that people were following what she said, and were interested. "The worst that can possibly happen is that it might not be quite as effective as the researchers hoped." She looked at Jacqui again, and smiled broadly. "But in this case, it worked even better than hoped. People are living longer, healthier lives because of these clinical trials. Many people were completely cured!"

"Yeah!" Jenna said and stood up and clapped.

APPLAUSE.

Backstage, Eleanor tapped her phone and returned Ryan's call. Fortunately, he was still nearby the phone he had used to call her, and after a few moments of shouted Spanish, Ryan came on the line.

"I have bad news," he said, straight to the point.

"Well, I didn't really imagine you were calling to tell me something wonderful," she said, letting a little of the acid she felt drip into her tone. "What is it?"

"Three things," Ryan said. "First—"

"Speak up, I can hardly hear you!"

The phone rustled, and after a moment the background noise dropped to a whisper. "Is that better?"

"Yes. Three points."

"One, one of the speakers from the U.N. conference has been kidnapped. Two, the main tent at the U.N. conference site was damaged by a bomb late last night. Three, the CUI offices here were blown up, a night watchman badly injured, and one of the bombers—possibly also one of the kidnappers—was killed."

"Kidnapped?" She tried to imagine why anyone would be worth taking from *that* conference…it wasn't Davos or G8. "Who was it?"

"A ransom note and videotape of the captive were left at the conference bomb site. The police here are keeping things really quiet, so I haven't been able to get a look at the demands, but I was able to get that much."

"And who was kidnapped?" She asked again.

"That professor I told you about—the falling-birthrates, all-children-are-unwanted-products-of-rape dude."

"Name?"

"Not released, but he was the second speaker at the conference." There was rustling again as Ryan apparently moved the phone around. "I have the agenda, here, just a minute…" after a brief silence, "…yeah, Dr. Liam Shaughnessy. I remember he was Irish. Short guy, red hair."

She shook her head. She had never heard of Liam Shaughnessy before the conference, and doubted anyone else had either. "Any idea why him?"

"Well, according to rumors, his mother is a wealthy lady."

She didn't recognize the name, but that didn't mean much. She had dropped out of high-income social circles years ago. "So money?"

"Apparently."

"Was a group name released, anyone claiming credit?"

"Nope. Nothing."

She wasn't a believer in conspiracy theories, but she didn't like coincidences either. "I'm thinking it's quite a coincidence that our, 'I'm anti-drug-testing' chica just flew into Iquitos two days before this bomb goes off."

"After she was arrested, I did a background check. No evidence of prior violence," Ryan said.

She ignored his play for praise, not trusting half of everything he reported anyway. "Do you know where she is?"

"Not in Iquitos." Ryan's voice sounded certain.

"CUI, eh. Were they active down there? I thought they finished their trials last— "

Ryan interjected, "The report in the daily news said they had just begun another phase three research project out in the villages along the Nanay River, a tributary of the Amazon near Iquitos."

"What were they testing?"

"Don't know, the reports didn't say. They just said their building was blown up, so whatever it was, it's gone now."

She could not recall any CUI projects in the area, but that didn't mean there weren't any. She could have her staff check on it.

"That isn't necessarily a bad thing, I think," she said, then realized she was musing aloud. She temporized and continued, "I don't wish anyone trouble, but having CUI as a martyr for the cause can't hurt. It might help fund raising and I can circulate the story among the WHO committee as a cautionary tale. All right. Do what you can to keep a lid on things; I'd be really happy if this didn't hit the international news."

"Yeah, I think the locals would like that, too."

"*The locals?*"

"The city, the government, the people down here. Terrorism is supposed to be all over with. The conference should have been safe."

"As best as I can tell, terrorism will never be all over, but it's nice they want to keep things quiet. Any chance you can hook up with their investigation, pose as a friend of the kidnap victim's family or something?"

"I'll give that a try. I was hoping you might have some background information on him or something that might make that kind of request more convincing."

"I will have Devon or someone from my staff email you a packet before tomorrow morning. I assume email works?"

"Yeah, so far it's more reliable than the phones. I'll look for info tomorrow."

Ever concerned about keeping him on track and in line, she reviewed, "Your first priority is quiet. Your second priority is to find that poor economist and get him away from those idiots that have him. Ransom for university professors! Bombs! Good grief."

"Yes, sir," Ryan's voice said, and he hung up.

She pulled her phone away from her ear and looked at it. "Well, I guess 'yes, sir' is not that bad a response," she muttered to herself, swiping the phone off. "So long as he keeps on task, I'm happy enough to have him treat it as a military operation."

16 ≡ MIKE

For the remainder of the trip, Mike carved nonstop, in a meditative trance of sorts, half remembering, half trying to center himself, find a balance within that would carry him through this upcoming action. The wiseman in the village of Chi's grandmother had taught him the Tao. The villagers didn't trust him in the beginning, saw him as an agent of death.

Of course they did. I was an agent of death.

But the wiseman saw that Mike was trying to make things right. The old man's gentle heart had touched Mike, and taught him much. Taught him to find a balance of action and peace. A balance of aggression and harmony. The villagers still did not always trust him, but they tolerated him from a distance. He missed the old man, who had died and been replaced by his son—who was not at all a gentle man—many years ago.

Mike realized now he had let the years pass too quietly. He had given up. Not given in to peace, but given up on making change. Too much harmony, too much yin. He had gotten too mellow, too quiet, too still. He needed yang. Much more yang.

Below his seat on the train, Cam lai wood chips covered the floor. The facing bench had filled with parents, children, packages, and a small potbelly pig in a wicker cage, which would eat the wood chips if they landed within reach. A carved blade with a dragon handle now was tucked into his jacket pocket, and a second blade with a leopard handle came to life in his hands. *Beautiful wood, strong and hard, doesn't float, but polishes like Xuan Huong Lake on a windless dawn.*

The small boy in the opposite bench watched him carve, wide-eyed. Mike smiled at him. The carvings were his one source of income, sent in small batches with the villagers who sold them for him, along with their vegetables and pigs, coffee and cardamom.

The little boy said something to his mother, which caused some sort of controversy Mike could not hear. The entire family was talking, and the volume escalated into a shouting match. Even the pig was squealing. Mike turned his attention inward, tuning them out as well as he was able.

After Mai Linh's baby, the couple in the park, and the train inspector, he was ready for some good luck, *chúc may mắn*. The afternoon sun lit up the dingy second-class cars as the train flowed out of the mountains onto the broad plain of the Mekong delta. Lush green disguised the battlefields he remembered from the war. Saigon in the past. Ho Chi Minh City just ahead.

Chi broke into his reverie. "You won't be able to rent a hotel room without ID, not in Ho Chi Minh City."

His focus returned to Chi and the mission. "Let's not do that lost passport thing again, that was a total bummer." He considered their options, his near-empty pockets. "Can we get some dinner without ID?"

Chi smiled. "No problem. But remember we can't get me a room and have you sneak in. That would mark me and invite others, like Mr. Between-the-sheets."

"How do you even know about things like that?"

"I'm not a child any more."

"I know that, but you were a *village* child. How do you know about the city?"

"Women's talk," she said and smiled at the woman in the facing seat who had cowed her entire family, including the pig, into silence as they approached the city.

Mike scowled. Why did it upset him so that Chi was almost an adult?

As they entered the city, shanties and billboards replaced rice fields and vegetable gardens.

Rather than fight off his feelings about Chi growing up and the dangers facing her, he tried to incorporate them into his new *yang* focus. Fear could be useful, could be energy and strength.

He pointed to a billboard. "Look, McDonald's! Let's get hamburgers. I haven't had American food since... " He didn't want to talk about "since" anything. Certainly not to Chi and not now. "I've forgotten how much I miss them."

"Never had one, but I'm willing to try. I hear that french fries are very tasty."

He chuckled. *Not so grown up after all. I can still show you a thing or two.*

"Look at that!" He pointed to a billboard advertising the Cu Chi tunnels. These were part of a complex tunnel system constructed by the Viet Cong during the war and now opened for tourists. "I bet some Saigon tunnels have never been found."

"Ho Chi Minh City."

Mike shrugged. Maybe he could spend the night in the tunnels, whatever city they were in.

As they left the Saigon railroad station, McDonald's beckoned with golden arches and the smell of bubbling fat. Chi agreed the odor was inviting. He ordered Big Macs, large fries, and Cokes. They ate the greasy meal like two starving refugees. Before they left, he ordered another round to go and stuffed the bags in his oversized jacket pockets next to the wooden knives. "Just in case. Or maybe breakfast."

He began to plan his embassy assault in earnest. He slipped into mission mode—focused on the objective.

"First let's find you a place to sleep."

It took a few minutes, but Chi seemed happy to show him she knew how to get the key for her room and arrange to pay the bill in the morning.

"All right," Mike said handing her half their remaining money. "Let's split up. You buy me a very large dress, a gray wig and a newspaper. I will scout out a tunnel for a place for me to sleep." They agreed on a meeting place later that evening.

As they separated, Chi turned and called, "A dress? Wouldn't you rather sleep in pajamas?"

With Chi out of the way, he made for the American Embassy. There was more traffic than he remembered, especially motorcycles. He remembered Saigon as a city of bicycles. Though he saw some bicycles and hand carts, the motorcycles had taken over. Buildings and street names had changed, but he had plenty of time to find his way.

While he wandered around, he looked for the telltale fresh air vents that identified the Cu Chi tunnels. As he walked it all came back to him: the pattern of five holes drilled in the sidewalk, the circle of missing bolts in the base of a fire hydrant, or an oddly placed fountain in a park. With so much new business on the streets, no one paid attention to the old tunnels below. At least, that's what he hoped.

He found an isolated tunnel access in front of Independence Palace. He tested the trap door with his foot, but didn't dare enter until after dark. He knew the Embassy was just behind the Palace, on Le Duan Street. With these successes, he headed back to the railroad station feeling a bright future unfolding all around. *Chúc may mắn.* Good luck had returned. More yang had already helped. This was the right path.

"Here's a gray wig, but I couldn't find a dress in your size. This big shawl might work." She held up a green knitted shawl with long fringe. It looked like a bedspread to Mike.

He took the wig. "Let me see." He squeezed his head into the wig, tugging the sides of the fake hair down over his ears.

Chi laughed. "Turn it around. It's backwards. Long in back."

He twisted the wig around. He frowned at the shawl, but laid it over his shoulders, like Aunt Josa used to do. He looked at his reflection in a shop window. It looked pretty stupid. He noticed the shopkeeper staring at him from inside the shop with an amused expression.

"I guess there aren't many six and a half foot tall old ladies in Saigon."

Chi clearly held back laughter while she added, "Especially with such dark complexions."

"Can you take them back?"

Chi nodded and put the shawl and wig back into the bag she had brought them in. Mike waited while she vanished among the shops on the street. That disguise would not work. The bag was a good idea, though. He wandered past a couple cheap souvenir shops, finally spotted what he was looking for, a discarded plastic bag with a tourist shop's name stamped on it. He put the McDonald's in it and continued looking. By the time Chi came back he felt they looked like two tourists accidentally passing in front of the U.S. Embassy with their bags of souvenirs.

The steel fences and corner turrets of the embassy looked like a cross between a medieval castle and a prison. "I wonder if security is as strong as during the war?" he mused in Vietnamese as they walked by. He smiled at Chi. "Shall we find out?" He explained his plan to Chi while they strolled. She nodded her understanding.

She stopped a motorcycle delivery boy. "Here is a quarter million dong if you can fall off your cycle in front of the American Embassy."

"You mean Consulate?

"Yes, Consulate."

The boy grabbed the money and took off. Honoring the deal, the boy fell right in front of the Embassy. Machine guns atop each turret aimed at the potential intruder, and growling motors turned three long metallic boxes towards the unfortunate cyclist.

The boy cursed loudly in Vietnamese and was on his way, a tiny bit richer.

"I am impressed," Mike said. "They were quick and prepared. Do you see those long boxes? Do you know what they are? Are they ray guns? Missiles?"

Chi laughed. "You are a big hibernating bear. Those are surveillance cameras." At his blank look, she said, "TV cameras. They have a station somewhere with someone watching the pictures. Cameras are everywhere."

"I wonder how many more surprises they have. I need to find out what's going on inside."

"How are we going to do that?"

"I want you to apply for what ID papers you would need to visit America. You would still do that here, at the Embassy, yes?"

"I think so, but I don't know how to apply."

"Just tell them you think your father is an American."

"But I was born decades after the war."

"Doesn't matter. Tell them something. Tell them your hair is too wavy to be Vietnamese."

She nodded. She handed him her bag of tourist collectibles and walked toward the consulate.

He smiled. *She's a brave one, isn't she?*

But after a few steps, she stopped. She turned to him. "You know, you may be right? Maybe my father *is* an American."

He slapped his thigh and laughed. "Maybe. But as you say, you were born two decades after the war ended!"

She narrowed her eyes at him, but turned back toward the American Embassy without a word.

While he waited for her to return, he sat on a park bench. He reached in his pocket for one of the cam lai knives, then dug in his bag of tourist food. In between carving more detail into the dragon scales on the knife handle, he took bites of his cold hamburger and fries. He carved and watched the tourists. He enjoyed the warm weather, well-kept park, and even the cold fries. This was a good path. Lots of energy, lots of light. He was building his yang. A change of luck, and a change of balance. It was good. It was far far better than standing in the stupid stream. *Far out.*

"**A**ll packages went through an x-ray machine. People went through metal detectors, and some people's bags were searched. Once inside, I waited in line. The counselor listened politely and scheduled an appointment for tomorrow to draw blood for a DNA test."

"What's that? DNA test?"

"They look at my blood and they can tell who my parents are. If I have an American father, they might give me a visa. What do you think of that?"

He sighed deeply. Now he had all the information he needed. Tomorrow he would attack. "You probably shouldn't go back. There's going to be a lot of trouble at the embassy tomorrow."

Chi gave him a silly grin. "Maybe I will and maybe I won't."

After dark he entered his tunnel. With his mind on the mission, on the new path he was taking, he slept soundly. Thick earth walls insulated him from the weather and noise. He awoke full of energy and optimism. First he bought tourist clothes from a used clothing shop—Levis, a Hard Rock Café shirt, and an Oakland Raiders cap. Aunt Josa had bought him an Oakland Raiders cap when their football team had won the AFL championship in 1967. He'd lost it when he had returned to camp after a mission to find the entire forward base just gone. His hat had been blown to bits, along with everything else. He was happy to have one again, it felt like home had hugged him. *So cool to see some things had not changed.*

He walked into the consulate. A Marine blocked his path. In his best Uncle Tom drawl, Mike asked, "Is this where I go for a new passport? Mine was stolen."

He waited while the Marine examined his hat, shirt, pants and shoes. He worried that he should have gotten better shoes. The young marine looked up at him. "You ever play football?"

Mike gave him a big smile, lots of teeth. "Yeah. I was pretty good in high school."

The Marine continued to stand at attention, staring at him.

"Fremont High, Oakland."

He tried again, "California."

"Linebacker?" the Marine asked.

Mike nodded, smiling again.

The Marine smiled back. "Okay, just step through the metal detector."

The metal detector beeped.

Another Marine went over him with a wand and found the brass rivets on his jeans. "You're fine. Good luck with your new passport."

He followed the arrows, took a number and sat down. The waiting room looked like the the train station, rows of wooden benches and a few small tables with old newspapers and magazines. The walls had posters that said, "Liberty" and "Freedom" in large letters and pictures of famous American landmarks. He recognized the Golden Gate Bridge, Yosemite Park and Disneyland. *California.* Maybe he missed home more than he'd thought.

He wanted to carve, but he had left his metal Army knife in the tunnel. He read a newspaper called USA Today. The color pictures were nice.

After he had sat there for forty-five minutes or so, Chi arrived. His leg moved back and forth as he stared at her from across the room. *I told her not to come, damn it.* He tried to ESP her. *Split! Get out of here!*

She ignored him, of course. He stared at her, afraid for her. Proud of her.

He took it as a lucky sign when a uniformed nurse called her name. Shortly she returned with a bandage on the inside of her elbow. She didn't look at him. He gave a sigh and held his leg still as she moved toward the door. He gladly waited another twenty minutes allowing her time to escape.

"Jack Mitchell."

He waited a second before he remembered he had given them the name Jack Mitchell. He stood up. Show time.

"I'm Bryson Smythe. You can call me Bry."

Bry leaned over his desk and held out his hand.

Mike shook and took a deep breath. He didn't want to say the wrong name. "Jack Mitchell—Jack."

Someone had sweaty palms. *Damn! It's me. Don't freak out.* Find the balance, move gently toward the yang. *Smooth action.*

The small room, with white walls and harsh fluorescent lights in the ceiling, had just one visitor's chair. He sat. His body hung over the gray steel arms, the seat padding had long ago compacted into uselessness. He would have been more comfortable standing or squatting like they did back in the village.

Bry—*maybe five-eight, five-nine, small guy, no problem*—sat behind a desk that matched the steel chair in style and age. He was clean-shaven and neatly dressed with a white shirt and blue blazer with an insignia on the pocket. He glanced at Mike while he typed into a computer.

"Where do you live?"

Mike regretted not rehearsing the interview. Luckily he remembered the answer he gave the Marine guard outside. "Oakland, California."

Bry waited and finally asked, "Address?"

He tried to remember. "Yes, of course, address, 3833 Redding, just off MacArthur. Big World War Two hero, you remember MacArthur?"

"That was a long time ago."

He started shaking his leg as he watched Bry. His knee bounced up and down. *Is he getting suspicious? Did I give a wrong answer?*

Bry kept looking toward the door as if he expected reinforcements. Mike figured he'd better make his move soon.

"What is your phone number?"

Phone number? Pushing down panic, retaining his cool, Mike took a deep breath. When Bry's right hand left the keyboard and moved out of sight, he thought of panic alarm buttons and jumped across the desk. The computer screen crashed to the floor as his fist hit Bryson Smythe. Bryson collapsed, but Mike had been too slow. An alarm sounded. He quickly stood up behind the desk with one foot on Bryson's neck and watched the door.

The door opened and a Marine rushed in with his sidearm aimed across the room at Mike. Before he could fire, a flying wooden knife bounced off his combat vest, but the second one stuck into his wrist. It must have hit an artery, because a lot of blood covered the Marine's hand very quickly. The gun dropped.

Mike wasn't too slow this time. He was already leaping over the desk. He kicked the gun away, pulled the Marine into the room and slammed his 300 pounds against the door. When the Marine lifted his head, Mike kicked it. The Marine grunted and blinked, not out, but clearly stunned and in pain. He lay on the floor and breathed, eyeing Mike. Mike picked up his knives.

Behind the desk, Bryson moaned. Still lying on the floor, the Marine struggled to stop the bleeding from his wrist. Mike took a deep breath. The Tao of violence? This was not what the old village man had taught him, but it felt great.

He picked up the Marine's gun. The grip said Beretta. It was lighter than the Colt M1911 he'd had during the war. It seemed to have only one safety, on the slide. He moved it up and pointed the gun at the door. "Stand back from the door," he called.

He pulled the trigger. Nothing. He quickly switched the safety the other way and pulled again. Bang! A nice hole in the door. He smiled. He checked the magazine. *Cool.* Fourteen left plus the one in the chamber. He grinned. He had plenty of ammo, so he fired at the door again, just to be sure the backup would think twice before rushing in.

He had scored two to their zero, but he was still outnumbered, not even counting the squad that had certainly mustered in the hallway.

He grabbed a roll of tape from Bryson's desk and field dressed the Marine's wrist. He then wrapped the Marine's wrists together using the rest of the tape. He turned to Bryson who was trying to stand up. "Stay down," Mike said. "For your own safety." Bryson looked at him, and lay back down on the floor.

A soft knock on the door preceded a woman's voice. "I'm unarmed. Can I come in?"

Cowards are sending in a woman. "Slowly." He bent down next to Smythe.

The door opened slightly. A Marine Lieutenant peered into the room. Mike watched her eyes pause at the bound Marine with a bloody wrist wrapped in Scotch tape lying next to a broken computer monitor. She looked at Mike with an automatic revolver in one hand and a bloody wooden knife held to the throat of Counselor Smythe in the other. Mike stared into her eyes until he was certain she understood he knew how to use both weapons.

She didn't open the door any farther. She pointed to the soldier on the floor. "He needs medical attention."

Mike pointed the gun in her direction. "Not yet. Get me the man in charge or he'll never need medical attention."

The door closed.

"Away from the door!" he shouted and put another slug through it just to make sure they knew he was serious.

His breathing slowed as he relaxed minutely. This was a good plan. He was going to make them help Chi, and Mai Linh and the others. *Chúc may mắn,* for sure.

17 ≡ LIAM

He realized he was going to have to try to escape. He had seen the statistics once, about the first twenty-four hours being the most important. After that his chances for escape, rescue or safe delivery in exchange for ransom would begin to decline. It was hard to concoct a sensible plan when he was berating himself, though. Carlo had seemed so nice, so helpful. Liam had been so willing to be the smart, rich, world-traveling professor— he had pretty much bragged his way into this. *How could I have been so stupid?*

He struggled to think clearly, but rivulets of sweat ran down his forehead. His tongue felt like a piece of stale toast, split and cracked as he tried to lick the salty crust from his lips. *Sweat? Tears? Blood?*

His arms ached and head throbbed; waves of chills and fever crashed across his prone body. His legs shivered, while his torso oozed with sweat. He fought against the futile urge to scream or cry. *I must concentrate beyond the physical distractions. Escape.*

Gradually a few orderly memories emerged from the jumble of agony and regret. *A tricycle taxi bounced me out of Iquitos. A motor boat churned me up the river. Two guys dropped me in the water and rolled me dripping wet up the shore; I gulped mouthsful of river water before I could get my head above water and breathe. I've been lying here awhile.*

I need to answer three questions: One: who did this?

Two: why?

The numbers were orderly. They helped clear his mind.

Three, how can I escape? It was dark. Was it the next night already? *Are my twenty-four hours already up?"*

He was in some kind of a tent. His elbows pushed the thin floor into the sand as he lifted his head, tried to look around. He rolled onto his side to squint through what must be mosquito netting beside him. He heard faint snoring from nearby. Someone was asleep in the tent with him, or very near by.

He rolled the rest of the way to his stomach, got to his hands and knees. All he could see were shadows amid shadows. After awhile his eyes adjusted enough to see the faint outline of the tent. He was facing the door. Or the back of the tent, he couldn't tell. He crawled toward the end in front of him, felt around for a zipper. Found one, slid it slowly, silently upward. Gentle snores continued nearby. Slowly he crept out of the tent, like a baby, on his hands and knees. Outside, faint starlight filtered down through dark tree shadows. A slight glimmer of moonlight on water showed him where the river was.

That was what he could do—get in the boat, drift away.

But when he got to the water, there was no boat. The shore was empty. He wobbled, getting to his feet.

Should he try to swim? He was not that good a swimmer, and he remembered how swift the current had been, tugging at him as the men had hauled him to the shore. That was probably not his best plan. He set off into the jungle, one slow tiny step at a time. The sand dwindled and faded into masses of leaves, tree roots, and mud, more vegetation the further he walked from the camp. One tiny step at a time, feeling ahead with his bare foot before he put his weight on it, creeping quietly away from his kidnappers.

Money, he thought he remembered—they had talked about money. Did they think they could ransom him, like he was one of those rich American businessmen? He had no company that would pay for his return. He had no family that would, either. He brushed against something wet that moved away from him with a slight rustle of leaves. He froze. Snake? *Must focus on what I'm doing,* he admonished himself. *Must get away, find a village, find a boat.*

He began moving again, feeling for a safe step before he put his weight down. It didn't matter why they had taken him, he simply needed to get away.

He estimated he had been moving about an hour before he came to a slight clearing where he could sense no bushes nearby him. He sat down and rested his shaking legs. Why did he feel so dizzy, so weak? He maybe should have tried to find some water to take with him, but it was too late now. He eyed the river flowing past a few yards away. It wasn't very clean-looking, but it might be better than no water at all. And he'd already swallowed some when they'd dumped him out of the boat.

He'd consider the water problem again later. Maybe he'd find a village first, or a park ranger. He was pretty sure he'd heard them say "Parque" a couple times, which he thought meant Park, or Preserve.

He got to his feet, wobbled and bent over. Without warning, his stomach heaved and he vomited. Feeling a bit better he stood up, and avoiding his mess, began slowly moving upriver again.

He didn't remember sitting down, but he was lying on his side when he was awakened by voices. He tried to crawl under some bushes to hide, but he was shivering so badly he could not make more than a couple inches progress before he saw boots in front of him. Boots connected to legs, connected to someone—was it one of his captors? Or had he made it to a village? The man tried to help him stand up, but he could not stand. He shivered and shook and sweated on the ground while the man yelled at him. He thought it sounded like his captor's voices swirling around him, then he blacked out for awhile.

When he woke, sweating, shivering, hot and cold at the same time, he was back in the mosquito-netting tent. He discovered his hands and feet had been plastic-tied together. He groaned and rolled over, blinking his eyes and trying to see better.

Before he could focus on anything someone shook him. Sweat, or blood, stung his eyes and he shut them. Rough hands kept shaking him and a man shouted something over and over. *Just leave me alone.* But they didn't.

He blinked and tried to understand, but it didn't even sound like Spanish. When he forced one eye open, the man stopped talking and held a bottle of water in his face. He realized he was thirsty. A shirtless man with a scar across his chest held the bottle with two hands and said, "Shhh. Shhh."

Shhh?

Baffled, he held his breath. With exaggerated motions, the man slowly twisted his hands in opposite directions and he heard the click as the seal snapped open on the water bottle. The man smiled and repeated, "*Dos soles, dos soles, agua bueno, muy bueno, agua bueno,*" over and over. He got the message. This was a bottle of clean water purchased for the extravagant amount of *dos soles*. They clearly wanted him alive.

He relaxed and tipped his head back to receive the bottle against his lips and suck the warm water into his mouth. Each time some water spilled, the man nudged him, scowled and repeated, "*Dos soles, dos soles.*"

After several gulps, he had enough and turned away. A second man shouted, "*Mas, mas,*" and pushed him back towards the water. Eventually he finished the entire bottle. They treated the water like some kind of medicine that came one dose to a bottle and had to be consumed immediately and completely before it was contaminated by some airborne toxin. He was thankful they hadn't bought one of the huge two and half liter bottles that he had seen children carrying around the market. When the bottle was emptied and his stomach distended, the men ignored him for a while.

This process was repeated twice more between bouts of sleep, shivering and sweating. Then it was getting dark and he could hear the men eating some kind of dinner. Given how his stomach felt, he was thankful they didn't try to force any into him. The water was plenty.

After some loud talk and drinking, they staggered into the tent and fell asleep—one on each side of him.

I should escape now, he thought, forgetting his earlier failure. He struggled to sit up without awakening his two sentries. Each time he contracted his abdomen, he became nauseous. Twice he almost threw up the precious water on his tent mates.

His belly ached. He groaned, but no one seem to care.

Without much confidence that he would awaken, he fell back to sleep and dreamed of Carlo's strange sister with her extravagant English vocabulary.

18 ≡ ANI

Ani required the help of both the men in the camp to get Carlo out of the boat. She woke them up, shirtless, shoeless, and one without any pants either. They stumbled along down to the narrow beach where she had tied up the boat. Later she learned their names were Pusac and Ruiz. They grumbled about being awakened in the middle of the night. She knew they couldn't have been asleep too long, since the campfire had still been glowing red with bright embers and occasional flames among the coals. They laid Carlo down close to the fire.

"Do you have a lantern or something," she asked, first in Quechua then in the Cocama-Quechua patois many *rivereños* used. One guy had already disappeared.

The other one didn't answer, just staggered off toward the mosquito-net canopy tent they had been sleeping in. She stared after him a moment, then threw some more wood on the fire and dug around in their makeshift cooking area to find a pot, finally finding an old battered one she thought she recognized from Mamí's kitchen. She trotted back to the boat landing, scooped some river water in the pot, brought it back and set it among the coals to heat.

By the time she had done that, Carlo's friend had brought her a freshly-filled kerosene lantern. She could still smell the oily petroleum liquid. He pumped up the pressure, lit it with a match he produced from some magic pocket in his jockey shorts, and still without speaking, stumbled back to his sleeping pad behind the mosquito nets. Someone was already snoring again, and she assumed the third shadowy lump under the canopy was the kidnap victim Carlo wanted help with.

She picked up the lantern and placed it down carefully near Carlo, but not right next to him in case he thrashed. He had been moaning and muttering and felt feverishly hot. She untied the soggy, filthy tee shirt that Carlo had wrapped around his foot, and sucked a breath in at the sight of the bloody bones and flesh. "Ai," she said. She had a little healing skill, first-aid-level *curandero* training, and some knowledge of useful plants. Nothing like what was needed to heal Carlo's foot.

She had definitely not brought enough bandages. She sat back on her haunches and wondered how she might convince the *curandero*—the medicine man who was so good with plants—to come and help with this. She could not obligate her family any further, and she certainly had nothing to trade or pay the man with. She glanced at Carlo's face, and realized his eyes were open and he was looking at her.

"Pretty messed up, eh?"

"Yeah, Carlito. You need that *curandero*, the one from Mamay village."

"We will have money soon," Carlo murmured. "Lots of money. I am sure he will come, then." He rubbed his left ear, where there was dried blood. "My head hurts," he said, then rolled his head to the side and passed out again.

She picked up the lantern and looked carefully at the ear, touching gently with her fingertips. The whole area was swollen, the side of his face distorted and bruised. She sighed, and picked up her backpack. She had a few things that might help. She would do what she could. She soaked some leaves she had brought in a cupful of steaming water from the pot on the fire.

Meanwhile she used her knife to start a hole, ripped Carlo's tee shirt in half, and then one half of it again in half. She dipped the smallest piece into the hot water and bathed Carlo's foot, taking a firm hold on his ankle with her left hand, while dabbing and stroking and cleaning with her right. Carlo didn't move, and after awhile she let go of his ankle and used both hands to cleanse and smooth the skin of his upper foot. She held the limb close to the lantern and examined it closely. It was not, perhaps, quite as awful as it had first looked.

To be sure, it was a nasty wound, but most of the bones were all in one piece. The delicate thin bones across the top of the foot down to his outer toes—that area was not in good shape. The machete, or whatever it had been that had been thrust through the flesh and bone, had completely torn away an area of flesh about as big as a sol coin in diameter. She cleaned that again and again, refilling and reheating the pot of water to make it as pure as she could. That would take care of the foot for the moment.

Meanwhile, she took the leaves she had soaked and laid them across the injured ear. She used one of the pieces of tee shirt dipped in hot water to tie the leaves onto Carlo's head. Almost before she was done knotting the bandage, Carlo's breathing seemed easier, and the tight muscles of his face relaxed.

Now, to bandage the foot. She needed some things she hadn't brought. She lifted the lantern and made her way down to the riverbank, and along it, as best she could, climbing over and around tree trunks, vines, lianas, dead plants and leaves, swinging the lantern from side to side, looking for a plant she did not even know the name of. But she knew what it looked like, and what it did. It took over an hour, but she eventually found some. A good-sized healthy bush. She collected a dozen leaves, and tried to mark the place in her mind's eye so she could find it again later. The leaves were only good fresh.

She aimed herself back at where she thought the campsite was, having gone a good kilometer or more downstream in her search. Moving through the jungle in the dark wasn't the smartest thing she had ever done—there were snakes that were poisonous, and cane toads that liked to lurk in dark places, and other hazards—but her luck or her prayers worked, and she made it back safely, to find the fire almost out again, of course. His loyal friends were both snoring loudly.

She built it back up, took a swig of now-cooling water from the pot, but didn't swallow it, and stuffed one of the leaves in her mouth. She sat and chewed, spitting the mouthfuls of soggy ground-up leaves onto Carlo's foot. She put the quarter-tee shirt that remained into the pot to boil along with another one of the leaves, and began chewing up another batch.

By the time she had enough of the poultice for both the front and back of Carlo's foot, there was a faint line of dawn showing in the east. She tied the boiled rag around her brother's foot, making sure some of the poultice was seated on both the top and the bottom of the main wound. When she finished, she warmed up another batch of leaves for his ear, and went to check on the hostage.

So tired she didn't really care if she woke Pusac and Ruiz again, she slipped between the overlapping mosquito nets, carrying the lantern underneath the canopy. She found the two friends of Carlo first and second, then on the third try, the lump that had to be their victim. She squatted down and pulled the light cotton blanket away from the man's face, and grimaced to herself in the dim light.

It was the young American professor Carlo had brought to dinner at their parents' house. "You are a fool and twice a fool, Carlo Moreno," she murmured, staring at the red hair and freckled skin of their *norte* captive. The eyes popped open. Even in the dim lantern light, she could see they were a fascinating shade of green.

"It's you!" the Professor said, and grinned. "I was dreaming about you."

"Oh," she said, though he had already fallen back to sleep.

Ani took advantage of the break in the action to consider. Carlo, the cause of this mess and the most in need had fallen asleep, and besides there was nothing more she could do for him. His two lazy friends were stirring with the rising sun, but not awake yet. That left the Professor. Carlo's sole preparation for the Professor was water, "Two cases, not refills, for him." She went to check the boat.

When she returned with several bottles of water, one of Carlo's friends was rubbing his eyes. "Who are you?" she asked. "Pusac," he said. "That's Ruiz." Ruiz sat up. She handed a bottle to the Professor, who didn't take it, holding up his hands, showing his wrists wrapped in zip ties.

"This is so embarrassing," the Professor said. "My pants are filthy, and I would be happy to wash them, but I cannot do anything with my hands tied."

Angeline glared at Pusac, and then, getting no reaction, at Ruiz. "Do you really think he needs to be tied up?' she said, voice dry as *altiplano* air.

"Carlo said," Pusac muttered, staring at the ground.

"If he gets away, we are going to have nothing!" Ruiz said.

"Just where," she said rolling her eyes, "is he going to run?"

Pusac scowled fiercely. "Away." He cleared his throat and spit. "He already tried to run away once."

"Well, look. Carlo is out of things for awhile, and I say we're going to have to untie him. If he should somehow find his way to someone who speaks English and get help, then I suppose we will have lost him, but that isn't very likely out here, is it?"

Ruiz shook his head. Pusac continued his dark scowl.

"And he's certainly not going to be able to find his way back to Iquitos without help, and who is going to help him?" She got to her feet, knife in her hand, and walked over to where the Professor was sitting. "Hands," she said to him in English.

The Professor raised his hands. She slid the blade of her knife between the pale, freckled wrists, and cut the plastic ties. The plastic sprang away, and the Professor rubbed his wrists, which were swollen and marked with a dark red line where the ties had been.

"Feet," she said, and the Professor tried to sit down and raise his feet at the same time, and ended up in a clumsy squat on the ground. The odor of loose bowels was strong when he moved, and she held her breath. Then he used his hands to brace himself, tripod-style, and raised his bound feet. She cut the plastic, then turned away, back to the fire. "There's some hot water you can use to wash up with. Take it inside the mosquito netting."

"I don't have any clean clothes," the Professor said.

"Ruiz, you are about the same size. Give him your extra pants."

"No!" Ruiz said, eyes flashing. "Let him poop on the ground, not ruin my clothes!" He gestured toward the tent with a jerky wrist movement. "Anyway, I don't have extra pants, just these."

"Okay, then you're going to have to wash his, so he has something to wear. He can't go out with no clothes on, or his skin will burn raw."

"You wash them," Ruiz said.

Ani moved suddenly, and Ruiz found her knife blade under his chin, and her with what she hoped was a fierce expression on her face a half-meter from his. "Listen, my man," she said softly, "I have been awake all night, and I am tired, and I have no patience, and you will help take care of this person you stole for money, and you will wash the pants or you will give him yours, yes?" She gave him an eyes-too-bright smile, and Ruiz scowled but nodded slowly. Across the fire, Pusac sat frozen and silent, staring at them. His scowl was gone, his face blank. *Probably wondering if he is next*, she thought. She looked at him. "You can help," she said, and Pusac was already nodding, getting to his feet.

She went over to the tent. "I'm not looking," she announced to the captive. "When you are washed, I want you to drink some of the tea I've prepared before you fall back asleep, and drink lots of water."

At the mention of water, he made a face, but she didn't have time to worry about such details. She just continued,. "Later, Pusac is going to make you some steamed rice, which is the only thing you should eat besides bananas that I'm sure they can find for you. Stay out of the sun. I'll be back."

Ruiz stood on one side of the fire, Pusac on the other. They both watched her, wary, as of a wild animal. However, when she stomped towards the river, Ruiz got up and took a few steps in her direction. Pusac followed more slowly. She untied the boat.

Ruiz yelped, "What are you doing with my boat?"

Without turning around, She stepped into the boat, "Going to Nanay Libre for more water for your sick *norte* prisoner."

"That's *my* boat!"

She used the paddle to push the boat away from the bank. "I'm going...in *your* boat. You're welcome to come and help paddle. Or make the motor work. Otherwise stay out of my way."

Ruiz stopped. Pusac took a few steps backwards. There they stood like two capybaras, confused and indecisive. Two stupid ground pigs, not moving, eyes flicking left and right in dawning sunlight, as the boat coasted toward Nanay Libre and Iquitos.

It was late morning when she returned. She gave a pill to the Professor, gave instructions to Pusac about water, pills and rice, then got some much needed sleep. She was awakened by what seemed like a loud celebration. She blinked sleepily into the late afternoon sun, hearing Carlo's voice.

"It just totally blew up, boards raining down, fire all over the place. We're going to be like Túpac Amaru," Carlo's voice said, laughing. "Except, we are going to be rich!"

She could hear Ruiz and Pusac laughing too. She sat up. Her brother and his friends were clustered around the campfire, holding tin cups they sipped from time to time. She thought she could smell *cachaça*—cane rum, but hoped that was not what they were drinking. She searched the campsite, finally finding the captive Professor standing under the canopy tent, clutching the mosquito netting in his fists. He had been listening to the guys boast about their rebel deeds. But they had been saying it in patois, so he must be reacting to their tone, she realized.

"What about Tito?" she called. "I don't hear you talking about him being rich."

Carlo immediately stopped laughing. Pusac turned to look at her. "What about Tito," he said. "Where is he?"

Carlo cleared his throat. "He didn't make it, man."

"What do you mean?" Pusac said, an ugly tone to his voice. He stood up, towering over Carlo, who lay back against a log on the ground, his bandaged foot stretched out straight in front of him.

"I mean Tito laid down his life for us," Carlo said, in as respectful a voice as she had ever heard him use.

"Do I understand you?" Pusac said, struggling to use only Quechua words instead of his usual half Quechua, half Cocama mix. "Are you saying my cousin is dead?"

She stood up, clutching her sharp little knife, wishing she had a machete. She didn't like Pusac's threatening tone at all.

Carlo nodded. "I'm sorry I couldn't tell you last night. The guard just shot him, blew his head off, right in front of me, and he was aiming for my head when I jumped off the dock." He raised his leg. "He got my foot, instead."

Pusac threw the rest of his cupful of rum into the fire, where it flared up with a whoosh. "What am I going to tell Tito's friends?"

"What friends?" Carlo asked, before she could. "I thought *you* were his friends."

"His guerrilla friends." Ruiz stared at Carlo. "You think the Túpac Amaru are so bad," he said and shuddered. "These guys are worse than even those Shining Path assholes. New Sun, they call themselves."

"I'll offer them Tito's share of the money," Carlo said. "They shouldn't mind that, eh? A quarter million dollars, U.S." He sniffed. "Yeah, because one of them is going to be coming round here tomorrow or the next day, according to what Tito was saying. To make sure we don't need any more explosives or stuff."

"I don't know," Pusac said, shaking his head. "I'm thinking I don't want anything to do with those guys. I hear things, they burnt out a whole village up near Puerto Maldonado."

"What village?" Carlo asked.

Pusac shook his head again. "I don't know. Some Guaraní speakers, didn't want New Sun making their headquarters nearby, so the guerrillas just burnt them up, with that napalm stuff. Village, school, trees, people. I don't even want them to know what happened to Tito."

She thought Pusac looked genuinely scared.

"He was only my cousin, man, I don't want to die for him."

"As soon as we get the ransom money, you can go wherever you want to, my man," Carlo laughed. "With a million dollars, you can go to the goddamned moon!" He yelled it in English, laughed again, emptied his cup down his throat, burped, and laid his head back on the log. In that moment, so quickly, he was snoring.

Pusac nudged Carlo with one bare foot. He got no response. He chewed his lip, staring at Carlo, then turned to Ruiz. She could see them look at each other. She didn't hear any words, but they were communicating. Silently, they both turned and left the campsite, trotting down the narrow slope to the river, where Ruiz' boat was tied up. Pusac tossed the second case of water onto the beach.

She wasn't surprised when she heard the motor start up, roar, then fade out, taking them both away.

Her heart was sad. Even his friends—supposed friends—had abandoned Carlo.

From the tent, she heard the Professor clear his throat.

"I hope they don't think someone's going to pay a million dollars to ransom me," he said.

She looked at him, her heart sinking even further. "What?" she asked, standing up. "What did you say?"

"Liam," the little man said, clearing his throat again. "My name is Liam, and I said nobody's going to pay a million dollars to ransom me. In fact, I don't think anyone will pay anything to ransom me at all, actually."

"You had better not let my brother hear you say that," she said walking towards him to keep their voices down.

"Yes, well, that's why I haven't said anything until now." He murmured something else, Ani thought maybe it was, "I'm not that stupid," but she couldn't be certain.

"Don't you have a rich relative or something?" She was trying to remember the details of Carlo's plan that he had ranted to her the night before in the moments he had been conscious.

"My mother has a fair amount of money, though I've no idea exactly how much. But she never wanted me in the first place. I'm quite certain she would not pay ten dollars to have me back, much less a million."

Ani's legs just buckled, and she fell to the ground, feeling like a rag doll some little child had dropped. She shook her head. "Of course," she said. "Why would that part of Carlo's stupid plan go any better than the rest of it has?"

19 ≡ MIKE

Waiting for the lady Marine to return with the guy in charge, Mike thought to settle Counselor Smythe, "Don't freak out. Mai Linh's baby died, but I want Chi's baby to live. The villages need doctors and hospitals. The old people need their families. What bugs me the most? The villages need people, young people, babies."

Smythe still looked scared, "Listen, I'm just like you. I'm a Tiger. I went to Fremont High—in the Media School. I also lived on Redding Street, one block from the freeway. I walked down High Street to go to school each morning."

Mike remembered the high school, an old, run-down building surrounded by run-down portables. A holding tank for girls until they got pregnant and boys until they were drafted into the Army. *Why had it survived and the jungle villages died? Why had the gods saved one and destroyed the other?* He knew the answer had nothing to do with gods: Fremont High was green and gold, while Vietnam was Agent Orange.

"Fremont was a dump. How come they didn't tear it down?"

Bryson relaxed, his voiced got louder, slower. "Tear it down? After all the money they spent to rebuild it? When did you graduate?"

Mike figured this was a good diversion while he planned his next step.

"1974."

"My grandmother graduated around then. Wasn't that during the Vietnam War? Did you know her, Linda, Linda ... I forget what her name was in high school."

He shook his head. Linda had been a common name.

The Marine on the floor with the bloody wrist started to move. Mike examined the man's pudgy face. He looked like Mai Linh's brother, not old enough to marry.

Mike let go of his hostage. "Bryson buddy, stand in the corner with your hands on your head."

He stood up and tapped the Marine with his toe. "Hey cat, roll over onto your belly." The Marine, still holding tight to his bleeding wrist in front of him, rolled on his side.

Bryson seemed happy to have the knife removed from his throat. He stood facing the corner.

Mike pulled a second pair of cuffs from the Marine's belt and cuffed him to the door. He pulled the guy's belt and tied his legs together with it. The belt released a cache of treasures—a radio, keys, another knife, a Billy club, and something that looked like a small cordless telephone. He put the stuff on the desk.

With the Marine under control, he returned to the Fremont grad in the corner. He removed Bryson's belt and his pants slipped down revealing red boxer shorts decorated with firecrackers and the words, "I'm Hot." He wrapped the belt twice around Bryson's ankles and buckled it.

He sat down in the desk chair and juggled his hardwood knives. He admired the intricately carved handles, an eagle, two dragons. He was especially happy with the dragon he'd carved on the train during the trip to Saigon.

There was a gentle knock on the door. "Would you like something to eat in there? Does anyone need medical assistance?"

He ducked down behind the gray steel desk, resting his arm across the top with the gun pointed at the door. "Are you listening to me? Who's in charge here? I told that Lieutenant I wanted to talk to him."

He'd forgotten how good tactics and strategy made him feel. Throwing knives and shooting guns rejuvenated his old body. *Zen of violence.* He felt sorry for the boy with the bloody wrist now acting as a door stop, but he was sure he would do it again if the situation called for it. His close combat reflexes ached for action like a tiger waiting for a pig to wander closer.

He thought about his real demands—a helicopter, like those helicopters they used to escape when Saigon fell, doctors to take care of the sick people in the villages. No—that may not be enough, maybe scientists to figure why people are dying, why the babies are dying. Last, but not least, a visa for Chi—some day she's going to get married and pregnant and I want her to have her baby back home, in the United States.

He was a little surprised to realize that he still thought of the States as home.

"**I**'m Consul General Hollingsdale. I have a squad of Marines out here very concerned about their buddy inside. You seemed to be a military guy, so you know how they feel about a man left behind."

Mike pointed to the Marine on the floor massaging his injured wrist. "Tell them you're okay."

The soldier squeaked out, "Marine Corporal Wilson, present."

"Hang in the Willie. You OK?"

"We're going to get you out."

Mike drew the eagle knife across his lips. "Shhh."

Corporal Wilson got the message.

Only Mike replied. "That's enough! Listen now: Agent Orange is killing my friends. Last week Mai Linh's baby died. Not in the jungle, in the hospital in Da Lat! In the hospital! Many other babies have died. There are so few children. They need help. Now."

"I can help you. You know the Veterans Administration has programs for veterans, wives, and children. I am personally working on programs for Vietnamese nationals. Who are your friends?"

He didn't trust this conciliatory, smooth talking politician. He remembered all the nice speeches the troops got during the war—from people who had never set foot in a village, never saw it blow up.

He shook himself. He was still in combat mode. "You promised us some food. We want McDonald's…Big Macs, fries and cokes."

"Okay," came a different voice. "Just tell us who you are and we'll get you some lunch."

"I signed in. Jack Mitchell. Nothing else until after lunch, and you'd better include some bandages and antiseptic for Corporal Wilson here."

"You're in charge, Jack."

Yes I am.

Even after all these years, combat felt better than the peaceful jungle village life. Screw standing in the river. He'd stood in the river far too long. The women and children needed action.

"**S**ergeant Michael Jefferson Johnson, U. S. Army Special Forces! Your lunch is ready and I want to be the first to welcome you home." Mike recognized the Consul General's voice.

They know who I am. How did they figure that out so quickly?

He threw a dragon knife across the room. It stuck into the wall just inches from Bryson's head. To no one in particular, he shouted, "How the hell do you know who I am?"

"We've been looking for you for years. You are one of 1,762 unaccounted Americans in Vietnam. I have a file on every one, pictures, dog tags, fingerprints, dental records, DNA, everything. You left prints in the waiting room."

He scowled at the terminology. Did unaccounted mean *deserter?* Must be. And DNA? They wanted Chi's DNA. What was this DNA?

So. They were still hunting down deserters after all these years. Well, he'd assumed he might be court-martialed. The Army, Marines—all of them hated deserters. All of them wanted to make sure the guilty were caught. Why else would they have those files?

His primary goal was to get help for Chi and the villages. He needed to be sure that help would come *before* he was arrested.

The voice came again. "I've answered your questions. I'm curious if you can answer one of mine. The Marines told me you threw a knife, with great skill they point out, at Corporal Wilson. How did you get a knife past security?"

Mike laughed at the change in subject. "I carved the knife myself from jungle hardwood. I guess your guards weren't looking for wooden knives."

"OK, soldier, listen to this clearly. As long as you don't kill anyone, you'll go home a hero. We haven't found any missing soldiers in years, especially live ones. Everyone will be so happy to see you. You'll probably be a celebrity—you know—fifteen-minute of fame, talk shows, book deals."

They must think I'm a fool.

Someone broke the silence, "We have your lunch and a field medic kit. You were a medic, weren't you?"

He realized he was very hungry. "Just open the door slowly and slide them in."

He ate his third, or fourth, McDonald's meal in two days. Bryson fed himself and the corporal, but Mike took charge of the medic kit.

He didn't recognize everything, but antiseptic and bandages don't change. He bandaged the wounded wrist. From the way Wilson's fingers twitched, Mike decided that the knife missed the critical parts. He allowed a half smile, more good luck—*chúc may mắn*.

Prepared for battle, he struggled with the story about files and heroes. Bryson threw away the lunch wrapper and shuffled back into the corner and put his hands on his head. This time he faced out. Mike studied his face. Perhaps he looked like one of the Lindas from high school. "Say Mr. Fremont Tiger, what do you think of this jive I'm hearing?"

"Not jive. They'll probably invite you to talk at graduation. Your picture will be all over the net. You'll have your own website, Mike Johnson dot com or something."

Net? Web sight? But Bryson, and even Corporal Wilson, seemed to be looking at him differently now, more respectful somehow. He pulled the knife from the wall next to Bryson. "You better be giving me the straight dope."

"Don't believe me. Here's my phone, call your family, your friends. I have international service."

Mike looked at the little phone. It was like the one from Wilson's belt. He wondered if everyone carried these little phones and how they worked. He had nobody to call, so he just threw the phone in the trash.

"You're right Bryson, I'll call someone." He walked over to the door and banged. "Hollingsdale, you still there?"

There was some shuffling and noise. "Yes?"

"A young woman named Chi Nguyen was just in for a blood test. Find her and tell her I want to talk to her."

He wondered where that idea came from. He had been such a loner, he couldn't remember the last time he'd asked advice or help from anyone. But just the possibility of her friendly presence made him feel better.

He thought about going home, about some of the things he'd missed out in the jungle—restaurants, movies, hot showers, air conditioning. It was a pleasant daydream to imagine himself as a hero. He could get his own doctors and scientists and medical supplies and return to help the villages. He wouldn't forget the villages like they've been forgotten for so long. The old people would laugh and take care of the grandchildren and the great-grandchildren. The forests would echo with happy voices. New generations could appreciate the waterfalls and trees, the birds and monkeys.

But no. It was just too fantastic. Had the bureaucrats switched his file from deserter to hero? How was that even possible? He couldn't believe it.

He was a deserter. As a deserter, he lined up his knives on the desk. He counted his bullets—eleven in the gun, and thirty more in two magazines. The room had one door and no windows. He had a strong defensive position for now, but could he really hold out against a squad of well-armed Marines?

Maybe. *Maybe.*

This *had* been a lucky trip. He and Chi made it to Saigon. Maybe he *was* a hero.

How could he find out? He certainly didn't want to walk out the door straight into jail. He'd come too far and waited too long for it all to end in a cell waiting for a firing squad.

What next? What next?

He noticed that Bryson and Wilson now seemed calm. Someone had pushed the door open and he could see the hall was deserted. If they were planning an assault, they were in no rush. He followed their lead and sat at the desk eating french fries.

It would be groovy to have french fries every day.

His reverie was interrupted by a knock. "Mike? Mike? It's Chi!"

He picked up the Beretta and crouched behind the desk, "Chi? Are you alone? Come in."

The door opened slightly. Wilson, still cuffed to the door, did his best to get out of the way. Not much space was needed for Chi to squeeze in. She ran behind the desk and hugged him. "Are you okay?"

"Of course. How are you? Did they hurt you?"

Chi got that twinkle in her dark eyes. "Hurt me? You crazy? They came in a limo. I had a full seat to myself, white leather, so big I could have slept in it. The car had a television and a refrigerator! They gave me a cold beer and delicious *Bánh xèo*."

Chi stepped back and spun around. "And look at this. They gave me this nice jacket with the seal of the United States on the back. Look at the embroidered eagle and gold threads! Beautiful, isn't it?"

The more excited Chi got, the more worried he got. "Can't you see, they're just trying to trick me. As soon as I let down my guard, they're going to rush in, and—"

Chi stopped spinning and frowned. "What? Are you crazy?"

"Don't you see? They're telling me I'm a hero, not a deserter. As soon as I let their friends go, those Marines outside will charge in and probably kill me."

The twinkled returned. "Marines? There no Marines outside the door, only that nice Mr. Hollingsdale. And outside the building, there were newspaper reporters asking about you. They took my picture, but they wanted yours. You're famous!"

Mike could not even imagine that scene. "Can't you see? It's all a trick."

Chi took off her new jacket and covered the wounded Marine, who seemed to be shivering. Was he shocky? If so, Mike should get help for him.

But Chi, addressing no one in particular said, "This is my friend Mike. He's not crazy. Really very nice. *Trong khốn khó, mới biết bạn hiền.* Always ready to help. Definitely not crazy."

Bryson seemed to be listening to her. The Marine on the floor was out of it. Mike scowled. He could not let this be over yet—he still did not have what he wanted.

Chi walked over to Bryson, "I have a cousin in America."

She turned to Mike, "You remember? You must remember, he has the same name as you—Michael, Michael Tran. He lives in Minot, North Dakota. Remember he wrote me a that New Year's letter when I was ten. He sent a million dong and an American doll. He missed home—the trees, the mountains, the waterfalls. You do remember, don't you?"

He made an excuse to himself, *Too much spinning through my head to remember anything.* But Chi was so happy. He said, "Maybe I remember, maybe."

Bryson took a cautious step toward Chi without taking his eyes off Mike and the gun. "You want to talk to your cousin?"

Chi looked at him, gave him one of those half-smiles she always used when she wanted something special, "Yes, please."

Bryson raised his hand. "Mr. Hollingsdale, sir! Can you please get someone to find a phone number for Michael Tran, Minot, North Dakota. I seem to remember an Air Force Base there. Perhaps someone there could find a phone number."

An unfamiliar voice responded, "It's the middle of last night there—dateline and all you know, but I'll see what we can do."

Who was that? The Marine that had poked his head in? Where was

Hollingsdale?

Mike knew this was a waste of time, they'd never find Chi's cousin. She just didn't realize how big the United States was. But, never one to smash her dreams, he sat silently and waited, worrying.

In less than five minutes, Hollingsdale himself announced, "701-555-2479."

Too fast, Mike thought. *Did they also have files on all the Vietnamese in America? Maybe this wasn't really Chi's cousin. Another trick?*

Bryson looked at Chi and pointed at the trash can. "Please hand me my phone."

Chi looked puzzled, but saw the shiny metal object, picked it up and handed it to him. It didn't look dangerous, so Mike just stood by and watched. Bryson tapped it. It looked something like a small TV screen. After a short while he held it against Chi's cheek with one end touching her ear.

"Hello," Chi said in Vietnamese.

He listened to half the discussion, all in Vietnamese.

"Middle of the night?"

Chi took the phone from Bryson, sat on the desk.

"Yes, of course. I'm so sorry? But I need your help."

"Who am I?" Chi seem surprised and indignant, making Mike again think that this wasn't really Chi's cousin.

"Your mother's brother-in-law's niece? You remember?"

"Yes! I remember the letter. I still have the doll. Thank you."

Mike blinked. Maybe— He didn't know what to exactly to think.

As the discussion went on Chi got more excited and she danced around the room. He was still afraid that Bryson might try something, so he placed himself between them.

Chi explained the story again and again. After almost an hour, she handed the little phone to Bryson and turned to Mike. "He checked the files and you are listed as missing. People have been looking for you and will be very happy that you've been found. Mr. Hollingsdale is telling the truth."

He was now very suspicious. He wondered about *the files*.

How can a Vietnamese immigrant, in North Dakota no less, find my name in some government files—in the middle of the night?

He might have been in the jungle for forty years, but how stupid did they think he was?

However, Chi was running around the room, hugging Bryson, uncuffing Wilson, packing up Mike's knives. "Come on, out of here! Let's go!"

She was jumping, laughing, and talking in Vietnamese and English, so no one could follow what she was saying, except Mike. He eyed Bryson, who was watching Chi. And perhaps *him*. Chi chattered about the villages having a hero, and who knew Mike was so lucky? Bryson had a gentle smile on his face.

Chi put her jacket on again and giggled. "U.S.A.!" She helped Bryson undo the belt from around his legs, and ran to help Wilson stand up while Bryson pulled his pants on.

Mike sighed. *Damn your mother. She raised a headstrong, spoiled brat*. He had never been able to refuse Chi anything, and that certainly wasn't changing today.

All of them exited the room together, but he was soon led away by four marines.

20 ≡ RYAN

Ryan hadn't found the information packet on the Shaughnessy family much help to his plan to pose as a family member. He'd forwarded it to Claudia. By some coincidence, she knew Shaughnessy's mother from her cat rescue work. Claudia seemed to know everyone, that was one of the reasons he liked her.

She'd summarized Mrs. Shaughnessy as "rich, arrogant, and rich. Not the sharpest kitten at the scratching post." She also managed to locate some additional photos. He'd looked at the pictures, read the information backward and forwards, finally falling asleep with photographs of the mother, the deceased father, and young Liam Shaughnessy over his face.

In the morning, he attended a couple of sessions of the U.N. conference to see if he could pick up any useful information from the rumor mill, but there was surprisingly little. Individuals shook their heads over the exploded tent, but aside from that and some loose folding chairs turned into kindling, the U.N. facilities had not actually suffered much damage. No one spoke a word about the missing Professor of Economics from the College of the Rocky Mountains, or anywhere else.

He glanced at headlines from the Iquitos daily paper, listened to news reports, and discovered the CUI building had been destroyed by a warehouse fire of "suspicious origins." *Not a bomb, huh? But my guess is a bomb would be included in "suspicious origins."*

He left the conference and had Roberto drop him off in the market area for lunch. He strolled around, chatting in his broken Spanish to a few shop owners, showing Liam Shaughnessy's current photograph and asking if they had seen him. No luck until he hit the herbalists' section of the market. There an old woman smiled and nodded at the picture. A young girl in the shop ran off and came back with a packet of red powder. Through gestures, the old lady indicated, Ryan thought, that Dr. Shaughnessy had purchased some of the powder. Wishing he had kept Roberto with him as translator, he tried a few more nearby shops, but no one else admitted to having seen the missing economist.

Later he met Roberto and asked him to drive to the Policia. Without comment, Roberto did so. "Would you mind coming in to translate, in case I need you?" he asked, and Roberto came, but more reluctantly than he had done anything else requested of him. So as they were walking through the gate into a patio area in front of the office door, Ryan queried, "Is there a problem?"

Roberto's mouth opened, but he didn't say anything. Finally he stopped walking and turned to meet Ryan's gaze. "If you are looking for the man in that photograph, you don't want these police," Roberto said. "They are traffic police. That," he pointed to the folio of Shaughnessy data, "is not what they are doing."

"Well, who do I want, then?"

Again Roberto hesitated, then came to a decision. "Okay, I take you."

They ended up at what looked like an army base on the outskirts of Iquitos. Roberto stopped his Saab off the road outside the gate guard's little kiosk, got out and glanced to Ryan. Ryan gestured, "Do you want me to come?" and Roberto nodded. He jumped out.

They walked towards the guard post. A young man in a military uniform stepped out of the little wooden building and stared at them. Roberto nodded at the man, and burst into a stream of not-Spanish.

The soldier glanced at Ryan, then back at Roberto, eyes narrowing.

Roberto stopped walking about two meters from the soldier, so Ryan stopped, too. "Show him the photograph?"

He opened the folio he had carried with him and withdrew the current color photograph of Dr. Shaughnessy. He stepped forward and handed it to the soldier, who took it from him with a grave expression. Ryan got a sense of negativity, of being too close in the other man's personal—or military—space. He stepped back beside Roberto.

Only then did the soldier look at the photograph and shake his head.

Ryan stepped forward to retrieve the photo, but the soldier shook his head again, putting the photograph behind his back.

Okay, looks like I'm not getting it back. What's that about? It was annoying, because if he had known, he would have stopped and made a copy of the damned thing. He sighed. Well, he could probably print another copy at the internet café.

"You are his relative?" the soldier asked, and Roberto translated.

"No. I am just a friend," Ryan said.

"U.S. government?"

"No."

At this, the soldier's till-now relatively pleasant demeanor hardened. "You are soldier or spy." Stated, not asked.

He shook his head. "Nope. I used to be Army Special Forces, but I'm retired. I'm just a Private Investigator."

When this was translated, the soldier looked a little more friendly. "Magnum, P.I., eh?" he said in English.

"More or less," he said. "*Más o menos*," Roberto translated, and the soldier laughed.

They stood there a few moments, looking not at each other, but off into the distance in different directions. Having begun to get the hang of the pace of things in Peru's Amazon district, he was willing to just wait, and see what developed.

A second guard in the wooden guard station called out something to the soldier they stood with. That soldier took the picture, looked at it and just shrugged. After a few moments, this soldier looked at him, and said something in rapid Spanish.

Roberto translated. "The terrorist's boots had white sand ground into the soles."

He tilted his head. *So they are kind of admitting there was a terrorist*, he thought, but what else that might mean he couldn't begin to speculate.

The soldier, whose big dimples, smiling brown eyes, and genial disposition made him look a lot more like a kindergarten teacher than a soldier, stood with his hands—and the photograph—clasped behind his butt, and stared off into the distance, where some palm trees were rustling in the breeze. Not excruciatingly helpful.

On a hunch, he said, and Roberto translated: "If someone who was not a relative or a government employee, who also wanted things to stay peaceful and tourist-friendly and *quiet* in Iquitos—if that person wanted to find a person who had disappeared, where do you think that person ought to look?"

After a brief "silence and staring off into the distance" interlude, the soldier said, "It is very interesting that the Amigos del Porvenir Preserve reports say that is the only place in all Loreto district where there is white sand ecology." The soldier smiled, eyes crinkling almost closed. "Is that not strange?" He nodded, turned and walked back inside the guard post, taking Dr. Shaughnessy's photograph with him.

Roberto promptly turned and walked back to his vehicle. Taking the hint, Ryan quickly followed. They got in, closing the doors, and Roberto started up the noisy little engine, made a U-turn in front of the razor-wire topped gate, and headed back the way they had come.

Roberto glanced over his shoulder at Ryan. "I am thinking you are going to El Porvenir Preserve, eh?"

"Can you get me there?"

"No problem, my man. No problem."

They rented a good sized boat stocked with gear for a jungle expedition, including tents, yards of mosquito netting, cooking gear and a few canned goods for when they didn't have time to live off the land. Ryan had said he had no idea how long they'd be out. Roberto helped him hire a couple of guys to porter the gear, and a jungle guide.

Ryan packed a small bag of personal items, change of clothes, toothbrush, toothpaste. He liked to travel light, so he could forget shaving for the duration. He slipped his trusty Glock between a light jacket and his clean underwear.

"Only one little *problemo*," Roberto explained at one point. "The Preserve, he is very large."

He nodded. "That doesn't surprise me much."

Well, maybe there was one last place to look for clues before they headed out. One of Roberto's friends had driven the red-haired professor from the conference to his hotel. Roberto spoke to Eduardo and found out Dr. Shaughnessy was staying at the *Hostal Rivereños*. Roberto took him there. Maybe some hint to reduce the search area, maybe nothing.

After a long discussion and a generous tip, they finally acquired the tidbit of information that Dr. Shaughnessy's local guide was a young man named Carlo Moreno.

Ryan's head came up at the name—but probably Moreno was a really common name down here.

Roberto knew where Carlo's family lived, roughly, some place along the Nanay River, on the way to the El Porvenir Preserve and the white-sand ecology.

Early the next morning, Ryan checked his dwindling wad of U.S. dollars. He'd paid off Roberto's cousin's husband's sister for his room and board, giving her the full week as agreed, though he'd only stayed a few days.

When they got to Port Masusa, the rising sun was reflecting a long orange stripe across the Amazon, impressively wide—he estimated the width to be over two miles—even though they were over 2,000 miles from the ocean.

They were immediately approached by a short man with enormous biceps wearing a khaki shirt with buttons, a collar, and long sleeves.

Practically formal wear, he thought. Written in what looked like black marker, just above his shirt pocket, was "Jungle Jurnees." He was a head shorter than the other two men, but his well-developed biceps matched Ryan's, bulging the shirt sleeves.

"*Rimaykullayki, hola* Roberto," the short man said.

"*Napaykullayki, hola* Wari," Roberto replied.

Roberto introduced him to Wari, jungle guide.

Eager to get started, Ryan explained the plan to access the Preserve from the Nanay, which on his detailed topo map looked a lot like an intestinal worm with hiccups. Looking over his shoulder, the jungle guide chuckled.

"This is always changing," he said pointing to the blue line of wriggling river. "It is why you always need a good guide." He smiled, baring snaggled white teeth.

"Yeah, I kind of figured."

They loaded everything into their boat, and Roberto did his final tourist guide tip-earner of the day by getting one of the porters to help spread the green canvas roof over the boat's framework struts.

"You sure I can't talk you into coming along to translate?" he repeated, letting a little pleading tone enter his voice. He'd come to like and rely on the young man. "Big boat, plenty of room!"

"No, man," Roberto laughed. "I am tourist guide of Iquitos. He waved a hand. Wari is tourist guide of jungle!" He laughed again. "Anyway, his English is better, my man!"

Ryan gave him two hundred *soles*, which he hoped was a generous but still within the bounds of reasonable tip. Roberto grinned and waved good bye as one of the porters, whose duties apparently doubled as boat operator, started up the twin outboard motors, and the boat leapt away from the docks.

He sat down abruptly and watched Roberto and the town of Iquitos disappear into the clouds and mist and rain. It took about a minute of jungle-level downpour to make him really grateful for the cover on the boat.

A helpful little white sign proclaimed that "Nanay Libre" was the name of the village where their boat tied up at the small floating dock. Leaving the two porters behind in the boat, Wari gestured for him to follow up the stairs cut into the riverside embankment.

"Water level is rising from rainy season," Wari said, as they clambered up the ten steep steps to the muddy path above. "Soon you can just step out of the boat," he grinned.

A couple of children passed them, carrying books wrapped in banana leaves against the rain. Wari said something to them that included the name Moreno and they pointed back along the path, giggled and ran on their way. "First school session already started. Those two are late," Wari said. "They have two shifts at these little village schools."

Ryan had been admiring the crystal-clear water dripping from various leaves and flowers when he skidded on the slippery wet clay. He spent the rest of the walk watching his feet.

They arrived at a pair of palm-thatched wood houses. "Carlo Moreno?" Wari called to a young woman who poked her head around the wall to stare at them. She called something back, not in Spanish.

"He's not here," Wari said.

"At least we're in the right place," Ryan said.

"*Donde está*"? Wari asked.

"*No sé.*"

His curiosity was going to drive him batty if he didn't ask. "Does he have a sister?" he asked, unable to pass up the opportunity.

Wari asked.

The young woman got a very serious expression on her face. She stepped out into the rain, down the wooden ramp to her house and approached them.

"Angeline is not here," she said, pronouncing it AHN-hell-EE-neh. He rehearsed it silently a few times. The young woman said something else.

"She wants to know why you want to know."

Seeing nothing to be gained by hiding the truth, he said, "There is an American Professor who is missing. "Red hair, about her height," he said indicating the young woman. We think Carlo might have been his tour guide in Iquitos, might know something about where the Doctor went, and that Miss Angeline Moreno might know also."

Wari translated all this, glancing from Ryan to the young woman and back. The woman glanced over her shoulder at the other house. He couldn't see anyone else nearby, and there was no smoke coming from that house. In contract, this lady's home fires were cooking up a storm. She rubbed one bare foot against her other ankle, smearing mud. Her hair began to drip water from her bangs down her cheeks as the rain drenched her.

She said something, in a very low voice.

Wari asked her a question, and she answered, again in a very quiet tone, this time talking for several long sentences. Wari nodded, asked another question, got another long response, among which he thought he heard the word professor. Then Wari turned to Ryan.

"Maybe you can give her a couple soles for her trouble," he said, "enough to buy a chicken."

"Of course," Ryan said, digging in his pockets. He came up with a five soles coin and reached out to hand it to her.

She stared down at it, glanced up at him with a sad expression in her eyes, then reached down and gently lifted the coin from between his fingers. It was like the touch of butterfly wings.

"Come," Wari said, turning away. "I'll tell you later what she said."

Back on the boat, Wari signaled the driver to start the boat and go further up the river. Then Wari huddled up next to Ryan and explained.

"Carlo is the brother of her husband," Wari said, "and the brother of Angeline." Wari made a face, as if trying to figure out the best way to translate something. "Carlo is a pretty good tour guide, but not pretty good at anything else." He looked sideways to see if his American employer was getting this. Ryan nodded. He got it.

"Kind of a ne'er-do-well, this Carlo?"

144

"Yes, a ne'er does well. He brings the Professor to this village for dinner, for a native experience. Angeline had come home from the American university she is going to school at, just this week," Wari continued.

"Yeah, I saw her at the airport," he said.

"Well, she disappears some nights ago. She wakes Tipa up in the middle of the night...that is this lady's name, Tipa. She want medicines."

He nodded again.

"Medicines for…um, you know *la turista*?"

"Yeah. Traveler's diarrhea."

"That's it. This medicine is not for Ani."

"Ani?"

"What they call Angeline."

He nodded.

"And she had on her clothes rain and mud and blood."

He frowned. "So, was she hurt out in the jungle?"

"Taking care of somebody who was hurt."

Ryan glanced at him. "Like maybe in an explosion."

"Maybe that." Wari said.

"Tipa has not seen or heard from Carlo or Ani since then, and Ani's mother is very sad."

He nodded.

Wari held up his hands in an international shrug. "That is what she says."

"That's all?"

"Yes." Wari looked at the porter running the engines in the back of the boat, then glanced at the front of the boat where the other porter was apparently taking a nap. "Except for one thing."

Ryan met his gaze, raising his eyebrows in question.

"Carlo's another-brother once made a place to build a house, to claim a piece of land in the jungle. In a white-sand place."

Ryan leaned forward. "Did she know where?"

Wari shrugged again. "*Más o menos*. It is not in the Preserve though. Someplace not too far from Yuto, near El Porvenir."

"You know where that is?"

"Yes, of course. It's all white-sand up there. Even not in the Preserve, it is not a small place, either."

He nodded again. "We can go there and look though?"

"We are on the way to there," Wari said.

He thought a few moments, then dug through their stacks of gear to find the satellite phone. He called Dr. Powell. It was interesting, but also a little bit sad how quickly the call went through. Here he was plowing up the Nanay River in the drenching Amazon rains of wet season, chatting on the phone with his boss, who was—somewhere—in the Northern Hemisphere.

"Saint Louis?" he said, as Eleanor explained where she was. "I bet it's sunny there."

"Overcast, actually. What's that noise?"

"The motorboat?"

"No, that rushing sound."

"That's the sound of the rain that makes the rainforest a *rain* forest," he said feeling momentarily whimsical. Then he cleared his throat and got down to business.

"We have a lead on where to find the Professor. But it looks like maybe your protest-march leader from San Francisco has been kidnapped, too. By her brother, who we think may have taken the Professor, and may have taken the sister to help him with, uh, a medical issue."

"Well, that's bizarre," she said. "Why would anyone want that little socialist troublemaker?"

"Maybe it's a family thing." He couldn't imagine why Eleanor Powell would care so much about a little jungle girl.

"So. Are things quiet?"

"Eerily so. It doesn't look much like the Peruvians are even trying to find this guy. Or if they are, they're keeping it incredibly quiet for reasons I can't figure."

"That's good, though. That's good. Keep it that way. And find the economics professor and extract him," she said.

"Yeah, he said. "That's what I'm doing." He cut the connection, stowed the phone back in its waterproof liner and nylon carry sack. He nodded at Wari who kept peeking at him sidelong throughout the phone call. Then he leaned back against the gunwale and watched the rainforest glide by.

21 ≡ ANI

The morning following Ruiz and Pusac's departure, Ani was up early boiling water for tea, *turista* medicine for Liam, and a fresh poultice for Carlo. As she carried the warm drink to the Professor, she reflected how little she wanted the role of *curandero,* especially when they should be getting away from here before Tito's friends showed up.

"I thought I heard you arguing about terrorists," the professor said to her. "Or did I hallucinate that?"

She reached through the mosquito netting to hand him the steaming tin cup.

"No, you heard us. I tried to talk in English so you could hear. The guerrillas are real. They are not nice people. My stupid-head brother invited their help to—" *well, to kidnap you and blow up buildings,* she thought, but it probably wasn't a good idea to just blurt that out and scare him more. She waved her hands, "to come here. We were supposed to join with those crazies, but I feel we must leave as soon as we can." She met his gaze. His green eyes looked miserable. "I cannot guarantee your safety, either way, Professor."

"Liam, please," he said.

She nodded. "Liam." She would remember that. If he was going to die because of her stupid brother, the least she could do was call him by his name. "I am taking my brother, who is out of his head with fever—no doubt you can tell this from watching—and I am going to leave here." She watched him blow on the tea and sip at it gingerly. "I think they would get you medical help if you stay here, but they might kill you as soon as they find out no one is rushing to pay your ransom."

She glanced up at the morning sun. Clouds were rolling in. "They could come today, or maybe not until tomorrow. I might be able to get help back to you in two or three days. I cannot leave Carlo here. His friends left us last night."

Liam nodded. "Yeah, I saw them. They took the boat, didn't they?"

"They did. We have to go on foot through the jungle. I have to pull Carlo; I cannot take the tent. It *is* going to rain, as you've seen already. We cannot stop to make a fire, so no more rice or tea for awhile. You are probably going to get more sick. And the jungle is not a totally dangerous place, but there are…hazards."

"I want to go with you. Please don't leave me here."

"Yes, if that is what you want. Just so you know the options."

"I understand. But you can maybe find us some food along the way, and you can speak to people." His eyes looked wild. "I can't. A professor without language is useless."

"Okay. Put on all the clothes you have and bring any extra with you," she said. "While we walk I will find…a native remedy for mosquitoes. It will help keep them off you."

She took out her knife, knelt and cut another strip of mosquito netting off the base of the canopy. It made good rope. She stood back up and noticed Liam had moved away from the opening.

He set down the cup of still-steaming tea and picked up his own pants. "Hey, they're dry already," he said. "I'm sure glad I went to a good outfitter. That was worth—" he laughed, sounding a little crazy to her, out of his head, just like Carlo. Then he cleared his throat, "—while."

He pulled Pusac's pants off, put his own on and she turned away, walking back to Carlo and her half-finished travois. She had cleaned and re-bandaged her brother's foot, but there wasn't much she could do for the head injury. It was a constant worry, and Carlo's crazy talk made it even scarier.

She knelt and used short strips of the netting to tie lengths of liana onto the travois frame branches. She tested it for strength, and made the decision to use the netting for the sling of the travois—like a net hammock —to lay Carlo on.

"I'm dismantling the canopy now, no more roof," she warned Liam, who grabbed his stuff, headed off, then turned back and snatched up the cup of tea. He stepped off the sand-strewn nylon floor of the pavilion-tent, and she removed the poles, stretching out the sheet of mosquito netting as far as it would go. *Good, there's enough for a double layer*, she thought, and cut it off as neatly as she could manage. She took the piece and laid it over the travois, tying it on every few centimeters so it would give a little, but hold together with Carlo's weight on it.

When she was finished, she glanced over at the Professor. Liam. He didn't look very strong. "Do you think you could help me get him on this?"

He nodded and joined her beside Carlo.

She gently lifted her brother's injured foot, setting it on top of the good leg to protect it as much as possible. "If you can lift his butt, I'll get his shoulders, and we can swing his legs on afterwards." They did that, Liam surprising her by managing Carlo's limp weight at least as well as she did. She lifted the crossed feet on, and began tying Carlo to the travois.

"Maybe you can figure out how to drag or carry as much water as possible," she told Liam. Sooner or later they were going to run out, and he was going to have to drink river water, as she did. She glanced overhead at the heavily-clouded sky. "Maybe we should also bring the pot. Perhaps collect some rain water to supplement what is in the bottles."

Liam nodded and looked over at the remnants of the pavilion. "Can I use some of that nylon to make a sack, or a bundle?"

She nodded, imagining he was going to have a tough time of it. "Use the floor or the roof, one or the other. I need the other half to cover Carlo."

"Can I use your knife, or do you have another one I could use?"

She looked at him a moment, trying to decide if he could more safely use her knife or Carlo's machete.

"I promise I won't try to escape," Liam said with a wobbly attempt at a smile.

"No, I was not imagining you would," she said. She looked through the pitifully small pile of gear Carlo had left, lifted up the machete, flipped it up and caught it by the flat of the blade so she could hand it to Liam handle-first.

"That's a big knife," Liam said.

"Machete. Multipurpose jungle tool," she said, managing not to laugh out loud at the expression on his face.

"Is there anything you cannot do?" the professor asked. He was staring at the travois.

"What?"

"I— You— Well, Carlo said you are a student at a fancy Institute in San Francisco, but also you cooked that wonderful fish dinner and now you are treating injuries and making—that. And, I just wondered if there was anything you are not good at."

She had no idea how to respond to that. Her brother actually said something nice about her? "*Rivereño* girls can all do this. Most do not get the opportunity to go to college in *Norte* America, but they would if they could. And we must know about herbs, the *curandero* cannot always come to us."

He nodded, then continued trying to construct a sack from the tent roof.

She estimated it was about ten when they at last left the campsite behind. She buried the remnants of gear, and raked leaves over the disturbed white sand with a couple of branches, but it still looked like a campsite to her. She didn't really believe it would fool the guerrillas for a minute—if they knew where they were supposed to meet up with Carlo's group with any exactitude at all. But if they did not, perhaps they would overlook the clearing, giving her that much more of a head start.

She knew for certain she could not hide their trail through the jungle. Not dragging the travois and a *norte* Professor along with her. Maybe if he'd been a biologist, or a geologist. She'd seen some of those Professors, and most of them did field work and were accomplished in the jungle. But this was a mathematician. The only field he worked was the inside of his head.

He kept surprising her, though.

It turned out that even burdened with his sack of water and the cook pot, Liam was some help with Carlo, lifting the trailing end of the travois over tangles of undergrowth, vines, and deadwood on the jungle floor. She led the way, dragging the travois, selecting the path, and watching out, as well she could, for snakes, spiders, stinging bushes, bad-tempered toads, and tiny poison-dart frogs that might be a threat to her *norte*...captive? victim? What was he, at this point? *A poor lost soul*, she thought. A very long way from home.

He didn't complain.

He didn't keep asking to stop and rest, though his steps trudged more and more heavily as the afternoon wore on.

He didn't even complain when she found a soldier termite nest, stopped and used a branch to knock a hole in the nest. The insects swarmed. She scooped handfuls of termites out and smashed them between her palms and rubbed them on every inch of his exposed pale, freckled skin. "Jungle mosquito repellent," she said. He just nodded and took some from her palm to rub down inside his shirt front.

Just before dark, she found a plantain with some very ripe fruit on it. She pulled out the machete from where it had been riding between Carlo's back and a travois branch, shinnied up a nearby ceiba tree, leaned over and whacked the bunch of plantains loose. They fell to the forest floor with a meaty thud. She climbed back down and smiled at Liam who was staring at her dully. "Dinner," she said. "They're not sweet like bananas, but this batch is quite ripe. They're better cooked, but they'll do."

She kept them walking just a bit farther, to get some distance between themselves and a black sinkhole of water that was in the process of breeding a couple trillion mosquitoes. This extra distance also revealed an inga tree with bright yellow pods. She took a few moments to scoop up a couple handfuls. "Inga beans. More dinner," she told Liam, who nodded without much enthusiasm as he trudged on behind her.

As darkness fell, she found where a big ceiba tree had fallen, taking a few smaller ones with it. She liked the little triangular space between the trees that required only a few whacks with the machete to clear of undergrowth. They lifted Carlo over one of the smaller trees and set him down inside the triangle.

As it got dark, she dribbled water into Carlo's mouth. It was very troubling that he had not returned to consciousness all day.

"Could we have just a little fire," Liam's voice came softly from where he sat on the damp ground, leaning against the smaller fallen ficus trunk. "Just for some tea?"

"I don't even have any matches," she said.

"I do," Liam said, fishing in his many pockets. He held out a pack of paper matches to her. "Pusac's."

She sighed and got to her feet. "Well we have this nice dead tree. Maybe some of the wood inside it is dry enough to use for kindling."

Liam patted his pockets again. Mute, he handed her a paperback book.

"Stephen King?" she said, looking at him. "I would have guessed you for, umm, Updike, maybe. Or Steven Leavitt?"

"One of the other tourists at the *hostal* gave it to me."

She noticed a dog-eared corner about a hundred pages in. "You haven't finished it yet."

"No." Liam looked at the ground, then back up at her. He snorted, a sound that to her sounded halfway between laughter and tears. "Maybe you can just burn the front half," he said.

This struck her as absurdly funny. "Sure," she said, "The first part ought to work as well as the last." She laughed softly to herself. "Burning King in the jungle!" That was even funnier. She started laughing out loud. It wasn't funny, but soon he was laughing too. She couldn't seem to help herself, and soon big whoops and snorts were coming out of both of them. Calming down, she wiped tears from her eyes. It took awhile before she controlled herself well enough to try to light a fire.

Still snickering from time to time, she used the machete to scrape layers of dead leaves aside, clearing a spot on the spongy damp dirt. She found some punky wood inside the fallen tree, collected a few more solid branches which she broke or hacked with the machete into small enough pieces. She tore out and twisted what were no doubt deliciously exciting paragraphs from the King, and built a small fire.

Liam splashed some of his precious water into the pot he'd carried and handed it to her. She set the pot over the green branches she was using as a grill platform. Then she reached over the fallen ceiba tree trunk and hacked a few plantains off the bundle. She poked these around the edges of the fire. Once there were some coals, they'd roast nicely.

"I hope they couldn't hear us," Liam said.

She looked at him.

"Laughing."

She gave him a wry smile. "Probably sounded like howler monkeys," she said. "If they're even back there."

"How far do you think we went, today," he asked with a hopeful tone in his voice.

"Oh, maybe a couple of kilometers," she said.

"How far to civilization?"

"That I don't know," she said. "My guess is it's about thirty or forty kilometers to my village, but I'm trying to go the other way, away from Iquitos and the guerrillas. If we are going in the right direction, we could be in El Porvenir Preserve tomorrow. Late, tomorrow. Assuming all goes well. Through the jungle, one never knows."

"Oh. Okay," he said.

She rummaged through her nearly-empty backpack and found the typical *curandero's* anti-diarrhea remedy. She opened the little cotton packet, pulled out the last two whole leaves and crumbled them into Liam's pot of water. It wasn't going to help him much, but let him enjoy the illusion as long as possible. They were already out of the store-bought pills, not that those ever helped much.

A few raindrops rustled through the leaves nearby, and she jumped up.

She grasped the canopy—the roof part of the pavilion tent—from where it had covered Carlo, and shook it open. She laid one end across the big ceiba tree, then turned and tossed the other end over Liam's head and over the ficus trunk. They ate crouched under their rain shelter, Liam washing down the dry plantain with his tea. She showed him how to open the inga pods. They ate the sweet white pulp along with the seeds, licking their fingers like children with a fancy dessert.

They fell asleep beneath their makeshift tent roof, rain pattering down all around them.

Sometime much later, she was awakened by Liam shaking her shoulder. "Ani! Ani!"

"What?"

"What's that noise?"

She listened. The rain had stopped. Then she didn't need to listen because the troop of monkeys were practically on top of them, and dreadfully loud. How had she slept through that?

"Howler monkeys," she managed to shout into a break between their roaring, thumping, hooting calls.

"Monkeys?"

"Go back to sleep!"

P+P BLOG POST

Pride and Prejudice (apologies to Jane) aka Lies, Damn Lies, and Statistics (apologies to whomever said it first)—A blog dedicated to odd stories about numbers

Some Subjective Statistics

Unemployment

An old joke among economists is: What's the difference between an economic slow-down and a recession?

"Easy," the economist answers, "In a slow-down my neighbor is out of work, but in a recession, I'm out of work."

Behind this humor is the real problem of subjective statistics. The Bureau of Labor Statistics states:

"The basic concepts involved in identifying the employed and unemployed are quite simple:

• People with jobs are employed.

• People who are jobless, looking for jobs, and available for work, are unemployed.

• People who are neither employed nor unemployed are not in the labor force."

While there may be general agreement about who is employed, the differences between unemployed and not in the labor force are highly subjective.

Miscarriages

An even more subjective statistic has recently surfaced around an unhappy Vietnam Vet who took several hostages at the U.S. Consulate in Ho Chi Minh City. He was upset by his belief that Viet Nam is experiencing a high level of miscarriages and that Agent Orange caused them. Miscarriages, technically called spontaneous abortions, are when a small fetus (less than a pound) is lost in the first half of the pregnancy. Unfortunately for the statisticians, many spontaneous abortions are unnoticed and/or unreported. The result is that the literature reports the "normal" rate to be somewhere between 1.2% and 50%!

Our Vietnam vet attacked the consulate because a close friend lost a baby in childbirth—technically not even a miscarriage, but a significant statistic to this man. Given the subjective nature of the data, we are not surprised many groups include "increased miscarriages" in their laundry list of dire predictions.

Here are some of the explanations of miscarriage.

Africa: AIDS and poor nutrition.
South America: smoking and drug use.
China: husbands who smoke or work in chemical plants.
Indonesia: pesticides.
Australia: drinking.
Europe: heavy lifting.
United States: illegal abortions and pollution, depending on your political leanings.

That explains things, doesn't it? Or maybe not.

22 ≡ TOMITO

Tomito helped Señora Verde every day, taking the kindergarten and first grade niñas and niños outside for an extra play and exercise time while she was teaching the arithmetic session to the older children.

Today he was refereeing a *fútbol* match on the rough grass field. He couldn't run up and down the field with them, but his presence minimized arguments about penalties and goals. The younger ones were building a house with banana palm leaves and the legs of the broken swing set. Mostly, he leaned against the school stairs and kept an eye on them all.

Mañuel had gone off to the back fields with Papa that morning, so Tomito also watched the village. He noticed some activity all the way over by the dock. A large *americano* was talking to Tipa. By the time his step-swing-step gait took him around the *fútbol* match, he could see a boat leaving the Moreno dock and heading upstream. The *americano* was gone.

It had been sunny, but sudden clouds blew in for the morning rainstorm. He took the niños under the vendors' canopy to play. The boys practiced kicking and blocking the ball, and some of the girls played jump rope, a new craze begun by a visiting tourist who had brought enough jump ropes to equip the entire school.

He grinned as two of the little sparkly-eyed girls began a game of peek-a-boo with someone's little three-year-old brother who had been left at the school during a family emergency.

Out on the field, the house builders stacked more palm leaves on their house, hoping to have a waterproof shelter. Instead, they just got wet amidst much shouting and laughter.

Eventually the rain stopped. He kept looking up at the heavy metal frame for the swings, imagining braided ropes tied on at the top, attached to little wooden seats at the bottom. Didn't Mañuel have a few extra flat boards left from putting the walls on his sleeping area? His big brother would surely donate them, if Tomito himself braided the ropes. Then the children could swing again. Everyone liked the swings.

Marya came running to him holding out her hair ribbon which had come undone. He pulled her hair back into a ponytail, then tied the ribbon on, double-knotting the bow. It would slip off her sleek black hair again as soon as she ran, but she seemed to like coming to him, assured he would always put the ribbon back for her.

The cheerful scene was interrupted by what could only be automatic gunfire, some kind of machine gun noises rattling through the trees upriver. He jumped to his feet, scanning the schoolyard from one side to the other. It sounded like it had come from near his family's home.

"Inside! Now!" he shouted in Spanish, then again in Quechua.

A worried-looking Señora Verde stuck her head out the back door, as the children lined up, still chattering innocently, and began marching back inside the classroom.

He shook his head. "It sounded like—"

More bullets were fired, much closer this time. He could hear them ping and whistle through the leaves of the banana trees along the pathway. He wonder if the *americano* had returned, but he didn't see the big boat. *If it wasn't the americano, then who was it? Guns were not welcome in the villages. Children could be hurt.*

"I'll get them on the floor," Señora Verde said in a hoarse voice. Her eyes were very wide. Her parents had lived through the times of the Shining Path; she knew what automatic weapon fire sounded like, what it might

J. & D.R. Oestreicher

mean.

He nodded. "I will go see if I can get them to stop."

She reached a hand toward him, and started to say something, then just stopped and nodded. "*Cuidado.*"

He nodded back, walking his hitch-stepped walk toward the path to his home. Step with the good leg, swing the club foot and bad knee around and forward, step onto and off it as quickly as he could. He didn't think much about it anymore, only regretting he couldn't move faster in situations like this, where speed would have helped.

Except there have been no situations like this ... until now, he thought. Not with guns firing for no reason.

As he got to the path he saw the reason. A group of five young men dressed in various types of camouflage-colored clothing and military khakis were marching down the path toward him. He was frightened. *Guerrillas!*

Two held their guns up straight in the air, their other hands grasping the arms of a struggling Tipa. She looked terrified. Her dress was tight against her pregnant belly, but the men did not seem to care. The other three held their weapons at an angle, and as he watched, one of them fired shots randomly into the air. Their faces were very grim.

He felt his heart bang in his chest, as his stomach roiled. How could *he* stop these guys?

"You!" one of the ones holding Tipa called to him in Quechua. "You are Carlo's brother?"

Carlo! What was he doing now? "Yes," he said. "Carlo is my brother, but I don't know—"

"Come with us! Now!" the man said, shoving Tipa aside into the bushes.

It seemed to him that there was a moment of intense silence, when all the birds, bugs, wind and rustling noises stopped, as if to listen to his answer.

He looked at Tipa, meeting her eyes, which were welling with tears as she stood up. She pulled her dress straight and rubbed her upper arms. She seemed okay, aside from being scared and shaken.

"What do you want me for?" he asked aloud, stepping toward them.

"Where is Tito?" one of the others asked.

The two who had been holding Tipa now grabbed his upper arms and began marching back the way they'd come, toward his house. He was happy enough to swap himself for Tipa, whose pregnancy and quiet sweetness had not stopped these bad men from taking her hostage. He knew he wasn't much use to anyone; it was far better that he went with these pretend-military bullies than that they took her, or Ani or someone. But why did they want anyone from his family?

He shook his head. "I don't know anyone named Tito. I do not know where he is or where Carlo is."

"Did Carlo bomb the CUI building?"

He just looked at them.

One of the guys who had been firing his weapon now lowered it, pointing it back toward Tipa. "Where is Tito?" he asked, separating each word and yelling it at Tomito.

He stepped in front of the man's weapon, dragging the two guys who were holding him along with him. He'd surprised them. Now they tried to jerk him back onto the path, away from the rifle. One of them said something to the guy aiming at Tipa.

Then the leader, the guy that had asked the questions, said, "Pedro, *no más*." That one, Pedro, made a face, but turned back to walk with the rest of them, without firing any more shots. The two holding Tomito push-pulled him along with them again. His bare feet left crooked footprints in the dirt of the path.

"Jesus! You could go faster if we just cut that damned thing off," Pedro said staring down at Tomito's club foot. One of the other men laughed.

He decided to ignore the comment. He couldn't walk any faster, but that was fine with him. Give Tipa plenty of time to get to the school or other safety—away from these crazy men with guns.

A part of his mind was amazed that he was so calm about things. But what was the worst they could do? Kill him instead of Tipa. That was an acceptable trade, so he had nothing to lose that he wasn't willing to lose.

They were approaching Tipa and Mañuel's house now, and he could see bullet holes in the flat boards of the house. He stopped breathing, *Where was Mami*? Finally, his brain recalled Mamí was visiting her sister upriver. She would not be back until dark. He disguised his sigh of relief as a gasp when he caught his toe on a root and stumbled a bit.

Pedro and the other guy laughed at him again, but the men holding him helped him keep on his feet.

"Does Carlo live here?" the man who seemed to be their leader asked.

He nodded. "Yes, he sleeps here now and then, but he does have other places he stays."

The man nodded. "And when was the last time he was here?"

He thought back. "Not last night, nor the night before. Maybe the day before that, in the afternoon, he brought one of his tourists home for dinner. Then he took the guy back to Iquitos, but he did not sleep here or come home afterwards." He shrugged. "I don't know where he is."

The leader stared at the silent houses, Mamí's and Tipa's, for a moment. Then he turned abruptly toward the river. "We will go back to the Nanay camp," he said. "Bring the boy." They descended the bank, Tomito awkward on the steep steps, slipping as they half-pushed, half-carried him. His right leg went deep into the mud at the bottom, wetting the hem edge of his shorts. They tugged him out of the hole and onto the tiny floating dock.

A man holding a machine gun sat alertly in a long canoe at the Moreno family dock. Without another word, they all got in the canoe, pushing him onto the floor. Three of them traded their guns for paddles and the canoe glided silently and swiftly downstream.

The *norte* in the big boat had gone upstream. He was strangely comforted that the two groups were headed in opposite directions. Maybe they had nothing to do with each other.

"You see," the leader said, digging the toe of his boot into Tomito's ribs, "there are supposed to be people here. Your brother. The American Professor. Tito, and his cousin Pusac, and another guy who is Pusac's friend. Where are they?" The guerrilla prodded his ribs again. Tomito rolled onto his stomach and managed to get himself into a kneeling position on the roughly carved deck.

"I have told you before, I don't know. I have not seen Carlo since more than three days ago. I do not know these other people."

"Where is your sister?"

Tomito felt as if the man had kicked his stomach; all the breath flew out of him. *Was Ani involved with this*? He and his parents had wondered where she had disappeared to. Did she bring this trouble? It was not like her to just vanish without saying something.

But yesterday, Tipa told him that Ani had borrowed some herbs and medicine in the middle of the night, and Ani had been very careful not to tell Tipa anything. So, Tipa told him nothing, and now there was nothing to tell these guys, right? He shook his head. "She has not been home for two nights," he said.

"Was she helping Carlo?"

He shrugged.

"Your brother will be sure to hand over the rich *americano* in trade for you," the leader said. "We will not hurt you, if he gives us what we want. We just need funding."

"For what?" he blurted before he thought about it. He really did not want to know their plans, did he?

The man laughed, looking much older than Tomito had originally thought him. There was gray in the dark hair, and deep wrinkles at his eyes.

"You do not need to know, boy. But I will tell you this for free: Aren't you tired of the *anglos* trying to get rid of us? Aren't you sad that there are so few babies in your village? We are fighting against genocide, that is what."

One of the other guerrillas brought the leader an icy cold American soda. He could see the condensation on the side of the bright red and blue can as the man tipped back his head, swigged and burped.

They did not offer anything to Tomito. He squirmed backwards until he could lean his back against a seat board. He thought about how strange it was to have two groups of visitors on a single day and how he preferred no visitors at all.

He watched them sit and talk as it began to rain again. The heavy drops were pleasant against the bare skin of his legs. He tilted his head back and opened his mouth, drinking in the fresh wet droplets. He didn't need their stupid cola. But he would like to get his two good hands on one of their automatic weapons.

"If they weren't in Nanay Libre, we'll check the camp next."

He couldn't imagine where a camp could be so near to Iquitos, but soon enough the swift current took them to Port Masusa. There, they carry-dragged him to a jeep and were soon speeding southwest on the Nauta Highway, which ran parallel to the Nanay for many kilometers before diving into the jungle to reach Nauta.

23 ≡ MIKE

Mike stood tall, a head taller the the Marines around him, and marched in step with them. Special Forces had never let the Marines outshine them, and he took this responsibility seriously. Each neutral blue hall ended at a pair of closed doors guarded by a pair of steel-straight Marine guards. After salutes and the display of proper identification, the doors opened to admit Mike and his four escorts.

In the first hall, the walls were hung with famous Marine operations like Guadalcanal and Okinawa. Later these were replaced with documents like The Act Establishing the Marines in 1778, and various treaties. These gave way to organization charts, and warnings like, "The price of peace is eternal vigilance," and finally blank walls. As they moved through this progression from the public spaces, the hope of welcome home banners, garden parties, news reporters or indeed civilians of any kind became remote.

Sure enough, the final door opened to a room with bars across its small window. The two forward guards stepped aside to let him in. On the left was a cot, maybe six feet long, fitted exactly between two concrete walls. The walls were scratched with comments, signatures and tallies by previous occupants, all covered over with a thin, ineffective coat of paint.

The bare mattress had a pillow with a blue-gray blanket, sheets and a pillowcase stacked on top of it. The other side of the room had a sink and a slot in the floor. There was one light shining in the ceiling, and no light switch.

A layer of dust covered the bedding and mattress. Obviously the cell hadn't been used recently. Mike just stood in the doorway, reluctant to trap himself inside, but also certain he couldn't overpower four alert Marines, especially since they had confiscated three of his four wooden knives.

"Step inside. Don't bother to make the bed, you won't be here long." They seemed like grunt-level guards, and he wondered how they knew what would happen next. Do they know something, or are they just trying to be nice? He stepped inside.

The door slammed closed. He used the slot in the floor, threw the dusty linens on the floor, and laid his head on the pillow. He folded his knees toward the ceiling to fit himself between the walls on the bed, and imagined the immediate future—interrogation, court-martial, death sentence. Going to Saigon didn't seem like such a great plan just then.

On the other hand, it was more than he had accomplished in the previous 40 years. But how was he going to help Chi and Mai Linh from here?

He thought back to his military training. What was his first responsibility? Survive to fight another day. Well, he doubted the Marines would kill him, at least not here, and not before the court-martial. Survival seemed assured, at least for the short term.

He stared around his cement holding cell. After living in the forest so long, straight lines, walls and corners confined him, compressed him. His head felt as if it was being squeezed. He pressed his hands over his face to block the glare of the light and the smell coming from the slot in the floor and the dusty concrete. He shivered as he realized he'd lost most of his options when he'd allowed himself to be captured. Nothing remained on his agenda but escape.

He must have slept. Or was he drugged? Even before they removed Mike's blindfold, he knew he was airborne from the acceleration of the take-off that rolled him around on the floor. He blinked, trying to focus. His head felt a little better, in fact he felt relieved of the pressure he'd felt before. The open cargo hold dwarfed the concrete box at the embassy. Steel bars, horizontal and vertical, lined the walls along with an assortment of d-rings. Ropes, chains, strapping, and tensioners hung everywhere. Most of the cargo was packed in wooden crates, tightly lashed to the walls and each other, along with a few miscellaneous bundles and oddly-shaped items. He tried to read the markings to discover his destination, but he didn't recognize the codes.

A Marine sergeant walked up to him and nudged his feet. "You awake yet?"

Mike nodded, sat up straighter, and rattled the manacles that connected his wrists and ankles.

"Hungry? Thirsty?" The sergeant didn't wait for an answer. He handed Mike a cup of black coffee to one hand and some kind of food bar to the other. "That's the entire menu, so I recommend you enjoy it. We have a long flight ahead of us."

"Where we headed?"

The sergeant looked him in the eye. "Home," he said, and turned away.

He sipped the coffee and took a bite from the bar. It was sweet and crunchy. He thought it tasted like raisins or apples with some kind of cereal mixed in. His empty stomach welcomed the warm liquid and sweet solid. Quickly enough, he finished both.

The young sergeant returned to take his cup. "As a friend, I want you to understand your situation. You are being flown to an Air Force Base where you will be interrogated about your part in the war and these last 40 or so years. I recommend you do everything in your power to cooperate. You could be welcomed home as an MIA, but it's more likely you'll be handed over for a General Court Martial. There you could receive a lesser charge, maybe even a medical discharge. Or a death sentence for desertion. A lot depends on your attitude."

Mike studied the sergeant. The kid looked barely old enough to drink. A few blonde curls touched his pale forehead. He stood over Mike with his hand on his sidearm, the same one the Marine at the embassy lost so quickly.

"Look at me," Mike responded. "You see my gray hair. I'm not worried about a death sentence. They get nothing from me unless they do something for the Agent Orange victims I left behind in the mountains."

"That's what I'm talking about. A lot depends on your attitude and that particular one isn't going to help."

A corporal walked over from the small seating area at the front of the cargo hold. Her black hair was barely long enough to show under her beret. She reminded him of his cousins back in Oakland. She stood at attention except for her facial expression, which was disgusted. "Listen, you. Personally I don't care that it's been forty years. If you're a deserter, I'd be happy to shoot you myself, right now."

With that conversation-ender rattling around in his head, Mike leaned back and closed his eyes.

The interrogation room at the base held a long wooden table covered with scratches and cigarette burns. He sat at the middle of the table with a couple of empty chairs on either side, a bare wall behind, and a single door across the table from him. In addition to the two grunts he could see standing at attention with shouldered rifles, he knew there was another guard stationed on the other side of the door. The walls were blank, except for a large mirror on the end wall. He looked into the mirror, assuming people sat on the other side, staring back. Across from him in chairs were two shiny new lieutenants. He never liked officers and these youngsters would not be exceptions. Their name tags said, "K. Yamamoto," and "L. Ramirez."

He stood up. The two guards immediately took firing positions. The lieutenants looked maybe just a bit intimidated as they looked up at his six and half feet, 300 pounds. He smiled confidently and reached across the table. "Mike Johnson, Special Forces, retired."

Lieutenant Ramirez sighed, stood up, and offered his hand.

"Leon Ramirez." He was relaxed, with a slight grin and looseness in his stance that reminded Mike of a quarterback weaving down the field.

They shook hands. Ramirez indicated his fellow Lieutenant, who had remained seated. "This is Kathryn Yamamoto."

Lieutenant Yamamoto nodded at him, unsmiling. She sat very straight, making the most of her five feet two inches. It was her deep brown eyes that rarely blinked and seemed to look through him that gave her a commanding presence in this room of men. They stared at each other for a moment, then Mike seized the initiative. "I imagine you understand the awful damage the U.S. Forces inflicted on the civilians with Agent Orange, Purple, Pink, etcetera. I'm here to get help for them. Am I talking to the right people?"

Lieutenant Ramirez held his palms up, pushing Mike back. "Please have a seat. Can I get you something to eat or drink?"

"Not yet. I'm not planning on staying if you aren't the right folks."

Leon smiled tightly. "Well, we're from the JAG Corps, but we're happy to talk about anything you wish. You've been away for a long time and I'm sure you have a lot on your mind."

"I need to go back. I need doctors and supplies to take with me. Too many people, especially babies, newborn and unborn, have died already. The villagers are dying out. I, we, don't have time to waste."

Lieutenant Yamamoto whispered. Everyone else stopped breathing to hear her. "Listen carefully, Sergeant Michael Johnson. You are under investigation for desertion. This charge has priority over everything else. If I were you, I'd sit down, as Lieutenant Ramirez suggested."

Mike sat down, comforted slightly by the shadowy pressure of his last wooden knife still wedged between his buttocks. There would be time for force later.

"Tell us about your last mission," Lieutenant Yamamoto said in her soft voice, the only soft thing about her.

He put his elbows on the scratched table, rested his head in his hands, and stared at a burn scar in the wood. The image of himself carrying the charred corpse of a woman-child through the jungle floated before his eyes. "Honestly, after forty years, I can't separate the nightmares from the realities."

Lieutenant Ramirez leaned forward. "Relax. Try to remember. I know it's hard. Just try your best. Start with the beginning of that day, the day of your last mission." He cleared his throat. "You're Special Forces. You can do it."

Mike laughed softly to himself at the blatant false-comraderie. Well, he had had plenty of time to think about that last day. "It was March 28, 1972. My twentieth birthday. My unit had taken many casualties. We had inflicted even more. Of the original group I'd shipped out with, I was the only one left. I was on a recon mission. I called in Charlie's location, but something went wrong."

Lieutenant Yamamoto looked up from her note pad. "What happened?"

"Napalm rained down everywhere. It missed me, but nearby me women and children died, burned alive. I snapped. The next thing I remember is rain. It was probably May or June, and I'd lost a couple months."

"Did you try to make contact with your unit?"

He realized he hadn't explained this very clearly. After recalling the story so many times, some details became too obvious to keep repeating. "My unit was gone. It wasn't 1972 any more. It was 1975 and the Americans were gone. All gone, except me."

The Lieutenants asked him about this several more times, in different ways, and asked many questions about his life in the forest. He answered as well as he could.

"You studied Taoism?" Lieutenant Yamamoto asked softly, a look of disbelief on her face. "Be still like a mountain and flow like a great river."

Mike blinked at her.

"Lao Tse." Her face was cool and hard. "As you would know if you had studied."

"I didn't learn from books," Mike said. "I learned from an old wiseman in the village." He placed his palms flat on the table in front of him. "I learned I need to balance yin and yang." He curled his hands together in a lumpy yin-yang shape, fingertips to palms.

It was Lieutenant Yamamoto's turn to blink. Then she asked another question about his last mission. And he answered, as best he could.

As they marched him to another cell, an eerie copy of the one in Ho Chi Minh City except the plumbing was better, he wondered if they understood. He'd lost *years*. It was still painful, but he wouldn't let them see that; he was still Special Forces, at least for awhile yet. He sat silently on the too-short bed, tense, ready for fight or flight. He knew he'd never chosen flight, ever.

He might be many things, but not a deserter.

As the door clanked shut, he turned inward, seeking the balance he had learned from an old tribal villager. The Tao grated with his Special Forces identity until he remembered standing in the stupid stream. If nothing else, the years of standing there had taught him how to relax and center himself.

So: he was moving, he was changing, the yang had worked, had brought him here. Chi, his ying, was missing, but he could still remember her gentleness, her sweetness. He needed that to keep himself from derailing into senseless violence. She wasn't here, but he could still find a balance.

It struck him then, that maybe Chi wasn't his ying at all.

Maybe she was his luck: *chúc may mắn.* He had gone to Saigon with Chi. He had gone to the Embassy with Chi nearby. His standoff with the Embassy Marines had ended with Chi's arrival. She wasn't here; he was locked up. Suddenly he was grateful for the quiet of his cell. He needed to think about this.

24 ≡ RYAN

After a running up the Nanay River for a couple hours, Wari turned to Ryan and pointed to the riverbank on their left. "White sand ecology begins along in here. It goes west along the river, and north through the jungle, all the way into El Porvenir Preserve."

He nodded. "Are we going to stop and check it out?"

Wari handed him a well-used pair of binoculars. The black paint was worn down to the aluminum case where he placed his hands. Wari explained, "It's a big territory and there are few places where a big boat like ours can safely stop."

He understood jungle surveillance. He knew better than to prop the powerful binoculars on anything connected to the gently rolling vessel. He dialed down the magnification as far as possible and did his best to stabilize his observations. He spotted small black and white birds with long, sharp beaks, parrots of every color between yellow and blue, but mostly greens, and even a snake sunning on a low branch. But, no signs of a camp. The boat moved slowly along.

Farther upstream, the sand was white on both banks. He scanned left and right looking for any movement or sign of a human camp. It was too much to hope for a tent or a campfire, but he examined the white sand for trash, or footprints, drag marks, anything marking human presence.

He settled into his task. Thirty seconds from nine o'clock to twelve o'clock. Thirty seconds from three o'clock to twelve o'clock. Rest. Repeat and repeat. After so much white sand, green jungle, and black birds, at eleven o'clock, he saw them.

"Wari! Look over there on the left!" he whispered.

Wari shaded his eyes. "I see them. Men. What should we do?"

"Can you find a safe place to dock, before we get there, before they hear us?"

"There's a little inlet stream just over there, we can go up that and maybe find a mooring site."

"Good," he said, nodding again, and collecting his gear.

They entered the side stream. One porter—he had found out their names were Chuki and Orqo, but he still didn't know which was which—cut the motors down to a purr. The stream disappeared behind the branches of drowning trees and snags, but Chuki, or Orqo, steered the boat between the obstructions. The stream rapidly became narrower and shallower, and the driver ran the boat aground at a sandy shelf between two trees with enormous many-legged root structures.

Shrugging on his backpack, Ryan glanced at the sandy beachlet. It didn't look very white. Then he saw the footprints. Someone had been here, very recently; the rain they'd just had hadn't even begun to fill in the inch-deep heel marks. "Boot," he said. He stepped out of the boat, squatted down to look at the print, and thus saved his own life.

A bullet whined above his head, tore through part of the boat canopy, and encouraged Wari, Chuki and Orqo to drop flat in the boat. Ryan threw himself behind the cover of the thick root tangle to his left, pulling his pack off and throwing it down. He reached inside— *Knew they were there. Wasn't prepared. Getting soft*—and yanked out his Glock, trying to ignore the bullets that were still whizzing by around the tree, over the boat—he hoped *over* the boat—and through the nearby leaves and bushes.

Someone in the boat got the motors started. Still ducked down below the gunwale where they couldn't be seen, they backed the boat rapidly down the stream, until it hit a snag. He could hear one of the propellers kick, catch and hang up in something, coming to an abrupt stop. The other kept going though, the boat turning itself slowly, slowly around the pivot of the motor and snag.

The firing slowed and stopped, and he heard low voices. He peeked around his root shield, ready to fire. Some guy dressed in jungle camo saw him, exclaimed, and fired his pistol, but by then Ryan had nailed him, the triple-burst from the Glock catching him across the chest. He dropped. One of the other two forms beside him dove off into the bushes. Another, in the center, dropped to a knee, aimed and fired his submachine gun at Ryan. The bullets tore up the roots in front of him, spraying wood chips everywhere. He leaned way back, hoping the knee of the tree roots was thick enough to stop the barrage of bullets.

It occurred to him this could be a Peruvian Army contingent. Had he just killed one of his supposed allies? He took advantage of a pause in the firing to glance over the roots, checking out the clothing of the two opponents he could see. Paramilitary. No rank or insignia was showing, just tan pants and a camo shirt you could buy at the Peruvian equivalent of Army surplus. He hoped. Then he noticed the second guy's feet. Flip-flops. Not Army issue, one would think. The submachine gun started up again.

Between bursts, he could hear the sound of the boat backing and restarting, and finally breaking itself loose of the snag. *They're just going to abandon me here? That's real nice.* Well, he hadn't actually hired them to be shooting and dodging bullets. *Maybe they'll come back with the Army*, he thought, *The real Army. El ejército.*

The submachine gun stopped firing for a moment. He stood up, leaned forward and fired another burst from the Glock. The submachine gunner went down, but the guy who had dived aside earlier had apparently been waiting for his chance. His pistol cracked, and Ryan felt the burn of a bullet past his right bicep. "Damn, that hurts!" He roared, stepping out from behind his tree and firing three or four bursts at the pistol guy. That one went down with a yelp, but not before letting off one more round that missed Ryan's hip by so little it actually burned a hole through his dangling canvas and nylon belt strap.

He ducked back behind his tree, listening as he pressed a kerchief to his upper arm. Just a crease, but it stung like blazes. The enemy was down three, but how many more were there? And who were they? They seemed awfully well-armed for kidnappers. But maybe not for the terrorist bombers who had attacked Iquitos.

Unhelpfully, it began to rain, going from a drop or two to a full downpour in a single breath. He checked his flanks, making sure no one had managed to find a path alongside the stream to his left or right. He didn't see anything, but in the heavy rain her couldn't be sure.

He peered around the tree again, and saw only the three fallen bodies. He reached into his backpack, grabbed two spare magazines and dropped them in his cargo pocket. He marked his next piece of cover, and moved smoothly from behind his tree roots several yards to a solidly leafed little bush. He crouched down, reached his pistol way out and snagged the first guy's rifle, dragging it to him. A piece-of-crap Russian model. He chucked it behind him, into the stream. He checked his flanks again, then leaned out and grabbed the submachine gun from the middle guy, whose brown eyes were wide open in surprised death.

His weapon was a nice little 360 Mini Uzi. *How did you get all the way from Israel to the jungles of Peru*? Ryan asked it, but it didn't have anything to say for itself. If he could get some cartridges off the dead guy, this would help his minimal armaments situation. He tucked his Glock through his belt, wishing he'd had time to find his holster. The Uzi was going to be a big help. Especially since it seemed to be just him against he didn't know how many of these guys, whoever they were. *Three less than there were*, he thought, with a tight little smile.

He heard or sensed movement to his left, peered around his bush, and fired a burst from the Uzi. His target ducked down, firing some kind of automatic weapon back at him. *You can't hit the broad side of a barn, fella*, he thought, and let off a burst from the Uzi at a patch of blue-green shirt he could see through a break in the leaves. The guy cried out, dropping with a thud. Four down. That was good, but the Uzi was out, and that was bad.

He stood up briefly, making himself a target. A calculated risk, but these guys had not demonstrated themselves to be well-trained marksmen, no matter how many armaments they carried. No one shot at him. He took the chance, ten running steps in a crouch, presenting his side as a minimal target. He got a grip on the dead machine gunner, dragged him off to the right behind the cover of a mossy, slender tree, where the third guy, the one that had hit his arm, had fallen. He wiped rain off his brow, scanned his full perimeter. No one. Lots of rain and leaves.

On the dead guy, he found two magazines for the Uzi, reloaded it. He checked the pistol guy that had hit his arm. That one was still breathing. He took the guy's gun, a decent enough though older Beretta. He made sure neither the live guy or the dead one had any kind of weapon left. Then he moved ahead to the cover of a fat tree with another tree in the process of wrapping itself around it. *Strangler fig*, his brain commented. Soon the tree underneath would die, leaving the fig triumphant.

He checked around himself. The rain began to slow down a little. He moved inland, away from the stream, toward the next bit of cover. He could see around this tree into a small cleared area. Here the sand was actually white between the brown and black fallen leaves. He grunted to himself, scanning behind and between trees, leaves, flowers.

There were three more of these guys, and that was all he could see. One was prone on the ground, unmoving. The other two were crouched down nearby the fallen one, at the edge of the cleared space in plain sight. One of them saw him. That one said something to his companion, and they both stood up, showing Ryan empty hands.

"Yeah, I just bet you're unarmed," he muttered. He held the Uzi steady on them, checking all around himself again, in case this was a diversion. There really didn't seem to be anyone else. He stayed behind his tree.

"You speak English?" he called.

One of them answered him in Spanish too rapid for him to pick out more than the word, "*uno.*"

"One, what?" he shouted. "One me? One wound?" His arm burned like hell, he was stranded here alone and feeling crankier by the second. "Put your hands behind your heads," he tried.

They looked at each other, still holding their hands in front of themselves, palms up.

"Great," he said.

He pulled what he hoped were the right vocabulary words from his faint high school memories. "*Sus manos sobre sus cabezas,*" he yelled, knowing he was mangling it, but maybe it would be good enough.

They put their hands on top of their heads.

"Okay," he said. "Simon says 'sit down.'" He kicked his memory again, and it coughed up, "*Sientate!*"

They dropped to their butts on the sand.

"Cool!" he said. He did one more visual and auditory scan, heard something behind himself. He spun, the Uzi set in firing position.

Wari waved his hands frantically, eyes wide, from the little beach where they'd landed their boat the first time.

Ryan smiled at him, and waved him to stand behind the nice tree roots he'd used as a shield earlier. Wari nodded. Ryan couldn't see the boat anywhere, so how Wari had gotten back was a puzzle. He was grateful, though. "Can you talk to these guys?" he called.

Wari peeked around the tree roots. Evidently he couldn't see the surrendered guerrillas from where he stood; he shrugged.

"Ask them to say how many of them there are."

Wari yelled something. It didn't sound like Spanish.

One of the two seated prisoners shouted something back. "*Seis,*" he said, and even Ryan knew that meant six. But that was no good, he had counted seven. Why would they lie unless more of them were sneaking up on him? He stood there listening carefully for several minutes. The rain was no longer falling, but drops still pattered down, emptying over-filled leaves and dripping off branches. A bird chirped nearby. Something else made a sound like a drop of water falling a long way down into a pond. The two prisoners sat in the clearing with their hands on their heads, the guy on the ground near them still unmoving. No, not unmoving. That guy sat up, calling something out loud, not in Spanish. Ryan could now see this was just a kid, and his hands were bound.

Ryan glanced at Wari. Wari grinned. "He says, 'Don't shoot, he's a prisoner.'"

"Okay," he said, and stepped out from behind his tree toward the two captives and the kid. They stared at him as he moved into the clearing, the muzzle of the Uzi clearly pointed at one head and then the other. He could hear Wari following a few paces behind. He stopped, Wari stopped, then took another two steps to join him in staring at their two prisoners who had their own prisoner, if he could be believed.

"Can you find out who they are and who their captive is?" It wasn't Liam Shaughnessy, that was certain. This was a native kid from the look of him. Black hair, not red. Dark skin, not fair.

After an exchange of dialogue, Wari said, "They claim they are an Army patrol, but I do not think so."

"I do not think so either. They have no insignia, and their weapons are the crazy kind of mix you buy from gun-runners. And who's their prisoner?"

"My name is Tomito," the boy said in quiet Spanish. "They are not Army. They are guerrillas," he added in weirdly accented English.

Ryan scowled. "Wari, I'm going to stand guard here, while you search them, one at a time. Can you do that? Make sure they're not hiding a gun or a knife?"

Wari swallowed, then nodded. He said something to the guy on his left. That one stood up slowly, and began removing his clothes, which took some time while he unknotted the assortment of laces on his boots.

"Good thinking," Ryan said.

When the first was completely naked, Wari instructed him to sit down, hands atop head, and the other one to strip.

Ryan kicked their clothes into a pile. It looked like they'd been telling the truth with their empty hands.

Then Wari said the same thing to the kid, whose hands were still tied. Tomito—was that his name?—held up his wrists to show Wari, who grunted, then emitted a rapid stream of language at the kid, who sat down and extended his legs in front of himself. Ryan noticed one of the boy's feet was deformed, thick and blocky from the ankle down.

"Any more prisoners?" Wari asked, beginning to look a little more sure of himself. "Ours or theirs?"

"Three bodies," Ryan said, "and one wounded."

They used the captives' belts to tie their feet together at the ankles, and Wari guarded them, holding the captured Beretta on them as a threat while Ryan went and disarmed the fourth, green shirt guy he'd shot, who was quite thoroughly dead. Then he went back and dragged the wounded pistol guy into the clearing. He tossed one of the other two captives a shirt from one of the dead guys.

"Tell him to stop the bleeding," Ryan said, indicating their wounded comrade.

At the riverbank, Ryan heard the twin motors of his boat, and smiled.

"Tell me about Tomito, here," he asked Wari later, as they checked the camp area for weapons and gear.

Tomito told his story, Wari translating, about how the guerrillas had come looking for Carlo and someone named Tito, and had taken Tipa hostage, terrifying her. Tomito exchanged himself for her, and as far as he knew she was safe, and the rest of his family was safe. He knew nothing about an American Professor, except that Carlo had brought a tourist home for dinner at their house a couple nights previously, and that man had been some kind of Professor. Was that the same one?

"Dr. Shaughnessy," Ryan said, and Tomito nodded, eyes wide. Ryan shook his head. "The good doctor is still missing." Tomito said nothing to this, his face creased in a frown.

Ryan and Wari, Orqo and Chuki cleaned out the terrorists, leaving them with nothing but their clothes. Chuki and Orqo were delighted with the military-style boots a couple of the guerrillas had had, each finding a pair that fit pretty well. When it turned out Orqo knew a little bit about weapons, Ryan turned the Beretta over to him along with all the ammunition they could find for it. Chuki made sure he had collected all the machetes in camp, and he'd also found a nice cooking pot. Wari found a lantern and some fuel tucked into a hollow tree. They stashed everything in their boat.

"Find out where *their* boat is," he said to Wari when he came back.

There was a long involved argument between Wari and the two unwounded captives. Finally Wari looked up with a triumphant grin. "They don't have a boat. They have a jeep." He pronounced it "yeep" so it took a couple seconds for Ryan to figure it out.

"There's a road here?"

Wari nodded. "The Panjil road. It's a spur up from the Iquitos to Nauta Highway about three kilometers west of here. They just drove in as far as they could, parked about a half a kilometer from here, and walked the rest of the way." Wari held up the key, which dangled from a black metal chain.

"Nifty," Ryan said. At Wari's obvious confusion, he chuckled. "Uh, it's like: 'cool!' except way older."

"Nifty," Wari said, practicing it. "Nifty!"

"Thanks for coming back for me, man," he said making sure Wari knew he appreciated what a risk it had been.

"Hey, I saw the tip you give to Roberto," he laughed, making little of it, but Ryan clapped him on the shoulder and nodded.

"Now," he said, looking at their captives, "I wonder if they know what became of our missing Dr. Shaughnessy."

Their captives had no idea where Dr. Shaughnessy was. Carlo was supposed to have brought him here. They'd not found him at the Moreno home and no one knew where he or the Doctor were, or even if they had been together. Someone named Tito had done the negotiating on this deal. Their group was going to come looking for them at any time, the prisoners said.

"It may be a real threat," Wari said. "They claim to be part of a guerrilla group seeking independence for Loreto from the rest of Peru. I heard they were banding together up near Pantoja."

Ryan glanced at him, back at the prisoners. "Where's that?"

"Way up north, by the border to Columbia and Ecuador. The government is trying to wipe them out; they are very tough on terrorists since Shining Path."

"That's a good thing," he said. "These guys shoot first and talk later." His arm, cleaned and bandaged, had begun to stiffen up. It had swelled enough that his shirt sleeve had to be slit open. It still seemed to hurt a lot, for such a small wound. He'd taken worse hits and didn't remember them bothering him like this. Of course, he'd been somewhat younger then.

Orqo, who had been circling the campsite in a spiral search pattern, came into camp with a grin. He said something to Wari, who also grinned, and translated for Ryan: "Found a trail. Leads off into the bush, toward the Highway. There's more than one person, and they're dragging something."

"All right," he said. "Let me make a phone call. I'll get someone to come and pick up these guys."

He went to their boat, got out his satellite phone. First he called Claudia. One of her contacts at Amazon CARES had a cousin stationed in Iquitos who would be happy collect the terrorists. That taken care of, he called Eleanor.

She answered saying, "Give me good news."

"I've captured a bunch of terrorists, and am on the trail of the kidnapped economist. Claudia has some friends in the army here who will pick up the prisoners."

"So you don't have him yet? What about the girl?"

"We think they're together, but they're maybe a day ahead of us."

"Can they find Dr. Shaughnessy?"

He didn't need to feign confusion. "Who, the terrorists?"

"The Peruvian Army!"

He tried not to show his frustration, "Yes. I imagine they could, but they don't seem to be looking. I'm told they're waiting until they can spring an attack on the whole group."

"I should have thought you'd have this all wrapped up by now, Mr. Special Forces Army."

"Yes, ma'am, well, we've had some people shooting at us. That tends to slow me down."

"Any losses?"

"Yes, but all on their side." He decided not to mention his wound.

"Good grief. You're killing Peruvians?"

"Only bad ones, ma'am. They shot at us first."

"You sound a little too eager to play cowboy, Mr. Kolnikoff. I just want you to get Dr. Shaughnessy out of there, quickly and quietly. No more shoot-em-ups."

He flashed a big smile at Wari. "Fine ma'am. I'll tell them to stop shooting at us."

"Are you getting smart with me? You know, I can hire one of your buddies instead. I even have a Special Forces guy available, saved all the way since Vietnam."

He didn't say anything. It wasn't the first time she'd threatened him. He doubted she had any ready alternatives. And he had an in even the knowledgeable Eleanor didn't realize. Yet.

"You're spending a great deal of my money and not getting anywhere... Just a minute."

There was a silence, while Eleanor apparently spoke to someone else. When she came back her voice was even more irritated than before. "I've changed my mind, Mr. Kolnikoff. I want you to break it off right now. Turn your gear in where you got it, and come home."

"What, without the Professor?"

"You mean the one you haven't found yet? Yes, without the Professor. Return your gear and get your butt back to D.C."

He thought about telling her where to stuff her gear, but he managed to just say, "Yes, sir," and hang up.

He sat for a minute in the boat.

No, he was not willing to give up on the stranded American. Particularly when they were already all the way out here looking for him. She might be willing to abandon the poor man to these guerrilla wackos, but he was not. Of course, they hadn't been shooting at her, so that might be part of it. He grinned. Well, he already had transport and guides. She wasn't going to notice an extra day or so, and if she did, she could take it out of his bonus that was owed in any case. Claudia would make sure of

182

that.

He climbed out of the boat and walked back up to the campsite.

"Here's what we'll do," he told Wari.

He passed along his plan to separate. Orqo and Chuki could stay safely with the prisoners waiting for *el ejército*. He would take the jeep to find the growing list of missing folks. He needed Wari, though.

Wari nodded throughout his recitation. "They will want to continue with us," he said. "For no pay—just to clean up this mess. Besides they have gotten some very nice boots." He laughed.

"They're welcome to any of the rest of the gear, too," Ryan assured him.

Wari nodded again, his wide face split with a wide grin.

"Let's find our trail makers," Ryan said. "Which I believe will be Carlo and the Professor."

"And my sister," Tomito said, from his place on the ground.

Ryan looked down at the boy and saw the determination in those dark eyes. "And your sister."

25 ≡ ANI

Ani stopped for a moment to check Carlo and allow Liam to catch up with her. They were trudging even more slowly that morning than they had at the end of the day before. She was worried about both her brother and the American—at this point, it was difficult to determine who was more ill.

Although Dr. Shaughnessy—Liam—was on his feet, his conversations weren't making much sense and he wasn't remembering to drink the water he was carrying. He fell and dropped it repeatedly, then he would pause and carefully pick it up bottle by bottle—and not drink any of it.

She pushed her hair back behind her ear and began to wonder if she could do this. Perhaps it would be wiser to leave Liam and Carlo behind and run until she could find help.

Liam caught up with her and stopped, staring at her like she was a tree or some other object in his path. She nodded at him and smiled encouragingly.

When she turned forward and looked ahead on their trail, she saw something that froze her in mid-step.

A man stood in the narrow track they had been walking. A man in khaki pants, a camo shirt, carrying an evil black weapon. Despair filled her as she realized she had not even managed to get the two men away from the guerrillas. Would they just shoot her? Shoot all of them and leave the bodies out here?

The man moved toward her pushing away the undergrowth. As he approached, she recognized him. It was the man from the airport in Quito. In fact, it was the pro-drug-testing man whose face had appeared beside her own in the San Francisco newspapers after the riot; she was suddenly as certain of it as she knew she was standing there. Had the drug companies sent him to follow her? Were they somehow connected to the guerrilla terrorists? Nothing made any sense.

Exhausted, certain that death was near and her efforts had failed, she set the travois and her brother down on the ground and looked up to meet her executioner.

"Miss Moreno!" the man called.

She blinked at him, and brushed her hair back out of her face again.

The man looked beyond her, back to the stumbling Liam Shaughnessy, and last at the burden she had laid down on the ground. "And Dr. Shaughnessy," he scowled at her brother, "and...Carlo Moreno?"

He stepped up within touching distance, which she thought was odd, since the gun he carried was certainly designed to be used farther away.

She could see his eyes watching her as she looked at the gun hanging from his shoulder by a black nylon strap, then up at his grinning face. "A captured weapon, Miss Moreno, from back at the clearing—where a group of rather nasty guerrillas attacked us, me and my tour guides." He pointed a thumb over his shoulder. Behind him, another man appeared. This one was wearing the local uniform of shorts and a cast-off American tee shirt, but had exchanged the usual flip-flops on his feet for a pair of black leather boots.

"So are you going to kill us all, sir, because I marched against you in a legal protest in San Francisco?"

"Kill you?" He thrust his head forward, giving her a disbelieving look. "I'm here to rescue you!" He pushed the black gun behind him with his elbow, and reached his right hand forward. "I'm Ryan."

Still feeling numb with shock, she took his hand. He shook, and her hand went with his, her arm feeling as limp as a rotten banana leaf.

"Ani," she murmured.

"Angeline," he said, pronouncing it properly.

She looked from their joined hands back up at his face. He was still smiling. "We spoke to your sister-in-law, Tipa?" he said, tilting his head.

She nodded.

"And—" he paused with his dramatic tone, turned and pointed to someone behind him, "—your brother!"

"Tomito?" she dropped into a squat just in front of the travois handles, feeling quite dizzy. What...? Why was Tomito involved? Had Carlo dragged him into this? Or was he a terrorist, too? She shook her head. That was impossible to believe. Not Tomi.

The still-smiling Ryan went on, "Tipa was quite concerned about your safety. I guess your brother, uh, *this* brother was kidnapped. And that brother," now he nodded his chin toward Carlo, "has made friends with some bad people."

Fearful now he might rescue her but hurt Carlo, Ani stood up straight, stepped back to block his path toward the travois.

"Dr. Liam Shaughnessy, I presume?" Ryan laughed, looking beyond her. "I always wanted to say that."

She heard Liam clear his throat. "Who are you?" the Professor managed.

"A friend," Ryan said.

"Are you?" she challenged.

"Well, unless those terrorists are your allies. I'm afraid I killed a few of them, trying to defend myself." He touched his right arm, and beneath his ripped shirt sleeve, she could see a soiled white bandage.

"The terrorists are not my friends," Ani said. "And they are responsible for kidnapping Dr. Shaughnessy."

"Liam," Liam said.

"And your brother?"

"I—*which* brother?" she leaned and looked past Ryan to where Tomito stood on the little path. He waved at her, smiling his little shy smile, then gestured toward Carlo with a questioning look on his face.

"Not that brother," Ryan said. "Carlo."

"Carlo made a stupid mistake, which he is about to pay for by dying out here," she said loudly enough so Tomito could hear. Tears welled up in her eyes, blurring her view of everyone. Carlo was a stupid-head, but he was still her brother.

"I have a jeep up the road just a couple hundred meters from here, and a fast boat docked at a small inlet off the Nanay."

She did cry, then. She felt the tears slip down her cheeks and did not care. "You can do whatever you want with me," she said, trying not to wail, "if you will bring Carlo to the *curandero* at Mishama."

"Mishama," Ryan said and turned to the guy behind him, his guide. "Wari, are we close to Mishama?"

"Next town down the river. On the way to Iquitos."

"Good, then. Good," Ryan said and began easing past her.

They shifted, Ryan and Wari coming forward to pick up Carlo, leaving Ani to stare at her little brother.

"Tomi? What are you doing here?"

Tomito hitch-walked up close to her, arms open. While he hugged her, he said softly into her ear in Quechua, "I have been rescued by him," meaning this Ryan person. "They were going to take Tipa, but they took me instead, those bad men. Then Ryan came shooting them all!"

Behind Tomito, another local man approached, grinning at Ani. "I'm Orqo," he pointed to himself. "That's Chuki my cousin, and Wari my friend." She nodded at the smiling, friendly guy.

"Let's get everyone going!" Orqo announced in a cheerful mix of Quechua and Cocama. He made his way past the siblings and stood in a tiny clearing while the travois passed by. Then she could see him taking Liam's pack and helping the American to walk, following behind the others.

As Ryan passed with his end of the travois casually held in one big hand, he grinned at her again. "How does this sound, then? We'll drive to get the boat, go to Mishama and the *curandero*. Then we can take Dr.

Shaughnessy to Iquitos, and you—wherever you want to go. Home? Airport?"

Wari loaded Carlo into the back of the jeep. Ryan drove and Ani was given the only other seat. Tomito and Wari fit in the back as best as they could around Carlo's limp body. That left Chuki and Orqo to hang off the running boards, which they seemed quite happy to do swatting at the brushes and grabbing bananas and palm fruits as the jeep slowly navigated the narrow track.

When they arrived at the white sand camp site, she noticed blood on the ground, staining the sand black-red. She made a disgusted face.

Ryan must have noticed, because he said, "Claudia is certainly efficient. All the bodies are gone. The live ones *and* the dead ones."

Ani took a deep breath. "Who is Claudia?"

"My friend," Ryan said.

They abandoned the jeep at the deserted camp, but cleaned up everything else. Aside from the empty vehicle, it looked like no one had been there at all.

Meanwhile, Chuki and Orqo had managed to capture a small pig. Wari hosted everyone on the *Jungle Jurnees* boat, playing maitre'd, chef, and server, three roles he seemed to enjoy. He cooked slices of pig and bananas on his little grill and served them with a flourish.

Chuki headed the boat downstream as they ate. Even several hours later, she still did not know where she wanted to go. It seemed this man Ryan was going to do just as he had said. But what should she do? The guerrillas had already found her home and taken Tomito. Her parents must be crazy with worry about three missing children, but would it be better to go home and reassure them, or stay away and perhaps lure the guerrillas elsewhere?

She sat under the green canvas canopy of the boat and watched the rain drip through a row of ragged holes at the edge that must have been made by gunfire. She felt certain New Sun guerrillas were going to be looking for Carlo—and Dr. Shaughnessy—back in Iquitos. That did not seem a safe place at all. But was home any safer? And was it safer for her parents without her and Tomito?

She stared at the unconscious body of her brother. How much had Carlo promised those guys? Probably everything, knowing Carlo. *He probably said, "I'm Carlo Moreno and I live in the village of Nanay Libre on the Rio Nanay, and I know how to get you a million dollars!"* She thought, despairing of ever being free from those crazies. They had stopped and grabbed Tomito as insurance already—would have taken Tipa if Tomito hadn't come along.

Maybe the best thing would be for her and Liam to get on an airplane and go to the States. At least Liam would be safe.

Of course, that would leave Carlo, Tomito, Mamí and Papa, and Manuel and Tipa behind in the guerrillas' gun sights. Mamí and Papa did not even know that crazy men were stalking them.

She could not do that. Could she get them all to move, though?

She was mulling this over when the Wari cut the engines, the boat drifted through a thick mat of water lettuce, then nudged up against the dock at Mishama village. Ryan handed over the keys of the abandoned jeep to the local Mishama Policia in exchange for watching the boat. They seemed surprised but pleased with those arrangements. Grinning they played a kids *fútbol* game with keys, kicking them back and forth between them.

"Do your job," she snapped at the grinning young men in Cocama as she went past. Their eyes widened and they nodded at her.

"Where is this *curandero*?" Ryan asked.

"Out in the jungle," she replied.

"Of course he is," Ryan said.

It took several hours for them to locate a canoe big enough to get them all in, yet small enough to navigate the narrow stream that led to the isolated Cocama village, but they finally arrived. "Everyone please stay here, until I talk with the village headman," she said.

Ryan glanced at Wari, who shrugged. "I don't speak Cocama," Wari said.

She nodded at him. At least he knew this was a Cocama village. She walked from the landing up into the village itself. There was a single tall triangle-shaped building, the *maloko*, where about a dozen families lived. Here she would find the headman, or mayor, with whom she would negotiate for the *curandero's* services.

It took awhile. First she must discuss local news and weather. Then she must introduce herself and explain why she was there. Then they must discuss what was wrong with the "young man." Then the headman called for the *curandero* to join them. The old man sat on his heels in the comfortable native squat he could maintain for hours. She had once had the knack of it, but soft living in *el norte* world had left her unable to hold the position for more than a few minutes without shifting. The *curandero* watched her squirm, amusement glinting in his wrinkled old eyes, behind the cataracts that had begun to blind him.

But she knew he did not need to see to work his medicine. He saw with an inner sight that now seemed to her to truly be magic. The old man rocked slightly on his heels, humming a melody of patience and negotiation.

"Let us see this young man," the headman said.

She walked outside the *maloko* and waved at Ryan to bring Carlo, as they had agreed. With help from Wari, the big American got Carlo out of the canoe. Wari lifted his limp body in his muscular arms and carried him. He paused at the entrance to the *maloko*, and Ani formally asked the headman's permission for Wari to bring her brother in.

The *curandero's* song had a laugh in it. The headman gave permission.

Wari laid Carlo down at the *curandero's* feet.

The old man stopped rocking, stopped humming. He sniffed, and wrinkled his nose. He reached a wrinkle-skinned hand out and held it, palm flat, above Carlo's head. He started humming again. The headman watched all this with no comment.

After awhile, the headman spoke to the *curandero*. His Cocama was mixed with something else, and she only got about half of it, something about "contamination" and "healing" and "foreigners."

The *curandero* hummed louder, almost a buzzing sound. His hand

190

hovered above Carlo's body, moving from head to toe and back again.

"I can cure him," he said. "My price is high." He grinned up at Ani with a gap-toothed smile.

She nodded. "I thank you. I will pay the price."

"No, *he* will!" the *curandero* laughed, wheezing, at his own joke. He said many rapid words to the headman, again in the mixed dialect Ani did not quite understand.

The headman nodded, a half-smile on his face. He looked at Ani. "Your brother will be his apprentice," the headman said.

Ani knew her surprise showed on her face by the headman's laughing reaction. "He can be a *curandero*?" She said. *Carlo?* Of all the things that had happened recently, this was the most shocking. "You want Carlo?"

The old man rocked on his heels again, both hands held palm down above Carlo, now.

"He should be dead," the old man said. "Twice again dead. He has been curing himself! He is *curandero*."

The headman nodded.

Ani squatted down. She did not wish to interrupt the *curandero's* work, but she would not just leave Carlo here without speaking to him. "Here you are safe, my brother," she whispered in his ear. She knew he heard her. She did not know how she knew, but he heard her. "Go with the gods." She stood up, thanked the headman, and turned to leave.

She brushed past Ryan who had a quizzical expression on his face.

"Come," she ordered him, and Ryan complied.

Back in the canoe, they paddled in silence, her and Wari, Ryan and a fumbling Liam. When they got back to the Mishama dock and into the *Jungle Jurnees* boat, she looked at the big American, "So you work for the American drug companies?"

"I am a private detective. I work for a lot of people, but none of them are drug companies," he answered her. Then after a moment, he added, "In this case Eleanor Powell is my boss."

"And what are you being paid to do with me?"

"Nothing," Ryan said. "I was supposed to quietly rescue Dr.

Shaughnessy. Now I'm supposed to go home."

That seemed a little too simplistic to be believed. "Does your employer know where I live?"

"She probably does," Ryan said. He looked away. "She knows everything else." He rubbed his chin. "She has a lot of people that do research for her."

"So my village is not safe from her?"

He seemed startled. "No, your village is perfectly safe—from her." He waved an arm, out at the dark jungle. "I doubt your village is safe from the guerrillas. They took Tomito. I don't know how they missed your parents. And they could go back for Tipa."

She shook her head. "I don't know. Carlo's such a stupid-head, he might not have mentioned parents." But she wondered about her opinion of Carlo. If he was gifted enough to be a *curandero*, maybe he wasn't such a stupid-head. "They know he's a tour guide in Iquitos, where he snatched Dr. Shaughnessy," she said.

"Liam," Liam said.

She turned to him with a wry smile. "Liam," she said with a nod. She turned back to Ryan. "So Iquitos is not safe. Nor our village, really. I am trying to think of a way to make Mañuel and Tipa and Mamí and Papa to go away for a little while."

"I see."

"Does the *Ejercito* know about any of this?"

Ryan nodded. Supposedly they are looking for Dr. Shaughnessy. Liam," he said, with a quick grin. "New Sun killed some villagers up north, and destroyed a building in Iquitos, so the army is on alert."

All right. Tomito needed to go home, and she— she thought about it some more. "Well, I need to go home and explain where Carlo is and what has happened." She turned to Liam. "What do you want to do? It seems we are not safe anywhere."

"I think we need to go to your village," he said. His color looked better, and he had stopped shaking. Ryan had given him the magic pill called Cipro, and his improvement was startling. "We need to lie low until those guerrillas are rounded up, don't you think?"

It was true that if the Army captured all the terrorists, her village would be safe. She wasn't so sure they'd be safe in the meantime, but she couldn't just abandon them to whomever might show up at their dock. She nodded. She looked at Ryan, then bit her lip.

"What?" he asked her.

"Do you think—" she wanted to ask for a weapon. But he was her enemy, wasn't he? She pointed at the guns.

He reached behind himself. He lifted two machine guns off the stack of weapons in the back of the boat, and offered them to her. She stared at the guns, suddenly unsure she would even be able to use one to save her own life.

Tomito had no problem with that. He leaned back from his bench alongside the bow and took one of the guns, a fierce smile on his face. He seemed to know how to hold it.

Then, surprising her even more, Liam gingerly took the other weapon. "Please show us how to use these," he said in a firm quiet voice.

"Of course. To Nanay Libre?" Ryan asked.

"Yes," she agreed. She glanced at Tomito. He grinned. "It will be all right," he said.

Ani smiled, but inside there was nothing but confusion. When did her littlest brother become so strong?

She was glad they were going to try to protect her village, at the same time she hoped it would not be necessary. Maybe the remaining guerrillas did not even know about her family, about Carlo or Pusac or Nanay Libre. Maybe Ryan had killed or captured the ones who knew and the rest were as confused as she was. She could hope.

Thunder rumbled, and the skies opened up, dumping centimeters of rain into the jungle, the river, but not their green canvas-covered boat. It was a little floating island of calm amidst the storm.

26 ≡ LIAM

Tomito stood guard at the Moreno family dock holding his machine gun and smiling like a kid who'd won the lottery two days in a row. The green canopy glided down the river taking Ryan to Iquitos. Ani and Liam stood on the shore among the banana plants as the boat moved towards the center of the river searching for the fast current. Liam gripped his gun, squeezing as much courage as he could from the cold metal. *It's not too late. Ryan wait! Take me to Iquitos. Take me home.*

Rain dripped down his neck and arms. The weather reminded him of guerrillas, jaguars, snakes, spiders and diseases hiding in the jungle. His feet sank slowly into the black mud as he waved goodbye to his only safe passage home. He turned to Ani, realizing she was the reason for his missing the boat. "Don't you think we'd be safer if we took the next plane home?"

"That works for you, if that's what you want, but *this* is my home."

He looked around Nanay Libre. *Of course. But what kind of home is this?*

Mamí and Tipa struggled to drag large sacks of rice into the center of sleeping platforms where it was dry. The breeze blew the light rain into their mostly open-sided house. The chickens collected under one corner of the floor, while the small children played tag among the stilts. The older children deserted the soccer field and retreated to the one room schoolhouse. Several of the adults, along with the dogs, gathered under the thatched shelter where they sold banana-leaf baskets and seed bracelets when the occasional tour boats stopped by. Two monkeys chattered loudly in the rafters, seemingly fully aware how the roof amplified their discussions.

A small garden of squash, papas, and yuca in front of the house and the larger plot of corn and cane behind soaked up the moisture. Liam wished his camera hadn't been stolen. These would have been perfect pictures to show his students or put up on a the web. The village embodied his every vision of idyllic and innocent life in the rainforest, so different from the smoggy trash-strewn streets of his home.

He looked at Ani. *You have a wonderful village.*

He watched her hair sway across her breasts, and her tan arms flex and relax as she grated the yuca against a number-ten can punctured with numerous rough nail holes. As happened so often down here, he had nothing to do. Dr. Shaughnessy, a highly educated college professor, had few useful skills in this jungle village. He checked the ground around his feet for ants, termites, cane toads and snakes before he sat down under the shade of a tree fern. Torn between Ani and home, he offered, "Maybe I could stay here a while and we could fly back together, as least as far as San Francisco."

She didn't look up. "Carlo's not coming back, so I'm sure Mamí and Papa will let you sleep in his hammock. Maybe you could help in the fields or.... " Her voice got soft and she started to mumble as if she were reconsidering.

He pulled up his sleeves and held out his skinny, pale arms, soft palms up. He shrugged his shoulders. "I'm a college professor, not much use here."

"Maybe you can help in the school. With one *maestra* to teach over thirty students from kindergarten to sixth grade, she can always use an extra hand."

He dropped his arms and thought of the foreign teaching assistants he'd been saddled with over the years. "I'd only be in the way. I don't know any Quechua, and very little Spanish."

She went back to grinding the yuca. He watched her, embarrassed to be staring, but afraid that if he turned away, he might never have another chance. *Another chance for what?* He asked himself.

"Maybe if someone helped me at first, so I wasn't in the teacher's way all the time," he offered, still unsure.

She looked up and smiled. "Okay, then it's settled. Tomito already assists *la maestra*, he'll help you too." She glanced to the soccer field where Tomito now sat at the sidelines making souvenir bracelets and necklaces from jungle vines and seeds, the machine gun propped on his feet.

He wondered what exactly had been settled, but she went back to making flour, so he understood it was too late to back out. Now that he was staying, he worried again about the dangers. He had two bottles of water left, and he couldn't imagine drinking the river water, either black or brown, like the *rivereños* did. All the preparation he'd made for the trip, Deet bug spray, sun block, malaria and diarrhea pills, mosquito nets—all were gone, lost somewhere in Iquitos.

"I can't leave anyway. My passport and tickets are in my hotel room in Iquitos." He thought back to the many warnings he'd read on the internet, "That is if they haven't been stolen too, like my wallet and my camera."

As soon as he said this he regretted it. *I'm getting paranoid ... and probably insulting too.*

She didn't look at him. The yuca grater growled at him for a long minute. Then, "Who stole your wallet and camera?"

"Well, my wallet wasn't really stolen."

She looked up with a serious expression, slowing shaking her head, "I see. And where were you staying?"

"*Hostal Rivereños.*"

"Pasquale's place?"

"How would I know? But I can tell you he recommended Carlo."

"That would be Pasquale. Not many others recommend my brother."

Ani spread the grated yuca out in the sun to dry. "You're in luck. I can assure you your suitcase is safe with Pasquale, safer than if you left it with the *policia* or one of those fancy new tourist hotels.

"Great. Could we go to town and get everything? I'd feel so much better with some clean clothes."

Ani went back to grating yuca.

He tried a different approach, "I have pills, you know for malaria and, and…stuff."

Ani still didn't say anything. He imagined she was just going to see how much trouble he could make for himself.

"Beside, I'd like to buy some more bottled water."

Finally, she responded. "In town the guerrillas have sympathizers and spies everywhere. Recall Carlo's craziness killed their friend Tito, and who knows how many our friend Ryan took care of. There could be many more. If we're seen, we're dead. That guy Ryan won't rescue us again. He's probably left the country already."

"No way to sneak into town?"

"Eh." She brushed her hair back with a forearm. "Maybe at night we can try."

"I**t's so dark. How are we going to navigate when we can't see?"

Ani held the dugout canoe steady. "Get in."

Liam crawled towards the front, holding tightly as the dugout rolled side to side surely intent on dumping him with every step. Ani rocked the boat some more as she got in and he dropped his paddle and grabbed the sides for balance. She laughed. "If you can't hold on to your paddle, just leave it in the bottom of the boat. We can't afford to lose it."

She pushed the boat into the current with a stick. "The Nanay flows directly to Iquitos. We just follow the current; there is no navigating. It should still be dark when we arrive."

He heard her paddle dip into the water and pull a long stroke. In front of him, the water bubbled as the canoe glided down the river. Another stroke and he felt a breeze against his face. He imagined her strong arms flexing and relaxing and she propelled the boat down the river. After a few minutes, his confidence returned and he reached for his paddle.

As soon as he dipped his oar into the water, his clumsy motions rolled the boat. Afraid of falling into the water with the piranhas and crocs, he froze, holding tightly to the precious paddle. When she didn't say anything, he made a second try. In spite of the boat rocking, he wasn't dumped into the water and his efforts appeared to propel them in the desired direction. After a few more attempts, he looked over his shoulder and she smiled at him. He smiled back and picked up his pace pulling harder with longer strokes.

"Relax. This is a long trip and we want to let the river do most of the work. You'll have your chance on the return trip. Upstream."

He had forgotten that after Iquitos they were returning to the village, a thought that filled him with both anticipation and anxiety.

The effervescence at the boat's prow blended with the whistles, chirps, and buzzes of the jungle night. Liam recalled, just a few short days ago, Carlo's light was searching for red eyes. He rested his paddle on his thighs and marveled at the reflection of the Milky Way on the black surface of the river. The Milky Way reminded him of home. The band of stars disappeared in the light of the college campus, but after a short drive west into the National Forests it shone like the crystal rainbow reflected in the river tonight.

She woke him from his reverie. "Tell me, Assistant Professor of Statistics, what do you actually do?"

He gave his elevator answer—the quick one between the lobby and mezzanine. The one he used at parties or when he met curious strangers. It was as much a test as an answer. "Data mining. Cross correlations. Database linking. Population Studies."

"Really? Why did the U.N. invite you to the conference in Iquitos?"

He assumed that she had no idea what he was talking about. He was embarrassed to have given her the test that she failed. He started over.

"Most statisticians and governments study population in the aggregate, looking at big groups."

"I'm not a statistician, but isn't 'aggregate' just a fancy word that means you mix up all the information?"

"Sure, I guess…"

She continued. "You aggregate data for privacy, don't you? Individual information is hidden in the mix. When I study indigenous people, I do the same thing, to protect their private information."

This is going better. "Absolutely right. However, they also aggregate the data because it's easier. Considering each individual separately requires too many data and too many calculations. Everyone looks at averages because anything else is too hard." He thought, *Or at least it used require too many data and too many calculations.*

"I see."

He doubted she understood, but he'd learned in his lectures not to repeat each concept over and over. It was better to move forward and return to difficult concepts after the students had more background.

While he was thinking about what to say next, she jumped in, "Statistics might be useful in North America where you have big governments and big computers, but anthropologists have learned that the sophistication and complexity of so-called-primitive societies are best understood through the lives of the individuals who make up that society. So while I sometimes use aggregate data, I mostly study people."

Now it was his turn to reply, "I see."

Liam picked up his paddle and stroked strongly through the dark river. The pleasant, intelligent voice seemed to surround him, even caress him. "I think my research does the same thing." Not wanting to be presumptuous, he added, "At least in theory. I don't observe people in the field, as you say. I observe them in the cloud—also called big data."

"Big data?"

"Big data is the universe of all data. I combine government databases: census data on births, deaths, marriages, divorces, occupations, residences and records from taxes, licenses, and legal proceedings. This government data provides a wealth of information, but combined with information from search histories, social networks, call records, and credit card transactions, my computer programs can construct a good picture of each individual. All together, my research method isolates the lives of each individual."

"Doesn't that take a big computer?"

"Oh yes, petabytes and petaflops." He realized he was slipping into techno babble. "You're right, it takes a big computer, but big computers are not as expensive as they used to be. Even assistant professors can get big computers these days."

He saw a light ahead. "Is that the sunrise? Have we been rowing all night?"

"No, that's the airport. We'll stop near there. *Mi amigo* Guillermo lives nearby and will sneak us into the city."

Ani motioned for Liam to follow her. She quietly approached one of the open-sided houses, climbed up onto the sleeping platform and shook one of the hammocks. Even though the sun wouldn't rise for a while, when the man saw Ani he jumped off his hammock in one smooth motion and smiled.

Ani and Guillermo hugged. Lima recognized just a few of their words as they talked in what must have been a combination of Spanish and Quechua. Or something. *"Hermano Carlo...guerrillas...Hostal Rivereños... Peligro... "* Liam felt a wave of despair. There was so much he did not understand.

Guillermo started up his tricycle. Iquitos had few street lights and the taxi had no headlights. As they roared down the street, Liam was convinced Guillermo could see in the dark, until they bounced into a parked truck. A little while later they tipped over into a drainage ditch. No one said anything while all three of them lifted the vehicle back into the street.

Soon enough they stopped in front of *Hostal Rivereños*. He looked at the driver and realized that this was the same one who drove him to the *Mercado* with Carlo. Ani hugged the driver again. "Can you pick us up tonight when it gets dark?"

"*No problemo.*"

As with Carlo, Liam noticed that she didn't pay Guillermo either.

She held open the *hostal* door. "Hurry up, the sun is rising."

She opened a door behind the front desk and jiggled the hammock suspended in what looked like a storage closet. As before, when the man saw Ani, he jumped up and smiled. Liam recognized Pasquale in the early morning light. Ani and Pasquale embraced. He listened to another incomprehensible discussion.

Ani turned to him. "It is good we were careful to hide," she said. "Men have been here looking for us. Bad men."

Liam nodded slowly. "So I am not going home."

Ani shook her head. "Not yet." She turned to Pasquale. "Now for your things, so at least we have the passport all ready once things quiet down."

"*Aqui. Aqui.*" the man pointed to the corner of the closet. There was Liam's suitcase and the braided rope sack containing all his souvenirs. He shook Pasquale's hand and quickly unlocked the suitcase. He pushed past his passport and pills to find his wallet. He took a worn hundred *soles* note and handed it to Pasquale. "*Gracias, mucho gracias,*" he said in his best Spanish.

Pasquale put his hands in his pockets, pressed his lips together and turned his head left and right. Liam looked to Ani.

"Now that you're sleeping in Nanay Libre, especially the home of Papa *y* Mamí, you are *rivereño*. He can't take money from you. Most definitely you *owe* him, but money will never do."

Then Ani grabbed the bill and handed it to Pasquale saying something Liam didn't understand. This time he took the money. Liam shook his head, completely baffled.

"We can't leave here until dark, so he will go to the market and buy some bottled water for us to take back to Nanay Libre. In the meanwhile, I rowed the most, so I get the first shift on the hammock. You can sit in the corner with your suitcase. Please do not let anyone see you, besides Pasquale."

Liam nodded and sat on his suitcase for a bit, then sat on the floor.

"**D**esayuño! Breakfast!" Pasquale kicked the door open, his hands full with a wooden tray of hot coffee and cut papayas. Even before Liam opened his eyes, the bright sun seemed more like lunchtime. He straightened up, leaning against the wall, and reached for a cup of coffee. It smelled wonderful.

When Pasquale left, Ani took a cup of coffee and some papaya and ate and drank, swinging gently in the hammock. She turned to Liam, licking papaya juice from her fingers. "So, you have a big computer with data stories about individuals. So, what is that for?"

He shifted, bumping his elbow against a stack of a half-dozen cases of bottled water. He shook his head. "Huh? Computers?" He rubbed the dry sweat from his eyes and blinked. Ani's hair sparkled in the light, still wet from the shower, which explained somewhat how she was so alert. He stretched and sipped more coffee. "Give me a minute."

"Wake up Professor. It's almost noon. Why does anyone care about your data stories?"

He felt at a severe disadvantage. "Data stories?"

Her eyes smiled at him and he wanted her to understand, but, *What should I say? It's so complicated....*

He took a mouthful of papaya. The juice spilled down his chin. He wiped his chin, chewed slowly and collected his thoughts. "Okay. Before my research, the conventional wisdom stated that global over-population threatened the planet. As Malthus predicted almost 200 years ago, we would over-breed ourselves into war and poverty."

"That's true. Isn't it?"

Liam took another bite of ripe fruit and stood up. "Not exactly. In the first world, where most of these studies happen, the population is increasing for two reasons. First, there's the influx of people from poorer countries. Second, for some reason that I haven't been able to get the public health types to adequately explain, people are living longer. Lots of people are living lots longer."

Ani sucked the papaya before she took her bite, managing to avoid a drippy mess.

So that's how it's done!

She chewed and swallowed. "No surprise, yah? Hasn't all this been in the news? For years?"

"The surprise was hidden from the aggregate data, but my research reveals— " he paused for emphasis, "—that the local population is not breeding. The birthrate among the native, indigenous populations—here I mean the people born and raised in the first world, for example the big cities like Tokyo, Chicago, and Munich—has fallen dramatically. These populations are in danger of extinction."

"Are you saying that those *city people* are not having babies?"

He marveled at how fast she picked this up. *If only she'd been on the tenure committee.* "You're absolutely correct."

Ani frowned, seeming to be deep in thought.

That night Pasquale and Guillermo helped them tie the suitcase, souvenirs, water, and some other supplies onto the back and floor of the tricycle. Then they waved goodbye to Pasquale and rolled into the darkness towards the airport. They transferred everything except Guillermo to the canoe. The canoe rode low in the water carrying them and all the cargo. As they pulled away from the lights, Liam and Ani strained to keep the boat moving upstream. Each time one of them rested, the boat stopped, or worse floated downstream. He couldn't imagine how they would ever make it back to Nanay Libre.

"We need to stay near the shore and look for reverse eddies. When we find one, you'll feel the current pulling us upstream. If we don't take advantage of them, we'll soon tire and be washed downstream to the Amazon itself."

He didn't understand until they were suddenly gliding upstream. He put his paddle down for a much needed rest. There was so much to learn. When they were out of sight of the airport, Ani sang a soft song. He enjoyed the gently flowing words interspersed with wild whistles and chirps. As the time went on, her voice blended in with the jungle choir. When they entered a particularly swiftly moving eddy, she spoke. "Why do you think the birthrate has crashed in your big cities?"

Surprised at her continued interest, he turned around to see if she was serious. When the boat entered the downstream current and stopped, he lost his balance. She laughed. "Watch where you're going."

At the next reverse eddy, he put down his paddle. "Easy question. Everyone knows that, given a chance, women won't have children. From a women's point of view, children mean work and pain, and sometimes even death. Women mostly become pregnant through rape or other coercion."

He wasn't sure of what she intended when she said, "Really?"

He didn't dare turn around to check, so he continued. "The women I've been studying are educated and have access to birth control. More importantly, these women have real power, so the traditional methods of breeding—arranged marriages and societal pressures—are less available, therefore, less babies."

He could hear her paddling just before they hit the downstream current. *How does she know when to start paddling?*

Explaining his favorite theories to a beautiful woman, alone, on a dark night, gave him new strength to pull them forward to the next eddy. He raised his voice like he did during the key points in his lectures. "Think of the benefits for *your* family and culture. With the decline, and possible extinction, of the profligate consumer societies, your native people will have the opportunity to start over and hopefully do a better job."

His paddling and talking got faster. "It's the Fall of Rome and the Bubonic Plague all over again. Out with the old, making way for a new Renaissance!"

Behind him a soft voice interrupted. "I don't recall a rebirth after the Fall of Rome. More like the Dark Ages, eh?"

He shut up. They hit a downstream section and he took long strokes to keep the canoe moving forward. Sweat dripped into his eyes, but he didn't pause to wipe them. *Now she thinks I'm crazy, just like the tenure committee.*

"I'd welcome some restraint on the part of you folks in the northern hemisphere, but I don't know if extinction is necessary. Besides, did you know we're having population declines down here also?"

Her voice got softer and he tried to splash less so he could hear her. It seemed like she was talking to herself.

"Some villages have died out completely. I can assure you women in the Amazon *want* babies. Tipa wants more babies, but has had a hard time. It's from miscarriages and infant mortality the birth rate has dropped."

When a helpful current pulled them forward, he put down his paddle to wipe the sweat out of his eyes. A flock of parrots took off from the tall trees announcing sunrise. They'd been paddling all night. A troop of monkeys responded, shaking the branches as they left their arboreal nests. Pink dolphins breached in the river ahead of them. A gentle breeze brought the scents of unseen blossoms. He turned around. "You don't understand. What's happening down here is completely different. The Amazon is… another world."

She spoke with the forced, non-judgmental voice adults so often use with small children. "Is that so?"

27 ≡ ELEANOR

They had had to get special permission to land at Minot Air Force Base, but Eleanor's Personal Assistant, Devon Snow, had managed it. Yet again, he had pulled a miracle out of his pudgy butt. Pudgy, but Harvard-trained, and well worth the hundred-plus grand a year she paid him to put his masters in political science to work. They were not what could be called friends, but after a dozen years together, they knew each other's habits.

"He's on this flight, Ma'am," Devon said, leaning over closer to her ear to speak over the roar of jet engines.

She nodded, and they stepped forward to stand next to the small group of reporters.

"Stay behind the ropes," an MP hollered. He indicated the red velvet ropes that formed three sides of a rectangle. The open side collected a few more people, a camera crew and her and Devon.

Her patience was still thin, but her advancing years had given her experience which she wielded in the same way she did her money: to support the projects of most personal concern to her. The reporters would offer a barrage of questions, the camera crews would film their news bites, and then they would leave. And she would still be there, waiting for her moment to talk to Mr. Mike Johnson, MIA for forty years in Viet Nam, advocate for indigenous people, and minor celebrity—all elements she could use to further publicity for her programs, if he could be persuaded.

She waited. She was good at persuading.

The cameras turned to the east to track the C-17 landing and taxiing around to the awaiting reception. Several groups put up "Welcome Home" banners and filmed news anchors with the banners and the majestic C-17 in the background.

Everything followed the expected script, until four Marines escorted someone who had to be Sergeant Michael Johnson from the transport. She immediately knew something was wrong seeing him in a brown prisoner's uniform, not dress blues. When they bypassed the press and marched him off the field, she turned to Devon, "We have some extra persuading to do."

They moved their operation to the Minot Frontier Lodge, located on quiet grounds between the Roosevelt Park and Zoo and the Souris River. She personally called her contacts at the Pentagon, especially an old friend in the Office of the Administrative Assistant to the Secretary of the Army, but left the rest of the operation in Devon's capable charge. He coordinated the researchers who worked their contacts from Minot to Washington. He assigned himself the important congressional committees, Armed Services and Veterans' Affairs.

Everyone understood that she preferred to work behind the scenes, so she was confident no one would contact the media. Since marching a prisoner was not news, the arrival was not covered nationally, and even the local Minot outlets, barely mentioned it.

By morning, the press returned and Sergeant Johnson was presented in dress blues, with a chest full of ribbons, including a Vietnam Distinguished Service Order. She marveled at Devon's efficiency and effectiveness, making a mental note to give him a raise and, maybe, a nice expense-paid vacation when this was all over.

After the press conference, she and Devon Snow were the only civilians who remained in the room where everyone had interviewed Mr. Johnson. Devon swooped in, introducing her.

Mr. Johnson seemed more startled by her attention than he had been by the news people. He listened carefully as Mr. Snow introduced Dr. Powell, including her degrees and philanthropic associations. She leaned forward, reaching out her right hand and he put out his big fist to shake with her.

Aware of the incongruity of their relative heights and weights, she took a step back and looked up at him. He seemed about twice as big as she was. "Well, Mr. Johnson—"

"Mike, ma'am. Just Mike."

"Mike. I would like to make a proposal to you. Frankly your visibility as a returned MIA is going to be useful for about a week, and then will fade away…unless we take advantage of it, and put you into the public eye at every opportunity. These opportunities must be nurtured and managed, which I am willing to do, provided you are willing to assist me with a project of mine. A project you may be interested in also."

"Are you a doctor, Doctor?"

"I am not a practicing physician, if that is your meaning. However, I have extensive medical and biological training."

Mike looked at her, glanced at Devon Snow, then back at her. Clearly he knew who the important one was in this pair. "So what do you know about Agent Orange?" he asked her.

She smiled at him. "I like a man who comes right to the point, Mike. I think we may have several programs that can aid your Agent Orange victims, with new medical tests, new drugs, and clinical trials of developing drugs." She smiled with gentle encouragement. "In exchange, I would like your help as a spokesman for clinical drug trials to benefit indigenous peoples."

Moving slowly, Mike went over to the coffee service area the military had set up in the press conference room. He examined the coffeemaker, picked up the pot of hot coffee, set it back down on the warming burner, fooled with the pressure pump thermos jugs of hot water and cold milk, and eventually worked his way through pouring a cup of coffee and loading it with sugar and cream. She could see by his expression he was thinking, thinking the whole time—she hoped—about her intentionally vague proposal.

He took a sip of his coffee and turned to her. "If you want to buy me, Dr.—"

"Powell," Devon supplied helpfully.

"Powell," Mike repeated, meeting her eyes with a deliberate, steely-eyed stare. "If I do as you wish, can you send a fully-supplied medical mission to the mountain communities surrounding Da Lat? One with enough physicians and gear to examine and treat for the effects of Agent Orange on about 500 people? Can you do that?"

She looked at him, allowing a small smile to touch her lips. She admired his courage and conviction. *He'll make a great witness.* "That's absurd, sir." She calculated rapidly. "That would involve costs many times what I anticipated reimbursing you for your ten or so hours of help."

He looked at her blank and silent.

"I've been vague," she confessed, "and your request is excessive, but I expect I can deliver what you *need*."

In a softer voice, thinking aloud, she continued, "Yes, Mr.— Mike, I'm sure you can make a valuable contribution to my projects"

Mike finally spoke up, with his own small smile, "We can help each other, but without that medical mission, I'm not your man."

She thought, now is the right time. She stepped closer to Mike and raised herself on her toes. Probably without realizing it, Mike tilted his head down so they were face to face. Out of the corner of her eye, she saw a proud smile on Devon's face.

"I pulled a lot of strings to put you in dress blues, instead of that brown prisoner garb you were wearing yesterday. You do remember yesterday? Don't you?"

She paused to let him think. He stepped back and blinked three or four times. *He's a smart one. He gets it.*

"You owe me...and you know it."

He took a deep breath, "I do. I do. But I also owe Chi and Lei Minh and

An Ly, and there will be a medical mission. There will."

She reached up, slapped his shoulder, allowed herself to laugh. *Well, you are signed up, sir, it's just a matter of details, now.*

P+P BLOG POST

Pride and Prejudice (apologies to Jane) aka Lies, Damn Lies, and Statistics (apologies to whomever said it first)—A blog dedicated to odd stories about numbers

International Census Data

FACT: Around the world, even as the population is increasing, the number of population centers is decreasing. Big cities are getting bigger and small villages are disappearing.

Did I hear you ask, "Why?"

FANTASIES:

In the mountainous areas of Western China people are abandoning their ancestral homes to participate in the economic opportunities of the new factory cities.

In the Amazon rainforest government programs teach nomadic hunter-gatherers agricultural skills. As result, small groups now consolidate around large plantations.

In an innovative program to improve health care in the Siberian tundra, the government has opened modern hospitals. People have moved to take advantages of these facilities.

In a continuing effort to clean up the environment, several south African nations require villages to install modern sewage systems or relocate to places where sewage system are already available.

In Afghanistan, aid groups have refused to supply winter food into the mountains held by rebels, so as a result many people have moved.

In the Urals, labor unions have refused to allow truck drivers to risk their lives their lives on icy mountain roads. Villages, thus cutoff from food and energy supplies, have just disappeared.

As we have seen over and over, these felicitous correlations are rarely the full story, or even any part of the story. So...

That explains things, doesn't it? Or maybe not.

28 ≡ LIAM

Liam rolled his shoulders and stretched his legs in another attempt to get comfortable in Carlo's hammock. He felt like he was sleeping on an old sagging mattress. His body just wouldn't adjust to being curled up. He even considered sleeping on the floor, but he feared he'd insult Papa and Mamí if he refused the hammock. He had no choice but listening to monkeys and frogs night after night while he struggled to fall asleep.

The sun rose slowly, shining across the glassy, early morning calm of the Nanay, through the fields of bananas, cane and corn, eventually to reflect a faint glow into the wall-less house. He awoke before the dogs and chickens. He felt like a child, not daring to stir until some responsible adult signaled the time was alright.

If I could only do something useful. The youngest children had the job of chasing birds from the crops, and the infirm told the stories filled with history and wisdom. Only Liam and babies still too tiny to walk were useless.

Today, he vowed, *I'll find a way to contribute.*

When Papa rolled out of his hammock, Liam did the same. Together they walked down a trail, a different direction each day, and provided their nitrogen-rich contribution to the washed out rainforest soil. After a breakfast of fresh papaya and leftover rice, Papa prepared to go hunting.

The dogs sensed his plan and ran in circles chasing each other. The dogs flushed and cornered game for Papa to kill—his bow and arrow for small game like iguana or monkey or his spear for a tasty pig. The dogs only got fed when they caught something. No kill, no food.

He wondered whether they enjoyed to hunt or were just hungry. Ani returned from the river carrying a basket of black fish that looked like they wore armor. He ran over. "Please ask your father if I can go hunting with him."

She had a long discussion. He listened nervously. Papa seemed to be asking a lot of questions and she gave same answer repeatedly. Eventually, she returned. "He said he'd be happy for you to join the hunt. Just be very quiet, follow the dogs and do what they do."

He repeated, "Just do what the dogs do." He ought to be able to accomplish that. Except maybe for the frisking about.

Ani went back to the women. In a few minutes the dogs quieted down and the hunting party moved down a trail that went along the river. As soon as they passed the last house, the dogs got very quiet. Liam took his lead from the dogs. They walked without snapping a twig, crinkling a leaf, or kicking a rock.

High above them the trees with umbrella shaped leaf clusters asserted their rights to the sunlight. Any animals that lived in the canopy were safe from this hunting party and invisible to Liam's untrained eyes. Except for the hanging weaver nests the forest heights looked lifeless. At a more convenient level the ficus trees bore green bumps—tasty iguanas—or furry tufts—monkeys hiding in the branches. Nothing lived alone in the forest. The trees shared their space with lianas, bromeliads and epiphytes.

They stopped and Papa put his hand to his ears. Liam strained to listen. He heard whistles, chirps, and tweets, but he couldn't tell a capuchin from a katydid or a macaw from a frog.

In the midst of this cacophony, there was a faint snort. No one breathed. The snort repeated. The dogs were focused on a spot among the trees. Papa petted them and pointed, making a sweeping arc shape with his arm.

Everyone moved silently, circling around the pig. Liam followed the line of dogs, silent until he tripped on a liana and fell on his face with a thump. Not ten feet away there was a crash in the forest. He saw stubby legs moving as the pig retreated into the thick underbrush. The dogs took off in pursuit, but it was too late.

He sheepishly retreated back to the village to sit with the women. Papa didn't return until afternoon, with sad, hungry dogs. The pig would live for another day, the only winner of Liam's clumsiness.

He thought of returning to Iquitos, no matter the danger—better risk running into the guerrillas again, than to burden Ani's family so.

Ani looked disappointed when he walked into the central area where the women were chatting and twisting rope from tree bark collected by the children. "You can't just hang around like a pet monkey. You're a college professor. Go to the school and see if you can be helpful there."

This was the second time Ani suggested that he teach. He still couldn't imagine how a college professor who didn't speak the language would be anything but a disturbance, much like his attempt to go hunting this morning. But he didn't want to say all this in front of the group of cheerful women, so he headed towards the school.

As he crossed the soccer field, kicking rocks and stirring up the grasshoppers, he thought about multivariate analysis and statistical significance—over twenty years of education and not a single useful skill. Afraid to return to Ani without even trying, he slowly scaled the wooden steps to the one room school.

He stood in the back of the room observing the teacher. She was explaining multiplication to the older children. When she noticed him, she pointed to him and then to the younger children. He walked over the little ones. He stood there silently.

She wrote some problems on an old, chipped chalk board and walked past him to a supply box. She dug through the box and found pieces of construction paper with writing on them and strings attached. She hung one around each child's neck. After saying something cheery to them, she returned to teaching multiplication. He guessed these were name tags, but he didn't dare use them. When he was in elementary school, teachers always mangled is his name as Lime or Lam or, most embarrassing, Lami.

The students sat at their desks with their hands folded and looked at him with smiling anticipation. He was on the spot. He thought back to second grade. His favorite activity had been reading. Reading wasn't going to work here.

The longer he stood in front of the group, the straighter they sat up, and the tighter they folded they hands. Slowly their smiles faded.

He didn't know enough Spanish to play the only games he could remember from school—Simon Says or Heads Up, Seven Up. Big brown eyes stared expectantly at him. When he moved, those eyes followed. He folded his hand together and tried to smile in return.

Finally he got an idea. He went back to the box with the name tags and wrote an X on one and an O in the other. He selected two students. He anointed one X and the other O. The rest of the class watched with rapt attention. They were much more attentive than his college class.

He drew a tic-tac-toe grid on the black board. He pointed to X, a girl with the biggest, blackest eyes, he'd ever seen. He pointed to the different squares waiting for her to make a choice. At first the she was silent, but slowly the class figured out the question and shouted *"Tres en raya,"* along with lots of advice. Finally, he pointed to a lower corner and she squeaked, *"Si, si."*

He pointed to her name tag and drew an X in the square she selected. Now he went to the other child, a boy—barefooted, wearing a Dallas Cowboys tee shirt. He quickly selected a corner and Liam repeated the action of pointing to his name tag and drawing an O in his square. This game continued with much discussion among the students, until someone got a tic-tac-toe. Liam said, "tic-tac-toe," and drew a line through the three Xs.

The class shouted, *"Ta-te-ti"* and, "Tic-tac-toe."

As X had won, he removed the boy's O tag and pointed back to his seat.

He held up the name tag and the students caught on immediately and excitedly raised their hands. Liam chose another boy. This one had a Bay-to-Breakers tee shirt. The game went quicker this time because the boy won in three moves. When Liam said, "Tic-tac-toe," and drew the line through the three O's, the class went wild, except for the little girl. She took off her X and handed it to him.

The next game was a tie and the game after that. Finally, the new X won. The students cheered. The teacher finished with the older children and poured each student a glass of UHT milk. They went out for recess. He sat on the stairs until the little girl with the big eyes came over to him. "*Ta-te-ti?*"

He picked up a stick and drew a grid in the dirt. He drew a circle and handed her the stick. She shouted to the other children. "*Vamanos!*"

They gathered around her yelling until she finally drew her X. He let her win and everyone clapped. He erased the dirt with his foot and drew another grid. He handed the stick to another child. He played with the girl three times until he won. She graciously stepped aside for another student to play.

In a little while there were tic-tac-toe grids all around the schoolyard and the younger children had interested the older ones. Ani came over to watch the excitement. "Maybe you *should* be a teacher."

He smiled. "I am a teacher." He looked out at the children. "Just not for students this young."

When Ani returned to making rope, he watched the children and was reminded that he had no idea what they were saying. He couldn't even tell what language they were speaking. What good is a teacher that doesn't know the language?

His tic-tac-toe friends surrounded him after lunch. The little girl with the big eyes pointed to herself and said, "*Eckees? No!*" She shook her head and laughed. "*Zero? No!*" Again she shook her head and her long braids whipped back and forth. "*Rosa? Si!*"

He touched her nose and said, "Rosa." He touched his own nose and said, "Liam."

The students chanted. "Liam. Liam."

"Alejandro."

"Yessica."

He attempted his limited Spanish. *"Hola Rosa. Hola Alejandro. Hola Yessica."*

After the teacher dismissed the class, Rosa and Yessica grabbed his hands and dragged him to the garden. The irregular shaped field, no bigger than twenty-five feet in any direction, looked like an abandoned lot, a random assortment of green sprouts. Alejandro ran around the field and pointed to one green seedling after another and shouting, *"Bueno! Bueno! No! No!"*

Next Rosa pointed to a different seedling, *"Malo, malo, no es bueno!"*

With an exaggerated struggle she pulled up the *malo* green sprout, threw it on a pile of similar greens and jumped on it. The other students applauded. With the pantomime complete, the children swarmed across the field pulling weeds. He watched until Rosa pulled his arm. He hoped she didn't expect him pull weeds. All these green things looked the same to him.

They all smiled at him, so he reached down to pull out a weed. They all laughed, *"No, es bueno!"*

He reached over to another and even before they started shouting, their laughter let him know, wrong again.

Third time was the charm. He guessed again, this time they applauded. He pulled out the weed and placed it on the pile and jumped up and down, stomping it flat. They clapped and all went back to work. He never figured out exactly how to tell weed from plant, but with all the seven-year-old helpers, he got the job done. *Well, part of it, anyhow.*

Ani came over and watched. "You're such a good teacher."

She looked into the forest. "And I'm glad the children have an adult with them in case those guerrillas show up."

Guerrillas? He didn't even know where that gun Ryan had left for him had ended up. He felt almost completely lost as a teacher, to be also considered a guardian for the children was—he just shook his head. "They're better teachers than I am." *I don't know about protecting them. Can I?*

Ani smiled at him, then waved and walked off toward her home. He used his thumb to roll dirt and sap off his fingers, watching Ani till she disappeared into the banana trees, then watching the weeding crew turn their chore into a game of tag.

The teacher stepped out of the schoolroom door and clapped her hands. The children lined up and went back into the classroom. Liam wiped his hands on his pants and followed.

29 ≡ ELEANOR

One window in Eleanor's home office, the entire second floor of her Sands Point, Long Island home, looked out over a timbered lot, a pond, and a meadow—no man-made constructions. She had paid to have trees moved to screen the electrical wires. She had even had a small hill built behind the pond to hide a neighbor's barn-like house. She had purchased an adjacent home, had the house demolished and an assortment of fruit trees planted, so that throughout the year she could stare at blossoms, or apples, or bare branches, rather than someone's SUV on an asphalt driveway or swing set on their lawn.

She was effective at dealing with people, but she did not like it, and she much preferred the quiet peace of nature to the distractions of human busyness. This was her refuge, her focus, a few days to recharge while Devon settled Mike in Washington.

Her respite ended when she received notice that the U.N. resolution to restrict drug testing among indigenous peoples had passed.

Now she stared at the bare apple branches—still bare? Or could she see tiny buds?—considering her next move.

Somehow, she must stop the U.S. from signing the resolution. This blow to the creation and dissemination of new drugs could not be allowed to stand. If the United States and one or two other big spenders in the U.N.'s programs, notably the World Health Organization and UNICEF, refused to support this anti-science nonsense, maybe even threatened to pull funding, then she still might be able to do her work: Promote clinical trials, get new treatments out into the mainstream, save lives.

She was not any particular friend to the DRMAA—Drug Research and Manufacturers of America Association. She laughed to herself, recalling that they pronounced their acronym, "Drama." But they had the kind of power and influence she needed. Those people spearheading the anti-clinical trial movement must not be allowed to mislead everyone, especially native groups. Otherwise, a lot of people were going to die that didn't have to. People who probably didn't even know this battle was being fought for them. Unknowing victims.

Worse, the people supposedly fighting for them, were not of them—and they—the victims—didn't know that, either. Rich groups and individuals who had managed to escape tribal life, those were the ones screaming "my culture will die!" Right. Your culture, that you don't even belong to any more—you ensure that those you left behind are trapped there to live and die in ignorance of their options. For the sake of your misguided, stupid, stupid!, stupid!! beliefs!! One could really question your motives! She scowled, and rubbed her temples. Those people were such hypocrites.

A migraine was coming on. She could feel it ready to pounce. She groaned in irritation.

She didn't have time for a migraine. She had to pull a plan together to defend against the U.S. supporting the U.N. resolution. She congratulated herself on recruiting Sergeant Johnson, *Nice move, Ellie.*

She closed her eyes and rested her head on her arms. Maybe a little nap would help. Just for awhile, for she'd be in Washington soon enough.

It wouldn't be the first time she'd slept at her desk. Rest today, fly tomorrow.

Devon escorted Sergeant Johnson into Eleanor's Washington, D.C. office.

The sergeant was wearing a light brown suit with the jacket unbuttoned, a pale blue shirt with a spread collar, and tie embroidered with small crossed arrows. She recognized this as off-the-rack tailoring, but he still looked good. Certainly another demonstration of Devon's deft hand. Mike would be an excellent witness.

She'd hoped that given the time elapsed, Devon had come to an agreement with Mike, when she saw Mike's expression, she could only describe it as suspicious.

Good thing I decided against meeting with him at my home, she thought, *We need to get down to business here*. Once again, her instincts had been correct. She'd also made the right choice to move out from behind her half-acre of rosewood desk. She'd greeted him from her comfortable chairs in the quiet sitting room adjacent to her office. *Much friendlier, less intimidating, the right balance*. Who could get nervous, sitting in an overstuffed armchair upholstered in giant yellow daisy fabric, ever so slightly silly, ever so slightly soiled and worn on the edges? She'd fought with the decorators over that one, and had never regretted her stubbornness on that point.

"Well, Mr. Johnson, have you made a decision about joining my team?"

He frowned, and would not meet her eyes. He toyed with the china cup and saucer of tea Devon had set on the table beside him. She tried not to let the persistent tink of the spoon against the porcelain bother her.

"Well, have you decided whether you are going to sponsor the medical mission I asked for?" he said, eventually.

"Yes. I believe we can agree on such a project, if you agree to help support my indigenous peoples' testing project."

"The thing is, there's no way for me to be sure you'll hold up your end of the deal, once I've gone and spoken in your favor. You want me to— What? Talk on television?"

She nodded. When he didn't go on, she added, "And testify before Congress once hearings are set up about whether the United States will support the U.N. resolution about drug testing in third-world countries."

"So what is this resolution about?"

"Some individuals believe native peoples are being injured somehow by participating in clinical trials for new drugs."

"And, are they?"

"No." Eleanor rested her elbows on her knees and leaned forward. "The worst that can happen is these drugs are ineffective. But often they are so effective the company stops the test and gives everyone the drug, because it is obviously helping. These tests save lives, Mr. Johnson. They save lives in the testing phase, and they save many more lives later when the drugs are released for use by everyone."

"Is this the same thing as FDA approval?"

She blinked at him, unsure of his question. Over many interviews, she'd learned not to assume too much knowledge or understanding behind such questions. Best to start with the basics. "Well, such tests are required before the FDA will approve a drug," she said, "if that's what you mean."

Mike's response surprised her—after all this guy had been living in the jungle for the last forty years. "The U.S. drug companies test their drugs—for the FDA approval, right?—on people outside the U.S., in places like Viet Nam and Africa."

It was more of a statement than a question, but she did not hesitate to refute it. "No, Mr. Johnson. Many, many tests are done here in the U.S. Most in fact. A well-designed program tests across an assortment of populations. However, some diseases they are testing drugs to cure simply do not occur in the U.S." She leaned back and watched him take a sip of tea. "You know malaria does not occur here, except sometimes in travelers just returned from a visit to a nation where it is endemic."

He raised his eyes from his teacup to glance at her, then back down. He nodded.

"So we cannot possibly test a candidate malaria cure here. It has to be done somewhere the disease exists."

"Like Viet Nam or Africa."

"Like Viet Nam or Africa," she agreed. "Some diseases only appear in one small area of the world. For example, consider a disease called "river blindness" among natives along the Congo in Africa. Recent trials have shown great success."

"Huh," he said. "Well, I could support that kind of testing."

Arrogant, isn't he? She smiled. "Good, Mr. Johnson. That's very good."

"Mike," he said. "It sounds pretentious for you to call me Mr. Johnson."

Pretentious? she thought, *There is more to this sergeant than —*

"All right," she said, "Mike."

"But I am going to insist in my payment up front!"

"How's that, Mike?"

"You are going to fund the medical mission to the Viet Nam highlands *first*." He nudged the handle of the teacup so the cup rotated in the saucer with an annoying squeaking sound. "Then I will make your speeches and go to your hearings."

"That's fine, Mike. I am happy to do things that will help the people you love. And you will be helping them twice, the second time when you speak for the drug testing."

He met her eyes and smiled. It still wasn't a warm and fuzzy smile, in her estimation. But they had an agreement.

"Would you be more comfortable with a formal contract?" she asked him. "I can have my legal staff draw something up."

He sipped his tea, flicking a glance up at her over the rim. He set the cup down with a clink. "If that makes you happy, it's fine with me," he said. "But mostly what I want to see is a medical team and clinical gear being loaded into a Vietnam Airlines jet, headed for Saigon."

"Saigon?" she said, surprised to hear that old name.

"Ho Chi Minh City," he said with a crooked smile.

"Mike, there's an ex-Special Forces guy who sometimes works for me that I'd like to assign to assist you."

"What for?" he asked, suspicion entering his expression again.

"To handle logistics for this medical mission." She shrugged, "If you don't like the idea, it's not necessary. I just thought he could be of some help to you." She waved toward the Priscilla curtained window. "After forty years, a lot things probably don't make much sense to you."

"That's true enough," he said.

Eleanor smiled. "His name is Ryan, and I'll have him drive you back to your hotel today, so you can get to know each other."

He nodded. "Fair enough."

"Dr. Roseman, please."

"May I tell him who's calling?"

"This is Dr. Powell."

"Connecting."

"Hello?"

"Hi, Rosie, it's Eleanor."

"Hi, Ellie. What can I do for you?"

She chuckled. "I'm glad you asked…" She went into her spiel, that she was calling in favors, and he was perfect to head the expedition.

"Expedition? God, Ellie, where are you sending me?"

"Viet Nam. Highlands."

"Okaaay… and what are we doing there?"

"Countless villages have died away. The data are anecdotal, so I can't say if we are talking a handful or hundreds. Many older villagers are left alive, but they've gone to the city or other villages as the younger ones dwindle. Very low birthrates. Lots of miscarriages, spontaneous abortions, difficulties becoming pregnant. My man there thinks maybe it's an effect of Agent Orange residue—in the population or in the environment. We can probably rule that out, but let's collect the data first and see."

"That could take months!"

"Mmm," she said, letting a little edge creep into her voice. "How many times have I saved your collective butts over there at your clinic?"

"I know, I know. It's just—"

"I have transport arranged, I'm putting together appropriate vehicles and technology for you to have mobile laboratory support. First class accommodations in tents, generators, porters, guides. All you have to do is clear a bit of your schedule and show up."

Roseman groaned. "And when does the plane leave?"

"The day after tomorrow."

"Oh my God. No. I can't possibly—"

"Rosie, don't make me threaten. Either the plane or the media leak about certain test results takes off the day after tomorrow, with you either way."

"Oh, thanks. Thanks for ruining my life, Ellie."

"Surely not! I've saved it, and will continue to…just as long as it's in my best interests to do so at least some of the time."

"What do you care about Agent Orange and villages in Viet Nam?"

"Rosie, I'm surprised at you. I care about the people. Why are the children dying, Dr. Roseman? That is what I care about."

Rosie groaned again, and she smiled her cat and canary smile. "I'll have my staff send you details. You can provide them with a wish list of equipment if you like. I will have it there waiting for you."

"I hear and obey," Dr. Roseman said, "though not without protest."

She smiled at the phone. "You might even have fun, Rosie," she said and hung up. She checked off "Roseman" on the list in front of her, stared out at the start of the cherry blossoms budding along the Potomac, then dialed the next name on the list thinking, *At this rate, I'll clear my list in a few hours, I hope tomorrow's enough time for Devon to perform miracles with* his *list.*

30 ≡ ANI

Ani stood looking down at a dugout canoe in progress on her father's handmade stretcher stand. Boards were tied at either end to pinch the canoe in to a point. Sticks were pressed into the center areas to force the wood to bow out, making room for passengers and supplies. She ran her hand along the skinned log, wondering who the canoe was for. Mañuel had already had one, of course, when he married. He had made a second one for Tipa when they first were married, even before their house was finished, because Tipa needed to be able to go up and down the river, and everyone used their canoes to sit in and do laundry during the high water seasons.

She heard footsteps and looked up to discover Liam walking toward her. He was staring at her, or at the canoe, and not watching his feet. She was going to warn him about the pile of bark scrap he was about to walk through when he looked where she was looking and managed to sidestep in time.

"Is that a canoe?" He asked walking around it. "Of course it is," he answered his own question. "Are you making it? Can I help?"

She shook her head. "It is Papa's job. Or Mañuel's."

"You don't think I can be of any help," Liam said, his shoulders slumping.

"Liam, you don't understand. I don't even help, not with canoes. It is my father's task, and he does it very well."

He looked at her suspiciously. "You mean you've never made a canoe?"

He held out his wrist and showed her a bracelet made of different seeds. "I asked Tomito to create some more of these for special souvenirs. Why can Tomito make bracelets, but you can't make canoes?"

She laughed at his disbelief. "Never. Nor Mamí, nor Tipa. Though I will tell you, there are some villages, some families, where the women prepare the canoes. But it is almost always men's work, because the women do not have the time."

He nodded, folding his arms across his chest. "What do they do all day, then?"

She raised her eyebrows. "You want to know what women's work is?"

"I'm curious. What could they do all day, that they do not have time to make a canoe."

"Well, you can come and help me today. Mamí has had no one to help her, and Tipa has her own household to take care of, so there are some jobs that are not getting done."

With a mystified expression on his pale, freckled face, Liam trailed along behind her.

"First we need to harvest and clean some breadfruit, and process the yuca Papa brought in yesterday. Then, Mamí needs a new sieve. She has dried and cleaned several big gourds, and we will make the holes in them and polish the nicest one so it is even better than your plastic colander at home."

He glanced at her with a thoughtful nod, forehead crinkled in thought.

"If we finish those chores, we will walk down to the school to see if they can use some help in the classroom today. Mamí used to go everyday to help, but she cannot, now. So we will be her substitutes."

"Um, school again?" Liam asked.

"You were very good with the children. They love the game you taught them yesterday. I think you make a good teacher."

227

They spent the morning on the yuca, grating it and letting it soak and mashing it. Liam managed to only grate his fingers twice.

"No blood in the manioc, please!" she teased.

He gamely wrapped his fingers with shredded bark for a bandage, and continued.

Some of the grated yuca would be pressed dry in the sieve. The sieve had a big crack in the side, and she showed Liam how it could not be used much longer before the entire bottom would break out.

"That's why we have to make a new one."

Once sieved, pressed yuca mash was spread to dry, and the juice turned into a drink. The wet yuca would later be mixed with eggs and a little corn flour to be turned into a kind of biscuit with bacon rind inside, that her mother was famous for in their little community.

Having eaten dim sum in San Francisco, she explained to Liam, "They are a little like pork sticky buns. Have you ever had them?"

When he shook his head, she shrugged.

"Well, you will be able to try Mamí's tonight or tomorrow."

They did not do the other things they had planned because the shaman arrived just as they strolled onto the *fútbol* playing field, heading toward the school. Escorting the shaman from the dock to her home was Ica, Toqui's mother. "Toqui was my best friend from back in school," Ani explained to Liam.

She did not explain that she and Toqui had become less friendly when Toqui had taken to flirting with every boy in town. She scowled. She had never heard that Toqui had gotten married. *She's probably still flirting*, she thought, feeling protective of Liam's innocence.

She nodded to Ica as they passed. Suddenly, Ica turned back and grasped Ani's upper arm.

"Angeline?"

"Hello Ica. This is—" she said, but was interrupted when she started to introduce Liam.

"Oh, please can you help?" Ica's face was all worried wrinkles, and Ani noticed a tightness in her eyes and jaw that spoke of fear or long worry.

"It's Toqui," Ica said. She waved a hand at the shaman. "Her baby is sick inside her." Ica's eyes were moist. "Oh, Angeline, can you please come and help? It would comfort her."

Angeline doubted that Ica knew of the angry words she and Toqui had spoken. "I have not seen her for years," she said gently. "Is there not someone Toqui is close with that could help?"

Ica's face crumpled and she wept, shaking her head.

Ani looked at Liam, who was staring, looking confused. She realized the entire conversation had been in Quechua, of course, and Liam had no idea what was going on. "An old friend of mine is sick; the shaman has come to help, but her mother," she indicated Ica, "wants me to come and be with her, too." She glanced across the playing field at the school building. "You go on to the school," she said. "They would be happy for your help."

Liam's eyes got big. "Can't I come with you?" he said. "I cannot even talk to them," he glanced at the school.

She sighed. Why was he so reluctant to go teach? He hadn't said a word when he'd demonstrated the game to the children the previous day, but that had worked quite well.

Behind her, the shaman said a word of impatience.

"Fine, come along. You may not like what you see," she said. She took Liam's hand in her right and Ica's hand in her left, and smiled pleasantly at the shaman. She asked him if it was acceptable for her to come and bring the American stranger.

His old, old face was so wrinkled she could not tell if he smiled or grimaced, but he said the equivalent of, "Yes."

They walked inland behind one of the *fútbol* goals, continued past the school buildings, down a short slope and back up, with a turn to the left. Ica's husband's property had once backed up with Angeline's father's, but then Mañuel had built in between them—one more bit of distance between Ani and Toqui.

Ica let go her hand and led the way into the house. Angeline was surprised and saddened by the run-down state of Toqui's house. Or, Ica's house, since Toqui was clearly still living at home. The ramp to their kitchen had a board missing, and the floorboards of the house were cracked and warped. The roof thatch was dry and slipping loose; it must leak a lot in the rains. There weren't any boards making the sleeping area quiet, though Ica or someone had tied a couple of pieces of woven matting and some mosquito netting to screen it from the casual viewer.

Toqui, big with pregnancy, lay listless and sweating in her old red hammock, the very one she had used when she and Angeline went to school together. It had holes in it, where Toqui's dress poked through. Ani scowled and looked about. Where was Toqui's father? He should be here for the ceremony.

But he did not come, then or later, and Ani came to understand Ica's husband was gone—either he had abandoned them or died, the other kind of abandonment the *rivereño* women dreaded.

The shaman said a few words, and Ica asked Angeline and Liam to help her lift Toqui from the hammock down to the floor. Ani explained in English and Liam suggested where they should stand to distribute the weight as they rolled the pregnant, moaning girl from the hammock into their arms. The shaman marked an area on the floor where he wanted Toqui to rest, and the three of them, grunting, bent and set her there.

Ica brushed Toqui's hair back from her face, and Ani took it upon herself to go get a basin of water and a rag, and wash Toqui's face and hands. The shaman nodded approval and asked for a fresh basin of water for himself and the others who would be present to cleanse themselves in.

Once this was done and they were arranged the way the shaman wanted them—himself at Toqui's head, Liam at her feet, and Ica and Angeline to either side, he began the formal ceremony, making himself the *paco*, the connection between the spirits.

He placed his beaded and embroidered and brightly tasseled cap on his head. He pulled his woven pack up beside him, reached in his pouch and withdrew a pinch of coca leaves which he set onto his tongue and began to chew. He pulled a small glass dish and another pouch out of his pack. He lit a tobacco cigarette which he set down on the dish to smoke, using his hands to waft the smoke over Toqui and down to Liam, who sneezed, then looked very apologetic.

She held her finger over her lips, and he nodded, nostrils flaring, eyes watering. He managed not to sneeze again, but she noticed his eyelids got very red.

She returned her gaze to the shaman, who chewed more coca leaves. Chanting softly, he removed wrapped packets of offerings from his pack, resting them in his lap. Then he took the altar cloths out of the pack, setting them atop the pile of offerings. With everything transferred from the pack to his lap, he put his empty pack down on the floor, smoothing it as flat as he could to serve as the altar.

Then he set the base altar cloth over it, not allowing any part of the cloth to touch the floor. Over that he spread the white cloth upon which the offerings would be placed, also keeping it from the floor.

Keeping up his gentle chant, he unwrapped the first set of offerings. One at a time he raised the items in his cupped hands, then lowered them to the altar cloth, placing each item separate from the others on the cloth. Chanting.

Ani watched, at peace, as the traditional coca leaves, grains, and beans were raised and placed. Instead of the traditional llama fat, difficult to get here in the lowlands, the shaman used a pad of yellow chicken fat, for fertility. He placed the seashell representing the daughter of Mother Lake with great reverence in the center. He placed gold and silver charms for sun, moon, and stars, a tiny book for wisdom. He placed a small wooden madonna figure to represent the earthly mother, in this case Toqui, and a small pink plastic baby doll to represent her healthy baby. A magnetic stone for drawing energy, candies for mother earth, who liked sweets.

Angeline happened to glance at Liam as the shaman placed the candies, saw him raise an eyebrow, as if to ask, "Really?" This cracked the ceremonial flow and all her American education pounced upon her, telling her this was nonsense. What could the offerings do to please the spirits, and what could the spirits do to heal Toqui? As her focus and her belief wavered, she met the shaman's eyes. He gave her the sweetest smile she had ever seen on a human face.

All her disbelief rush out of her as though sucked away by a vacuum—leaving peace, and trust, and hope. She smiled back at him, and bent her head in prayer as he began to fold the altar cloths closed.

He finished folding the cloth then indicated everyone, except Toqui, should stand up. Then he cleansed each person, beginning with Ica, brushing her shoulders and arms with the offering packet. He held it in front of her, and Ica blew on it three times, and the shaman rang a small brass bell. Ani stepped up next, with a glance at Liam to warn him he was next. She was brushed, she blew, the bell rang. Liam, blinking furiously at the tobacco smoke which still drifted about, stepped forward, was brushed, he blew, and the bell rang. Then the shaman carried the offering packet to Ica's stove, where her cooking fire was banked. He added some sticks, building up the fire, then placed the offerings on the fire.

"The offerings are burned so the smoke goes to the upper world, and the ashes go to the lower one," she explained to Liam in a whisper. He nodded, and stepped back, trying to stay out of everyone's way. Ica prepared some tea; Ani hoped it was for Toqui. The shaman was going to need a chicken, or at least a bunch of bananas as his thanks, but she did not see any such gift in Ica's kitchen.

Then she knelt beside Toqui, taking the girl's hand in hers. Toqui was very warm. The shaman knelt beside her and placed his hand on Toqui's belly. He sensed something about the baby that made him shake his head. "It is not alive," he said in Quechua. "I think it was not alive for several days."

From the kitchen, Ica looked at them, clearly unaware of what the shaman had said. Angeline did not know much about birthing babies, but she knew a fever when she saw one. She pinched Toqui's skin, and the skin bunched up and wrinkled easily between her fingers. "Very dry," she said. "Many days of fever."

Toqui's eyes opened for the first time since Ani had arrived. Toqui saw the shaman and smiled, then saw Ani and smiled even more. She clasped Angeline's hand. Her mother stepped over with a cup of tea, and Toqui smiled at her.

Then Toqui's eyes rolled up, her grip on Ani's hand went slack, and she no longer breathed. Just like that, she had died. Ica dropped the cup of tea, splattering hot liquid everywhere. She dropped to her knees beside her daughter, caught her up in a hug, and wailed. The shaman put his hands on her shoulders, holding her, and rocking her and Toqui's lifeless body.

Tears started in Ani's eyes, and she had the weird thought that she had cried more in front of Liam than she had cried the entire previous year. What was wrong with her?

Suddenly a pair of pale freckled arms went around her, and then she was crying on Liam's chest, his hands patting her shoulders in a rough rhythm. She swallowed, thinking of Toqui's short life, her dead child within her. She thought of Tipa, her lively, sweet sister-in-law, and choked back a wail. Was Tipa going to die, too?

It turned out Ica did not have a gift for the shaman. She had planned to cook him supper, but in her grief only wanted everyone to leave. By this time the sun had set, and Angeline was more than glad enough to do so.

She invited the shaman to her house, knowing her mother would welcome the old man, perhaps could even provide him with something to take home in addition to a full belly. Beside her, walking in the dusky light streaked with orange sunset glow, Liam was silent.

She glanced at him. "You should know that most shaman's ceremonies do not go like that. Ica waited too long to ask for help."

Liam nodded. "I'm sorry for her, they sure didn't have much."

She shook her head. "For Ica, now things are even worse." She sighed, but brightened considerably when the lights of her family's house showed ahead of them. Mamí had the cooking fire going, making something that smelled delicious. Beside her father, outside in the yard, she could see Tomito, Mañuel, and a third tall form.

"Marco?" she called, and then ran to her biggest brother.

Marco laughed, and swept her into a big strong hug. Somehow, he had gotten all the tallness of the family, as though once the eldest was tall, there was no need for anyone else to be any bigger than Papa. Marco had always made her feel safe.

She turned back and made sure her father saw the shaman, and that the old man had been properly welcomed at their home. Then she introduced Liam to Marco, and left the men to stand and smoke and talk while she joined her mother and Tipa in the kitchen.

Without thinking, she blurted, "You are drinking your cat's claw tea, aren't you, Tipa? And getting enough—" she stopped when she realized there was no word that she knew of for *calcium* in Quechua. "Bone meal," she finished in Spanish.

Tipa's eyes widened. "Yes, and yes, little sister," she said. Tipa also had no sisters of her own. She had only three brothers, not five, like Angeline. They had pretended to be sisters since before Tipa and Mañuel were married. Ani had helped Tipa when Chaya was born. She made a vow at that moment to be here when this next baby came, no matter what she had to do to get home.

"Good," she said.

"Why is the shaman here?" Mamí asked.

"Toqui," she said.

"Oh, Toqui," Mamí said.

"She died, mama," Angeline said. "She just died."

"What?" Tipa asked. "Just now?"

She nodded.

"Oh, I knew she was sick, but—"

"Her baby was dead inside her." She looked at Tipa with clear- eyed determination. "We will be certain this does not happen to you!"

"Oh!" Mamí said. "I am happy the shaman is here!"

"He will be needing supper," Ani said with a little shake of her head. "Ica is—"

"Oh, Ica!" her mother said. "That woman!"

"She has had a lot of bad luck," Tipa said in her usual generous way.

"Of course the shaman is welcome to eat with us. We have plenty," her mother said. "We will have him say a prayer and look at Tipa, who is just fine as you can see." She made shoo-ing motions. "Go join your American friend," Mamí said. "I am certain the men are terrifying him."

Angeline laughed and went outside. She rested a hand on Liam's shoulder, letting him know she was there. He turned to her, murmured, "I am sorry about your friend," he said. "I wish there was something I could do to help."

Ani started to shake her head, then looked at him. "Did I see some vitamins in your gear?" she asked.

He nodded, clearly puzzled how vitamins were going to help a dead girl.

"Can we give them to Tipa? It would...just make me feel better," she said.

Liam smiled. "Of course," he said.

31 ≡ MIKE

Mike turned in a full circle on the tarmac, seeing cargo handlers everywhere, with cargo sitting variously on the ground, on a loading conveyor, or still on tractor-pulled carts on both sides of the Airbus A400M.

There was more angry dialogue between Ryan and the homeland security inspector. Meanwhile Eleanor's United Earth Logistics ground crew ignored the altercation and continued their pre-flight checklist. The men in white coveralls with yellow reflector stripes and UEL stenciled in large black letters swarmed around the airplane. They definitely looked more professional than the homeland security team that was still attempting to inspect each and every crate UEL was trying to load. Meanwhile Ryan's men, para-military guards with HK45s tried to remain in the background, but Mike certainly noticed them. The homeland security inspector did too, eyes sliding to the right and left.

Ryan yelled at the inspector, who grimly attempted to continue his job.

The UEL supervisor stood nearby, ticking off her checklist with a thick black marker.

"Fuel, 105 thousand. Any weekend plans?"

"Girls' night out."

"Antiskid, checked and off. You need an escort?"

"You offering?"

"Forget it, his mama don't let him out after dark."

The supervisor ticked her checklist as the UEL crew burst into laughter. A team of three rolled the boarding stairway up to the plane. Mike shaded his eyes against the bright sun still coming under the wings, as he watched them open the hatch far above his head.

Ryan's argument with the inspector got louder. Mike didn't want to get involved. He drifted up the stairs, increasing his distance from the shouting match. He stopped on the top platform when Ryan lost his temper.

"Inspection is *over*! Stuff your damn homeland security regs. We're flying *out* of the country, not in. We're late and I'm not opening any more crates!"

The inspector signaled his two rent-a-cops with DHS insignias safety-pinned to their blue blazers. As they approached, two of Ryan's guys wearing black vests stepped forward and flicked the safeties off their HK45s. The rent-a-cops stopped. They looked toward their boss as if to say I'm not getting killed for this thankless, minimum wage job.

Ryan waved to the cargo handlers. When their boss yelled, "Go ahead," the forklifts started rolling again. Ryan turned back to the inspector. "Just have whoever gives you your orders contact Claudia." He offered the inspector Claudia's camo-patterned business card. The inspector just stood there, so Ryan shoved it into the inspector's shirt pocket. The breeze carried Ryan's voice up to Mike quite clearly. "You might want to wait a bit, since Claudia and DHS Secretary Linstret are taking advantage of some spring skiing in Jackson Hole for the next couple of days."

The inspector frowned and made a big show of writing everything down on a small pad that reminded Mike of one he used for homework assignments in grade school. The inspector snapped the little notebook shut and marched away. The rent-a-cops followed. Their out-of-shape bodies swayed. They looked like two ducklings following the mother duck to the pond.

Mike gave Ryan a thumbs-up. "Nice work." He gladly let Ryan bully the bureaucrats and technicians, especially as it seemed Ryan really enjoyed doing so. But Mike didn't want him to forget this was Mike's mission.

The containers, crates, personal luggage piled around the plane disappeared into the ample cargo hold. Ryan turned his attention to the other passengers who had begun filing out of the small waiting room.

"It's already oh-six-fifty-four; everybody on board, please. I'm not your babysitter. Doors close at oh-seven-hundred, sharp. We've gone to a lot of effort for a daytime departure and if we miss our window, domestic flights will lock us out. That's not going to happen, but Ellie'll be really unhappy if we have to leave you on the runway to get off on time."

Mike thought about Ellie. *She is one righteous cat.* He'd only known Dr. Eleanor Powell a short time, but she was Ellie and she had put together a lot very quickly. She was a lucky find.

In the back of his mind he thought, *What is her real interest in this mission?*

T he Airbus cruised at 33,000 feet. The turboprops reminded Mike of the C-123Ks in Nam, except that the airbus had twice as many engines and was twice as long. He found the rhythmic beating of the blades soothing.

He unbuckled his seat belt and polished his lucky knife. He admired the delicate blood-red grain along the blade and the dragon carved to look fierce while still fitting in his palm with comfort. Through all the search and interrogations at the old embassy in Ho Chi Minh City, he managed to keep his weapon. Always knowing he had one more option let him drive a hard bargain. But he never could have imagined an angel like Dr. Powell.

At first Eleanor seemed to be just another slippery politician like that General Consul bastard, Hogshead, or whatever his name was. But she delivered everything she promised and more. Mike pulled back the canvas divider and looked at the cargo in the hold. He recognized some of the military stuff, but the crates of scientific equipment meant little to him. He had ditched most of his science classes back in high school, so aside from the microscopes, he didn't recognize anything. A lot of it seemed to be *imagers* and *analyzers*. And computers. Little computers in little boxes. Nothing like the rooms full of monster machines he'd seen pictures of before he'd shipped out.

He grunted in satisfaction, and sat back down in his soft armchair. He swiveled it to study his fellow passengers. In his mind he stared at an empty seat where Eleanor might have sat. She said her goodbyes last night at a grand dinner at her horse ranch in Maryland. In his honor, she had served McDonald's on fine china with real silver and cloth napkins. He'd encouraged everyone to stuff themselves, since they wouldn't see much American food until they returned.

From Dr. Roseman's comment, "Science never solves one problem without creating ten more," it sounded like this mission might take a long time. After forty-plus years, he had patience, especially as things were moving forward. *Thanks to Ellie.*

Dr. Jacob Roseman, the toxicologist who Eleanor called "Rosie," brought stacks of magazines, most with plain covers and pages of small print. Though younger than Mike, he looked unprepared to live in the wild. Salt-and-pepper hair covered his head like bird feathers, each hair so perfectly fitted to another that they all fused into a single smooth surface. Mike could not imagine this man—with his fingernails sparkling like polished seashells—hiking through the undergrowth or sleeping in a hammock.

Next to him was Ryan—retired Special Forces—private investigator—Eleanor's muscle. If things got dangerous, he felt he could count on Ryan, but if there wasn't any trouble, he feared Ryan would get in the way. Ryan didn't talk much, but Mike suspected he and Eleanor differed on something. Mike admired Ryan's combat readiness, but recalling Eleanor's unblinking eyes and barely upturned lips, he decided that if he had to choose sides, he'd go with the mysteriously confident Dr. Powell.

Ryan's guys, armed as usual, and a couple of technicians occupied another half dozen seats. One of the techs was named something like

"Stinko," Mike remembered, but the other's name he had completely missed. And the cook. He couldn't believe they were taking a cook.

That left Dr. Zaara Yassin, the epidemiologist. She wore baggy camouflage pants with lots of pockets and a sweat shirt, also several sizes too large. He leaned back in his chair, pulled his Raiders cap down and stared at Dr. Yassin from under the visor. Everything about her face interested him, not in a sexual way—after all she was so young, she could be his daughter, but as a thing of beauty—her golden eyes, delicate ears decorated with two simple gold rings each, her broad nose, much like Mike's, and her translucent skin with just a hint of dark green like the summer forest.

She carried two electronic boxes at all times. Even during dinner last night, they sat next to her on the table. The larger flat black box was her own computer, and the small white one played music. She ignored everyone on the plane, her eyes focused on the computer screen and her ears connected to her private music. He didn't care; he just stared at her face as it reacted to the images on the computer screen.

Consul General Hollingsdale—Hogshead—met them at a military airport outside Ho Chi Minh City. Mike again marveled how Eleanor, or was it Claudia, had arranged clearance to land at a Communist Vietnamese military base. The Consul General didn't say anything as he escorted everyone through customs. He was sure Hollingsdale recognized him—after all he'd been interrogated at the embassy before Eleanor had sprung him free.

Four vehicles waited beside the plane. They reminded him of jeeps, only bigger, much bigger. He had expected military surplus, but these looked and smelled new, and were painted orange. He thought of Cinderella's pumpkins. He felt a little like Cinderella with Eleanor as the fairy godmother.

Ryan referred to the big jeeps as Humvees. He supervised unpacking the A400M and loading the Humvees, several equipped with trailers, while

Mr. Hollingsdale took Mike, Dr. Yessin, and Rosie into the VIP lounge. The whole time Hollingsdale only spoke to the two doctors. Mike was clearly the second-class citizen. Another reason Mike was eager to move out of a city that held bad memories of both his recent interrogation, and the war.

Soon enough they were driving out of Ho Chi Minh City, heading towards Da Lat, almost 200 kilometers up Highway 20. Ryan sat in the front of the lead car with a local driver. Mike, Dr. Yessin, and Rosie sat in the back seat with Mike in the middle. The rest of the team piled into the other Humvees, packed in tightly with the crates and supplies.

Claudia had gotten them hotel rooms for the first night in Da Lat where she was invested in coffee plantations and had a rescue operation for small wild felines, especially fishing cats. This was a nice treat. If they had taken a commercial flight, they would have arrived at night and had to stay over in Saigon. After this it was to be tents and air mattresses, or hammocks outdoors for the hardy.

He thought back to his train ride with Chi not that long ago. With pride and satisfaction, he reviewed his long journey from the jungle to Ho Chi Minh City, to Minot, North Dakota, to Washington D.C., and now back. As promised, he returned with American scientists to help Chi and Mai Linh and the other young women still living in the hills. He closed his eyes to rest as they passed by rice fields.

Dr. Yessin admired the countryside. "Can we visit the Cu Chi tunnels?"

Ryan laughed. "Maybe on the way back."

"Stop! Look at those waterfalls."

Ryan said something in his radio and the caravan pulled off the road, unconcerned by the soft dirt and lack of a proper shoulder. Dr. Yessin jumped up on the Humvee's hood and took about a dozen pictures with a camera the size of a pack of cigarettes.

He warned her, "We're going to be far from any stores. Be careful you don't run out of film."

"No problem, it's digital."

He had no idea what she was talking about, but that was her answer to most of his concerns, so he just let it go. A little way farther there was another waterfall.

When they stopped, Rosie complained. "I'm only here for a week. I've got to get back to my clinic. That's not much time to get everything done, so let's keep moving." He turned to Dr. Yessin. "Do your sightseeing when we're done with the real work."

She didn't reply, but turned to the window and took the rest of her pictures without stopping.

Mike turned to his left. "Rosie, what do you think we're going to find?"

"Nothing."

"What?"

"Oh, sorry. I meant, 'Nothing new.' I've been reading the Agent Orange literature. For example, here's an article from the Institute of Medicine on veterans and Agent Orange. It's almost 20 years old, but we stopped using Agent Orange in Vietnam over forty years ago. It reports on a large number of studies in Vietnam, both north and south and every one found an increase in miscarriages."

He looked at the journal, but the print was too small for him to read. "That's what I've been telling you: there are so many miscarriages, whole villages are disappearing."

"Not so fast. The largest effect was an increase from 4.3% to 18.1%, long ago, 1978—certainly significant, but nothing like villages disappearing. And those numbers have been dropping as the concentrations drop. So, as long as we investigate Agent Orange, we'll find nothing, nothing new. If that's our mission, we might as well go home today, which is fine with me."

Dr. Yessin put down her camera to add, "Your disappearing villages could be nothing more than anecdotes, family stories. Like myths, legends, or fairy tales, they get passed along from generation to generation, but are based on no facts at all. Science needs data not daydreams."

Ryan turned around to Rosie. "For the sake of your clinic back in the states, I hope you're wrong, otherwise we're going to be here a long time."

Mike appreciated Ryan's support, but also wanted to tell him to mind his own business. Ryan turned back to watch the road, so Mike didn't say anything.

Rosie muttered, "I'm leaving in a week," and tapped Ryan on the shoulder, "I'm the toxicologist, dragooned on this mission for my expertise. If you don't want to believe me, where are you going for a second opinion in the middle of nowhere?"

Ryan turned around towards Dr. Yessin. "What do you think?"

Rosie grimaced. "He's going to ask an epidemiologist about toxicology?"

Dr. Yessin's headscarf flapped in the wind as she stuck her camera out the window to take a couple pictures. She rolled the window up and smiled, "You want to know what I think?"

Ryan and Mike said, "Yes, yes please."

"As an epidemiologist, my first choice would be some mysterious new disease, never observed by western scientists—Yessin's Virus. That would be wicked cool."

Rosie laughed.

"But, that's unlikely, high unlikely, probably impossible. I did an extensive internet search and no one has seen anything. It's next to impossible that there's a new disease lurking here without being mentioned on the internet—*virtually* impossible."

Rosie laughed at some private joke.

She repeated, "Virtually impossible."

Ryan turned front and the discussion stopped. Dr. Yessin rolled the window down for some more pictures of waterfalls.

When Mike saw train tracks, he told everyone about the Swedish engineers hired by the French to cross the rugged terrain. "It's really a beautiful ride. You should all take the train back to Saigon when this is over." Dr. Yessin took a picture of a tunnel.

Ryan turned around again. "The toxicologist says it's not poison, and the epidemiologist says it's not disease. What the hell is it?"

He wondered about Ryan's response. Ryan was certainly more than an angry tough guy.

Dr. Yessin closed her window again. "Too much wind." She tucked her thick, wavy black hair back into her scarf. "I think Mike is basically right. It's something in the environment. The question is: what?"

Dr. Roseman repeated, "I'm out of here in a week."

The caravan stopped in front of the sparkling white, international-style Palace Hotel. The building had clean lines, with a few carefully chosen curves, emphasizing the height of the three-story building sited majestically atop a wide staircase. Ryan announced. "We'll be staying here. The drivers and the others have rooms close by."

Before Ryan could say anything else, Mike reached across Rosie and opened the door. "I'll go up and make the arrangements with the front desk and get the keys. Dr. Yessin and Rosie, please come with me. Ryan, can you arrange for our luggage to be sent to our rooms."

The two men stared at each other for seconds, until Ryan finally said, "Good plan, and let's meet in the dining room at nineteen-hundred hours for dinner. Claudia said the menu is excellent."

Mike walked up the white marble stairs with Rosie on his left and Dr. Yessin on his right. "This is one of those times when it's good to be able to speak the language."

32 ≡ LIAM

"**P**_uka_."

Liam wrote a large numeral three on the blackboard and repeated, "*Puka.*"

Rosa and Alejandro passed out the baskets of beans. The school didn't have many supplies, but the village had plenty of beans and baskets. When he asked for baskets, each family donated a few and some of the older girls proudly wove more from river reeds and banana leaves.

With their wooden desks pushed together, each pair of students shared three baskets of beans—*puka* red beans, *yurak* white beans, and *yana* black beans. He felt like a kindergartener, learning his colors. Each student counted three red beans into small pile. The youngest ones struggled, not with the counting, but coordinating their short thumbs and fingers to close with a slick bean between them. He reached out to help, but shoved his hands in his pockets remembering their teacher's admonition, "Hands only learn what hands do."

Rosa finished first and couldn't resist helping the others, especially Yessica, her partner. Alejandro was also quick, but he was content to hold out his handful of beans for Liam's approval. Liam walked around the room and touched child's hand, saying *bueno*, or *excelente*, or *perfecto*. The students accepted his praise with big smiles of white teeth.

When three red beans sat proudly in front of each child, he went back to the board, wrote a five, and said, "*Yurak*." The students scrambled to select five white beans. After everyone was ready, he put three reds in one hand and five whites into his other hand, said "*y*," and cupped his hands together. He opened his hands and asked "*¿Cuántos?*"

They all yelled, "*Ocho*."

Liam had learned his numbers, anyway up to *veinte*—twenty, but only in Spanish. His Quechua was limited to these few colors and little else.

Each day he played this game with them. Some like Rosa caught on very quickly, while others like Yessica needed more time. Sometimes he said, "*Solamente Yessica*." He gave her five black plus five red.

After she cupped her hands together, she counted all the beans and proudly announced, "*Diez*." He made little clapping motions and the class broke out in real applause. Everyone cheered except Javier.

Javier sat at his desk and looked around the room. Nothing caught his interest or held his attention. Liam thought he might be deaf, but when the big downpour beat on the tin schoolhouse roof, and the other children shouted over the noise, he put his hands over his ears and held them there until the rain stopped. At least he could hear the cacophony of the large tropical raindrops drumming on the roof.

Even though he successfully engaged the other students in his math games, he continued to worry about Javier.

His pride in his teaching far exceeded what he felt in his college classes. Back in Colorado he had 200 students, most of whom hated statistics. Each student meant little more than another test to mark and grade to calculate. He rarely learned their names, except for the problem students. Here he knew each student—Rosa's eyes, Alejandro's quiet determination to excel, Yessica's shy desire to please. Each student brought his or her own unique contribution to the little kindergarten through second grade class in the jungle.

Even Javier, who seemed isolated in his own private world, added something. Liam thought, *especially Javier*.

After math class, the beans were all mixed up, so Liam usually gave the baskets to Rosa or Alejandro to sort. Today he noticed Javier staring at the baskets of beans. This spark of light excited Liam—his heart raced. *What should I do? What should I say?* He thought of asking Javier to do a math problem, or telling him to sort the beans, but Javier often got frustrated. He did not want that spark to fade and die. He had every reason to expect Javier to throw the beans across the room, as he often did with his crayons, and sometimes with the blocks. He had been warned to never to let Javier play with the blocks—"*muy peligroso*"—very dangerous.

He watched Javier's eyes follow the baskets, as they were collected. Finally it came to him: *Javier knows what to do; I don't need to say anything.* He placed all the baskets of mixed-up beans on Javier's desk and went off to teach the older children.

Later he had the grade three-to-six students. Liam wrote 4 x 9 = on the blackboard and held his hands in front of his face with the fingers spread wide. *Jazz hands*, he thought. The older students had figured out the *muy loco americano*. They all held their jazz hands, palms forward, in front of their faces. Keeping his hands in front of his face, he pointed to the four written on the board with his elbow. Everyone laughed and shouted, "*Quatro!*"

Now he started on his right, their left, and counted fingers with his nose. "*Uno*," he touched his pinky with his nose. "*Dos*," his nose touched his ring finder. "*Tres*," his middle finger. "*Quatro*," he stopped with his pointing finger delicately placed on the tip of his nose. Everyone counted fingers with their noses and laughed. He pretended to eat the finger touching his nose and folding it down as if he'd chewed the finger off and swallowed it. The class copied his pantomime. The boys shouted; the girls giggled. Now, moving quickly, he counted the fingers still up on the student's left, "*Uno, dos, tres*," and wrote a three on the board. Next he counted the fingers on the other side of the digested digit, with his nose as usual: "*Uno, dos, tres, quatro, cinco, seis*," and wrote the six. The board now showed, 4 x 9 = 36. Everyone applauded and shouted, "*Una mas. Una mas.*"

He wrote 6 x 9 = this time. They all performed the same trick with their fingers and found the answer to be 54. The excited chatter died down as he handed out a nine-times practice sheet that the regular teacher had prepared for them. Liam's chest felt warm and he wanted to call Ani to come see as they all made jazz hands and counted with their noses. He tried to think of one reason why he had ever taught classes of 200 "Introduction to Statistics" students.

He couldn't.

When he returned to Javier, an unexpectedly happy Javier, he was pleased to see the beans were sorted and none had been thrown across the room. There were four baskets of red beans, four of white and four of black. Javier held out his hand. It had one bean. Liam reached down to pick it up and throw it in the correct basket when he realized there wasn't a correct basket. He couldn't decide whether the bean was white with large black spots, or black with funny long white stripes.

When he examined the white-bean baskets more closely, he discovered one basket had pure white, clean and unblemished beans, another had off-white beans, some with a few small spots, the third had beans with medium size black spots, and the last had white with medium sized brown spots. Certainly this odd bean didn't fit in any of those baskets. At that point he realized, Javier had done more than sort *puka, yurak, yana*. Each of the twelve baskets had a different set of beans. Since the reds were all uniformly colored, Javier differentiated them by size. He segregated the small black beans by shade. Liam took the extra bean and put it in his pocket to remind himself that people only looked the same if you were too busy to see the differences.

Javier smiled when Liam put the extra bean in his pocket, like he knew all along that that was where it belonged.

When morning session was over and the children were dismissed, most children stayed to play in front of the school. Some played jump rope, others *fútbol*, and Liam was gratified to see some still playing tic-tac-toe. Javier's sister came over and hugged Liam before she took Javier home. He watched as she led him across the *fútbol* field, past Ani's house and into a small garden where his mother was planting squash. When she saw Javier, she immediately jumped up and hugged him. She was so glad to see him.

While his mother kissed his rubicund cheeks, Javier's arms hung limply at his sides. He didn't smile or laugh. Liam recognized his "nothing interesting" expression, staring into the distance with a slight space between his flaccid lips. None of this detracted from his mother's happiness.

Liam remembered returning home from school in Colorado, running up the long dirt road from the school bus, searching among the paddocks and outbuildings until he found his mother. "Look what I got!" Turning his backpack upside down in front of her to find the day's class work, each page with a sticker saying "Good Work!" or "Well Done!"

For a moment he imagined a connection with Javier, their eyes meeting as if Javier could feel Liam's pain from long ago when his mother didn't kiss him, but rather said, "Now your papers are all dirty, throw them away."

"**A**nd after everyone left, I counted the beans in each basket. Each basket had exactly the same number of beans! I thought about how difficult it is to devise a sorting criterion that results in equal sets... " *In the general case, I expect it's an unsolvable problem.* "But this six year old, who won't talk and can't look you in the eye, did it. He did it!"

Ani stared at him. Surely she noticed his excitement and maybe his indirect pride. She said, "I'm sure his mother will be very proud."

He jumped up. "That's the most interesting part. She's already so proud of him, I doubt this would make any difference!"

Ani smiled faintly, and walked past him towards the river. She clearly did not think Javier's small success was anything special.

She looked up and down the river. "Did you just hear a motor boat?"

"Are you still worried about guerrillas? I thought the *Ejercito* was rounding them up."

"Yes. They are. But who knows how many hide in the jungle, who maybe want revenge. Who maybe come back here."

Liam took a deep breath. "I hope not."

They both could hear a boat motor now.

"I am wondering if I will ever feel safe again. If my family will be safe." She stared silently until a tourist boat came into view. "Oh, just *turistas*." She sighed a long, shuddering sigh. "What were you saying?"

Liam just shrugged. Javier's bean-sorting paradigm could just remain his own little treasured memory. It didn't seem very important against the backdrop of guerrillas and wiped-out villages, he had to admit.

The next day the students colored a line drawing of a shaman. Rosa started with his hat and selected the brightest colors for his tassels. Alejandro found the sharpest color pencils to delicately color the offerings set out before the shaman. He colored the moon and stars silver, and the sun gold. He tried several pencils before he selected the perfect olive green for the coca leaves. Yessica ignored the picture and planted a circle of flowers around the shaman. Every child created his or her own interpretation. Javier picked up a black crayon and scribbled over the picture.

Liam's shoulders got heavy with disappointment. Javier did so well yesterday and now he just scribbled. He remembered reading a joke about a child who colored all his pictures black. The school psychologist predicted dire consequences, until someone asked the child, "Why are all your pictures black?"

The child had replied, "That's the only crayon I have."

Liam thought about that another moment, then gave Javier a blank piece of paper and a blue crayon. When he returned, Javier had created an intricate geometric pattern that Liam was sure had something to do with the golden mean and Fibonacci numbers.

After school he sat on the stairs and watched the children play. For some reason Javier's sister didn't come to get him. Javier just stood in front of the school; arms limp, not looking at anything, the light rain dripping down his face like tears. Alejandro waved for him to play *fútbol*, but he didn't respond. Yessica invited him to play tic-tac-toe, but he ignored her. After the longest time, we walked over to Liam and sat in his lap.

Liam didn't know what to do, but was willing to wait for Javier to make the next move. "Hands only learn what hands do." He had seen a glimpse into Javier's mind and saw no reason to second-guess Javier's judgment now.

That night before he told Ani about his day with Javier, she said, "I'm glad you're doing so well at the school." She was silent a long moment, chopping vegetables. "So. My classes start next week. I am trying to decide if it is safe to return to the Academy in San Francisco. The *Ejercito* claims it has rounded up the last of the New Sun. Or so the Captain said who came here this afternoon."

Liam leaned against the wall frame and scratched his head, trying to process what she just said.

She added, "Do you think it is a good time for you to return also? Certainly you have classes to teach at the College of the Rocky Mountains."

He had been thinking about Javier, not returning home. He didn't want to think about home or the tenure committee or his mother.

He had forgotten that Ani lived in San Francisco, and that he lived in Boulder, Colorado. Not only had he forgotten, but also he was not at all certain he wanted to go back and teach college students, even assuming his fight with the tenure committee was over, and he was going to be *allowed* to teach there.

After dinner, he sat on the floor by the kitchen ramp and stared out at the river, next to Papa, who offered him a hand-rolled cigarette. He smiled and shook his head, then stared out at the water again. Was it time to go home? The river coiled by, an occasional undulating streak marking an eddy in the black water. Very much like his goals—murky, confused. What was he going to do now?

33 ≡ ANI

Ani could not believe it was almost time to go back to the Academy. The time had gone much faster than two weeks ever did in San Francisco.

She wanted to walk around the village and begin making her goodbyes, so she accompanied Liam to the school, through the drizzling rain. She watched with a crooked smile as the children mobbed him, laughing and screaming his name.

"Liam! Liam!"

"*Mi nombre es Elena, si?*"

"Tic-Tac-Toe?"

"Liam! *Seis y nueve son quince!*"

Others picked that up and they chanted it: "*Seis y nueve son quince!*"

He must have been drilling them in arithmetic. The children's regular teacher clanged the remnant of steel drum that served as a school bell. The older children lined up promptly, but the younger ones still clustered around Liam.

She waved goodbye as he turned briefly to smile at her before his red head disappeared through the door into the classroom along with his escort of dark haired children.

She glanced around as one older child sprinted toward the door. She noticed a roiling column of smoke rising from the jungle behind Mañuel and Tipa's house, and headed quickly in that direction. She made her way down the muddy path, knowing nothing could possibly be dry enough to burn in the rain—thinking, *The guerrillas are back. They're attacking Nanay Libre.* She crouched down and crawled through the thickest parts of the vegetation, listening for men's voices or gunfire.

She realized as she got closer that the smoke was coming from Ica's house. She jumped across the gully which had now turned into a runoff ditch almost a meter wide with muddy water sluggishly making its way down and around to the Nanay. As she moved up a low rise, first she could see the smoke thicken and darken, and then flames appeared, licking the dry roof thatch, and then the blackening house itself, and finally Ica, crouched in the rain, watching her house burn.

Ani joined her, crouching down to be at Ica's level. Two pathetically small bundles sat at Ica's feet: everything she had wanted to save before burning her house. A few items of clothing or cloth, wrapped up in a hammock. A good canvas sack filled with kitchen gear; Ani could see the curve of a pot, and the handle of a knife, and other lumps that comprised Ica's belongings. Beside the woman on the ground were a pair of machetes.

Ica turned her head just enough to see who it was beside her, then slowly, like a lizard in the cold dawn, rotated her head back to watch her house burn.

Ani sat there with her in silence until the floor collapsed, shooting up sparks. Then she jumped to her feet and leaned forward to brush an ember from Ica's canvas sack. With another pitifully tiny whoosh, the rest of the floor caved in, and Ica's old house was now just a pile of embers and half-burned logs, smoking in the rain.

"I am going to live with my brother in Nauta," Ica said in Quechua. "He is all that is left for me now. My husband is dead. My children are dead. Their children are dead, before they were ever born." Ica turned, like a robot Ani had once seen in a movie, very mechanical-moving and stiff, to stand up and face Ani. "My brother also has no one. Our family is cursed."

She opened her arms, offering a hug of comfort, but Ica pulled herself up. Standing straight with a flash in her eye, she said, "No. It could jump to you. I would not tempt the spirits to curse your family as mine as been." With a stiff dignity that was all she had left of her family and her pride, Ica bent and picked up the machetes, fitting them by a thin leather strap to hang from the canvas bag. The old woman picked up her hammock carry-sack and her canvas bag, nodded to Ani, and made her way toward the river.

"I pray for you, Ica," she said, small comfort though it would be. Ica disappeared without a backward look. Ani turned and looked at the smoldering embers. She would tell Tipa what had happened here. The shaman could perhaps come and bless the place, and maybe after a time of regeneration, Mañuel could use the land for his cane sugar crop. If the village didn't use the cleared space, the jungle would simply return.

She continued along the inland path, past Ica's place and on to where three more houses crouched against the shade of the jungle. Before she'd left for *el norte*, she knew everyone in her small village, but now her circle was only her family and childhood friends.

One house was abandoned, she could see immediately. She thought, *Perhaps this too should be burned, before the rats become a nuisance*. The other two were ill-kept, in her opinion, one of them had a gaping hole in the thatch that must let in nasty amounts of rain, and the other was in need of new floorboards. An old woman glanced up from the pot she was stirring and grinned a gap-toothed grin. Beside her, a younger woman, grossly pregnant, stood sideways at the stove, keeping her big belly out of the way as she chopped tomatoes. She did not look at Ani at all. Unless someone was asleep in a hammock, there were no children that Ani could see.

At the other house, a very bony man was smoking fish over a cane-scrap fire out in the yard. A sickly-featherless chicken scratched in the dirt beside him. Inside the house a woman a little older than Ani was weaving thatch—to patch their hole, no doubt—and singing to a boy about six-years old. *Who should be in school*, she thought, but she didn't say anything. There were only three hammocks swinging in the sleeping area—so only the one child. She could understand how the mother would want to keep him close. Just as Tipa had kept Chaya close by her, until, at last, she became pregnant again.

This path didn't go any farther. She nodded a greeting to the family, then turned back the way she'd come. She crossed behind the schoolhouse, walking in the downriver direction to the rest of the village on the other side of the school.

Again, she was disturbed to see in that direction also there were very small families, with no new babies. Not even a pregnant wife. Three homes on the jungle side of the path, one in nice condition, two starting to show signs of need. It was hard to take pride in your home when you had no children to think of passing it down to. Only two houses survived on the river side of the path, at the east side of the school. There also: no babies, and no one pregnant.

Thoughtful, she walked back to her home. *Deforestation? No. Along the Nanay, reforestation seems to be more likely.*

Marco waved to her as she approached the house. He had come back again from a short riverboat trip. It looked like he had *just* gotten back; his suitcase was on the ground at his feet as he talked to Papa. He must have come in on the morning *peque peque*. She hadn't heard the little river taxi, but here Marco was. He reached out an arm, and hugged her against himself one-handed, while Papa finished what he had been saying.

Then Marco turned to her. "Good news!" he said.

"Good news would be nice," she said.

"The New Sun is definitely gone."

Was he teasing her? She looked at his face, which showed triumph, but not the twinkle he would get when he was "putting her on," as he liked to say in one of his tourist-ese expressions. Then understanding dawned.

"What, all of them?"

Marco nodded, squeezing her against his shoulder again, then dropping his hand as she stepped back a bit to look at him better. "If there are any left, they're just new recruits or perhaps one or two loose patrols. The Army had infiltrated the group; they had a man inside, which is why they weren't too helpful with your Mr. Shaughnessy," Marco said. "They needed to protect their *hombre* until he could get word out where the guerrilla main base was. Doesn't make any sense to just round up a few patrols."

"No, it doesn't," she agreed, dubious about the full truth of that, but whatever. The Army had a plan, and they followed the plan, and it had apparently succeeded.

"Chinca, and the leader whose name they had never known, which turns out to be Carlo," he said making a face, "but of course, not *our* Carlo," he grinned at her, "were all captured. And about fifty of their soldiers, too. Yesterday morning, up somewhere by Triunfo Nuevo off the Tigre."

Ani nodded. "Yes, the Captain came by yesterday and told us of the capture. But not that they were that close." But in truth, it wasn't as close as she had feared. "Someone said they were at Diamonte Azul, but I guess that was wrong."

"Good thing. It's only half as far, and still on the Nanay." Papa said. "We don't need those crazies around here."

Marco swept his fingers through his hair, brushing it back from his forehead. "They'd been recruiting in Nauta and Iquitos, which is how the Army got someone in with them. It's probably no surprise Carlo got hooked in by them, too." He stared deeply into her eyes. "Is he really going to be a *curandero*?"

"Yes!" Papa said.

She nodded. "I don't think he has much choice," she said, and laughed. "He can't get away from where he is with a bad foot and no boat, and he was pretty weak and sick when I left him. He probably doesn't even *know* where he is." She sniffed and shrugged. "And before he finds out, he's going to have to learn Cocama."

Marcos eyebrows went up, but he laughed outright. "Well, that's good. That's very good."

"I'm so glad you got back again before I had to leave," she said.

"Well, of course," Marco said, though he really did not have much control over his schedule. "What's to eat?"

"Would you like to come with me this afternoon?" Ani asked Liam as he added his banana leaf plate onto the stack of trash and picked up the stack to throw it in the compost pile.

He glanced at her. "Well, where are you going?"

"Just down to the next village or so," she said.

He looked uncertain, and rather foolish standing there with his hands full of banana leaves and scraps from their meal.

"It would be nice having help to paddle," she said—and it was the truth, for Liam had become fairly proficient at paddling, and it was always nice to have company. "Or if not, maybe I can drag Marco out of his hammock for a couple hours."

"He's already snoring," Mamí said.

"Okay," Liam said. "It's not like I have anything else to do now that school's done for the day."

It was very muggy. No doubt they'd have rain on the way back, if not before. She dipped her paddle. Liam dipped his. They were going upstream, and had stayed to the edge of the Nanay, picking up eddies to help them along. Before long they were in Mishama. A villager self-importantly pushed her dugout onto the dock to make room for more arrivals. Mishama was much larger than Nanay Libre, so it took awhile for Ani to do her rough head count.

The totals were very troubling. There were very few younger children— she had counted only eleven, out of a total population of eight hundred and six. There were only two new babies on the way.

She scowled as they made their way back to the Mishama dock and their canoe.

Liam tilted his head, and she said, "Later." She didn't really want the Mishama village elders asking any questions, not that she expected any of the villagers could understand English, but you could never tell anymore. They pushed away from the dock, and she lazily guided the canoe, letting the Nanay current pull them back toward home.

"You look unhappy," Liam said.

"The villages aren't just in trouble; in twenty years they are going to be extinct," she said.

He looked confused.

"Actually, they won't be extinct. There will only be old folks." She threw her arms out wide, nearly striking him with her paddle. "There are no children! Can't you see?"

He was still confused. "There's lots of children at the school."

She shook her head. "No, not like it was when my brothers and I were little. And there are so few babies, and even fewer women who are pregnant."

Liam looked off in the distance, then back at her. "Yes, I noticed that."

"I would be very interested to see what the numbers look like in villages where there *hasn't* been any drug testing."

Liam's expression changed from puzzlement to one of alarm. "My God, you don't think there's something about the tests…?"

"I don't know what else to think. In the villages where I know there was drug testing, the birth rate is very low and still dropping. That's what I know." She dug her paddle into the black water of the Nanay. "You can be sure I will know more once I get back to the Academy and get my hands on some research data about other villages. These tests and drug trials have been done all over the world. In your cities, too. There must be some other reports of results like this. Maybe even scientific proof."

P+P BLOG POST

Pride and Prejudice (apologies to Jane) aka Lies, Damn Lies, and Statistics (apologies to whomever said it first)—A blog dedicated to odd stories about numbers

Correlation Paradox

When people observe that two events are related, statisticians say they are "correlated," but most people ascribe causation. Common examples are:

People who eat more, weigh more.
Fertilized crops have higher yields.
People who engage in risky sexual practices are more likely to contract HIV.
Washing hands reduces the spread of disease.

Most people make little distinction between correlation (People are happier on sunny days) and causation (Sunny days cause people to be happy)."

Imagine a statistician wants to test this. Each day she could stand in the town square and observe the number of hours of sunshine and the percent of people smiling. This might give her a nice graph showing more smiling when there is more sunshine. She would conclude, "Sunshine makes people smile."

But her data also support, "Smiling makes the sun shine." Since the sun is 93,000,000 miles away, she doesn't make this mistake.

Unfortunately causality is not always that clear.

Consider: Cleaner water improves life expectancy—a recent global study declared that people with access to cleaner water lived longer.

Imagine a beautiful graph showing water quality and life expectancy increasing together (correlation). Since we don't believe increased life expectancy could cause the water to get cleaner, we happily accept: Cleaner water improves life expectancy.

This is a correlation paradox—correlation is not causation.

A more likely explanation is that both clean water and life expectancy are caused by economic prosperity. Neither one causes the other. Often two statistics that are correlated are caused by a third factor. Gray hair doesn't cause wrinkled skin, and wrinkled skin doesn't cause gray hair—age causes them both.

That explains things, doesn't it? Or maybe not.

34 ≡ MIKE

"This is my pad."

After Mike said it, he felt unsure. The caravan came to a stop. He recognized his isolated home, but somehow it was different. The woven walls and thatched roof seemed primitive, almost uncivilized. The raw-wood stilts that kept his floor above the rainy-season mud embarrassed him. The noise of the Humvees had scared the family of chickens; they ran among the forest trees in a frenzy of squawks and flying feathers. He didn't know what to say. He'd always been proud of his little space when Chi or other villagers came to visit.

Dr. Yessin ran around taking pictures of the stilts, woven walls, thatched roof, and the chickens in the underbrush. "Wicked! You actually live here? Can I look inside?"

He did his best to put up a brave front. "Sure, come on in."

Only Dr. Yessin and Ryan followed. Rosie went back to sit in the car. He had a sick look on his face. He took out his stack of journals.

Dr. Yessin ran around the room. She stopped in front of the ceramic brazier. "Do you use this for cooking?"

"Yes, and for heating in the winter."

Ryan picked up Mike's M21.

He snapped, "Be careful with that!"

Ryan's arms tensed as he slowly raised the gun and looked through the sight. Ryan chuckled, "I'll be careful. It's an antique." He admired the wooden stock. "Nice. Were you a sniper?"

"I did a lot of different things."

"What're you doing for ammo?"

"I found a cache. Not much left now."

Ryan returned the gun to its resting place beside the 50-pound sack of rice. "You eat a lot of rice?"

"Yep."

Dr. Yessin took a dozen pictures of the dragon chair. She folded the interlocking pieces together and opened them up again. "Did you make that?"

"Yes."

He felt a little better, but wanted them out of his house. "Thanks for visiting. I just need to pick up a few things and we can get going." They took the hint and headed outside.

He reached in his carry-on bag and took out the huge wad of cash—both dong and American twenties—that Eleanor had given him, "For whatever." He split off a small portion and put it in his pocket. The rest he stuffed deep into the rice in his rice sack. Even if one of the villagers came and "borrowed" some rice, he knew they would not touch the cash. It was safer here than in an American bank.

He grabbed a clean tee shirt and his spare carving knife. They had confiscated his other one at the embassy. Since he was just the native guide, he expected to have lots of free time to carve while the scientists did...whatever they did. He realized he had no idea what Rosie and Dr. Yassin intended.

"**W**elcome to my village."

Mai Linh welcomed the caravan in Vietnamese and Mike translated.

He looked around the village and tried to imagine what the visitors were thinking. Three long houses lined up side-by-side, with one wall of each facing south for the best sunlight. Fences of woven branches protected small vegetable plots from the pigs and chickens that roamed freely. The largest cultivated area contained coffee plants, but even this small commercial enterprise looked wild—no uniform rows, just a thicket of small trees with cardamom growing wherever it could find sunlight and pigs sleeping where they could find shade among the ferns under the keruing trees.

Mai Linh walked in front of the houses. She rested her hand on the floor of the first house. "The grandparents live here. My parents and I are proud that our village has so many wise ones."

Dr. Yessin acted as if she'd never seen such a house before and took pictures of the stilts, thatch and woven walls, just as she had of Mike's home less than an hour previously. Mai Linh smiled proudly at all the attention and moved on to the next house. "This is where I live with my parents, brother, and husband." Her hand traced her empty abdomen, and Mike knew she was thinking of her lost child. "That last house is empty. You're welcome to sleep there. It has been empty for a long time and the ghosts have left."

Dr. Yessin yelped, "Look! Look, an elephant," and rushed between the last two houses to take pictures of the animal chained to a tree stump.

Mai Linh covered her mouth and laughed. "She is a very funny lady."

He didn't translate.

Ryan looked at Mai Linh and pointed to the open space in front of the houses where the Humvees were parked. "Can we set up our tents there?"

Mike and Mai Linh discussed the question in Vietnamese, the group's mission, how long they might stay, and whether they would be respectful guests. Finally, Mai Linh said in English, "Okay, okay."

Ryan turned to his team. "Move the Hummers off the flat ground, down to that path area. In these hills, level land is scarce. Set up one tent for sleeping and supplies, though I expect most people will sleep there." He pointed to the third house.

Rosie whispered, "Not me, I'll sleep in the tent, thank you."

"Fine. Set up another tent for Dr. Roseman and his lab. He'll let you know which equipment he wants up immediately and what can wait."

"All of it. Now."

The guys looked at him questioningly.

"I wouldn't have brought it 10,000 miles if I didn't need it. The sooner you get it ready, the sooner I can get out of here."

His lab tech smiled.

Rosie looked at the tech. "I expect you to help, Stenko, especially with the gas chromatograph."

"No problem. I insist. I don't want anything broken," Stenko said, moving toward the crates. "These are delicate instruments."

Mike wasn't sure what all the gear did, but it sounded impressive.

"Next, a tarp roof for the cooking and eating area," Ryan directed. "It doesn't look like rainy season, but we better be prepared."

Ryan's guys were already moving when he added, "Put the generator and the refrigerator down by the Humvees. They don't need flat land either."

In an unexpected agreeable moment, Rosie smiled. "Good idea. I don't have much faith in my portable air filtering system, and see no reason to make it work harder by being close to the diesel fumes."

Mike stepped forward. "I can't tell you folks how to do your jobs, but we need to maintain coordination. We'll meet every night at seven o'clock for dinner and debrief. Ryan, can your group have dinner ready at seven? Everyone else, let's not waste the rest of today."

Rosie took out a carton of small bottles packed in a cardboard array like so many delicate eggs. Each slot also included individually wrapped tweezers and picks. He disappeared behind the long houses.

Dr. Yessin snagged Mike, "Can you translate for me? I have many questions about their health and village life and so on."

Without waiting for an answer, she dragged him to the first long house. Several elderly men and women sat on the floor in a circle. He bowed, then joined the circle and took out his knife and a piece of wood to carve. Dr. Yessin took out her small digital thing to take notes with. After some polite preliminaries, she started with the oldest looking woman. "How old are you and how long have you lived in this village?"

He translated.

The small wrinkled woman put one of her swollen arthritic finger joints up to the lips of her toothless mouth. Her fingers moved against her lips, joint by joint. The raspy voice replied, "Seventy-two years, born here, always here."

"How big was the village when you were a child?"

Again she counted on her knuckles. "Eight long houses, four here, four there." She waved her hand along the current row of houses and again toward where Ryan's crew was raising the tents.

"Where did everyone go?"

The woman talked to the others. They argued back and forth with feeling and energy. Mike summarized, "Moved to cities, killed by Americans, cursed because husbands sent them back to their village when they didn't have any children, kidnappings, miscarriages, two died in a flood, someone was bitten by a snake."

Dr. Yessin tightened her headscarf. "Mmm—anecdotes—mixtures of facts, memory and superstition. This is not going to be easy." She tapped her abdomen with a fingertip. "How many children did you have?"

After the same counting ritual, the elder announced proudly, "Nine."

Dr. Yessin asked about each one individually—name, spouse, children, and what became of each one. She did the same for the children and the children's children, and siblings and cousins. "Only by collecting data on individuals can we get past the vagaries of human memory, inaccurate generalizations and unintentional misconceptions." Mike did not translate that.

Dr. Yessin moved on to one of the elder men, and on around the circle of elders, asking names and ages and all again.

When Dr. Yessin finished, Mike handed the first old woman a carved dragon, bowed, and offered his gratitude to the house. She bowed also.

Meanwhile, Dr. Yessin walked to the next long house. Mai Linh's house. "I have all these people listed by the grandparents. Now I'd like to see if the younger generation agrees."

Mike nodded. "No problem, Dr. Yessin."

"Zaara, please."

"Zaara." Mike smiled.

"Mike," Duong said, greeting him just inside the door to Mai Linh's house. They hugged in sadness, in memory of the last time they had seen each other. Mai Linh ignored them, inviting Dr. Yessin inside.

After introductions, the questions continued. "What happened to your mother's sister, Su Linh?"

"I remember her well. She escaped to America. We got a postcard with pictures of American presidents carved into a mountain."

Dr. Yessin—Zaara—leaned toward Mike who had started a new carving, a tiger this time. "The grandparents said her husband divorced her because she was barren."

He smiled. "Both stories are true."

"**I** could have told you." Rosie put a spoonful of kosher beef stew in his mouth straight from the can. Whatever Ryan's cook had prepared was apparently not appetizing to Rosie. "After we dumped almost twenty million gallons of this stuff, I'm not surprised I can still find levels measured in hundreds of parts per trillion. This is not good. For comparison, the EPA standard for drinking water is 0.03 parts per trillion. This is thousands of times not good."

Mike looked up from his noodle soup, compliments of Mai Linh's mother. "Good work. What else did you learn?"

"I took blood samples. The blood levels are fortunately just a few parts per trillion. While that sounds good, the WHO standard for human blood is 0.01 parts per trillion—hundreds of times not good."

Mike leaned his head back and finished the last of the soup, drinking it from the wooden bowl. "See, I told you it was Agent Orange. What next."

"Not so fast. I've read papers from all over the world, and while these concentrations are not good, they have never caused the symptoms you report. I can still say with 95% certainty the low birth rates are not from Agent Orange. It's probably a biological, not chemical, agent."

The heat felt oppressive under the tarp. Mike wanted to roll up the walls to catch the breeze, but Dr. Roseman complained about the diesel fumes, so they sat in a sweaty funk.

Dr. Yessin put her fork down with an audible click on the aluminum folding table. "First of all, the only hard fact I have is that the population of this village dropped from over 160 to 13 in the last seventy years. Why? Everything from the ordinary to the supernatural has been suggested. I don't have enough data, but that's pretty slow for a disease vector."

Mike had finished eating and was carving his tiger. "Tomorrow we'll go to the higher altitudes to find some remote villages that haven't heard all the gossip." *And visit Chi!* Trying to sound very scientific, he added with his best educated accent, "We'll find cleaner data there."

He looked at Dr. Yessin, but she didn't seem to notice.

Rosie chimed in. "As long as you're going, collect some more blood samples. I'm sure Dr. Yessin knows how to do it."

Mike thought Dr. Yessin made an angry face at Rosie. Happy to be useful, he volunteered. "I was a medic. I can do it. Give me the syringes and test tubes."

Ryan, who had been quiet to this point, murmured, "I remember...you did do a lot of things during the war, didn't you?"

Dr. Yessin picked up her fork and pointed it at Rosie. "The population decline has been really slow. It must be something in the environment, a pollutant of some kind. Disease just doesn't work that slowly." She put a bite of what looked like mashed potatoes in her mouth.

Rosie scoffed. "Pollution, pollution! Since Rachel Carson's lucky guess, you lazy biologists blame everything on pollution—chlorinated hydrocarbons, heavy metals, trace radioactivity, manufacturing residuals, whatever."

"Environmental poisons like mercury, PCBs, estrogens work slowly. Biological agents like bacteria and viruses work fast. You've got that fancy lab setup. Put it to work."

Rosie shot back. "How fast was HIV leading to AIDS or HPV and cervical cancer?"

Dr. Yassin sat up very straight and smiled, "Lentiviruses like those are very rare. I'm with Mike—Agent Orange or some byproduct. Don't bury yourself in the literature. You're in the field. Do your research."

Mike took advantage of the momentary silence, "Lentivirus?"

This time Dr. Yessin laughed, "Latin for *slow virus*."

Rosie clenched his jaw. "We've researched Agent Orange to death. That's not it!"

"Fine! Check for something that's *not* dioxin."

With that Rosie left the tent. Dr. Yessin followed shortly after.

Ryan made his second comment of the evening, "Good work, Eleanor. I don't think either one has any idea what to look for." Ryan pulled the tarp aside and looked up at the stars. "Not a clue."

Mike left Ryan standing at the tarp door. He headed for Mai Linh's house and a little intelligent conversation before he went to sleep. He felt as frustrated as that day in Da Lat after Mai Linh's baby died. Too many questions, no answers.

They pulled out of the village after an early breakfast prepared by Ryan's cook. Mike had planned to return to his regular diet of rice and fresh vegetables, but the smell of powdered pancakes and artificial maple syrup drew him to the table. Leaving Ryan's guys to clean up, he got the jeep loaded.

He sat in the front with the driver and gave jungle directions, "Look for any path that heads uphill."

Dr. Yessin watched over the syringes, test tubes and lunches on the back seat. The driver turned left and shifted into low gear. Everything and everyone slid back hard against the seat backs as the Humvee headed up on a road that was little more than a wide trail. The American vehicle built for open deserts knocked down brush and small trees on both sides. Occasionally vines were pulled tight until they snapped with a deep "sproink." Odors of cardamom and sweet nectars filled the air as the wheels crushed the foliage. Occasionally a wild pig squealed. They moved higher and higher. The vehicle bounced over rocks, but nothing stopped its steady progress.

Villages were sparse on this side of the mountain, but after an hour climbing the driver pointed to the right. Mike concurred, "There's one! Let's go there."

The driver crashed right into the brush—there was no trail at all. As they got close, Mike could distinguish a single house, much like his own. "You'll find clean data here," he announced proudly.

He heard a loud report and a characteristic star crack appeared on the windshield. The driver hit the brakes. Mike looked back over the seat. "Dr. Yessin, are you okay?"

"Sure, what happened?"

The driver shifted into reverse. Mike grabbed his hand off the lever. "What are you doing?"

"Are you crazy? We're being shot at. We're leaving. If you wanted to go to war we should've come properly armed for it and Ryan should be here."

"Well, you don't back up downhill, fool."

There was another shot, followed by shattered glass this time. He guessed that they had lost a headlight. He didn't remember how many they had, but he thought there were more than two. "Stay here. The two of you get on the floor. You'll be safe there. You'll be protected by the engine."

There was another pop at the front of the car as if to emphasize the location of the shooter. He opened his door and rolled under the car. He shouted in Vietnamese, "We're friends."

A bullet answered. The jeep jerked, sliding off a rock and helpfully nudging the door shut. "Hey!" he shouted.

"That wasn't me," the driver yelled.

Mike checked the other tires, which all seemed to be on flat ground now. He looked out between the front wheels. Less than a hundred yards ahead—one football field—a single house commanded the high ground. In his favor, small trees provided cover above and a clear crawl space below. He recognized the trees—coffee. Ah, shit. The shooter was a farmer protecting his coffee crop.

Well, they had asked for trouble, blindly driving over the coffee bushes. A bullet ricocheted off the chrome bumper. Mike covered his ears as the sound reverberated and echoed. He crawled into some cardamom and headed a short way down the hill before turning upward to circle towards the house.

He flashed back to hiding in the brush as Chi's grandmother caught fire carrying her chickens, moments before the napalm burned her life away. He looked back toward Dr. Yessin on the floor of the Humvee thinking he would hate to fail at protecting her, too, but he kept crawling towards the house. He stayed low and thumped and scratched the ground to announce his progress to the fauna, watchful for snakes and monkeys who could be aggressive if frightened. It was dangerous to surprise the wildlife. Another shot reminded him that the natives were also dangerous.

He stopped at the open space around the house. Of course, the woven walls gave the occupants visual access in all directions. He needed a diversion. No radio. No gun.

He reached in his pocket and pulled out his lucky knife—the one with the dragon handle. He spotted a pig on the far side of the house and threw his knife. The wooden knife wasn't heavy enough to penetrate a pig at that range, but it surprised the animal and it ran in circles squealing. An old man with an AK-47 ran out the front door and turned to see what was upsetting the pig.

In high school Mike ran forty yards, in full uniform, shoulder pads and helmet, in a little over five seconds. The old guy was less than ten yards away. Mike crossed the open space, leaped onto the platform and tackled him while he was still looking at the squealing pig. The AK-47 flew into the dust firing one more round which pinged off a tree.

He repeated, "We're friends."

The old man tightened his fists, but when he saw Mike the fight drained out of him. He put his hands on his head like a POW. Mike repeated for a third time, "We're friends," and added, "The war is over." The man sat on the platform in front of his house and cried. The forest came back to life. Birds whistled, chickens scratched, and three piglets squeaked for the sow. An old lady emerged from a dark corner of the house and sat next to the man. She whispered to him. Mike couldn't make out what she was saying. Mike picked up the AK-47 and removed the magazine. He shouted towards the Hummer. "Leave the car there. Bring everything—especially lunch and some money."

An apology for the coffee plants, a hot thermos of Mai Linh's mother's soup, and a couple of million dong cured all hard feelings. Zaara got her interviews and he took the blood samples.

Next was Chi's village. Mike smiled in anticipation. He directed the driver to the three longhouses that seemed invisible until they were less than 30 yards away. The forest and scrub brush parted into the peaceful, sunny clearing. Mike could hear a happy shriek as the motor turned off, and Chi came flying around the corner of the closest longhouse, her hair a long streak behind her.

"Uncle Mike!" He barely got out of the Humvee in time to capture her in a hug as she flew into him. "I was so worried! But here you are!" She paused and took in the rest of the people in the vehicle. "Oh! Hello," she said in her best English. "Welcome to my home."

The small propane-powered generator kicked on behind the third longhouse, where Thuy Qui ran a tiny village shop, breaking the quiet.

Mike couldn't stop smiling as they made the rounds of introductions and moved toward the elders' house. He wanted to see Chi's mother, but it would be very bad manners—and bad luck—not to start with the elders first.

Zaara repeated her questions to this group of four elders, while Mike quietly received permission to do the blood draws. He was meticulous about labeling the samples and placing them in the small insulated box in the back of the jeep. He returned to the elder's longhouse in time to see

Zaara bowing and thanking them. He grinned at Zaara, bowed and gave the eldest grandmother the carved leopard he had made the night before.

Outside, Chi was jumping up and down like a school-child. "Mama wants to talk to you! Come, come!"

They entered the middle longhouse, where Chi's mother knelt, chopping vegetables at the low table Mike had made for her so many years before. She glanced up at him. Her eyes smiled, but she ducked her head back down to her work as was proper before an unmarried man. Mike introduced everyone, and explained what Dr. Yessin would be asking about.

Besides An Ly, there was also her aunt, Thien Thuy—Chi's great-aunt—who was not yet considered an elder, and her son Dai Ba who was so bad-tempered he had never found a wife who would have him. Finally Thuy Qui, her husband and her two daughters, who were so excited they would not sit still. They giggled and fired off questions non-stop, interrupting the translations Mike attempted for Zaara. Thuy Qui finally chased them outside. Mike handed Thuy Qui a handful of dong and asked for cold beers all around. Thuy Qui disappeared, and after a few moments the little girls popped back in, handing out beer and giggles.

"So here are some children," Zaara said watching them chase each other back down the ramp to the ground as if this was the most fun amusement ride they'd ever seen. "At last."

While Zaara spoke with Thien Thuy and Chi translated, Mike again got permission and took blood samples. When he finished, he spoke softly to An Ly. "Chi said you wished to speak with me?" She glanced up at him. A beam of sunlight highlighted silver strands in her hair. She picked up her untouched bottle of beer and took a delicate sip.

"It is time you should meet the man Chi will marry. His family will be here in four days. Can you come?"

Mike looked at the commotion around him with a sinking heart. He had no idea how long the Doctors were going to take, and whether he would be able to break away for such a visit before Eleanor brought him home to speak to Congress or whatever he was doing for her.

The husband-to-be's family visit was an important event. He took a deep breath. "I cannot promise this," he said. It was awkward in Vietnamese. "Though I will try." He idly picked up the discarded head of a carrot by its greens and nibbled the crunchy orange stub. An Ly had always grown wonderful vegetables. "Is Chi happy with him?"

An Ly nodded, eyes cast downward. "He is a nice boy. From a nice family, with eight pigs. And coffee plants."

That was quite wealthy, in villager terms. "I will provide for her gowns, and fireworks, and the food," Mike said. "Whether or not I can be here to meet him, I will have those sent to you." He took out his remaining cash and gave it to An Ly.

Ay Ly nodded again, eyed the money and finally reached out and took it. She tucked it into a pocket. Mike frowned. The wedding would not be for the traditional six months. The party gown, and maybe a wedding gown, could wait. But Chi would need the traditional *áo dài* for this celebration; he would have to be quick to have it here in four days. Maybe he could get one of Ryan's crew to go to Da Lat.

Aware of the silence in the room, Mike glanced up. Chi was watching Zaara who was watching him. Zaara glanced at An Ly and back at Mike with a small smile.

"Are you ready to speak with An Ly?" he asked, rather artlessly.

"Aside from the excitement of the being shot at in the forest, today's interviews were more of the same—gossip, superstition, and rationalizations. I now have over 200 individual stories from a couple of different locations. Unfortunately most of the data is useless—unscientific nonsense—barren daughters—sons moved to the city—Americans killing everything from the soil and birds to the fruits and vegetables."

Zaara turned to Mike, "I don't know what you and your buddies were doing here, long before I was born, but you weren't making any friends." Her eyebrow quirked. "Well, maybe one friend," she amended with a teasing smile.

"Aggh." Sweat made stripes on Rosie's dirty face; his fingernails were cracked and dirty. "We've been screening samples all day. The gas chromatograph-mass spectrometer has a big database. It screens automatically for 1,722 pesticides, endocrine disruptors, and Homeland Security HazMats." He wiped his face with a clean white paper towel. "I've been all over the village—under houses, on roofs, digging in the dirt, in pig shit, chicken shit. I've been everywhere. You're safer here than at home... well except for the dioxin...which we've already discussed." He grimaced at the now-filthy paper towel, crumpled it and tossed it in the trash can. "The ball's in your court Zaara, figure it out."

"There's nothing in my court."

Ryan took control at that point. "Good work all of you, especially Mike. I didn't think you had it in you old man...to disarm an even older man."

His guys laughed. Mike didn't think it was all that funny.

"At least no one got shot."

"Indeed," Ryan said. "Doctors, you should get some rest and you'll be able to think better. Dr. Roseman, why don't you go into the field with Mike and Zaara tomorrow? The change of scene might do you good."

Zaara chewed on the oatmeal cookies that had been offered for dessert and straightened her headscarf. "I don't know. I just don't know. There has to be an answer somewhere."

Dr. Roseman abruptly turned to his tech. "Start packing up in the morning, Stenko. We're done." He stalked out. Stenko got to his feet, nodded at the rest of them, and followed him.

Ryan jumped up and went out. Mike could hear him ordering his men to make a call to Ellie.

Mike had a feeling Rosie might not be done just yet.

Zaara sprawled in her folding chair. "So." She looked Mike in the eye. "An Ly says Chi's father was an American soldier. She never was able to marry any local boy, because that was considered shameful."

Mike said nothing, just took out his carving again.

"So why didn't you marry her?"

Mike sighed. "That is also considered shameful. More shameful. Like consorting with the enemy. To the villagers, I'm still that, still not wholly trusted."

"*She* trusted you. An Ly."

"I saved her life," Mike said. "I saved the lives of her whole village, several times." He studied his piece of wood, intent on finding the animal in it.

"But the rest of them still don't trust you?"

He shrugged. "It's the way they are. Insular. And paranoid from the war. I'm not one of them." He thought he could see a tiger's strong jaw and ears. "They don't even interact with other Vietnamese that much."

"Chi is a beautiful girl," Zaara said.

"I need to go to Da Lat and get her dress," Mike said. "Or get one of Ryan's guys to get it, maybe."

"I think Chi would want to pick it out, don't you?"

Mike shook his head. "There's nothing to pick. The *áo dài* is always the same, and always red. The headdress, the *khăn đống*, is always the same. Red and white. The nicest you can afford. She would wear her mother's if An Ly had had them."

"Just the same, she may want to try them on."

Mike shook his head, got up and walked out of the tarp tent.

35 ≡ LIAM

Papa shook Liam's hammock. "Psst, psst"

Liam had been dreaming of small children with big dark eyes, bright teeth, and straight black hair, saying, "*Uno, dos, tres...*"

He leaned toward the hissing noise and almost fell out of the hammock. He knew he couldn't fall out of a hammock, but every time he moved, he felt like he was going to be dumped on the floor. His motivation to puzzle out this paradox disappeared when he remembered this was his last night. Sadly, he realized he was going to miss the hammock. He looked at Papa, "*Hola.*"

Papa smiled and Liam regretted that he hadn't spent more time with this gentle man. Even now, he was unsure how much Spanish Papa understood, but he had grown to appreciate the old man's warmth. Liam looked around. Somebody had already put his suitcase in the canoe. The night birds and frogs were still singing. He picked up his souvenirs—a plastic sack of bracelets, a tube with a rolled oil painting, a paper sack with baskets, and a bag made from woven twine filled with various other trinkets.

He and Ani were to be chauffeured to the airport in two canoes paddled by Mañuel and Tomito. Afterwards, the canoes would bring back some supplies from Iquitos. He'd left the remainder of his *soles* with the teacher for her and the children to buy school supplies. As he waddled to the canoe juggling his souvenirs, he left a trail of handicrafts. Chaya followed him, picking up his valuables and laughing.

Ani sat in the front of Tomito's canoe. Liam balanced in Mañuel's while Chaya rocked them back and forth delivering rescued valuables to him and kisses to her daddy. The sun would not arrive for hours, but everyone got up to wave goodbye—Papa, Mamí, Marco, Tipa, everybody. Mamí and Tipa sprinkled coca leaves in the water for good luck. Somewhere in the distance a monkey woke up and screeched. Papa and Marco gave them a starting push and waved goodbye while the current carried the canoes away.

Guillermo's tricycle dropped them off in front of the single, low terminal at Iquitos airport. The sky was still dark as the small airport parking lot filled with tourist buses sending their tired passengers back to Lima before the vultures laid siege to the airport for another day. For a one *sol* coin, a porter in a colorful wool hat with ear flaps and a tassel carried their suitcases. Liam picked up his souvenirs and followed. "Are the porters wearing the same hat as the shaman?"

Laughing, Ani picked up his souvenirs as they dropped. "You're very observant. Some times you're so smart, and other times… "

He didn't have time to think about her comment. All his energy concentrated on keeping up with the porters through the crowds. By the time they were in the terminal, Ani's arms were full and the porters had vanished.

He stopped in the middle of the terminal with tourists and locals rushing every which way around him. "Where did they go?"

"Don't worry, they know where to go. I'm taking you to the little shops and we're going to buy you a carry-on bag."

"Do I really need one?"

He looked at Ani with her arms full of his dropped souvenirs. "I guess I do."

She took him to a stall that displayed blankets and shoulder bags made from thick wool. They were all colors, but reds and purples seemed to be the most popular.

"*Rimaykullayki.*"

"*Napaykullayki,*" Ani hugged the girl sitting in the back nursing a baby. The two women spoke quickly and the only words he recognized were "Liam" and "*americano.*"

She turned to him. "Ten dollars. Take your pick."

"Do you know everyone in Iquitos?"

"No, just my relatives and a few friends. Anyway, Iquitos is pretty small."

He chose a red and white bag with stylized llamas woven into the material which seemed to be a popular design. He stuffed everything in. They found their suitcases, checked hers to San Francisco, his to Denver.

He must have seemed confused as he juggled, his wallet, passport, souvenirs, and luggage, because as they walked to the waiting area, she reminded him, "Remember you claim your bags in San Francisco to go through customs, then return them for your Denver flight."

Thanks to the vultures, they had a twelve-hour layover in Lima after their extra-early start from Iquitos. After they disembarked the bus at the terminal, he walked about ten steps and stopped. He didn't have a plan. Ani walked a short way ahead and also stopped. He watched her turn around, looking for him. Just as their eyes met, an American bumped into him.

"Excuse me. I wasn't looking."

"No. My fault I shouldn't have stopped in the middle of the door."

She shouted, "Liam, over here."

He acknowledged her waving and headed in that direction.

"Follow me; we're going to my favorite restaurant in Lima."

Before he realized it, they were sitting in a cab, a real taxicab with four wheels and four doors. His new bag with the llamas was on the seat between them. The road from the airport was lined with shops: hardware stores—*ferreteria*, hair salons—*unisex peluqueria*, Chinese restaurants—*chi fa*, and casinos—signed in English. He could tell they were in the big city now. The stores and residences were protected by walls topped by razor wire and broken glass set in concrete. Only the casinos offered a friendly greeting with open doors, large windows and neon lights, though the plenitude of armed guards added some ambiguity to this welcome. The traffic made it too noisy to talk.

It was definitely settling into his mind that his Amazon adventure had come to an end. *In a few hours I'll be asleep on the plane to San Francisco and when I awake we'll go through customs, separate, and it will be all over. Ani will be gone.*

I should say something like "Do you want to keep in touch," or "Can I have your email?"

Should I try to hold her hand? Can't do that with mother's baskets between us. Damn mother, always in the way.

He weighed his options and decided he was too old and she wasn't interested.

"Here we are—Miraflores district. It means look at the flowers. Look at the flowers."

They walked through a park with formal gardens and a tiny amphitheater. "This is Central Park and if we came at night we'd see dance contests over there." She pointed to the amphitheater. They passed vendors selling corn bread and candy apples, and crossed a small street, blocked off to traffic.

He felt he should say something, "I'll bet it is colorful and fun to see."

Ani smiled, "The restaurant is just past there."

They headed to a smaller park in the direction of the restaurant. She pointed to a bust of John Kennedy, but he only saw the children playing in the playground. He hadn't left Peru and already missed the *chicos* and *chicas*. His *real* students, it suddenly seemed to him.

They had lunch, the big meal in Lima, across from the Kennedy Park at

Café de la Paz. They ate outside. She ordered. They started with Pisco Sours—a specialty made with grape brandy and lemon juice. They were too strong for him, but she had two. Then they enjoyed a delicious Peruvian fish and ended with a delicate flan. With a few more hours left they wandered through the beautiful Miraflores district looking at the flowers.

His bag got heavy, so he switched shoulders every few blocks. It seemed to have its own plan, insinuating itself between her and him.

"Sunset!"

Straight ahead of them the sun approached the Pacific Ocean. "I didn't realize we were so close to the ocean."

"That's the main road ahead. We'll get a taxi back to the airport there."

As they approached the ocean, he saw a park with colorful mosaic benches in undulating shapes reflecting the ocean waves, but when they arrived he saw the centerpiece, a statue: *El Beso*—the kiss—by Victor Delfin. A huge couple reclined on a fifty-foot long platform, intertwined in a passionate kiss.

How did we end up at Parque del Amor—*the Love Park*? Changing the subject before it was mentioned, he pointed at the sky. "Look at the hang glider." A red and white striped paraglider gently hung in the air above the bluff.

"The warm ocean current and the cliffs make this a great place to fly. People come from all over and down below you can see the best surfing beach in Lima."

"Not much surfing in Colorado."

"Nor San Francisco."

They paid their departure taxes, moved through security and sat in the waiting area. She read an English-language magazine, *Around the Globe Today*, she'd picked up at a newsstand just inside security. He looked around. Families sat close together, mothers hugging their children close and fathers telling stories. *Would things have been different if my father hadn't died so young?* There was no way to know. His mother was his mother; she probably would not have been much different if his father had lived.

As he scanned the waiting crowd, he snuck glimpses at Ani. Sitting so close, he noticed how her smooth skin seemed to glow with some inner light and how gently she held the magazine with her fingertips.

Again he felt the pressure to say something; time was running out. He opened his bag and found a copy of his paper. The paper had all his contact information—phone, address, email—printed at the top. "This is the paper that describes my work. Would you like a copy?"

She barely looked at it, folded it in half the long way, and stuffed it into her backpack. "Thanks."

He didn't think she'd read it, but he hoped she wouldn't just throw it away. He watched a family line up to board a flight to Miami. The children were giggling and poking at each other.

Ani swapped her magazine for his paper. She read several pages, spending a little time on the charts. He stared at her expectantly.

"I don't understand your statistics, but if you say the birth rate is falling, I believe you."

The tenure committee arguments flashed back, so he didn't say anything. He hoped she wouldn't notice the arteries throbbing in his neck.

After some silence, she said, "However, I doubt the cause is birth control."

He didn't want to argue with her, not on their last day together. Besides, he was realizing that though he was well educated, he didn't have the data or experience to understand this problem he had uncovered. He knew statistics, not the social structures or societies the data had been pulled from.

Also, since his time in Nanay Libre, he was uncertain that rape and coercion were the primary reasons for having children. What had his mother's life been like, that she believed this? That she had told him this, over and over? He felt a deep sadness, thinking of all she had missed, all they had missed as a family.

But some of the fault lay with him. He had believed his mother's explanations without examining them. What kind of scientist did that? How had his mother brainwashed him like that?

Ani interrupted his reverie, "I think that all the places you studied, and also my home along the Nanay River, have allowed drug testing. I still think maybe drug testing is the cause."

Her breasts rose and fell in time to her breathing. His professorial instincts took over and he began a short lecture, "Umm. That may be, but all those places did not test the same drugs. It is difficult to support the idea that the same results might have occurred from different drug tests. More importantly, my results are only correlation... "

Before he could add, *and correlation does not imply causation*, he saw her hold her breath, a slight frown on her face. He stopped and changed his direction. "You have an interesting suggestion. I'll research that when I get back to Boulder." He took a deep breath. He should ask her now for her contact information, so they could discuss this....

"LAN Peru flight 2311 to Los Angeles and San Francisco, gate two now boarding!"

He pulled out his earplugs and blindfold so he'd be ready when they took their seats.

36 ≡ ELEANOR

Eleanor stepped out of her conference room, leaving her staff to discuss logistics for the presentation to the congressional hearings regarding the U.N. resolution. Devon could figure out what materials needed to be kept back from the hearings, so they had material available later in support of their rebuttal to the idiots from Save Our Native Cultures. Those people weren't saving *their* native cultures from anything; they might have had good intentions at one point but—

The chirp from her cell phone confirmed the connection was made. She was live with Ryan from Viet Nam, via satellite phone. She stepped into an alcove away from the door of the conference room where voices had been raised just enough to interfere with her hearing of the phone call.

"Hello, Dr. Powell."

"Why can't they fix these things with closed captioning?" she asked. She waited a beat while Ryan processed that. "It's probably already been done, right?"

"Yes, in a way. The real problem is that it requires voice recognition software, which still is not one hundred percent effective, and even less secure. Either that or a person to type, live."

"Which we neither want nor need."

"Yes."

"So how are things?"

"They're worse than kids," Ryan said.

Eleanor remembered her daughter, who had always been reserved and dignified, even at the age of six. She did not imagine that was what Ryan meant. "How's that?"

"It's like living at home again, with my three squabbling sisters and my dad," Ryan said. "The doctors argue constantly, bitching about conditions and calling each other names and disagreeing about what to look for next, and your ever cheerful Mike just wants everyone to get along like some middle-child peacemaker."

He startled her into one of her rare laughs. "I can see the picture," she said. "I'm sorry you have to baby sit."

"Mike's okay, I didn't mean to imply he's a problem. I think he's got a better idea about what's going on than the doctors do."

"Have they made any progress?"

"Not a damn thing that I can see. They haven't eliminated Agent Orange, but they haven't verified it as the cause, either. So they're running more tests, just to be sure, or something. There's some technical arguments about methodology and testing that I don't understand."

"That's okay," she said. "I'll get that from Rosie, in a minute."

"Good. But what's most irritating, is Roseman and Yessin can't even seem to agree on whether to look for a disease vector, a genetic factor or an environmental something, whatever all that really means anyway. I had thought you'd given them some...uh, guidelines or instructions, – "

"It's research, Mister Kolnikoff." Her voice went very dry. "You aren't expected to understand."

"Well, what am I *expected* to *do*, then?"

She took a deep breath, "Just make sure they're working and they have everything they need. The results are up to them."

"Do you really expect them to find anything?"

"I don't know, Mr. Kolnikoff. I don't know whether they'll find an answer or not. That's why it's called *research* and not *conclusions*. But I do know they can't possibly find anything if they don't look, so keep them looking."

"Yes, ma'am. I'm doing that."

"Good. Put Dr. Roseman on."

"Yes ma'am."

There was rustling and what might have been voices in the background.

"It's the middle of the night, Ellie. When are we supposed to sleep?"

"Since when do you sleep when you're working on a problem, Rosie?"

"Since I got to be old!"

"Sir! Sixty-three is not old! Take it from me; you're just getting into the arena where experience and training make an enormous difference."

"Only if you've got some kind of energizer bunny genetic thing going on."

"What have you found?"

"Very damn little. No epidemiological linkages, nothing environmental."

"No Agent Orange?"

"Yes, there is still a lot of environmental contamination, I didn't mean to say there isn't," he said, irritation in his voice. "It's just not relevant to the problems people are reporting here. No research has ever linked their level of symptoms with chemical effects from this stuff."

"Is there a third factor that has been overlooked in the studies?"

"Possibly. That's the only thing keeping me here. That, and there isn't any *other* explanation for the population aging and decline, either. Unless it's a statistical illusion, there's got to be something causing the low birth rate, and so forth."

"What are the symptoms, exactly? Has Zaara got a short list?"

"No. Declining population for a number of reasons, including low birthrates. Nothing glaring us in the face. I still think people-move-away-and-nobody-remembers-why is a reasonable explanation."

"But they aren't anyplace else, either, Rosie, so that's not it."

"Emigration? Statistical anomalies?"

"Some relevant statistics indicate low birth rates. Possibly across the globe, though that has not been confirmed yet. There's a couple of economists I'd like to pick the brains of. But that's not your job. I want to know why the villages in the mountains of Viet Nam are empty, Rosie. That's why you're there."

"You'll know when I know."

"Is Mr. Johnson available?"

"He's whittling."

"What?"

"He whittles. You know, carves figures out of little pieces of wood."

"Ah. But can he come to the phone?" No answer.

Then, "Hello Dr. Powell. What time is it there? It's close to midnight here." Mike sounded wide awake.

"Late morning."

"Really? And what day?" Now he sounded like a kid watching an exciting science show.

"Same day as it is over there. So Mike, how's it going? Are you getting your money's worth?" She tried to match his upbeat tone.

"Well, they aren't finding much, but they are looking, and thinking."

"Yes, that's good. You know I warned you it might take some time."

A moderate silence responded to her words.

"Mike? Are you there?"

"I'm here, Dr. Powell."

"You were smart enough to see there's a problem, Mr. Johnson. I hope you can be patient enough to wait for the solution."

"Yeah. I'm waiting."

"Is Dr. Yessin there?"

"She's asleep."

"Uh-huh. Okay, any problems? Anything you need?"

"Nope."

"All right, I'll be in touch."

"Neat. This satphone is far out."

"It is, isn't it? Talk to you later."

She pressed END. She stood in her office hallway, thinking. What she had told Mike was correct. There wasn't much more they could be doing to solve the problem than what was already in progress. It was just going to take time. And he wasn't going to speak in her favor on the drug testing issue until there was an answer for his Vietnamese villages, that seemed clear. It would be better when he did, though; even more evidence for her programs.

She wished there was some way she could expedite the slow progress of science, but wishing wasn't going to make it so. She would just have to find someone else to testify at the congressional hearings.

The conference room door opened a crack, and Devon peered out. She raised her eyebrows at him.

"We think we have the SONC issue solved. On to the databases item?"

She sighed. She was starting to feel wilted. It seemed to happen earlier and earlier each day. Just like Rosie's "getting old" comment. Or was that a statistical illusion too?

Then she brightened, recalling databases were the last thing on the agenda, or at least she hoped they were the last item. "Let's go," she said.

37 ≡ ANI

The airplane flight was the worst part of visiting home, Ani decided after the first two hours of flight. This time she went through Lima instead of Quito. The total flight was a little over eight hours. She was only one fourth of the way through the flight, and it was already too long, too loud, too crowded with people.

She had prepared for the flight dressing in her favorite jeans, too hot for the jungle, too loose for fancy dress, but perfect for relaxing on the plane or her apartment in San Francisco. Mamí had supplied her with delicious fried and salted fava beans, wrapped in paper. They smelled great, but she didn't eat them. She knew she couldn't bring them into California, but she wasn't hungry right now. It seemed like no preparation could make the flight go quickly.

Even though this time she was seated next to Liam, instead of a stranger, it wasn't quite as wonderful as she had imagined. She was afraid she was going to bump him. He seemed able to sleep in the darkened cabin, but she was wide awake. And she hadn't been able to talk to him as much as she would have liked because he was so bothered by the noise of the plane that he wore earplugs—and he couldn't hear her.

She moved, shifting a little in her seat. His eyes popped open; she smiled at him, and he smiled back, and then closed his eyes again, this time pulling down his blindfold, and turning to snuggle his little pillow against his headrest.

She returned her attention to the *Around the Globe Today* magazine she had picked up at the Lima airport. She wanted to be up to date when she got back to San Francisco, or she'd be teased by her friends. She had an internet at the Academy, but wouldn't be able to read that until she was already home.

She folded back the first couple of pages after a brief glance at headlines. It was the usual worst-case reports on the first two or three pages—the war stories, world-ending kinds of bad news. But one of the reasons she made an effort to seek out this obscure publication was that the *AGT* editors made an effort to report scientific and other *good* news, as well as that bad stuff. The good stuff generally began about page four or five and continued for eight or nine pages. The last couple of pages each week were also worth looking at. Typically those were dedicated to editorials, opinions, a few wicked little political cartoons, and the "weird news around the globe" section which sometimes she thought was the best news of all.

Two articles caught her eye. The first was about a medical mission to explore the causes of miscarriages in Viet Nam. She could feel her heart rate speed up. She leaned forward as if to suck every word and punctuation mark of the article off the page. *Could this possibly be the same thing as in my village?* She pulled her highlighter out of her backpack and marked the doctors' names. Maybe there would be a follow-up article or some way to contact them.

Then she stared at the seat back in front of her. She remembered Liam's paper was about low birth rates in First World countries and his odd interpretation of the causes. And, she knew drug testing happened all the time in the U.S. and Europe. Was it possible this was part of a global problem? She looked back at the magazine.

She noted the article also referenced some web sites about drug testing and medical problems. She highlighted the addresses of those, as well. She could look those up as soon as she got back to the Academy and had access to their wonderful computers and internet connections.

What if all the low birth rates were in nations where clinical trials regularly went on? She knew Liam's comment about them testing different drugs was a strong argument against her theory, but it could be the testing itself, or possibly some vehicle used to deliver the shots or pills used in the tests....

She read that article again, committing it to memory to be certain she had not overlooked anything. It was a recent project, and so might not have any real data yet, but she would definitely watch for further reports.

The second article that she read avidly was about some congressional hearings in Washington, D.C.—about a United Nations resolution to prohibit drug testing on native populations. She'd have to rush her research, but if her speculations were right that would be the perfect venue for a protest; a big march publicizing the connection between drug tests and population decline.

Her hand trembled with excitement as she folded her highlighted copy of *Around the Globe Today* and put it carefully, safely into her backpack. When she sat back up, she realized the cabin lights were back on, and the stewards were preparing to serve breakfast. The airplane food didn't smell very appetizing, so she was grateful for Mamí's fava beans.

Beside her Liam was awake and watching her. He smiled, stretched and put away his earplugs and blindfold.

"You're different," he said.

She looked at him, unable to fabricate a response.

He looked into her eyes, searching for something, "I mean, you're studying and planning, and it's all...different. Different from how you were at home, I mean."

"Oh," she said. *Was this why he hadn't wanted to talk to her during the flight?* "You just like the barefoot *rivereño* jungle girl?" she said.

He paled, then turned red. "No, that's not what I said. I didn't say I liked either style of you better or worse. I just observed that you're different. It surprised me."

"Hmm," she said.

"**I** have hours to catch my plane to Colorado," Liam said as they waited to get off the plane. "We can get a cup of coffee while we wait for the baggage; I can walk through customs with you, and get back in plenty of time to make my flight."

She was surprised that he suddenly wanted to spend more time with her after ignoring her on the airplane.

Or maybe he hated airplane flights as much as she did, and had just prepared himself to endure. Now they were back on the ground, he opened up again?

"Well, okay," she replied.

They deplaned and walked through the airport. Ani hadn't been through SFO that many times that she didn't find the displays along the concourses interesting. They looked and laughed at some of them, then stopped at a Starbucks. She ordered a small latte, he got a venti cappuccino. They sat in a quiet area where a row of rocking chairs had been set out, and sipped and rocked, watching the planes taxi in and out.

Afterwards, they got their bags and went through customs. Of course Liam went through the citizens' lines, and she had to go through the visitors'—her dark red Peru passport standing out amongst the ones from China, Japan and the Philippines.

Liam got a cart and put their two suitcases and all his souvenirs in the llama bag on it, wheeling it to the AirTrain where the red line would take him to his terminal and the blue line would take her to BART and her home. *Her San Francisco home*, she thought, surprised that she had ever come to think of her little dorm room as home, much less look forward to getting there.

Liam lifted her suitcase off the cart and stood holding it. "Well, while I'm glad to have met you, and that I got to spend some time with your family, I can't say I was thrilled to be kidnapped." He laughed, looking at her face as if he wished she would laugh with him, or so she imagined.

She shook her head, letting her eyes smile. "I'm sorry too. Carlo is a stupid-head," she said. "At least, he *acted* like a stupid-head trying to get money he didn't earn by stealing you. But I think he did do one part of what he intended, after all. He did manage to steal someone of value."

She saw the blue AirTrain coming. She leaned forward, kissed his chin, then turned and boarded. Liam pushed her suitcase past the automatic door and quickly backed away. She grabbed it, sat down, and turned to the window. He did not seem to see her wave goodbye.

38 ≡ MIKE

The discussion continued after Eleanor hung up. Ryan, Rosie and Mike sat in the dark, under the dining tarp. Any light brought an unwelcome assortment of flying insects and with the insects came bats and with the bats came curious monkeys. They drank warm coffee from a thermos. Ryan told his staff to have coffee available 24/7, but wasn't too firm on the temperature. At 2:00 AM, they all had bigger issues to complain about.

Dr. Roseman turned to the other two. "You know she made me *promise* to go out with you guys tomorrow? That bitch drives me crazy. I don't know why I accept her help."

Mike was learning to ignore his complaints, "Glad to have you along. We leave at 7:30 AM."

Rosie said, "Great. Well, I'll be awake anyway, when that damn generator kicks on." He paused to watch Dr. Yassin stumble toward the table. "I guess we woke you up," Rosie said. "Did you hear Eleanor called?"

Zaara grunted. "You stopped packing."

Rosie made a face. "Yah. Not going home. Yet."

Zaara blinked. She poured herself some of the tepid coffee.

"She says we're missing something,"

Ryan added. *"You're* missing something."

Zaara took a sip of the coffee and shuddered. "So. Unh. Let's assume Eleanor's right and we're missing something. Maybe you're right too—the environment's not the problem," she said, nodding to Rosie.

"I can assure you I'm right."

"Great attitude," Mike muttered as he walked over to the refrigerator. "Coffee's terrible. Anyone want a *Ba-ba-ba*?"

They'd drank all the American beer they'd brought with them, so only the local beer Ryan's crew had picked up in Da Lat remained. *Ba-ba-ba* or 333 was from Saigon Beer company. Mike preferred it because it used the old name for Ho Chi Minh City.

When no one responded to his offer, he grabbed himself a beer, went back to the table and rested his head on arms, half listening, half snoozing between sips of beer. For what seemed like the fifth or fifteenth time, Zaara repeated, "I think Eleanor's right, we just haven't found it yet."

Mike suggested, "Animals, you think it could be something from animals?"

Zaara seemed to perk up, "Good idea Mike," and looking over at Roseman, who was pulling his hair, "That's the kind of outside-the-box thinking we need to solve this."

Mike sat up a little straighter until she added, "But yes. I contacted the U.S. Veterinary Organization and they got an intern to check with their zoonosis collections. Short answer? Nothing."

His head returned to the table pillowed by his crossed arms.

Zaara said to the trees, "We're missing something. I know we're missing something."

Rosie shook his head and yawned, "Whatever you say Zaara, but the only thing I'm missing is sleep. Why don't—"

The generator kicked on with a bang drowning out the rest of Dr. Roseman's bitching. His mouth stopped moving and after a short while his eyes closed. His coffee cup slipped from his fingers dumping the dark liquid in his lap. He jumped up shouting, "Between that bitch calling in the middle of the night, the infernal generator, and my leaky air mattresses,

I'm not getting any sleep!"

Zaara also ignored Rosie's frustration, "If it's not the environment, what is it?"

Rosie kicked his coffee cup into the jungle outside and asked for a beer. "I'd vote for some tropical disease, except no one's sick."

"That's exactly what I told Ellie—no one's sick. The old people still hanging around have hundreds of different stories, but none involve sick people—no sick people. Just healthy old people."

Mike retrieved the coffee cup and handed Dr. Roseman a beer. He put one in front of Zaara before he remembered she didn't drink, so he took it himself. It was good beer. "I'm not a doctor like you folks, but isn't it odd that all these old people are so healthy? That guy shooting at us today was in pretty good shape."

Roseman took a long swig of his beer. "Clean living. I'm too tired to think. If you want to leave at 7:30, I have to get some sleep. If we just had brought a DNA analysis lab over here, we wouldn't be having this discussion."

Mike stared at Rosie in surprise. He had been sure they have brought everything—absolutely everything they could need—in that enormous plane.

Zaara just laughed. "Sure, like we have room for all the robotics, computers, PCRs, centrifuges, electrophoresis equipment, sequencers and techs, to say nothing about the size of the clean room we'd need. Dream on."

Roseman walked toward the sleeping tent. "My plan exactly."

Zaara stared at nothing for a few moments, then jumped up, chasing him into the dark. "But you're right! DNA analysis is the next step! Rosie, collect all those blood samples and pack them in ice. We're shipping them to San Francisco."

Mike was half asleep when she returned and shook him awake. "Can you please find Ryan and tell him we need one of his guys to drive these packages to Ho Chi Minh City?!"

"Now?"

"Remember what Hollingsdale said? International flights to the U.S. only leave in the early morning. Rosie wants to go home. Eleanor demands action. Let's not waste another day!"

Saigon? Now? That was perfect. Just perfect. "I'm going too," Mike said. He grinned at her. "Dr. Roseman can sleep in a bit tomorrow."

He found Ryan in the back of his tent, washing out tee shirts. He explained. Ryan got it set up. In moments, Mike was seated beside the driver, grinning as he took the white Styrofoam packages into his lap and on the floor by his feet as Rosie and Zaara handed them in. The driver turned the key and the Hummer roared to life. They bounced down the road, throwing rocks, knocking over small trees and leaving a cloud of bugs, bats, and monkeys behind as the headlights dove into the night.

They paused for a moment at Mike's house so he could dash in and grab his money. They rolled into Ho Chi Minh City well before the morning flights took off. They got the packages set up for the next flight out direct to Los Angeles, connecting to San Francisco and the lab Dr. Yessin wanted them to go to. Mike abandoned the driver to do as he wished—pick up some more beer maybe, while Mike tracked down a traditional wedding shop among the rows of shops in the old town section nearest the airport.

It did not take long to find a beautiful áo dài with a headdress to match in the window of a small store. He called up to the shop owner whose living quarters were upstairs. The man opened his window, nodded at Mike's polite request and offer of a large tip. He came down and opened up the shop just for Mike. He was helpful in choosing a size based on Mike's description of Chi. Mike made sure to give the man a generous tip in thanks, and also to thank him for wrapping up the gown and *khăn đống* so beautifully. They were pure silk, very nice quality, and wrapped in lovely red tissue papers. Mike bowed and smiled so much his face was aching. He met the driver at the airport taxi stand and they headed back to Mai Linh's village, arriving just before 10:00 in the morning.

The two doctors were sitting in the tent nursing their coffees—looking grateful for hot morning coffee even though hot was its only positive attribute. Rosie mumbled. "They grow the stuff here, why can't we get a decent cup?"

"We ready to head out?" Mike asked.

Zaara eyed the red-tissue-wrapped package Mike carried.

Mike smiled and stowed it in his tent with his gear.

They loaded the Humvee for the day.

Mike navigated again, telling today's driver which way to go. "Keep on truckin'. We'd like to get ten or twenty miles away before we go into the forest," he said, smiling.

In the early morning light, the rainforest presented a green mosaic filtered through the canopy leaves and the understory palms and ferns. The greens ranged from the palest new leaves, almost yellow, to the deepest fronds, almost black. He thought of the small green predators—snakes, frogs, lizards, insects—who lived in the foliage, and the large dark predators—bears and boars—who lived on the ground. Beyond all the green beauty lay a world of red violence.

After bouncing along the dirt road for an hour, he shouted. "Turn here."

The driver headed up the mountain, widening a track worn through the forest by elephants or the few small vehicles found in the area—nothing like this huge, clumsy, American Humvee.

Zaara tapped the driver on the shoulder. "See those low trees? Those are coffee trees. You don't want to drive over them. It makes people really mad."

The lack of sleep subdued Dr. Roseman. His complaining had stopped and he stared at the coffee trees in silence.

They found the small village, and the driver parked on the main track, right in the middle of the path. They approached on a narrow trail, single file. Rosie had his collection bottles and Zaara brought her notebook.

The small village consisted of three longhouses, a small coffee plantation, and as they approached, they could see two vegetable gardens surrounded by fences of woven branches, an assortment of pot-belly pigs and chickens, and a few dogs running wild. Mike knew the dogs might be pets, but back in the hills here they could just as well be for special dinners.

About half way to the houses, they spied a man. Zaara smiled. "That's a very good sign. He's not carrying a gun."

Rosie maintained his sleep-deprived tranquility. "They live such a peaceful life here."

Mike shouted, "*Xin chao*," good morning in Vietnamese.

The old man waved, seemingly happy for visitors. He pointed to the longhouses, where another man sat on the part of the floor platform that extended beyond the front of his house, with a wild cat purring in his lap. He brushed away some large green insects from the platform and said, "Please join me. My wife can bring us some tea."

Mike translated.

Rosie looked at the bugs and said, "Thanks, but I'd like to look around and collect a few samples."

Mike negotiated permission for Rosie to wander around, but warned him to be careful as he disappeared into the coffee trees. Zaara sat down. After tea she introduced herself.

When he translated that she was from the U.S., the man interrupted. He held up his cat, "Do you know Claudia?"

He had to discuss Claudia, her cats, her coffee business, and her friends in Da Lat, before Zaara could continue. "How old are you?"

Everyone seemed very proud of their age and ascribed their health to a variety of causes—good spirits, living the right way, not getting killed long ago by the Americans (usually followed by a nervous laugh), or secret herbs. Mike quietly did the blood draws while Zaara interviewed.

When she asked about children, the people got sad. Asking about grandchildren usually killed the discussion entirely, and no one seemed to have any great grandchildren.

The wife cried. He translated. "To be blessed with such a long life, but denied many grandchildren is a curse worse than any other."

The sun shone straight down and Mike was getting ready to share their lunch with this couple living alone in the forest, when they all heard a frenzied scream. Mike ran into the coffee trees. The distant scream flashed him back to one he'd heard so many years ago. Fright and horror urged him into the brush. He kicked through the ferns, held his arms up to protect his face from the palms as they whipped by. Finally, he saw Dr. Roseman on his back, pinned under a black bear. In one automatic motion, he withdrew his knife from its sheath and threw it.

The startled bear stood up with the heavy knife stuck into its shoulder. Blood covered Dr. Roseman. While the bear's paw batted at its injured neck, Mike moved closer and dragged Rosie away. He put the bloody body over his shoulder and headed for the car.

He might have heard the bear collapse to the ground, but he didn't turn around to check. Secretly he hoped the crash was something else. He didn't wish anything bad for the bear. Bears rarely attacked people. *What did grumpy Dr. Roseman do to upset it*? Regardless, his combat medic training drove him to save the life of anyone in his group, and he certainly didn't want to repay Ellie's help with something like this. This was just damned bad luck.

When he got to the jeep, he laid Rosie on the back seat, broke open the first aid kit and waded though the blood to find Dr. Roseman's injuries. He shouted towards the village, "Zaara, we need to go! Now!" The doctor had three deep scratches across his back with one white rib visible, lots of blood there. Also three more across his belly.

Zaara arrived with the driver who tossed their gear in and jumped in the driver's seat. Zaara knelt on the front seat, looking over into the back. Mike squatted on the floor, holding Rose's limp body stable on the seat as the driver jerked the jeep into motion.

He glanced at Zaara, whose face alerted him to bad news before it came. "It looks like the peritoneum was pierced."

"I was afraid of that." He had seen similar injuries during the war—due to bullets, not bears. Rosie would probably live, but his injuries were serious. He cleaned him as well as he could while the car bounced down the mountain. He found a syrette of morphine and injected Dr. Roseman. During the war, morphine syrettes were more important than bullets. Even when the wounded couldn't be saved, their last hours, or sometimes days, could be eased with regular injections. He had seen soldiers without obvious wounds inject themselves daily just to kill some pain deep in their souls, and that was more important than bullets, also.

He liberally sprinkled antibiotics on the wounds and wrapped the entire torso firmly in gauze bandages to stop the bleeding.

Back at base, Ryan helped change the bandages. They administered field stitches, more antibiotics, and more morphine, but Dr. Roseman needed to be in a hospital, soon. Ryan turned to one of his guys, "Get Dr. Roseman to the hospital in Da Lat. I'll call Claudia to set things up. The Chief of Staff moonlights as a vet at her feline rescue farm."

As the guy ran to the car, he added, "Make sure he's in good hands, then head back here. We're going to need to pack all this up. Rosie's going home for sure, this time."

Mike could still hear the Humvee crashing through the brush, when Ryan turned to Zaara and Stenko and the other technicians. "So, I need to speak with Eleanor, but I think we are done here."

Zaara blinked. "We just got here."

Ryan shook his head. "I think Dr. Roseman's part was the biggest push."

"I'm just the afterthought?"

Ryan seemed startled. "Oh, no, I didn't mean that. It's just that your research requires a lot less...stuff."

Zaara chuckled. "Well, yes." Zaara leaned back and put her feet up on the aluminum table. "Damn. Well, she wanted action, and I guess we got that. Just not what anyone expected." Ryan headed off to inform Ellie and supervise packing.

Mike took out a half-carved bear from his pocket before he realized his knife was gone. "It's not her fault, but it does look like we're done here...for now."

Zaara took two bottles of cold water from the refrigerator and placed one in front of each of them. "What are you going to do now?

"I don't know. I owe something to Eleanor. I promised her I'd testify before Congress, or talk on television, or something. It's all hard to imagine after forty years in the forest, but I enlisted and I'll report for duty." *Not a deserter*, he thought. *Still not.* "But I need to take Chi her dress. And maybe stay for the husband's family visit." He scowled, turning the bear carving over and over in his big hands. *If it won't embarrass An Ly. If Chi wants me there.* He realized he was almost afraid to ask.

He thought about the chaos this group had brought to these villages and wondered if this had even been the right idea in the first place.

"Is it too late to marry her?"

Mike started, thinking Zaara meant Chi's wedding, then realized she was talking about him and An Ly.

He shook his head. "I just don't know. Seems like it would be less shameful for Chi to have a real father, and An Ly a real husband, but...I just don't know."

"By my lights, these people have come to respect you, Mike. That's what I saw."

He sucked a tooth, then set the unfinished bear carefully on the table. "I don't know."

Thunder rolled through the camp. The generator kicked on and the rain started, so no one said anything for a while. The rain brought Rosie's lab tech under the tarp. He helped himself to a *Ba-ba-ba* and sat at a nearby table. "Is Dr. Roseman going to be all right?"

Mike laughed. "Don't worry, Stenko. I saw much worse during war."

"But didn't a lot of those war casualties die?"

"Just drink your beer. I guarantee we'll all meet on New Year Eve and laugh about this. Rosie will be taking off his shirt to show everyone his scars."

Zaara joined in. "*There's* an image! Rosie, rejuvenated with his perfect hair and manicured fingers, whipping off his shirt at a New Year's party to show his bear scars. I'll look forward to that."

Stenko cheered up. "Me too."

The generator stopped, as did the rain, and there was another silence.

"So, anyhow, I think I'll stay here—this is my home—for a little while before I report to duty," Mike said, finally answering Zarra's question.

She nodded. "Me, too, stay awhile. You know, I think I'm going to take that Swedish train—the engineering marvel you told us about."

Stenko asked, "Aren't you curious about the dying villages?"

"I will be after I come back from my train ride." To no one in particular, she added, "Anyone else interested in a train ride?"

Mike smiled. "I'm going to spend time with Chi and An Ly. They're my family and I'm going to have to go away again soon enough."

He looked at Stenko. "I haven't given up. If it's not Agent Orange, it's still something. I can't do nothing and watch my family just fade away." He stared into the jungle, "But maybe there's another way."

"Well," Stenko turned to Zaara. "If you can help me pack up the lab, I'd like to join you and see the country."

"Deal," Zaara said. "But I'm definitely not finished here yet. I want to come back with a fresh perspective. Maybe we can *both* come back to help Mike and his family find some answers." She put her empty water bottle in the recycle bin and headed toward the lab with Stenko close behind.

"It might be easier to come up with some fresh ideas without the good doctor's— uh— "

"Pessimism?" Zaara laughed.

"Uh, vast knowledge. Yeah. Contempt prior to investigation? Not to speak ill of the bear-mauled and half-dead, but sometimes he's really hard to work for," Stenko said, voice fading as they disappeared into the lab tent.

Mike finished his water, thinking about getting on his way to Chi's village. Ryan popped his head under the tarp roof. "Claudia was able to organize transport. We're cleared for takeoff tomorrow morning. Let's be there."

Mike got to his feet and explained that he, Zaara and Stenko were staying behind.

"Dude, I've got no idea how you're gonna get back to Eleanor's little shindig in that case. I'm afraid you're on your own."

"We weren't expected to be back for another couple days at best, probably a couple weeks. I'll still be able to do what she wants. We're just giving this a little more time. And I'm taking care of some personal business."

Ryan nodded. "Nice working with you. I wish you luck."

Luck, yes. He needed to take his luck her dress.

39 ≡ ELEANOR

Her limousine attracted no attention as it double parked to let her out at the back entrance of the *Female Entertainment Media* studios. *New Yorkers are just blasé*, she thought. They'd become so inured to rich visitors that even in the outlying districts, a fancy stretch limo was seen as pretty much normal. Her smaller-sized vehicle—even painted her preferred pearl gray rather than black or white—didn't seem to draw any eyes at all.

Her driver walked around, opened her door and helped her out.

A *FEM: News and Shoes* staffer bearing a big ID tag, a battered tablet, and one of those single earbuds, along with a flock of multi-colored earrings, pranced forward to greet her. A production assistant ran down the stairs, stuck a name tag sticker and segment number onto Eleanor's back and shook her hand.

She had been checked in, identified and given her appearance order all in one swoop. The PA escorted her to the modest green room, which while decorated in a tacky flocked and flowered wallpaper she loathed on sight, was at least clean and well-stocked with beverages (non-alcoholic) and snacks (organic). She settled herself onto a bright yellow sofa and thought through her presentation.

Her guest of a guest, Dottie Parsons—one of her "cured by early drug trials" people, had not yet arrived, making Eleanor uneasy. Dottie was usually early to everything, according to Devon's research report.

Dottie Parsons still had not arrived when the PA stuck her head in the door and signaled Eleanor was on in five minutes. Eleanor scowled. When the production assistant returned at three minutes to escort her to the stage, Eleanor whispered, "Dottie Parsons is not here yet."

The PA nodded and whispered back. "We know. Will you go on anyway? You can still talk about your issues. Perhaps she will arrive before Miss Brown has finished with your segment."

She didn't like the sound of that. She stopped walking so abruptly that a technician who had been following her, adjusting her microphone pack, actually bumped into her.

"Sorry," the technician mouthed, finishing her work and stepping away.

The PA figured out Eleanor was no longer beside her, turned back and frowned. "Is there a problem?" she mouthed.

Her mind quickly sorted through her options. It would look bad for her and her cause if she simply refused to walk out on stage. Besides, she didn't need the witness to back her up. Did she? She stood up straight, adjusted the jacket of her cream baby-alpaca business suit, smiled, and stepped forward just as, onstage, Miss Delilah Brown finished her introduction.

She walked out on stage to mild applause. She glanced out at the audience as she seated herself beside Miss Brown. Today she *noticed* the studio audience—as individuals, not simply heads out there in the dark. She smiled for the camera at the same time she was thinking, *How old everyone is*. It wasn't just the typical sampling of retired business people she presumed were found in most audiences. These were primarily folks her own age and up. Not that they announced their birthdays on their name tags or anything, but she considered herself a fair judge of such things after her many years of dealing with people.

While she had been thinking, she had missed Miss Brown's first question. Delilah was waiting expectantly for a response.

She concocted a way to cover her lapse. "Forgive me, Miss Brown, I was noticing there are both women and men in your audience, which surprised me."

Delilah Brown laughed her signature laugh: velvety and deep. So deep she wondered again if Delilah had begun life as the other gender, but that was irrelevant to this interview, wasn't it?

Why couldn't she focus? Had Dottie Parsons' non-appearance derailed her usual calm so thoroughly?

"Of course, Dr. Powell," Delilah said. "Many of our guests come expecting the Female Entertainment Media channel to cater exclusively to women. But as you know," she emphasized this with a subtle eyebrow, as if to goad Eleanor back on track, "our programs are designed to be of interest to everyone; it is our production staff, hosts and ownership that are predominantly female."

"Yes," she said nodding, and feeling herself settle in a bit better. "I do know that."

"So, today we are going to talk about drug trials, and how they may be of benefit to YOU out there, not just in our studio audience, but at home and throughout the world."

Distressed by the "may be of benefit" line, Eleanor couldn't imagine what her response was supposed to be. How could she follow the script if Delilah didn't ask the cue questions? She just smiled, vowing to cut off Dottie Parsons without a penny for her part in this betrayal. Even then, she had no idea how thoroughly she had been set up by circumstances.

"Now, Doctor, I have heard you say elsewhere that the medicines tested in drug trials are designed to cure specific diseases, and that testing is a required part of a drug's development before it can be marketed in the United States." She emphasized United States, leaning forward so half a hundred of her beaded, tiny braids swung forward over her shoulder, framing her dark face.

"That's correct, Miss Brown—"

"Oh, you can call me Delilah," Delilah said. "Everyone does."

"Of course, Delilah," she dutifully followed her cue. "The Food and Drug Administration—"

"Well of course if these are drugs designed to cure specific diseases, then they—the drug companies which design them—" the hostess said, glancing at her audience to let them know she was trying to be clear for them, "these drug companies choose particular diseases to work on, don't they?"

"Yes, they—"

"And they choose the ones which are causing the most problems in the world population, isn't that so?"

"That's often the focus," she said, speaking rapidly so as to finish her statement before Delilah could interrupt again. "Though sometimes they stumble across something that works better for a different disease than the one they originally aimed at."

"Um hmm. Now, during the 1980's, the biggest effort was to find a cure for AIDS, isn't that true?"

This wasn't in the script at all. "Certainly that was the concern of health agencies and drug researchers around the world at that time," she said. This *interview* had taken on the dimensions of a bad dream. "There still is work going on with AIDS, to find better treatments, less expensive ones, and the most helpful with the least side effects."

"But in fact they found a cure for AIDS that worked so well they stopped the drug trials and gave the drug to their control groups as a humane gesture."

She felt her cheeks going numb with a prickle of intuitive fear. She nodded but did not smile. "AZT was the drug, originally researched as a cancer cure. The side effects were very serious, but it was effective against AIDS."

"And isn't it true that at that time your daughter, Jane, still in high school, had contracted AIDS because of a blood transfusion that was tainted with the virus?"

Eleanor's entire face prickled with shock; the numbness ran down to her hands. She couldn't speak.

"And you," Delilah Brown went on, relentless in her attack, "*refused to allow her to participate in that drug trial?*"

There were harsh murmurs out in the audience.

"So, because you don't practice what you preach, your daughter died needlessly?"

She couldn't feel the tears on her cheeks. She didn't know she was crying until she saw a teardrop land on her skirt, making a dark spot on the creamy soft wool.

She had buried Jane in creamy white, because her daughter was so pure, so innocent. When her husband had died, shortly thereafter—many of their friends said of a broken heart—she had put him in the ground in his best navy blue suit. But not Jane, Jane wore white.

She gasped, and began speaking without regard for Delilah's questions or the audience's response.

"I advised my daughter's physicians not to try this dangerous, unproven drug, but to stick with treatments the FDA had shown were effective, with fewer side effects. I felt AZT was very cruel to the body, as well as to the AIDS virus. And at that time, I had seen too many false hopes raised by these new, supposed wonder drugs as they each came along. When patients died anyway, the families were devastated. Most of the new drugs had horrendous side effects—which AZT certainly does—*and* most of them *were not effective at all.*"

She felt as if she could not breathe. She took several deep breaths and sat up straighter. "You know, I did the best that I could. I did what any mother would do—what I thought at that time was the best treatment plan for my child."

Delilah said nothing, but handed her a tissue. She dabbed at her nose. "After Jane died, I realized that the AZT trials were indeed prolonging the life of AIDS suffers. If I had let her doctors try it on her, she almost certainly would have lived. She would be alive today, and I would have a daughter, instead of nothing but my guilt."

She gathered her courage and looked at the audience. "That is why I now support, promote, *urge and encourage* drug testing. Early drug trials save lives. They could have saved Jane's and they could save many more lives than they do, if people would only do what I could not—take a chance on an unproven treatment."

There was utter silence in the studio.

Then, "Wow," Delilah said. "I understand where you're coming from with that!"

The audience murmured agreement.

Delilah stood up, clapping her hands. "And I think you are one very brave woman to come and tell us your story!"

The audience stood up, too. They applauded and cheered with vigor.

"We'll be right back," Delilah said, signaling for the overdue commercial break. She turned to Eleanor. "I for one am really glad Missus Parsons couldn't make it today," Delilah said. "We never would have gotten here if she had."

"No," she agreed faintly. "We certainly would not."

P+P BLOG POST

Pride and Prejudice (apologies to Jane) aka Lies, Damn Lies, and Statistics (apologies to whomever said it first)—A blog dedicated to odd stories about numbers

Control Groups

One of the frustrating things about clinical trials for new drugs is the control group. Why does anyone volunteer to participate in the test of an investigational drug? One motivation is to get access to the newest treatment before it is available to the general public. Maybe you don't expect to live long enough to wait until the drug is approved, a process that takes years.

So you sign up and take your pills exactly as directed. What happens? Nothing.

Unbeknownst to you or your doctor or anyone you come in contact with, you've been assigned to the control group and your pills do not include the drug.

What a waste!

If you live long enough, you discover this cruel act of fate: You've been assigned to the group of people who are dying for science.

Why have control groups?

The answer is the correlation paradox. Without a control group, the scientists only know that people who took the drug got better. Their improved health could have many causes. The two most popular are: first, placebo effect —patients get better just by being in the drug trial, no drugs required. The second is selection bias—only people with improving health are signed-up for the drug trial.

A control group is otherwise the same as the group receiving the real drug. If either of these effects occur, they will be observed in both groups. In fact, in many tests, both groups show improved health relative to the general population.

One way to show causation is to have a control group. If the effect is only observed in the group receiving the drug, causation is established—the drug is effective.

That explains things, doesn't it? Or maybe not.

40 ≡ LIAM

When Liam saw the lakes from his small airplane window, he knew he would be landing in a few minutes. He'd gone from Iquitos in the middle of a jungle wilderness back to the middle of an evergreen wilderness. Looking west, he enjoyed the aerial view of bare granite peaks and tree covered slopes. Those were *his* trees: various species of pine, spruce and firs. He felt his body relax. He'd never imagined becoming a tree hugger, but it did feel as though the trees embraced him in a big, comforting hug.

On the ground, but still a mile up, he quickly acclimated to the thin, dry air. His arms moved easier as if he'd just gotten out of a pool where he'd been walking under water for the last weeks. The bluer sky and brighter sun sent him to his suitcase to dig out his sunglasses.

Unsure of what to do next, he didn't call anyone. He took a cab, an hour west into the foothills, to his suburban Boulder apartment—feeling like he was sneaking into town.

Once home, he walked to the grocery store for orange juice, eggs and a few microwave dinners. For the entire three blocks, he noticed how the concrete and asphalt, lawns, buildings, parking lots, even people's gardens, covered every inch of land. Not a wild spot remained.

Later he walked the other way to the post office. He passed a creek, but after looking carefully, he realized the channel was just as man-made as the sidewalk and bridge crossing to the other side.

As he carried home the heavy carton of mail, he considered just dumping the entire mess of glossy catalogs and credit card offers into the nearest recycling bin. Instead, once home he piled the mail on the bed in the spare room, and closed the door on it.

He made a cup of coffee and surveyed his tiny living room. Most of the space was occupied by a secondhand sofa, green and blue plaid from his student days. He had promised himself he'd replace it with his first paycheck, but that was years ago. The Formica coffee table was also a remnant from his student days and should have been discarded long since.

Strangely after a week living in Nanay Libre, his apartment looked worse, not better. He stared at the sofa, then sat on the floor. He rested the coffee mug beside his feet to let it cool a bit. He'd intended to sync into local time by staying awake until bedtime, but even the coffee didn't help. He fell asleep on the hard floor.

The morning sun penetrated his exhausted eyelids. He was still on the floor, lying against the sofa. He grabbed two sofa cushions and made a Liam sandwich—one pillow under his head and the other on top to block the light.

The next time he woke up, the sun was setting. He staggered into his kitchenette and made a six-egg omelet. He sat on the floor and ate it with four slices of toast dripping with butter and honey. He drank a quart of OJ while watching some cable news show. There was a segment about miscarriages in Vietnam. It reminded him of Nanay Libre, and their dwindling population.

He flipped the channels, landing in the middle of a talk show piece on FEM with some woman crying about her dead daughter. *For sure, there are women who want children and love them. How could I have been so confused?* He made another Liam sandwich and fell back asleep.

The next morning he felt great. He put on a pair of black nylon shorts, a Boulder 10K tee shirt, and his running shoes. He ran out the front door intending to find some natural terrain. He ran towards the post office, turned uphill at the creek. The creek, paths, and vegetation all screamed: landscape architect! *Nothing natural here.* He ran faster and faster as if chased by demons. Eventually the buildings disappeared, along with the few cars traveling the isolated road on his right. Ahead and above the raw granite, formed and cracked by unimaginable forces, cut high into the blue sky and soft white clouds.

His wet shirt stuck to him and his lungs fought to steal enough oxygen from the mountain air. He went higher and faster, until the pain in his calves and quads forced him to slow. He puffed and puffed as he came to a small opening between the rocks. He collapsed on a flat granite boulder, flat on his back, legs hanging over the edge. He could see his chest rise and fall as his lungs struggled for sufficient breath. He stared at clouds, listening to the rolling, rumbling roar of Boulder Falls.

Icy water crashed down the mountain driven by the spring thaw. Melting winter snow, so different from the dark gliding water of the Nanay. He closed his eyes and thought about miscarriages, drug testing, motherhood, and statistics.

As his lungs grasped for oxygen, his brain grasped for facts, hard facts. Low birth rates in Minneapolis, Berlin, Osaka and other cities in the United States, Germany, and Japan. These were facts from his own research. Declining populations in the Amazon—he'd heard and observed this first-hand, but observations were not really facts. Cause unknown, but low birth rates reported, and miscarriages and infant mortality part of the decline. Also declining populations in Vietnam. Again cause unknown, but low birth rates were one of many possible explanations.

Abruptly, he had his fill of nature and wanted more than anything a computer and an internet connection. A high-speed, fiber-optic, broadband internet connection. Maybe there was more to his happiness than just wild places and tranquil solitude; technology was nice, too.

All night he searched public and private databases, United Nations census data, and blogs. In the morning he called a friend of his mother's, an executive at a talk show run by women. In fact the very show on FEM he'd caught a glimpse of the previous evening. She was his mother's friend, so probably a radical feminist, but he needed a national platform and he couldn't think of anyone else.

"So, you say the population explosion is going to ruin the environment? That's old news."

"No. That is *not* what I said." He repeated his main thesis for the third time. "I said people are not having enough babies and the world population is *crashing*."

"By 'crashing,' do you mean falling?"

"Yes, that's what I said."

"Well that sounds crazy."

He couldn't tell whether the lady liked crazy, or hated it.

"Since you're Alexandria Shaughnessy's son—and we have a last-minute cancellation, I can put you on the day after tomorrow. Be at the *Female Entertainment Media* studios in New York at 9:00 AM."

He couldn't believe his luck, but, "I thought *FEM: News and Shoes* was an afternoon show."

"We tape in the morning. Be there."

"I saw an interview last night— "

But he was too late. The lady in New York had already hung up.

Delilah Brown leaned towards Liam. He tried to watch her eyes instead of her neckline. "If this is such a big problem, why haven't other statisticians, mathematicians, politicians, or magicians noticed this?"

The camera tightened on his face while he formulated an answer. Delilah continued talking in the background. "If you tuned in late, we have Dr. Liam Shaughnessy, exclusively on *Female Entertainment Media*, talking to us about the global population crisis."

He felt like she was making fun of him. He kept thinking of Samson and Delilah and couldn't concentrate on his answer. Finally he blurted out, "Because of the old people—there's so many more old people, no one noticed fewer babies."

"Too many old folk, eh?" She smiled into the camera and broke for a commercial.

During the break, Delilah spoke to him with a different tone.

"Liam, my producer just reached your mother in San Diego. She's saying you're a loony. Is this all a stunt? Do you want to put in a plug for some cause after the break, because I'm being told to end the interview. It might be cut from the on-air show all together."

He didn't know what to do. He yelled, probably the worst thing he could have done. "I have a Ph.D. in Economics! Do you think M.I.T. gives Ph.D.'s to loonies?"

Looking uncharacteristically serious, she whispered, "Yes, sometimes."

"Well, not in this case. This is deadly serious. You have the opportunity today to break the story of the century or look the fool in a week when someone else does."

Delilah pressed her lips together and looked thoughtful.

Some young girl yelled. "Sixty seconds."

Delilah responded, "Makeup."

Three woman came out; one to touch up Delilah and two to clean him up, wipe the sweat away, apply a cold compress to the back of his neck, straighten his tie, and fix his hair.

"Welcome back."

She looked towards him, the camera pulled back so they were both on screen, and she smiled. He tensed, thinking he might as well walk out now.

She leaned toward the camera as if she sat across from one person, her best friend in the world, and had something intimate and important to share. "Think about going to the grocery store or the post office. Think about visiting your grandmother or father in the nursing home. Think about all those elder-care communities."

She rolled her shoulders as if her neck was sore like her message was a heavy burden. "You see it don't you? There are more old people than ever. Lots more."

She looked back to him. "Is that right?"

"Yes, my statistics—"

She cut him off. "On the other hand, where are all those strollers and nursing mothers that disturbed you in restaurants, movie theaters, airplanes. Where are they?"

Show rolled her shoulders again. "Not so many? Right?"

She looked away from that single close friend sitting in the camera. "You can explain this, right Liam?"

"Yes. My research—"

"How about a few question from the studio audience?"

A woman with tightly curled auburn hair stood up. "I'm a Sunday School teacher and I think the problem is too much birth control, abortions and gay marriages. In my time, good girls automatically got married and had children. We better get back on track before we go extinct!"

He couldn't believe it, had Delilah convinced them? Maybe she believed him instead of his mother, or at least she recognized a good story.

"Good point. Anyone else?"

A man wearing wire-rim glasses, plain black slacks and a white shirt walked towards the front of the studio before he spoke. In a quiet voice he said, "I think this is the call to finally provide services, especially prenatal and early childhood, to everyone in society, not just the rich, but the poor, the unwed, the neglected. Before it's too late we must remember the forgotten."

Delilah nodded, a small, sympathetic smile on her face. Then, "Look at the time. Well there you have it folks. The human race is dying out. It's been an interesting show. See you all tomorrow."

He walked out of the studio in a daze. Evidently FEM wasn't just TV, because two reporters pulled him into an office and interviewed him for over an hour. When he complained he'd be late for his plane, they ordered a limo and accompanied him to the airport, asking questions until he finally escaped through airport security.

When he arrived home, his voice mail was full. He ignored the phone, put a *free-range, organic* chicken pot pie in the microwave. *Free-range, organic?* He grinned. *That's all they have in Nanay Libre.* He turned on the 6:00 news and stood paralyzed as he watched himself on television. He flipped among the channels listening to headlines like, "Humans going Extinct?" and, "End of Gay Marriages?" and, "Reducing the Age of Consent," and, "Tax Credits for Unwed Mothers."

Dr. Lopez, introduced by the Channel 4 reporter as "Professor of Gender Studies at University of the Rocky Mountains, where Professor Shaughnessy teaches," solemnly announced, "Dr. Shaughnessy and I worked closely together to evaluate the implications for women now, as the social priority for motherhood increases."

Dr. Li, "Mathematics Professor at the same university," added, "We always considered his research within the broader context. He's not just one of those narrow leave-me-alone-with-my-computer types. His work has true relevance to the world."

He ate his chicken pot pie and wondered if Ani would see him on the news, and if she would approve. He thought about calling her, but he didn't have her phone number.

He also wondered if this problem deserved so much hype and attention. It seemed his research had taken off and left him behind.

41 ≡ ANI

Ani realized she was leaning forward into her computer screen so far her nose almost bumped the screen—again. She sat back, rubbing her eyes. Making the text bigger on her screen might help her read, but it didn't help her remember to sit up straight. It was time for a break. She stood up, slid her chair back, turned and stumbled over her backpack, crashing into the sofa.

Maybe a long break.

"You…okay?" Connie's voice drifted out from the bedroom.

She leaned into the stubby hallway to her roommate's bedroom. "Sorry for all the racket," she said.

"Maybe it's bedtime," Connie suggested, and Ani also heard the rumble of Gregg's voice muttering sleepy agreement.

Is it? She looked at the clock, yawning. Only midnight. No, that was the clock that didn't work. It always said midnight. She leaned back over her little desk in the living room and read the time on her computer. 2:10. *Must be A.M., if Connie's asleep*. Her thoughts were muzzy enough for two in the morning, that was for sure. How was she ever going to get all the information she needed to present to the Save Our Native Cultures grant committee?

They had withheld her tuition monies for the quarter. They would reinstate her scholarship pending a statement about her activities, reassurances of good behavior from her—or, her adviser had suggested—a distracting new research project—and sleeping wasn't going to get that done in time for the hearing tomorrow.

Ugh. Not tomorrow. *Today, now.*

She shuffled into the little kitchenette area, opened the refrigerator and stared into its white and steel emptiness. No one had gotten around to going shopping since quarter break. Not that there'd be much in there even if they had shopped. *A root beer, at least.* She'd kind of gotten addicted to American root beer, one of the few things she had missed during her visit home. Now she was back, no root beer, and she found herself wishing for a bowl of fava beans cooked with salt pork, the way Mamí did it, soft and salty. She longed for the ones she was required to discard on the long walk to customs after she just couldn't eat any more.

She heaved a sigh, and rummaged in the "pantry"—a single cupboard dedicated to dry food storage. "Ooo. Popcorn!" She pulled out the last bag and stuck it in the microwave, tossing the empty box into the sink as a reminder to buy more.

She leaned against the countertop staring out the tiny third floor window into the foggy darkness. If she could put together her proposal to publicize the increasing rate of infant mortality, population decline, its links to drug testing, and present that to the committee, they might forgive her the violence at the protest march. Though—

She smacked herself in the head. "Oww! You are the biggest stupid-head of all!" She only had to tell them about the counter-protest people that Ryan-in-the-jungle had told her about. *What was the lady's name? Dr. Powell. Yes.*

She didn't need to get her presentation together for them. She could just give them Eleanor Powell, and that lady's connections with the group that had attacked their until-then peaceful march. Surely SONC wasn't going to blame her for the disruptions someone else had been paid to cause?

Her popcorn finished cooking and she pulled the bag from the microwave, tore the end open and dumped the salty white puffs into a bowl. She kept feeling she had forgotten something. Or lost it. She scowled, then got back on track.

She didn't have any actual proof, but if she could provide a one-page sheet on Dr. Powell's connections to other pro drug-testing groups or activities, that might be enough.

"Oh, her again!" one of the scholarship committee members muttered, when Ani had presented her defense.

"I did some research showing how and where she appears in support of drug tests, and—"

"Yes, dear," Akinyi Baako said, nodding her head so fiercely her red-patterned turban came untucked and began to unravel. "We know who she is. And you say this man, Ryan? You say he told you Dr. Powell paid him to harass your peaceful—"

"And legal," Dr. Lalande interjected in his raspy voice.

"—and legal march?"

"That's correct," Ani said.

"Who is Ryan?" Dr. Jameson said, raising one of her thick white eyebrows. "I'm confused."

"This is the man I told you was sent to Peru, following me, to make certain I did not make a problem at the Iquitos United Nations conference on Population. And—" Ani pushed on, over Dr. Lalande's mumble, "the one whose photograph is next to mine in that newspaper report about the violence at the demonstration march. He was the leader of the opposition group."

"Paid by Dr. Powell…"

"That's what he said," Ani reiterated. "But I don't have proof of this."

"No, of course," Dr. Lalande said with a smile on his wrinkled, ancient face. "How could you?"

"I also," Ani said broaching the new topic, "found her name in other places as I was researching for a new march I would like to propose in

Washington, D.C."

"I adore how you go straight to the heart of things with no fear whatsoever," Dr. Jameson said. "Now you want to take on Dr. Powell in the heart of deepest darkest Washington?" She laughed her old woman's laugh. "Well, what have you got?"

The others looked at her expectantly. She took a deep breath. Apparently her scholarship was no longer in question. Wishing she had finished her research the night before after all, she began laying out her arguments for the march on Washington.

"I have some interesting data that I have begun to collect," she said. "You may know of it, too, so perhaps it is not a new thing to you…"

Miz Baako, realizing her turban was coming unwound, reached up and began tucking it back together. Ani found herself watching the elegant black fingers at their work, awed by the woman's ability to put the complicated thing back together without looking, without help. "We cannot know if it is known to us until you tell us what it is, my dear."

"Well, there appears to be a serious decline in birth rates in a number of places around the world."

There were murmurs of surprise at that statement.

"And every one of those places is also a place where there has been recent clinical trials—drug testing."

A stunned silence descended on the little group.

Then, "My God," Dr. Lalande said.

"That's terrible," Akinyi Baako said.

"Where are you getting your data?" Dr. Jameson asked.

She licked her lips and picked up the slender printout she had thrown into her backpack at the last minute. "Well. The drug testing locations are available on line from the World Health Organization clinical trials registry."

They all nodded. They knew what that was. *They were probably part of the group that lobbied in the U.N. until that registry became fact*, she thought. *Well, perhaps not Miz Baako, who looked a little young. But certainly Doctors Lalande and Jameson could have been part of it.* She blinked and refocused.

"Then, the other half that I'm matching it to involves a lot of different studies." She bent over and pulled Liam Shaughnessy's paper from her backpack. She unfolded it with trembling hands. "This one, for example, did a statistical analysis of data from all over the northern hemisphere. The birth rate has seriously declined in Berlin, Minneapolis and Tokyo. And in each one, some time in the past twelve years, there has been a clinical trial of some size."

Hands still shaking, she separated the three pages she had printed from her previous night's research. "I am moving forward on smaller populations, for example my village of Nanay Libre has likewise had both drug testing and a decline in both pregnancies and new live births in the past twelve years. Also." She read one of the pages, hoping she wasn't mispronouncing the tribal names, "Also the same circumstances among the Xucuru, in Pernambuco district of Brazil, and the Beja people of Eritrea.

"Finally, one tribe, the Karajá indians of the Araguaia River valley in the Mato Grosso, Brazil, have gone entirely extinct. In 1999 there were about twenty-five hundred living Karajá. A clinical trial found them in about 2001—it's not well documented because that was before WHO Registry was required—and the thing being tested resulted in the deaths of many of the women of child-bearing age. Those that remained alive did not have children. The twenty remaining elders committed mass suicide as a protest against their treatment by the *norte* company—the people who ran the tests did not follow up, and gave the villagers no help."

Dr. Lalande was nodding his head. "Yes, I know about them. Very sad. Their culture is lost to humanity forever, now."

"I have to get citations for these things, but I thought we could get some media attention by staging a march." Ani bit her lip, looking from one of the committee members to the next. They seemed thoughtful. "Aren't there hearings in Washington beginning next week about this?"

Dr. Jameson's smile was predatory. "There certainly are—congressional hearings about whether the United States should support the United Nations resolution to prohibit drug testing among native peoples. And we are certainly attending. And this information is chillingly telling, Ani

Moreno."

"Are you thinking what I'm thinking? But she can't testify and do the research at the same time," Miz Baako said.

Doctors Lalande and Jameson looked at each other. "We have time, and we also have some resources at headquarters to do the research," Jameson said.

She looked at Ani. "The presentations have to be turned in to the congressional committee ahead of time. Then, you don't actually present what's in the paper, it's read by the committee, mostly likely their staffers, and they interview you. Can you do that?"

"I will need to know what's in the paper," Ani said.

"Certainly. So, you go to Washington, do the protest march—we can use the publicity, in any event—you read over the paper, we'll ensure you are invited to the hearings, you answer questions based on what you just told us and any details you remember from the finished paper," Dr. Jameson said. "I'll be there with my nice M.D., and someone else from the senior staff at headquarters with a Ph.D. in Ethnic Studies or the like, to impress the congress folk—"

"So it won't matter that you don't have credentials, my dear," Akinyi Baako put in as an aside to Ani.

"But you have the enthusiasm, the ethnicity, and the face to present this convincingly to our government representatives. Eleanor Powell will also be there, so—"

"Oh!" Ani blurted. *That isn't good, is it?*

"—you will have a chance to have your revenge right to her face," Miz Baako said. "You'll just tell them what you told us about this Ryan person making trouble at your San Francisco march, and following you home."

"She shouldn't have done that," Dr. Lalande said, shaking his very white head. "Nope, nope, nope!"

Connie nudged Gregg over on their tiny sofa and sat down next to him, still looking at Ani. "So," she said, adjusting Gregg's arm across her shoulders, "they just reinstated your scholarship *and* added you to the committee testifying before Congress?" she giggled, and Gregg tousled her hair.

"Yes," she said, watching the two of them cuddle. "And they want the march in Washington. They're securing the permits. They offered me an airline ticket, but I said I needed you two, too. So they gave us gas money." She looked at Gregg. "If your truck will make it that far."

"Ah!" he said cheerfully. "My truck! Well, my truck has collapsed into itself!"

"Folded up like a little origami toy," Connie added, laughing.

"So my Pop bought me a new one."

"It's not new, new," Connie said. "But it's waaay better than the other one!"

"Which we are going to respect the memory of for its many trusty years of service," Gregg said, smiling so his dimple showed.

He only had one dimple, Constance had explained when she first introduced him to Ani. A dimple in his left cheek, where a piece of flying glass had made a tiny scar during one of his and his brothers' magic experiments as kids. It gave Gregg a very charming smile. She smiled back.

"Ohhh, bless the old truck," Connie was chanting, waving her hands.

"So," Ani said. "I'm going to write to my family, and then I am going to pack," she said, hoping they'd take the hint. "Or vice versa." She walked off toward the archway to her bedroom.

"Pack? When are we leaving?"

"Well... " she called from what passed for her bedroom—a little niche that once might have once been a walk-in closet, "...we have to be in Washington by Sunday for the march."

"Sunday!?!" She could hear footsteps as Connie walked over to her workstation, where she kept her calendar. "Damn, I'm going to miss that lecture on Olduvai Man in Archaeology!"

"I'll give you the notes," Gregg said. "I kept all my notes from last Quarter, so you won't miss anything."

"Cool!" Connie said. "If we have to be there by Sunday, we should leave…"

"Tomorrow," Gregg said.

Ani stood there by her bed, staring at her empty suitcase. She kept feeling like something was missing.

She picked up her shorts and crop top outfit, a hand-me-down from Connie, and set it in the bottom of her suitcase. It was going to be hot in Washington, and they might have time for a little fun.

She considered the rest of her meager wardrobe. The SONC committee had warned her to bring business clothes for the congressional hearings. "Can I borrow a suit, or something businesslike?" she called to Connie.

"What, they didn't give you a budget for that kind of stuff?" Connie asked, standing in the archway to Ani's room.

"Yes, they did. But we need money for the trip, and money for the—oh, no, they're going to make the signs, aren't they, so we don't have to pay for those."

"How much did they give you?"

She reached for her backpack, pulled out the check. "Five hundred. Plus a card for the gas," she held up the prepaid gasoline card.

"Oh, good grief. We only need, like a hundred for the trip, tops. You've plenty to go shopping." Connie perked up. "Ooo. Shopping! You want to go now? Stores are still open until nine."

"Yes, I suppose that would be a good idea," she said as Connie dashed into her own room.

She picked up her favorite tee shirt and jeans and set them in the suitcase. From the pocket of the jeans a braided fiber bracelet stuck out. She pulled it from the pocket. It had gone through the wash with her jeans, but still looked okay.

It's one of Liam's, that he kept dropping, she thought. One that he had bought from Tomito, made to his special order with the beads and the pattern he liked.

She put it around her wrist, running the tie strings through the loop on the other end, then crossed them beneath themselves. She walked into Connie's room and held it out to Connie. "Can you tie this on, please?"

"Oh, going native, are we?" Connie teased.

"It's—" she stared across the room, not seeing anything. "It's something I want to remember," she said.

"Cool!" Constance said, grabbing a sweater. They walked out into the living room. Connie looked at Gregg. "Are you going shopping with us, or going home?"

"Um. Home?"

Connie nodded and Ani laughed. "Okay, we'll see you bright and early tomorrow morning, ready to drive to our nation's capitol. Right?"

"Yes, ma'am," Gregg said, and smiled his one-dimple smile.

She waved, her eyes caught by the bracelet. She liked the design, was glad this bracelet was the one she had accidentally kept.

Or…had Liam tucked it into her pocket on purpose?

That made her smile. Then she caught her breath.

Was that what she had been missing?

Liam?

42 ≡ LIAM

Liam, exhausted from his red-eye return flight from New York, contemplated his next move. His normal life of teaching and research seemed in the distant past. He wondered if there would be more interviews and travel. The pleasant, bright Boulder morning reminded him how little he liked crowds and cities. Did he want more interviews?

Deep in thought, he snacked on cold pizza. *How old is this? Certainly from before the trip to New York. Good thing I'm such a good housekeeper and stored it in the fridge.* The door bell rang. *Who's here so early in the morning?*

He swung the door open. "Mother?"

"I wouldn't have had to fly in from San Diego, if you'd have answered your phone."

She turned around and headed out to the street. Even though he was in flannel pajama bottoms and an old 10K tee shirt, he followed her, expecting to help with her bags. She never traveled light. She turned to the cab driver, "Drop my suitcases off at the Boulder View Suites. Have them taken to my room. The name's on the tags."

She paid with a couple of hundreds, way too much for the ride from the airport. Once back in his apartment, she began her inspection, pausing at the dirty dishes in the sink, shaking her head at the unmade bed in one room and the heap of papers in the other. "It's a good thing I got my own suite," she announced to the stack of unopened mail.

She cleared a corner of the coffee table to set down her leather purse, emblazoned with the logo of a Paris designer. In her two-inch heels, she was slightly taller than Liam. She wore a red, raw silk jacket with a white blouse and a scarf from the same Paris designer as the purse. It appeared that she still played tennis regularly—after all she had her own court and a private trainer—since her tan and athletic figure were well maintained.

He collected the dirty dishes from the coffee table and carefully stacked them with the others in the sink. He felt a need to explain the mess. "I've been pretty busy."

He thought of offering her a drink, but after a mental inventory of the fridge—a couple of beers, maybe a half a glass of OJ, a box of wine, and a pitcher of filtered tap water—he reconsidered. Besides, he hadn't invited her and didn't want to make her feel too welcome.

She picked up a throw pillow and used it to dust off the plaid sofa before she sat down. "That's why I'm here. I saw you mentioned on the news, and I knew you'd need my help."

He thought to say, I was doing fine without you, but only grunted.

She leaned forward and spoke quickly. "This is your chance of a lifetime—media deals, appearances. I don't want you to mess it up. You must already realize that the way you handled the *Female Entertainment Media* interview was a big mistake."

He couldn't resist a sarcastic reply, "You realize I was kidnapped by guerrillas and escaped through the jungle without your help?"

"Of course. A nice gentleman from the State Department called me. I did what I could, but it was the same time as my biggest charity event of the year."

He almost added, I didn't need your help anyway, but while he counted ten shallow breaths, he figured it out. Her child always came last. Why should this occasion have been any different? He smiled at her. He felt he understood a fundamental point about her.

But he also felt if he stayed in the same room with her any longer he'd completely lose his composure. He stalked into his bedroom, grabbed the recycling carton from next to the computer and took it into the spare room. He sorted the mail, crumpling each piece of junk mail before shoving it into the bin. She sat on the sofa, wordless.

He turned on the TV to break the awkward silence. It was still on the FEM channel.

Mother stayed on the sofa, Paris-designer purse in front of her, hands clasped together, ankles crossed. Finally she spoke, raising her voice above the television. "You can't ignore the business issues. I can recommend a good agent, a friend of mine. You should also talk to my lawyer. He already has show biz clients. Did you know that a lot of movie stars live in Rancho Santa Fe? Douglas Fairbanks and Mary Pickford played important roles in founding the community. It's a haven for the famous."

He continued sorting the mail. As he expected, except for a few bills—paid automatically anyway—it was all junk mail, except for one piece from the Social Statistics Journal.

She raised her voice, but didn't move. "You just don't appreciate all I've done for you."

He threw the recycling box into the living room, spraying wads of paper everywhere. He almost laughed when a crumpled ad for a tanning salon landed in her lap. Calmly he looked down at her while she brushed the paper onto the floor. "*What* have you done? You've complained about the inconvenience and ordeal of motherhood. You've griped about my every perceived fault and how I wasn't worth the trouble—whatever the hell that means. How can a child be measured for his *worth?* What did I ever learn from you, but that I was unwanted?"

She flicked her foot, banishing a few trash balls under the table.

He continued. "Hell. You never, ever loved—"

She jumped up. "Liam Aloysius Shaughnessy! If your father— "

"When other children got hugs and learned about love, I learned about guilt!"

Some lady was in tears across from the ever-composed Delilah. Liam grabbed the remote, shut the TV off, threw the remote across the room where it smashed against the wall. The batteries rolled across the floor.

"I did the best I could, you know." Alexandria pursed her lips. It was not a pretty expression on her. Liam stared at her mouth. It was as if she wasn't his mother at all, just some strange woman making excuses. She went on with them, "I was a surprise child and my mother never let me forget she'd never wanted me. I can still hear her. You— You came too late. I respected your father, but I think I never learned how to love anyone, and had no idea how to try."

He was barely listening, and the revelation sounded too melodramatic to be taken seriously.

He ripped open the envelope from the Social Statistics Journal. He unfolded the single page. SSJ was famous for terse rejection slips. He glanced at the page, ready to toss it, then read it again more carefully. "You have not responded to our emails, so we are writing you to let you know your paper, "Population Trends in Berlin, Minneapolis and Tokyo," has been accepted for publication...please contact...as soon as possible."

Yes! He wanted to shout, to hug someone. His mother still stood by the old plaid sofa. No. Anyone but her.

He took the letter into his bedroom; his own, private, celebration would have to wait.

"You know after your father died, you became sullen and distant, Liam. What was I to do with a moody child? I was only twenty-two and I had to run the ranch, the mines, everything."

"Mother, can you hear yourself? I was only two years old, *two years old!* How the fuck could that have ever been my fault?!"

She flinched visibly at his language.

He flung a heavy textbook catalog towards the recycle bin. It hit the wall with a thud. "Mother, are you ever going to grow up, take responsibility for your *self*? You always blame others. Especially me."

She picked up her purse. "I can see you're in one of your moods. Call me a cab and I'll retire to my hotel. Call me when you're feeling better— you don't want to toss away this opportunity to build a real career."

His mother stood by the door, feet together, legs straight, both hands holding her purse like a shield in front of her, matching scarf, closed lips. He stared. She looked like a plastic doll posed by a little girl. Then like origami magic there was a transformation in his mind. He saw she wasn't the doll, *she was the little girl,* lost and lonely.

Shocked, he rejected this image. He said, "You're a big girl. Call your own cab. You have a cell in your purse."

"You're going to regret this." She walked out and slammed the door.

With the bang of the door, the little girl image returned to his mind. He wondered what she'd have done if he had walked over and hugged her.

Liam drank the last of the OJ from the carton and collapsed on the sofa. He'd had arguments with his mother before. She always blamed him, her mother, his father, as if his father planned the hunting accident and his death just to make her life miserable.

But then, he always pleaded two-year old vulnerability. He thought of Ica and Tomito; they didn't blame anyone. He thought, it's time for me to take responsibility for my life, too. *I'm thirty-two, ten years older than mother was when father died.*

He walked around picking up paper and placing it in the recycling bin. He found an envelope from the tenure committee among the junk mail he'd been about to toss. He opened it. "The tenure committee, after considering recent positive events, wishes to meet with you at your earliest convenience." It was almost funny. He dropped it on the coffee table.

He stared around at the unwelcoming room. Maybe he should go buy new furniture, throw out this junk. New job, new furniture... ?

It was like a magic door had opened in his life. Television show, SSJ, tenure committee. Like he'd come back from Peru a whole 'nother person, on a different track. A success track.

He wanted to share the SSJ acceptance and the encouraging letter from the tenure committee with someone. He couldn't think of anyone at school and certainly not his mother. The only name that came to mind was Ani, Angeline, Angel...he smiled when he realized he had given it the proper

Spanish pronunciation.

He still didn't have her phone number. His cell with the dead battery rested on the coffee table. He found the charger and plugged it in. He went into his bedroom.

A queen bed, a large desk and an ergonomic chair comprised all the furniture. The chair and the desk reflected his occupation and regular paycheck. Both were top of the line, and designed for the "serious computer user." The chair had eleven adjustments, including dynamic lumbar support. It even included a heater and three vibrators. The desk had an integrated power system and a built-in wireless hub. And of course, his computers were always the best.

He sat down and searched for Angeline Moreno, or Ani Moreno. If she had a phone number, it wasn't listed. He quickly found her on a list of witnesses to testify before Congress about a U.N. Resolution on drug testing. The news services, never too good with technical topics, connected drug testing to the population crash story, now called the "Pied Piper's Revenge."

He read several of these stories. Other statistical economists, after reexamining their data, found additional examples of declining birth rates hidden by longer life expectancies. One of his old professors at M.I.T. came up with the name "Pied Piper's Revenge," and asked the musical question, "Where have all the children gone? (with apologies to Pete Seeger.)" Liam noticed that Ani Moreno received more links than Dr. Liam Shaughnessy did.

He searched for the academy she'd talked about in San Francisco. The small school's web site, with Flash animations and beautiful pictures of native children, made him homesick—odd word choice he thought—for Nanay Libre, but offered no information about Ani. He searched the Iquitos web sites, found lots of Morenos, but nothing helpful.

He found an old news story about a protest march in San Francisco and a picture of Ani getting arrested. He copied this as his wallpaper. This was the only picture he had of her, since he'd lost his camera before he'd had a chance to take any. He searched all the organizations listed as sponsoring the protest. One after another yielded nothing, until he clicked on SONC - Save Our Native Cultures.

His heart raced. They listed Angeline Moreno as a scholarship recipient —with a better picture, but too small for wallpaper. He saved it anyway. They had announced another march in Washington, D.C. "Interested organizations can contact SONC coordinator, Ani Moreno at the Dolley M Inn." *Yes!*

She wasn't in, so he left a message. Hoping.

T he doorbell rang. Liam rolled over to look at the clock. It was only 7:30. It rang again. *Second morning in a row with early visitors, is this a trend? I hope not.* "Coming."

He pulled on his jeans and took a clean shirt from a desk drawer. He closed the bedroom and bathroom doors, threw the OJ carton in the trash, missed, but opened the door anyway.

"Good Morning! Did I wake you?"

It was mother. Again. Tan and sparkling clean, dressed western—from a red bandana to matching snakeskin western boots.

"I brought you some coffee and donuts."

As if yesterday had never happened.

She walked in, cleared a place for the food and hiked up her tight jeans so she could sit down. "I thought we should get started early. My cell's charged. Do you want to start with agents or lawyers?"

He looked at her—fifty years old, rich, good looking. He wondered why in the thirty years since his father died she hadn't found someone else. He felt sad for her. The Beatles song, *All the Lonely People* popped into his head. No, it was called *Eleanor Rigby*. His mother, kind of. He couldn't remember all the words.

"I appreciate your help, but— "

"I spoke to my friends the College. I found out you've had some difficulties, but I straightened them out."

He didn't mention the positive letter he's received yesterday. *Before* her intervention. "I have a meeting with them at 9:00 this morning."

His mother's high-fashion plaid western shirt embarrassed the sad sofa plaid. She sat with her back straight, her ankles crossed, and her hands folded in her lap. He held his breath as he realized where he had seen that pose before.

Many years ago, they had visited his grandmother at her fancy condo in New York City. Mother had warned nine-year-old Liam over and over: "Sit still, be polite. Sit like this." *This.* This pose, as she had sat then, and her mother had talked on and on in a sharper and sharper voice, saying all the things Alexandria had done wrong with her life.

Liam had forgotten that visit—their only visit—utterly, until now.

Mother sat in that same pose, waiting for— *longing* for approval. She just waited. He shook his head. Surely one among her influential friends was capable of giving her the approval she desired.

He *saw* that little girl, still waiting for recognition and approval. But he could not give it. He wasn't ready.

All the lonely people.

Where do they all come from?

We make them, he realized. That is where they come from. We create them ourselves. And then we pass it down from generation to generation.

He took a deep breath. What he really wanted to do was get online and buy a ticket to fly to Washington. As soon as he'd met with the tenure committee.

Or maybe before he met with them.

He needed to break this pattern—the passing onward of the lack of love, the unwantedness, the inherited loneliness. *He* must break it.

He realized he was standing in front of his computer, without remembering he'd walked there. He looked up airline schedules.

43 ≡ ANI

Ani sat down and pulled her straight lavender linen skirt down to cover her knees. It fitted a bit too closely, she thought, though Constance had been excited about the outfit. After she looked around at the others in the hearing room, she was very glad her roommate had taken her shopping. She even had a different skirt and blouse to go with the linen jacket if she was required to return another day.

Doctors Jameson and Lalonde and others from the SONC offices had coached her on how to sit, stand and talk. But Akinyi Baako had been the most help telling her what to expect. The room looked just as Akinyi had described it.

The chairman of the congressional committee was a large, older white man, whose silky voice and long soft vowels sounded like a new kind of music in her ears. He brought the meeting to order, announced the two speakers for the day—Ani Moreno and Dr. Eleanor Powell—and asked a pair of young aides to read the first statement, Ani's SONC-researched piece, aloud. She thought it sounded pretty impressive.

Then the chairman called her name, asking if she was present. She stood up, knees shaky, and said, "*Presente*," before nervously correcting herself, "I am here."

The aides escorted her to the witness area with its microphone, low podium and chair, where she would sit to answer questions from the Committee. *Do they swear us in, like court? I forgot to ask.*

"Now, Miss Moreno," the chairman said in his flowing southern accent, "I would like to ask what a young lady like yourself has to say to us about cultural survival on a personal level. You are not a U.S. citizen, is that correct?"

"I am a native of Peru, studying here in the United States at the San Francisco Academy of Indigenous Studies."

"Please explain to me and the committee what your expertise is, and why Save Our Native Cultures asked you to speak in support of the United Nations resolution that calls for a total ban on clinical trials among indigenous peoples."

Taken aback at his ability to state all that in a single sentence, and as best as she could tell, with a single breath, Ani was silent a moment. Then she recalled what Akinyi had suggested she say at the opening of her testimony.

"First I want to state that I am not an enemy of the drug companies," she said. "They have a difficult task, and I myself am very glad of my polio, MMR, and DTaP inoculations which have helped to keep me and my family healthy." The audience chuckled, and some applauded lightly.

She nodded and went on, "What I am an enemy of is thoughtless and unsupported intervention into the personal lives of people of indigenous cultures which are very different, in structure, temperament, goals, and daily lifestyle from the culture which formulated the drug testing procedures. Everywhere there has been drug testing, native cultures have declined."

"You are speaking here," the chairman jumped in as soon as she paused for a breath, "of the drop in birth rates?"

"Yes sir. That, as well as villages which are now simply empty where once they were thriving—even the elders are gone."

"So this data you have presented in your testimony, tell me how you discovered this connection?"

"I noticed in my home village that birth rates had dropped. Then I read a report about low birth rates in Vietnamese villages, and I had seen other reports that show a decline in birth rates among locals within the populations of three major cities in North America, Japan and Europe. Also there are SONC data reporting serious declines in western, northern and east African nations, with the biggest drop in live births occurring among some of the smallest tribes.

"I wrote down the names of all those tribes and their locations. Then I went to the United Nations Registry where clinical trials are reported. In every case I found that these tribal groups in these locations had been subjects of drug testing within the last twelve years."

The audience murmured at that.

Then a small, white-haired woman out in the audience blurted out, "You are reporting a correlation between these data—"

The Chairman hit his gavel, "Dr. Powell, it is not your turn to speak."

Ani looked at the women who had become so intertwined with her life. *You don't look that scary.*

Dr. Powell just continued, "—and correlation does not mean causation!"

Along the committee tables a couple of people were nodding their heads in agreement. But not the chairman.

"Dr. Powell!" The chairman hit his gavel twice more, "You are out of order! It is not your turn to speak."

But the little woman kept on speaking. "Her incompetence to know the simplest facts about statistics is misleading you and the committee, Mr. Chairman!" Dr. Powell said.

Now the chair shouted. "*That may be, Dr. Powell, but it is not your turn to speak!* If you do not desist with your interruptions, I will have you escorted from the room, do you understand me? You will have your chance later." He glared at the little Dr. Powell, who glared right back, not at all abashed. But she did stop interrupting.

Ani stared at her nemesis while her mind ran around in little circles. Hadn't Liam said something about correlation? What had he said?

She held her hands together to stop them from shaking, "Excuse me Mr.

Chairman. I'm so sorry I don't understand all the mathematics, but I'm sure what I'm telling you is right."

Eleanor made a little laughing sound, and the congressman asked, "And why is that?"

Now her voice was shaking as badly as her hands. "A professor has published a paper about this. He even flew to my country to present it to a U.N. conference."

This time Eleanor was silent, and the next question was full of respect, "Can we get him to testify?"

She regained her confidence, "Of course."

"Sergeant at Arms, get the information from this lady and get that professor here for our next hearing."

She relaxed, confident Liam would straighten everyone out. *He's so good at explaining things.*

"Another question Miss Moreno. You said these studies have occurred within the last twelve years?"

"Yes, sir."

"Which is as long as the Registry has been functioning, is that correct?"

"Yes, sir."

"Was there any match-up in the kinds of drugs being tested, or diseases being treated in these tests?"

"No, there wasn't. In fact, it seems to be a result of the testing process itself. The drugs were assorted; the majority were various AIDS treatments, several were for cancer, and some were for completely different conditions."

"Now that is very interesting, Miss Moreno. Very interesting." The chairman sipped from a glass of water on the table in front of him. "That is all the questions I have. The witness will now answer questions from the Committee."

A young man stood up, holding a sheaf of papers. He gazed at Ani with intense dark eyes. "There are ongoing plans to fund drug companies to focus their research on diseases endemic in developing regions of the world," he said.

She nodded.

"These studies are designed to test drugs that will prevent or cure malaria, leishmaniasis, schistosomiasis, dengue fever, and other scourges of the developing world. Diseases which rarely occur in the developed nations. They affect people in Peru, all of South America, most of Asia, Africa and the Pacific islands. Are you saying you don't want *those* drugs tested? Because there would be nowhere else to test them, if indigenous peoples may not be asked, and indigenous peoples are the very ones who could be helped by these drugs. So, you see, you are effectively asking to let your own and other native peoples keep dying of such things." His dark eyes bored into hers like Papa drilled into a coconut to open it. She blinked.

Then she said, "Sir, at the rate little villages like my own are dying, if there is not a ban placed on testing among indigenous peoples *now*, there will *be no* indigenous peoples left in the world, at all. Any *cures* that might be developed would be useless because there would be no population left alive to cure."

There was restless murmuring at that point in the audience.

The chairman glanced along the table of seated committee members. No one else indicated they wanted to ask a question.

"Miss Moreno, you may step down. Your opportunity for rebuttal will occur later this afternoon."

She returned to her seat in the audience. Dr. Jameson patted her hand.

"I now call Dr. Eleanor Powell. Is she here?"

Ani thought that was peculiar, because he knew very well Dr. Powell was there.

"I am here," Dr. Powell said and stood up. She walked up to the seat Ani had just vacated as bold as an anaconda stalking a chicken.

The clerk read Dr. Powell's statement. It had a lot of discussion of alternate explanations for the results Ani had cited among the tribal peoples. For example, Dr. Powell claimed that the Barabaig people were being destroyed by loss of habitat. They could no longer hunt, and that impacted their culture by not giving the young men a way to win a bride. Fewer marriages meant fewer children. Among the Xucuru, in Pernambuco district of Brazil, there had been a measles epidemic because less than twenty percent of the tribe had accepted inoculation against the disease. Those twenty percent were the only ones left alive, so of course their birth rate had dropped. There were other examples.

"Dr. Powell," the chairman said with a grimace, "you seem to have formed in advance arguments against most of the information the Native Cultures proponents have presented—"

"That is because their data is erroneous, your honor," Dr. Powell said.

Ani scowled. *No, it isn't.*

"No, Dr. Powell," the chairman said. Ani blinked at this surprising support. "The conclusions they make may or may not be erroneous, but the data are accurate, as my committee informs me. But you interrupt."

"I'm sorry, sir," the Doctor said, and bowed her head. Ani thought Eleanor Powell was either a consummate actress, or she had simply been in politics too long. It was not good enough to convince Ani of the old woman's contrition, but either the chairman was convinced, or he was letting it slide for the sake of getting to his point.

"Now, as I was saying, I found myself very curious about the processes you used to gather information on each one of these tribal groups that the Save Our Native Cultures folks reported on…and no others. Dr. Powell, would you care to explain that odd coincidence in your presentation?"

Ani began to get a sense of the chairman's displeasure. He did not like anyone making light of his committee or its work here. He did not like the way Dr. Powell did not follow the rules. His rules.

"My staff used the same process to locate tribal groups that conceivably had been affected by drug testing. Then they went a step further and researched to see if there was another possible explanation for the low birth rates reported for these peoples."

"Um hum," the chairman said. "But how is it you used *exactly* the same tribes? Did you have a spy in SONC, or a spy on my committee?"

Dr. Powell made an angry face, but she did not have a ready reply. After a moment she said in a clear steady voice, "I have no spies, sir. We simply used the same lists the SONC researchers did."

"Well, doctor, when *I* look at those lists, I find other tribes not mentioned in your report, and not mentioned in the SONC report. Perhaps you could explain to me the decline in population under the age of twenty for the following tribal groups." He then listed fifteen or twenty tribes. Ani had only heard of a few of them. Apparently Eleanor Powell had not heard of them either.

"I do not have any explanation for the population decline of these groups."

"I see." He sipped his water and turned to one of the congressmen at his committee table. "Charles, did you have a question for Dr. Powell?"

"Yes, sir, I do." It was an older man, who gave a gentle smile to the chairman, then turned to Eleanor Powell with no smile at all. "We are informed that one of your paid staff, a Ryan Kolnikoff, has been employed in espionage and strong-arm tactics in acquiring your data."

There was no response from Dr. Powell.

"In fact, you obtained in advance the entire text of the SONC report by illicit means before this committee received its own copy of that document. It appears you made every effort to target your own report to specifically damage each item of SONC concern. I wonder why you should care so much about that? I also wonder how you managed in what was to be a specific report on a specific topic, to address in advance every item on this committee's agenda for these hearings. Can you respond to these concerns?"

Ani was startled. Was one of the SONC people in Eleanor Powell's pay? Ryan Kolnikoff had not mentioned anything like that. She could not imagine Dr. Jameson or any of the others being a spy for the opposition group.

There was a long silence. Then Dr. Powell said, "Sir, may I request a recess?"

The chairman raised one elegant gray eyebrow, but nodded his head. "Yes, you may. Ladies and gentlemen, it's almost lunch time."

He looked at the committee members. "I believe we've heard enough. I move we adjourn for the day. Seconds?"

Everyone on the panel immediately said, "Second."

The room emptied rapidly. Ani took a deep breath, stood up, and surrounded by all the pro-Native Cultures folks, including her SONC friends and a half-dozen others, she made their way out the doors. They paused only a moment in the echoing hallway, before they passed through a second set of doors to the outside. On the stairway of the Cannon House Office Building, they were greeted by a crowd of spectators and news reporters.

After her successful March on Washington, Ani was especially sought after. She found herself staring into the lenses of an alarming number of TV cameras and an entire flock of microphones.

44 ≡ ELEANOR

Eleanor didn't move as people streamed around her. Devon offered his arm, "Let's get out of here." They headed for the door.

Deep in thought, she let Devon lead her. On the way out of the hearing room, she tripped on a raised threshold. She wanted to scream, *I hate this old building*! Fortunately Devon kept her upright. Without thinking she said, "Thanks," but immediately followed up with the thought, *This is all your fault*!

They crossed through the rotunda area, voices of reporters and aides shouting for Eleanor, but Devon's firm, "No comment," and her not-now expression quickly discouraged the press. They arrived at the corner exit of the Cannon House Office. Blinking in the sun at the top of the stairs, she squinted at the intersection of Independence and New Jersey Avenues.

As she thought every time she stood here, *So typical of Washington politics having it both ways: a door on the corner to be on two different streets at once.* Today this just made her angrier. *Where were my supporters on the panel? Why was the panel so one sided this morning?*

She stumbled down the stairs, and into her waiting limo. She didn't say anything until they were parked in the garage under her offices in Alexandria. She turn to Devon, "You can get out of here. I need to think.

I'm going to the farm."

Just before he closed the door, she added, "You need to think also. That was beyond worst case. How did that happen?"

As the driver headed east on the Beltway, she rolled up the privacy window and thought about her private war. It seemed she was failing on all fronts, today. Ryan, back from Vietnam. *What did he accomplish*? Besides spending a lot of money moving all that lab equipment, Dr. Roseman was in the hospital. Dr. Zaara Yassin, epidemiologist, had gone native. She still had the satphone, over $1,000 worth of high-tech magic, but she hadn't answered Eleanor's calls in days. Eleanor was left with a stack of invoices and no results. *No results!*

Even worse, the congressional hearings were underway and Ryan returned without Mike. She had hoped for his home-grown support to be added at the last minute, but—Sergeant Michael Johnson had also gone rogue.

She picked up her phone and went to "Green Beret."

Ryan answered on the first ring, "Hello Ellie."

"Bad news and bad news. The congressional aides fingered you for improper access to their agenda and planning documents. More bad news? They connected you to me."

"I don't know how that happened. I've used these sources many times and they've never—"

"Don't bother. You're fired, and don't give my name for a reference… ever."

"Are you sure your office didn't—"

She hung up, swearing to stick with highly-educated university types from here forward, no matter what her crazy-cat-lady half-sister suggested.

Her heart had begun to beat more slowly, more regularly by the time the limo turned off the Beltway onto Maryland Route 4 which would take her straight to Anne Arundel county. AA County was more low-key than the areas north of Washington in Maryland and west in Virginia. That was why she liked it.

Fifteen minutes later she was at her home away from home, enough acreage to pasture and exercise a half-dozen horses, and an antebellum house with outbuildings, far enough from the mainstream to have passed through the war unscathed. She had always wanted to restore the place, but for now: the parlor, library, drawing and dining rooms on the main floor, and the many bedrooms upstairs were just what could be called serviceable. Long before she bought the house, indoor plumbing had been added after the next war, WWI, and the keeping room and kitchen were *modernized* after the one after that, WWII. With its mixture of historical, plain old, obsolete, and needs some TLC, not even any film crews or Civil War reenactors had the property on their lists.

She sent the driver to her favorite seafood restaurant, just a few miles east on the Chesapeake Bay, "Get the catch-of-the-day dinner and a bottle of whatever they recommend to go with it." She was in no mood to make any decisions. "Just leave it in the dining room and you can call it a day."

One of the things she loved about this old house was a large clawfoot bathtub installed in the master suite probably in the 1920s. She took the binder prepared for the hearings and settled in to the warm tub scented with cinnamon and sandalwood.

She'd hoped for relaxation, but each section, so nicely formatted on 100% recycled, organic-cotton-fiber, acid-free paper made her angrier and angrier. The binder alternated between presentation material and background material, confidential background information was interspersed with the formal submission to Congress. When she realized what happened, she dropped the binder in the hot water splashing bubbles across the floor and soaking her favorite braided bath mat.

She climbed out, slipping on the wet bath mat, but saving herself from a nasty fall by grabbing the massive tub. As the last water gurgled from the tub, she reached into the remaining suds, grabbed the binder and threw it across the room. It popped open and wet papers exploded into the air. "Good riddance!"

Once presentable, she fired up her teleconferencing setup. Though the bulk of the blame fell on Devon, she felt she needed to address the full staff. "When we prepare for public hearings, we always prepare two binders. The blue binder has the public presentation and the data to support those public positions. The red binder has response data, only to be used in response to arguments presented by the other side or questions asked by the committee."

The large screen combining all four cameras in the conference room, showed everyone silent and sullen. A few people, especially the new interns whose names she didn't even know, looked left and right to see how others were reacting. No one reacted. Some didn't even seem to be breathing.

"When I ask, 'What topics are on the committee agenda for this hearing?' that goes in the red binder."

Everyone just stared at the screen in the front of the conference room that was displaying Eleanor larger than life size.

"When I ask, 'What other testimony will be presented?'—RED binding again. Analysis of opposition? RED binder! Committee member biases? RED! RED! RED!"

She dropped the now empty black binder on the hardwood floor with a resounding thud, "What makes us successful is that we are thorough, so thorough that the red binder is usually three or four times the size of the blue one."

She paused, and several people, led by Devon, apologized, offered explanations, and blamed the interns.

She whispered, "Don't you dare blame the interns. It's your job to check, to supervise, to ensure things are done correctly."

Everyone got very quiet. Devon asked, "What should we do?"

"The hearing will resume tomorrow or the next day. When I wake up tomorrow morning, I expect to see three correct copies of the blue binder and one correct copy of the red in the limo when the driver arrives to pick me up. Have a good evening all."

She exited the conferencing software.

Feeling really exhausted, she knew she had to make things right with her sister's boyfriend. *Or whatever she calls him.* She called Ryan's Green Beret number to apologize and re-hire him, but there was no answer. She debated leaving a message, but this needed to be done at least live on the telephone, if not in person.

After dinner she called Mike, but the status was the same. He hadn't heard from Zaara and everyone else had long ago returned home. He promised to help her, but not right away. She had too many more immediate issues to argue with him.

When she hung up, she thought about how much of her attention lately had been on Mike Johnson's project in Viet Nam. That was her own fault. She really cared about those people in the jungle 9,000 miles away.

Some of her attention had been on Ryan, who wasn't the most subtle investigator she had ever employed. Clearly not, given the information the committee had been leaked.

She had no idea what to do about Mike. And she still had no idea exactly how the information about Ryan and his work for her had leaked to the committee. It could have been anyone on her staff. Evidently those fancy university degrees didn't prevent sheer stupidity, or now she wondered, *duplicity, dishonesty, or double dealing.* Suddenly she felt very alone.

She walked out to the stables. It was dark and the stable hands had left for the day. She went from paddock to paddock, petting noses, curry combing withers, and dispensing oats and carrots. The horses were calming, exhibiting a natural warmth and affections.

She went down the row until she got to Black Beauty, a sorrel American warmblood. Two-year-old Jane had named the filly and Eleanor never changed it.

When Jane died, beautiful, brilliant Jane, with all her potential, Eleanor's heart had shrunk into a kernel inside her. When she discovered the very drug she had forbidden Jane to try could have—*would have*—cured her, she had nearly taken her own life.

The doctor that had saved her had no sympathy. He yelled at her for almost wasting *two* lives. That therapy worked for her. She came to terms with losing Jane by putting all her time and energy into doing good works to educate others so they would not make the same mistakes. She turned her life around by trying to save others. And trying to apologize to God — or whatever had tried to answer her prayers.

She had prayed for a miracle for Jane, and when it had been set before them, she had spurned it.

She had been making up for it ever since.

Or so she had thought. The accusations of the committee chairman stung. Had she become so intense in her goals that she had sacrificed everything in the name of efficiency? It had all been in Jane's name, she thought. She had made the conscious decision to turn her mourning into a positive effort to better the world.

But it certainly did not sound like that was what she had been doing, not the way the chairman had worded his questions. She was appalled at the scheming, monomaniacal bitch she felt he had described.

45 ≡ LIAM

"**W**elcome back, Dr. Shaughnessy. Speaking for the entire Tenure Review Committee," Dr. Li began in her cheery, high-pitched voice, "We're happy you survived your ordeal in the jungle."

Liam had promised himself not to argue with the committee this time, but he thought of Mamí and Tomito and Ica, and felt he needed to stand up for their way of life. "More like a vacation than an ordeal."

He looked around the room. Most committee members were reading journals or grading papers. He thought, *Ivory tower scholars. It's a shame Carlo didn't kidnap them instead*. His best intentions disappeared like so many monkeys into the rainforest. Slowly he asked, "You don't really want me as part of your little club, do you?"

A few professors looked up.

"I disturb your little fantasy world, don't I?"

Some frowned, others smiled, but all quickly returned to previous activities.

His voice got louder and less measured, "You're all like my mother, self-obsessed. You don't care what's happening beyond your little academic—"

He just stopped. *Why am I arguing with them? I'd be better off teaching in*

Nanay Libre. And they probably would be also.

The few who were listening turned towards Dr. Li. She shook her head to indicate disapproval, while also allowing a small smile. He couldn't figure out what she really thought at this juncture, but he also just didn't care.

Dr. Li gripped the edge of the table, and stood up, "You are making this quite unnecessarily difficult on *all* of us."

Several professors shook their heads. Others made comments. "Hasn't learned, has he?" "Why did he even return?"

Indeed, why had he? He regretted showing up. He'd promised himself to keep his mouth shut—not get into a fight with them, but they were so smug.

"There is no reason to get personal here. The committee wishes for reconciliation, but we still require your cooperation." She stared at him. When he didn't say anything she continued. "Regardless, we're glad you're safe and with the new information we've received, I think we can resolve our differences quickly and congenially."

He did not say anything, knowing if he opened his mouth, sarcasm would erupt.

Dr. Li maintained her smiling demeanor. "I spoke to your mother this morning. She says you're under a lot of stress. If everyone can come to order and stay calm, we can still have a productive meeting."

He sat quietly wondering if Ani might be flying over Boulder at that very moment. He looked up.

"Dr. Shaughnessy, can you confirm you've recently had a scholarly paper accepted for publication at SSJ?"

The committee buzzed and fidgeted. He nodded. "Yes." He didn't dare say any more.

"The Economics Department sent your file to the review committee due to insufficient publications. I think we can all agree you have rectified that deficiency, and we now return your case to Econ with our recommendation for approval."

Committee members nodded and began packing up their folders and papers. Dr. Li tapped her gavel, making the "vote" official.

Instead of elation when he realized they were going to give him tenure, disappointment left him angry and tense.

He realized he'd actually wanted to be fired, so he could teach in Nanay Libre, or somewhere like it. He sat in his chair, a bit stunned.

On her way out, Dr. Lopez paused beside him. "If you're interested, I don't think you should be teaching college. Your behavior is more appropriate for a kindergarten." She stalked off.

He waited for everyone to leave. Then he sent an email to Dr. Li, and waved goodbye to his mother's stern, disapproving portrait.

He had a plane to catch.

During the ride to the airport, he searched for a plan. The familiar doors marked "professor," "researcher," or even "celebrity" all opened to images of his mother and vaporized if he considered them too long. Other doors were buried deep in the jungle and too far away to consider. One door said "Ani," but when he approached, it receded out of reach.

When the cab dropped him at the terminal, he paid, picked up his backpack and stood in front of the airport doors. Sunset light glared off the glass, obscuring all within. He sighed and stepped forward.

He was rather concerned that at that moment, his entire life plan consisted only of a ticket to Washington, D.C..

He arrived at Dupont Circle late at night. The park comprised several concentric circles—two circles of traffic, an inner circle of bushes, then benches, sidewalk, and finally a circular pond around the fountain. Protesters still occupied the park in the center. Upside-down pickets signs, with their long handles pointing up like spears, leaned against the benches and the pool wall. The fountain had been turned off for the night. Groups of three or four sat on the benches and larger groups gathered around the silent fountain dedicated to the sea, the stars, and the wind—two of which were evident on that brisk evening. Animated discussions competed in volume with the light traffic.

He ignored the protesters, most much younger than him, and walked through the revolving door into Ani's hotel. White marble and dark wood surrounded Liam as he crossed the lobby, his hiking boots muffled by the deep maroon carpet.

The uniformed attendants watched him enter and pause. He searched the clocks mounted on the wall behind them skipping over Paris, Tokyo, and Johannesburg until he found Washington, D.C. Both hands were close. It was almost midnight.

This was the end of his plan, from here on it was all make it up as you go.

He walked towards the registration desk and imagined what would happen when he got there.

He would say, "Angeline Moreno, please."

The clerk would respond, "We don't release guests' room numbers. Do you know what time it is?"

And he would....

That question baffled him and he struggled to imagine a response. *I'm a friend* didn't seem convincing or even appropriate. *Someone she met on vacation* might be true, but again not very helpful. Surely *a fool who quit his job and flew to Washington* might be dramatic, *even overly dramatic*, but this sleepy night clerk probably wouldn't be impressed, or even care.

He looked at himself and the spotless hotel lobby reflected in window of the little souvenirs and sundries shop—long closed. His red hair, a month past needing a haircut, a Boulder fleece, now a veteran of hours on airplanes, and jeans still with circles of Amazon residue around the cuffs, might be a fine on a western college campus, but here, among the Federalist chairs and tables, and oil paintings of colonial politicians—here he looked out of place.

The mirror also revealed a guard with epaulets and brass buttons approaching quickly. Liam turned around and headed back to the door. He crossed the light traffic to the circle. He pulled a College of the Rocky Mountains sweatshirt out of his backpack and put it on under his fleece.

He zipped the fleece up and folded his arms across his chest against the night's chill. This wasn't Boulder, but it was still cold.

He stood in an open space listening to several different groups hoping they'd mention Ani or give him an opening to join their discussion. One group discussed an altercation with the capitol police, but Liam couldn't even tell if it happened today or some other time, maybe months ago. Another group debated the merits of their favorite pop bands, but here too Liam had nothing to contribute. He'd never even heard of most of the bands. People were drifting away in ones and twos, emptying the park.

Finally, he overheard a group discussing a connection between drug testing and population. A tall guy wearing a bandana on his head said, "I hear every time a village allows drug testing people start dying."

A girl who looked like she was still in high school added, "My professor says it's a global drug company cover-up."

A boy who looked like Tomito jumped in, "The FDA and the CDC, they're in on it too."

He walked up to them thinking about the fallacy of basing causation on correlation, but with a new found restraint, he just said, "You don't want to jump to conclusions. People might be dying for some other reason."

The girl laughed. "Surely drug testing isn't making them live longer."

The boy who looked like Tomito looked at his watch. "It's getting late."

The girl said, "Even if the drugs were helpful, those people can't afford them anyway."

The Tomito-looking guy walked off with the girl. The other guy said, "You're right," to Liam and trotted off in the other direction.

Liam again stood alone. He sat down on an empty bench. He counted the cars circling Dupont Circle. Twelve in five minutes, 144 an hour. He considered returning to Ani's hotel, realized that was a dumb idea and, besides, he was too old for her.

A pickup truck with running boards crept by, its passenger darting out to collect the protest signs that were scattered about and place them into the truck bed. When the area was clean, the truck disappeared.

Liam rubbed his arms and stood up, encouraging himself with, *I'll never know if I don't talk to her.*

He marched back to the hotel and through the revolving door. The Washington, D.C. clock said 2:37. He took fifteen steps toward the marble counter. He puts his hands on the counter.

"How can I help you?"

"Angeline Moreno's room, please."

"We don't release guest's room numbers." The clerk scowled at him. "Do you know what time it is?"

Liam turned around and pretty much ran out of the hotel, across the street to the now-deserted center of the circle. He spied a bare spot in the bushes. He waited until there were no vehicles, no possibility anyone would see him, then crawled into the bushes, curled up into fetal position, put his backpack under his head, and fell asleep.

A garbage truck dropped a steel dumpster with a clang. He opened his eyes. In the early light, he saw two men jump from the truck and run towards the fountain. He grabbed his pack and rolled deeper into the shrubbery. The men emptied the trash and recycling receptacles and were gone. He tried to go back to sleep, but all he could think about was Ani across the street. *Now is the time,* he thought. He grabbed his backpack and walked into the hotel lobby.

Two men in gray sport jackets were at the front desk, so he walked over to the hotel shop as if to check what time it opened—6:00 A.M.

"There's no Dr. Shaughnessy registered here," Liam heard one of the clerks say to the gray sports-jacketed guys.

"If he shows up call us." They handed photographs and cards to the desk clerk.

The clerk glanced at the photographs, and looked up. "He was here, in the very early morning."

He watched the men's reflection in the shop window. They were big guys with short hair. They both had enough of a belly that their jackets could not be buttoned. "He was here? But he's not registered?"

The clerk nodded. "He was looking for one of our guests."

"Who?"

The clerk blinked. "Sir. I am not— "

"—allowed to give out that information, yes I know." The gray suit guy scowled and he and his partner turned around.

Liam saw a shoulder holster with an odd geometric pattern tooled into the leather when the first guy turned. Guns? Looking for him?

He couldn't imagine who knew he was here. These guys didn't look any friendlier than the guerrillas in the rainforest—better dressed maybe, but no friendlier.

He hid behind a column, studying the shop displays until they were gone, then quickly left himself.

He walked a couple of laps around the Circle then called the only person he thought might help him.

46 ≡ MIKE

Mike grabbed his gasoline can, hopped off the overloaded Humvee and waved it on its way. Ryan waved back. Ryan was an okay guy, Mike decided. A little abrupt, but he apparently had a soft spot for the underprivileged. Mike poured the gas into his poor old jeep. He gave it his usual pat; it wasn't a Humvee but it got him where he needed to go.

He did a little quick weeding in his vegetable garden, harvested some overripe bok choy and few almost-ripe squash. He grabbed a few green onions, too. He loaded a bag with the vegetables, along with some crispy fresh ginger root and the last of his small bag of sweet rice. He contemplated the big bag of regular rice sitting in the corner by his dragon chair, but left it. They should have plenty.

After twenty minutes of running around and a bagful of tricks, he managed to capture his pig, which he put into the jeep along with a couple of the better-looking chickens. He used his jerry-rigged shower to wash up and put on clean clothes, then got the jeep going and headed toward Chi's village.

Chi must have heard his old jeep clunking up the hill, because she was waiting for him beside the small, flat open area they jokingly called the "car park."

Suddenly nervous, shy, embarrassed and proud all at once, Mike gave her an awkward hug. "Maybe you could help carry the chickens?"

She smiled at him, eyed the red tissue-wrapped package with raised eyebrows, and grabbed the chickens, tucking each one under an elbow against her ribs where they seemed content to ride without squawking. He felt a pang, looking at her. So much like her grandmother.

Mike untied the pig, picked up the package from his seat, and the canvas bag from the floor. Leading the pig, he and Chi walked into the tiny village. An Ly stood at her door, wiping her hands on the towel she'd tied around her waist as an apron. Mike grinned at her. "Where do you want this guy?" he asked, indicating the pig.

"Maybe Chi can put it in the pen with Thuy Qui's." Mike handed the rough palm-fiber rope to Chi, who managed to take it without dropping the chickens. He moved to the doorway and stood beside An Ly as Thuy Qui scattered grain for the chickens and Chi let them loose, then settled the pig behind the woven fence to the accompaniment of Thuy's chattering girls.

Mike handed the bag of vegetables to An Ly. "Not as nice as yours, but maybe they'll make a good soup." An Ly nodded.

Gathering his courage, Mike called, "Chi, please come inside."

An Ly smiled at the tissue package, and nodded her head. They moved into the privacy of An Ly's house, which had been her aunt's house. The aunt who had died so long ago, childless. Mike bit his lip. This was not a day for sad memories. He wanted to celebrate life and love today.

Chi stepped inside the doorway and he handed her the red package.

An Ly made a soft exclamation, but Chi said nothing, staring down at the tissue in her hands. Her eyes were wet when she glanced up at him. She held the tissue wrapped package as if it was an emperor's treasure.

Mike chuckled softly. "Are you going to open it?"

Chi laughed, and with a choked voice, said, "Yes. Yes I am." And she did so, gently undoing the bow and ribbon, pulling back the layers of delicate tissue to reveal the red silk inside. Chi gasped, then suddenly pulled the *khăn đóng* out and placed it on her head, and shook out the *áo dài*, layers of tissue paper cascading onto the floor. She held the embroidered gown against herself and posed as if she was a princess in the royal court.

Now An Ly's eyes filled with tears, also. "I was so afraid we could not have this for Chi." She smiled at Chi, at Mike. She sniffed and patted her nose with her apron.

"Oh!" said Chi. "May I put them on?"

Ignoring the fact that the *khăn đống* was already on her head, Mike smiled and nodded. Chi ran behind the bamboo screens that closed off the sleeping area.

An Ly said in a voice almost too soft to hear, "You are still my miracle man. You found me after so long looking. You kept the promise you made to my mother. You kept the promise you made to me. And you are taking care of Chi."

Mike decided the time would *never* be more right. He must simply do it. "Is it— would it— be right if we were married An Ly?" It all had just tumbled out of his mouth not at all how he had wanted to ask her.

She looked at him in awe. "You would do this?"

Behind the screen there was absolute stillness.

Mike could hardly speak, his throat ached so. "I always wished to ask you, but it seemed...the villagers did not trust me, and they made such faces when I was visiting you— I thought it could not ever happen. They still think I am a stranger, one of the enemy," he said, thinking of the man with the coffee trees who had shot at them, and then "surrendered."

She looked up at him, eyes wet.

"And your— the wiseman said— "

"*What* did he say," An Ly asked, "that mean old man?"

Mike was astonished. An Ly never spoke badly about anyone, let alone a village elder. "He said I could never marry you. I was just bad luck and I would bring more back luck upon you and the village."

"Agh!" Chi's voice came from behind the screen. "He was supposed to be such a *wise* man, teaching the Tao, teaching everyone manners and what was proper! Yet *he* was the father of Thuy Qui, did you know that? Not Thuy Qui's mother's husband! I would not listen to anything he said! I am glad he died and let us free!" She stomped out from behind the screen wall, looking quite fierce in her wedding finery.

An Ly's face was white with shock and wonder.

"You should be married!" Chi said.

After a moment of silence, "Shoes," Mike said. "I forgot shoes."

They all looked at Chi's dirty bare feet peeking out from under the *áo dài*.

The shoes turned out to be a non-problem which An Ly was so happy to solve she actually giggled as she brought out a pair of delicate silk slippers that had been wrapped and stored in her "treasure chest." She also presented Chi with a pretty pair of earrings and a necklace from the chest, so Chi was nicely decorated to greet her husband-to-be's family.

During the preparations, Chi would stop at Mike's side and say, "You should be married."

The third time she did this, An Ly rolled her eyes, and said, "Enough. What a way for a daughter to behave."

"A daughter that wants her father's name to be official," Chi said archly.

I suppose I should not be surprised that she figured that out, Mike thought.

"We will tell the Giang family our name is Johnson," An Ly said. Then she flushed deep red and turned to Mike. "If that is fine with you?"

"Of course it is," Mike said. "I haven't stopped smiling since I bought that *áo dài*. You can wear it too," he said, "and then it *will* be passed down from mother to daughter." Both An Ly and Chi smiled at this.

"Too bad there isn't time for you to go to Da Lat before the Giangs arrive," Chi said.

"Oh, you think we must go to Da Lat to be married," Mike asked. "Even in the United States, you can get married by just saying you are married."

"Of course you can," An Ly said. She smiled, but Mike could sense disappointment.

"We will go after the engagement party," he said. "We will find a chapel to get married in. Chi will want to pick out her dress for her own wedding party. And maybe a Western style wedding gown."

Chi made a face. "And maybe not. Why do I need to spend money on a dress I can only wear once?"

"Well, a party dress anyhow," Mike said. "The villagers are going to want a big party."

"Yes. I can wear that dress for visits to Da Lat, and maybe someday to America."

"Oh, now you are going to America?

"My father is an American citizen," Chi said, a sly smile on her face.

Mike had still not acknowledged directly that he was her father. He blinked, not quite sure what to say.

"I have the blood test to prove it."

"Chi," An Ly began, but Chi interrupted her.

"My father bought the *áo dài* as was proper, and he will be here for my engagement as is proper. And perhaps I will go to America and see where he grew up, some day, and that is proper too."

"Perhaps," Mike murmured.

The next two days passed in a haze for Mike.

The Giang family arrived, gifts were exchanged, an auspicious wedding date was set that made both families happy. Mike studied the Giang boy, and decided he would do. He was a second son, so did not have much of the family wealth to offer. He seemed to appreciate Chi's enthusiasm and when he was away from his parents, he was a little more forthcoming and friendly. Mike just had to trust that An Ly had chosen as well for their daughter.

More pigs were brought, and prepared and roasted, sweet rice was made. There was a big feast after the formal tea ceremony that Chi served quite beautifully. Fireworks went off. And Chi was engaged to Giang Văn Tý. Chi Johnson was engaged.

Mike and An Ly ran Thuy Qui's tiny store for a day while Qui and her husband and her girls went to Da Lat to do some shopping. Thuy Qui needed supplies for the store, so it took a full day to get the tiny taxi from Trinh village to pick them up and drive them down and around town and back.

Mike planned to ask the man to drive An Ly and himself to Da Lat for a day, so they could officially get married. It seemed like a nicer way to go than his open air jeep. He was trying to figure out how to tell Chi she wasn't invited while he sat on the porch, enjoying his cold beer. But she still needed to go and pick her gown—or gowns. It was a puzzle. Maybe he and An Ly would just have to do without privacy. It was more Vietnamese, anyway.

"We also need to decide what we are doing about where to live," Mike said. An Ly sat down beside him.

"We should go to your house. Chi should live here."

"I guess it's nice in a way they can't go to the Giangs to live. I like having her close." He turned to An Ly. "In fact, I was kind of thinking I'd close down my old house and build here, so we could be closer to Chi. Would you like to stay here?"

"It would be easier than trying to help Thuy Qui from your house," she said. "I want to make the store bigger, have more things. People will come here instead of going to Trinh village, or all the way to Da Lat."

"Mmm," Mike agreed. *I'm going to miss my stream. Not much else, though.* Especially when he had his family together here. He smiled. "Well, I'm going to take a look at the footings in back again. Maybe we can just add on."

"No new house?" An Ly asked with a small smile.

"Is that what you would like? A new house?" She grinned at him, not quite asking. "Well, then. I guess we could build on the other side of the store."

There was about 30 meters between Thuy Qui's house and the steep cliff of rock that climbed up beside the village. He was pacing out measurements when the Trinh taxi pulled into the car park down slope. Luggage and boxes were tied on to the roof. Mike watched as Zaara,

Stenko, Thuy Qui, her husband and their two giggling daughters climbed out of the tiny four-wheel-drive taxicab. They unloaded luggage and packages. Stenko paid the driver, who jumped back in and drove off while Mike was still standing there, "With his face hanging out," as his Aunt Josa used to say.

"You came back!" Mike shouted. Zaara waved.

"We were trying to figure out how to describe where the village is to a driver, when Thuy Qui showed up and insisted we ride with them." She smiled ruefully. "It was a little packed, but here we are." Thuy Qui's little girls laughed and ran around the yard front of the longhouses, chasing the few remaining chickens. "They certainly are energetic," Zaara said. "I wish they could go to school."

Mike jumped a bit at a buzzing sound. Zaara grunted as she bent over and pulled the satellite phone Ryan had left with her out of her backpack. It was rapidly flashing a red light.

"My turn," Stenko said, reaching for the phone.

Zaara gave it to him, then turned back to Mike. "Eleanor's been keeping the lab working around the clock," she said as Stenko stepped out of range of the others' voices. "They've kept us updated on each stage. Sequencing for viral fragments is next." She bit her lip and looked over at Stenko. "We're running out of tricks."

Mike invited everyone to a seat on the porch while Chi and Thuy arrived with cold drinks to choose from. Zaara took water. Everyone else took a beer. After distributing the drinks, the two young women retreated into the house. Mike listened to their high-pitched, animated discussion, catching the drift without really hearing the words.

"What are they so excited about?" Zaara asked.

"Chi's getting married, and we all pray for a baby eventually. Did you find out anything?"

Zaara sighed. "Most scientific experiments answer the question, 'What isn't it?' After, 'It isn't this' and, 'It isn't that,' over and over, sometimes we find, 'Maybe it's this.'"

Mike swung his leg nervously. "I remember Edison failed hundreds of times before he was able to invent the light bulb. He found a lot of things that didn't work, first."

"We've found out a lot of those things that it isn't," she said, nodding her head. "Not STDs. Not Agent Orange."

"Bummer. But there must have been fancier tests that couldn't be done out here in the jungle."

Stenko jumped in, "They spot checked my toxicology results and ran more esoteric tests for rare earths, radioactive compounds, the lot." He crammed the satphone back into Zaara's bag. "Another 'it isn't that.'"

"And it isn't childhood diseases, tropical diseases or xenobiotic diseases."

"What's xenobiotic?"

"Just a fancy word for non-human. Like from monkeys," Zaara said.

Mike groaned. This seemed to be going nowhere. "So, nothing?"

"We were out of tests. So if there was something causing it, which there must be somehow, it had to be something new."

"'Something new'? How did you know that?"

"At the beginning, we used a centrifuge to sort everything in the sample by size."

"Okay."

"We found big things the size of red blood cells—undoubtedly they actually were red blood cells."

Mike crossed his arms. "Okay."

"The details of each failure are important," Zaara said, glancing at Stenko as if for support. "So, there's lots of other stuff in blood."

"Yah, I get that!" At his raised voice, Chi and Thuy ventured outside to see what was going on.

"Well generally speaking we don't expect to find viruses, not in blood samples. And we didn't."

Mike couldn't help himself. He jumped off the porch, flung his arms wide and yelled. "I don't care! I don't care what you didn't find! What *did* you find?"

Stenko jumped between Mike and Zaara. "Nothing, Mike. Nothing and more nothing. Zaara's been wracking her brain for an answer. She's barely slept since we left. Don't yell at her, she's trying."

Mike picked up a big rock and tossed it across the yard. It landed with a thunk. The chickens clucked and ran under the farthest house. "I am sorry, Dr. Yessin, but I attacked the U.S. Embassy. I've been interrogated on two continents. I've been shot at. None of that matters—I'm a soldier."

Mike put his big arm around Chi. "Look at her, hasn't she grown to be a beautiful young lady? She's getting married. She's *not* a soldier. I just want her to have a healthy baby!"

The satphone buzzed again, red light flashing importantly.

Zaara picked it up and listened. Everyone stood silently, watching her.

The phone call went on and on. Mike hugged Chi and let her go. She grabbed her mother's hand and followed her into the house. Their house. Mike went up the stairs and stood on the porch, in the doorway, watching as the ladies began making dinner. He'd waited over forty years. He must try to be patient for awhile yet, but the world didn't seem to be waiting for answers. Chi was getting married soon.

Zaara talked for a long time, addressing Dr. Bhave, exchanging glances with Stenko, and saying things like "CDC" and "epidemiology" and "Eleanor will want to know."

When she finally finished, Mike asked, "Can Chi have a baby?"

"Maybe," Zaara said carefully. "Maybe."

Mike smiled. "Maybe is so much better than, 'It isn't this!'"

P+P BLOG POST

Pride and Prejudice (apologies to Jane) aka Lies, Damn Lies, and Statistics (apologies to whomever said it first)—A blog dedicated to odd stories about numbers

Daughters

Studies around the world show a preference for sons—a persistent desire for male children. This has been true over time from early Sumer to the twenty-first century. This preference shows up in many ways. Unwed mother carrying daughters are less likely to marry the daughter's father. Wed mother who deliver sons are less likely to get divorced. This is not something restricted to Tudor kings.

The real question is why? As we have seen with other topics, the correlation is clear, but the causation is not.

Suggested Causes

One suggestion is that fathers intuit their responsibility in raising boys, but feel left out and unnecessary with daughters. A daughter represents an additional mysterious, possibly dangerous, female presence.

The next suggestion is that boys represent family power, both earning power and fighting power. The idea is that a family with a son is stronger and more successful.

Another related suggestion is that in some societies girls are more difficult and expensive to raise, requiring fancy clothes, expensive matrimonial arrangements, extra care, and more protection.

Strangely, in spite of the universal nature of this effect, researchers tend to attribute it to local cultural conditions and practices. It seems odd that something observed so widely is ascribed to a plethora of varied local conditions.

Not mentioned

The one possibility that no one mentions is that fathers very much love their daughters, but just can't bear to watch them grow up in a world where women suffer injustice. Maybe men just can't stand to be witness to the disrespect, pain, and abuse their daughters are likely to receive.

That explains things, doesn't it? Or maybe not.

47 ≡ ANI

There was still enough sunshine left that afternoon that Ani thought of the shorts and top Connie had given her. She went up the elegant staircase of the Dolley M Inn to her room and changed clothes. She took a magazine and went down to sit beside the tiny swimming pool with its brilliant blue water. A sparkle of sunlight gleamed off the surface of the crystalline clear water. She could see clearly deep into the pool, could count the slits in the small round grate at the bottom. She leaned back in her chair. She could also smell the chemicals that made the water so pure and so different from the black tea-waters of the Nanay.

And her room was a marvel. A huge soft bed, just for her. She kept feeling like she was going to fall out. Even in her dorm room there were walls close by so she had the illusion of being in a snuggly hammock. This, this bed was as big as their whole sleeping room at home. And there was a second room, with a sofa, fireplace, and a nightly tray of fresh fruit on a low table.

She shook her head and smiled at the waiter who walked out to the pool area to see if she wanted anything. SONC was paying for her room, but she would have to pay for anything extra she ordered, and she hadn't the money to do it. Connie had warned her about that when she had checked out the website for the Dolley M Inn, with its strangely anachronistic slogan *A woman's touch in a man's world*.

At first, when Gregg had pulled up at the pink and white building, she had thought it was a mistake. It looked like someone's house. It was almost ugly to her eyes. But she had gone in and found everything lovely and clean and far beyond the fanciest she had imagined. Connie had glanced around, and said, "Swank," before she'd left with Gregg to find the friend's house they were staying at.

Ani had tried to convince them to join her in her SONC-funded room, but they'd declined, laughing. "Believe me when I tell you we will be more comfortable on Sonya's floor than we would here on your sofa bed. But thank you for asking," Connie had said. "Have fun!"

Ani turned the pages of her magazine, trying to decide if she was having fun.

That night, she stood in her darkened hotel room and stared out the window at all the lights and busy-ness of the capitol city of the United States. It was the complete opposite of her jungle nighttime view, but it had a beauty and energy of its own. The stoplights glowed green, amber and red. Neon gave the skyline a colorful glow. The fountain in Dupont Circle, below, was unlit, but she could imagine the rush of the water, just as it sounded when a little *rio* tumbled over a cascade at home.

Her hand turned the bracelet around and around on her wrist. Liam's bracelet, that Tomito had made.

A sudden wrenching wash of homesickness flooded over her, and tears sprang to her eyes.

Then she realized it wasn't her home and her brothers and parents that she was missing. Oh, she did miss them. But she missed Liam more. This quiet emptiness beside her was the absence of Liam.

With an abrupt motion, she turned and went into her bedroom, switching on the overhead light. She rummaged through her pile of papers until she found Liam's. It had the address and telephone number of the

College of the Rocky Mountains on it.

She bit her lip, wondering how to pay for the telephone call. Then she decided it could be charged to SONC; she was calling Liam to...to get information so she could feel better about her statistics.

She dialed for an outside line as the instructions said, then dialed the CRM number. It rang several times, then someone picked up. "College of the Rocky Mountains," the voice said.

"I'm looking for Dr. Liam Shaughnessy," she said.

"I'm sorry, but Dr. Shaughnessy is no longer part of our staff."

"What?"

"Dr. Shaughnessy resigned his position, and left the College."

"When? Where did he go?"

"I'm sorry, I don't have that information."

"Well who does? I need to find him."

"I suggest you speak to his department."

"Can you connect me with them?"

"I'm sorry, we are actually closed for the day. You need to call back during our regular business hours, from 9:00 A.M. until 5:30 P.M. Mountain Time, Monday through Friday, and ask for the Economics Department."

"Oh. Thank you." She hung up. She could call tomorrow, but that was exactly when she would be back in the hearing room. Besides, she wanted to talk to him tonight.

She thought a few moments then called information at the College's area code. After a recorded message about charges, she decided SONC could pay this also. "A number for Dr. Liam Shaughnessy, please."

"How is that spelled?"

I have no idea, she thought, then realized it must be on—yes, she lifted Liam's paper. She found his name, read the spelling to the operator, who gave her a prerecorded number. She dialed, poking at the numbers so erratically she lost her place and had to hang up and try again. Clutching the piece of paper with the number on it, she got up and walked into the living room. She walked around the sofa, pausing at the fireplace and the window.

Then she sat down on the sofa, picked up the telephone from the end table and dialed Liam's number again.

The phone was answered, and she began to speak, then realized it *was* Liam's voice, but on a recorded message.

"I'm not here right now. In fact, I may not be here ever again," she heard, then Liam's dry laughter. "So I can't exactly tell you to leave a message, because I don't know if I'll ever—" it beeped, and she almost hung up. But maybe he was there, maybe he was screening calls. Connie said people did that, just listened....

She said, hoping he could hear her, or that the machine was recording, "Hello, D—Liam. This is Angeline Moreno. I—" she *what*? Shouldn't have called? Had no idea what to say? "I was just thinking of you. I am sitting in my Washington hotel room feeling lonely and a little bit sorry for myself so far away from home, and— " She thought an instant, and realized what to say, "and I remembered how you were so far away from home when you were at my house, and how nice it was for us that you were there. And I wanted to say hello. So, I hope you are doing well, and perhaps I can talk to you later. Goodbye."

She hung up, feeling quite silly.

But once the idea of talking to him had planted itself in her head, she could not seem to let it go.

Where was he? How could she reach him?

Wasn't Ryan Kolnikoff a private investigator? Wasn't he in Washington, D.C.?

She got up, found a dusty telephone book in the desk, and looked through the Private Investigations listings, and found his number.

She picked up the desk phone, pictured herself trying to talk to the tough ex-soldier about being homesick and lonely, and hung up the phone.

She walked around the sofa again, then sat down on it.

She sat on her fancy sofa in front of her marble coffee table, with the phone in her lap, chiding herself for cowardice. It was just a phone call. Why was it so hard?

The idea had lodged in her mind. It was like a parrot once it had grasped a tough Brazil nut in its beak. Her mind wasn't letting go of the idea of talking to Liam. And she really did need reassurance about the statistics. She dialed Ryan's number.

48 ≡ ELEANOR

Not much refreshed by the break, Eleanor stepped from her limo in front of the Cannon House Office Building and waved the driver on.

She climbed up the stairs to the corner entrance of the building, sipping her second morning latte and literally keeping her head down. She just wasn't up to taking on reporters that morning. Once inside, she took the first staircase up again, hoping to skirt around and above the inevitable crowds in the rotunda.

Perhaps she was getting too old for this sort of thing—not the first time the idea had gone through her head recently, but the first time she had seriously considered it worthy of further thought.

She saw Ani Moreno enter the rotunda. Reporters surrounded the young woman. The rotunda acoustics transmitted their questions quite clearly to Eleanor's ears where she stood above. She watched Miss Moreno. The Peruvian girl was passionate, but dignified. Concerned and intelligent —though utterly wrong with her statistical conclusions.

Eleanor blamed the ultra-liberal school the young woman was attending. Didn't they teach basic statistics any more? Moreno should have known better than to interpret her data that way.

She thought, *This is the young woman my Jane could have been.* She would have been older now, but just as bright, energetic, determined. She smiled to herself. *Just as wrong-headed, no doubt, and we would have fought about it.*

She heard Miss Moreno tell the reporters, "The native peoples take all the risks, but receive little or no benefits."

"Miss Moreno," the Female Entertainment Network news reporter called, thrusting her microphone under the young woman's nose, "are you suggesting that there is something nefarious going on in these drug tests?"

Eleanor raised an eyebrow. *Nefarious? That's a big word for a FEM reporter.*

"I don't know," Moreno said. "All I know is that wherever there have been drug tests, there are low birthrates and reduced populations. I cannot help believing that one is causing the other."

"And that is where you are making a wrong assumption, Miss Moreno!" she called down to them. The acoustics of the rotunda were also such that they heard her perfectly. Moreno, the FEM reporter, and the others in the little cluster looked up.

She went on, "Many studies, scientifically rigorous studies, prove just the opposite. I am sorry to be so accusatory, child, but it makes me angry when people misuse data in this way."

"What do you mean?" Moreno called, tilting her head back to meet Eleanor's eyes.

Was it possible the child actually wanted to know? My Jane would have wanted to know. "Let me come down; we will discuss it," she heard herself say. She made her way quickly to the stairs and down onto the rotunda floor.

Once there she smiled at Moreno. "Correlation is a slippery creature. It predicts things. All sorts of odd things are correlated, hence predictable. For example there is a high correlation between cell phone towers and white cars. Did you know that? They are correlated. From the number of white cars, you can predict the number of cell phone towers."

She tried to keep it light, not angry. "But that correlation does not mean you can say anything about *causes*. Do cell phone towers cause white cars? No. Do white cars cause cell phone towers? No, again. In this case, we know there is a third element that causes of both cell phone towers and white cars. People with disposable income buy cell phones and white cars. Does that make sense?"

She looked at Ani, and tried to keep smiling. The girl's very earnestness made it impossible for her to stay angry that she hadn't been taught better. "The same with the data on drug tests and the decline in birth rates. There does seem to be a correlation, but that does not mean that one causes the other. I believe we will find a third element that is the cause, though right now, I can't imagine what that is."

She sighed, "I have been exploring this issue with a team in Vietnam. So far, they have not found anything. But I will tell you, Miss Moreno, that there have been very few clinical trials in these areas my team is looking at —and the birth rates are still low, the villages there are dying. That is the point I wish to make in the committee hearing today. The only point."

"So there is a drop in birth rates among indigenous peoples, even where there *haven't* been drug tests?" Moreno asked.

"That is what it looks like."

The FEM correspondent jumped in, "This is that Pied Piper thing again!" She was so excited she spit on the lens of the camera that had been filming her. She wiped her mouth, the camerawoman wiped the lens, and they repeated her statement. Eleanor waited calmly til they were ready for her answer.

"While I detest the name," she said, "I agree with the observation. The children are disappearing."

The FEM woman attempted to ask more questions, but Eleanor brushed by her. "I'm sorry, this will have to wait. I have no desire to anger the chairman by being late on top of the other mistakes I have made."

When she reached the hearing room, one of the young staffers opened the door for her, making her feel even older. The woman looked like so many freshly scrubbed, business-attired youngsters that seemed to fill every free space in Washington. This one had two piercings on her left eyebrow and several purple extensions in her hair. She recognized the young woman from first disastrous hearing. She murmured, "Thank you," and walked in.

Before she could take a seat, the committee filed in through a separate door and the room got quiet. The chairman immediately called on Eleanor, reminded her she was under oath, and asked her to explain her testimony.

"Mister Chairman, I owe you, this committee and your staff as well as the staff at Save Our Native Cultures, particularly Miss Moreno, a huge apology. I do have one point I wish to make before the committee, but before I present that information, I would like to address your concerns from yesterday."

The chairman made a wry face. "I would love for you to address my concerns, madam."

She nodded. "My daughter died some years ago as a result of contaminated blood she received in a transfusion. That was no one's fault. However, she had an opportunity to be included in the testing of a new drug thought to cure AIDS, and I refused to allow her to participate in using this experimental drug."

The staffer with the purple extensions gasped. "Oh, my God, that was *you* on the *News and Shoes* show!"

Then the staffer's eyes got enormous, she blushed dark pink and blurted, "OMG, I'm so sorry to interrupt, Your Honor! I'll just resign and go jump off the Key Bridge right now, sir."

There was muffled laughter, but the girl was so obviously embarrassed and apologetic that the Chairman apparently forgave her. He chuckled along with everyone else.

"That was me on the show," Eleanor said.

She let the room settle.

"However," she turned her gaze back to the Chairman, "to continue. The drug I turned down would have saved my daughter's life. Thus, since then my work has been to be certain others didn't make a similar mistake. I have focused on educating people about the benefits of drug testing—that a new drug, still in trials, can save lives, even though it hasn't been approved by the FDA yet."

The Chairman nodded. "All right, Dr. Powell, you are tugging on our heartstrings, but I don't quite see the connection between this and your testimony."

"Mr. Chairman, my overzealous staff is responsible for the content of my testimony, though I am entirely to blame for allowing it to leave my offices, much less appear here. I wish to make a formal statement of apology, and withdraw my entire testimony in favor of one simple statement—"

Her cell phone rang; the chime and thump of Scarlatti's sonata in D major seemed to blast out over the hearing room. "Oh, dear Lord, I forgot to turn it off again," she said, fumbling in her pocket and thinking, *Perhaps I AM too old to be doing this.*

"Well answer it, Madam!" the chairman said, rolling his eyes.

I could just turn it off, she thought, but, already nervous, she simply followed the chairman's instructions. Just as she said, "Hello?" she heard the chairman thump on the table.

"Please leave the room! We will have a ten minute recess."

She walked out of the hearing room as fast as her legs would go. God, what a mess she was making of things!

49 ≡ LIAM

"Liam?"

He pushed his backpack aside to open a place on the bench. "Ryan, you came."

"You look like hell. Yep. Worse than in the jungle."

Liam noticed some dried leaves still stuck to his jacket and brushed them off. When he looked up, the sun blinded him, so he moved his head until Ryan shaded his eyes. He felt his pockets for his sunglasses. Not finding them, he got up and searched his sleeping nest, and finally retrieved them from the bushes.

"Did you sleep out here?"

He didn't want to fib and he didn't want Ryan's sympathy either, so he tried a light answer. "We all slept on the ground in Iquitos. It seemed like a good idea at the time."

Ryan didn't laugh, which wasn't surprising since Liam barely smiled when he deliver his line.

The traffic had picked up since last night. Two circles of traffic flashed by with a loud hum occasionally interrupted by the noise of horns and brakes.

Ryan's half grin didn't tell him whether he was angry about being called at six in the morning.

Well, Liam didn't make a habit of asking for favors at any time of day. This was uncharted territory, but those two guys with guns left him no choice. "I think I'm in some kind of trouble."

Ryan nodded. "Okay. You've called the right guy."

Liam opened his backpack, shoved his sweatshirt in and found his last clean shirt—an Iquitos tee shirt he bought during his tourist day with Carlo. He changed shirts in the middle of the park.

Ryan nodded again. "I need some coffee. Then, we can talk."

Ryan picked up Liam's backpack and led the way across the traffic to one of three adjacent coffee shops. Ryan ordered a regular coffee and a scone. Liam got a double shot of espresso.

"Do you want something else?"

He pointed to a pecan roll and a slab of carrot cake. He couldn't remember the last time he'd eaten. His chest tightened when Ryan reached for his wallet, but he couldn't let him pay, not after waking him—and he still needed to ask him for help. He put his hand over Ryan's wallet and took out his credit card. Again, he unsuccessfully tried for a casual tone. "I invited you—my treat."

He relaxed when Ryan put his wallet away without an argument. They sat watching the dress-for-success crowd walking to work with briefcases in hand and phones attached to their ears. He tried to collect his thoughts.

He silently rehearsed—*I called you because I didn't know anyone else*. That sounded insulting. He considered—*Do you know where Ani is staying*? Even worse, since he knew she slept just on the other side of the circle, and that wasn't the problem anyway. He looked up at Ani's hotel hoping to see her in a window.

"Ryan—regular and espresso."

Liam jumped up to get the coffee. After a gulp of espresso and a big bite of sweet roll smothered in pecans and molasses icing, he was fortified. "I've read that after guys went to war together they formed a bond." His foot tapped rapidly against the chair. He heard the noise and pressed the foot firmly against the floor. After more coffee and cake, he tried again.

"I've been a loner most my life. Did we form a bond?"

Ryan sipped his coffee. "You are an odd duck. What's on your mind?"

He wanted to tell Ryan about the guys with the guns, but instead he said, "I just quit my job. After the jungle, I couldn't go back to the politics and bureaucracy."

He finished the pecan roll in several quick bites and waited.

Ryan leaned back in his chair and put his hands behind his head.

"Me too. I didn't actually quit. The bitch fired me, but I was going to quit pretty soon. Like you said: politics and bureaucracy."

Liam put his arms on the table and leaned forward.

Liam was puzzled. "I thought you ran your own business. The listing said: Kolnikoff Investigations."

"No difference. I still have clients and the clients come with baggage, especially good paying clients like Dr. Powell."

"What will you do?"

Ryan looked at the ceiling as if the answer was there. "I have a girlfriend. I think maybe it's time to settle down."

He almost said—*You'd just be bored.* But he didn't. He did not really know Ryan, after all—maybe he wouldn't be bored at all.

"I'm tired of killing people," Ryan offered.

"Well, I've been thinking about going back to Iquitos. I liked teaching the little ones. They're full of enthusiasm, not like college kids."

Ryan sounded incredulous. "Teaching? You want to go all the way back to Iquitos to teach?"

He felt defensive. "Really, I felt useful teaching in that little village."

Ryan smiled. "I don't know. When I watched you and that young lady —what's her name?"

"Ani…Angeline." He pronounced the name very carefully.

"Yes, Ani. When I saw you and Ani, I was sure there was something between you two. Did you see how she paid attention when you talked?"

"Not really."

Ryan ignored his response and resumed, "She was concerned for you."

He didn't know what to say.

"And you looked at her the same way, didn't you?"

"I don't know."

"I bet you do."

He took a deep breath. "Last night I went into her hotel twice, but I was afraid to ask for her at the desk the first time. I just turned around and walked out. I'm afraid. I need to be sure."

Ryan was firm, "I told you. I'm sure. You should go up there right now."

"I did but they would not give me any way to contact her. And then, while I was still there, two guys with guns were asking about me at the registration desk."

He described the two guys. Ryan listened calmly until he sketched the strange geometric patterns worked into the holster straps on a napkin. Ryan grabbed the drawing and drowned the soft paper in his water glass.

"Why didn't you say so sooner? You need to get out of here. That leather work is from Baghdad. Those guys could be bad news."

Baghdad? Every time I see this guy, there are guns and trouble. Maybe I shouldn't have called him.

Ryan pushed him out of the coffee shop, "Come back to my place, get a shower? I'll make some calls."

He wanted let Ryan know he wasn't staying long, "Thanks, I'd like a shower before I get on my return flight tonight."

"You sure didn't give yourself much time to find your princess, but given those guys following you, getting out of town might be a good idea."

He followed Ryan to the metro station, barely keeping up.

"Keep your eyes open. Let me know if you see them."

He put his backpack on and tightened the straps. He had to run to keep up with Ryan's pace down the stairs. Ryan had already bought tickets by the time he caught up, huffing and puffing. He had never been in a subway and expected it to be claustrophobic, but this station was huge and brightly lit.

"This is Dupont Circle. We're taking the red line to Chinatown."

He counted the stops to Chinatown—four stops. It took about ten minutes.

The doors opened. They got off just before they closed again. He looked around. "This looks just like Dupont Circle."

"Just keep a lookout for your buddies. Let's go—green line to Columbia Heights."

He raced after Ryan, terrified he'd get lost in this maze of stations and routes.

Ryan's office and home occupied a second story loft above a Chinese restaurant, a couple of blocks from the Metro. "I'm out of town a lot, so Mr. Chang and his family keep an eye on my place when I'm gone and I eat a lot of takeout when I'm here."

Liam looked into Ryan's office. The large wooden desk held two computers and a printer. Ryan's big chair sat behind the desk overlooking a great view of the metro station. The back corner held a table with a large format scanner next to another computer and printer. There was a row of four wooden file cabinets against one wall and a bookcase against the other. The bookcase had a few paperbacks and lots of pictures of an older woman holding various exotic-looking cats, some teenage children, and a few of Ryan in military gear with a bunch of other guys. Three chairs were scattered around the room.

"Come back this way to the living quarters."

The 'living quarters' contained a couple of recliners, a 72" plasma television, a cheap dinette set and a kitchenette. The only window here opened into an alley.

"The door on the left is my bedroom and the one on the right is the bathroom. You can go in there to take a shower. The towels in the laundry hamper are clean."

Liam hadn't planned this trip to include so much exercise. His Iquitos tee shirt was soaked from running through the Metro. "Can I borrow a clean shirt?"

"In the laundry hamper, under the towels."

He put on a blue dress shirt. It hung off his shoulders and down to his knees.

He dumped out the hamper, and tried on one shirt after another. He felt like Goldilocks, except they were all too big. Finally, he found a smaller pink tee shirt that said "Hot Babe." Great. He smelled it. Sure enough, it was clean. He put it on, covering it up with his CRM sweatshirt.

He packed the clean clothes back in the hamper and opened the door.

"Just got an interesting phone call."

"While I was in the shower?"

"Yes."

Ryan turned towards him and laughed. "What are you wearing? Did you find a clean shirt in the hamper?"

He lifted his sweatshirt and displayed his Hot Babe shirt. "It was the only one that fit."

Ryan nodded. "Don't worry. I don't expect she's coming back for it."

"The phone call?"

"Oh yes, it was Claudia. My lady friend. I should have checked in with her earlier. You know she has a cat rescue shelter in southern Maryland, Ann Arundel Country, beautiful place. Anyway she's friends with a lot of the senators. Have I told you about Claudia? An extraordinary person. Lost her husband in Vietnam.... General something. She and Eleanor—"

"Enough—the phone call?"

"A certain Angeline Moreno wants me to find you. Evidently, you no longer work at the college and no one knows where you are."

"Yeah?" Liam said. He could feel his pulse in his throat. He counted the beats, in synchrony with his rapid breathing.

Ryan looked away. "Yep. You could have saved me a lot of trouble if you had just called her hotel last night when you arrived."

Liam turned off the burner of Ryan's electric stove. The coil was still red hot, even though the eggs were done. He looked around, grabbed a towel to use as a potholder and pushed the pan off the coil. He found clean plates and slid the eggs onto them.

Out in the living area, he heard Ryan yelling at someone on the phone. Thinking, *let him take care of the bad guys*, he picked up the plates and walked through the archway into a roomful of guns.

Ryan faced the wall with a white zip tie binding his wrists. Two guys in gray jackets stood on either side of him, guns in hand. One guy rubbed his jaw and the other was straightening his jacket. His first thought was these guys must be good if they captured Ryan. *He's tough.*

One man pointed his gun at Liam. He didn't move.

"I'm Officer Jamalka. I want you to turn around and put your hands behind your head."

"Ryan, what's going on?"

"Shut up and turn around,"the other gray suit said. Liam looked around for a place to put the plates of eggs.

Ryan laughed softly. "Seriously guys, he's a college professor, a college professor. Handcuffs are *so* not needed."

Officer Jamalka ignored Ryan and stepped towards Liam. Liam turned around and put his hands behind him.

"We were just told to bring you in. No one warned us about your friend, but after that little scuffle we're taking you both in. Hands behind your head." He did so, and the officer patted him down. Liam could hear the other guy speaking into a radio. "Mall, Dupont Circle, report in."

After some chatter obscured by static, he said, "We apprehended the subject in Columbia Heights, after some resistance from his friend, here. We're bringing them in. Meet us at Cannon."

"**W**hat's going on?" He leaned against Ryan in the back seat of a black and white cruiser and whispered again, "What's going on?"

Ryan said, "I don't know."

"Who are these guys?"

"From their badges, they seem to be Capitol Police responsible for protecting Congress. They're taking us to the Cannon House Office

Building."

He guessed Ryan knew more. "And...?"

"Well, they're after you. What did you do?"

He shook his head. He had now been kidnapped twice in the last month. As he saw the Washington Monument and Capitol Mall come into view, he reflected how being held at gunpoint took his mind off concerns about a job or a girlfriend. The car with the seal of the United States on the side turned left at the mall and headed towards the Capitol.

He wracked his brain for some infraction that would interest the United States Congress. Prior to a month ago, he'd never been in any trouble. He always filed his taxes on time, probably paying too much. He never looked at porn on the internet. In fact, the only people he knew who ever got arrested were Ani, in San Francisco, and probably Ryan, if he ever got caught doing some of the stuff he did.

Liam frowned thinking that maybe this had to do with his mother. Who knew what that witch was messed up in?

They stopped in front of a two-story marble building with a broad staircase leading to a corner entrance.

Ryan poked him with his elbow. "We're here."

Officer Jamalka had another discussion with the static in his radio. He cut their zip ties and in a friendlier voice said, "Please follow me."

Liam looked back. Two more officers followed them.

Liam looked around the small waiting room. The only furniture consisted of three wooden benches, lined up like church pews. Liam and Ryan sat in the first one facing the door. Officer Jamalka locked the door. Liam could read "Room 108" through the frosted glass in the door.

Officer Jamalka started the conversation, "You are Ryan Kolnikoff?"

Ryan looked up smiling, "Dude, I know you know my name by now. You looked at my wallet, didn't you?"

Jamalka ignored this comment. "You're free to go. Ms. Moreno and Dr. Powell vouched for you. Sorry for any inconvenience."

Ryan didn't move. "I think I'll stay with my buddy here, if that's okay with you." He glanced at Liam. "I don't want to miss the end of the show. I certainly paid for a front row seat."

"Suit yourself. By the way, you're in pretty good shape. If you're looking, Capital Police are hiring."

Ryan shook his head. "I'm retired. Really retired."

Jamalka turned to Liam, "Dr. Shaughnessy, you've been summoned to answer questions about a paper you wrote which Ms. Moreno submitted with her testimony to this congressional hearing."

Liam collapsed thinking, *She just wanted someone to explain the math.* Once again he had the numbers, but missed everything else. He sighed, got to his feet, and walked towards the door. He noticed how slowly Ryan got up, then he saw that Jamalka and his buddy moving quickly to block his way.

Jamalka put his palm up, "Not so fast."

What is the problem now?

"We've been chasing you for hours, man, why did you run?"

Liam scowled, "Look, I was kidnapped in Peru, beat up, shot at and held captive for no reason at all. Why on earth would I stop and chat with two guys with guns?"

Officer Jamalka laughed. "Sorry man, we didn't know all that, but there is one more thing. You shouldn't testify before Congress in a sweatshirt and dirty jeans. Here's some more appropriate attire—fourteen-inch collar and size 30 jacket—okay?"

Liam took the offered package and tore open the brown paper.

"You have to return the shirt and jacket, but you can keep the Capitol Police insignia tie. It's our gift to you."

He also handed a tie to Ryan. "No hard feelings?"

Liam turned to Ryan. "I'm going to take off my sweatshirt now. If he says anything about my shirt, you kill him."

Ryan laughed. "You heard him."

Jamalka smiled but didn't say anything as Liam removed the pink tee shirt.

Once properly attired, they were led to a waiting room. Liam sat on a hard wooden chair and wondered if he would even have a chance to talk to Ani. It didn't look like it so far. If he was testifying with her, why wasn't she in this room with them? Where was she?

50 ≡ WASHINGTON, D.C.

Still breathless from the news she had just gotten, Eleanor's smile was savage as she returned to her podium in the hearing room. From besieged, she would become world savior.

"Mister Chairman," she began before everyone had finished settling in their chairs. She spoke loudly, projecting her clearest voice to be heard over the rustling of reporters, staffers, observers and the Representatives on the committee. "I apologize for the interruption, but the news I have received will answer everyone's questions about low birth rates."

"Is this *information* new testimony, Dr. Powell?"

"Yes, sir, it is."

"It had better not be designed to embarrass this committee *any further*, or to slander others who are testifying here, Dr. Powell, or I will charge you with contempt and throw you straight out of here, as I perhaps should have done twice over by now!"

"I appreciate your patience, Your Honor, as will the entire world."

"Now that is a bold statement." He sighed and leaned back in his seat, a disapproving expression radiating from his face. "You have five minutes."

Eleanor wondered how to explain her news and not sound like some crazy lady. "The evidence comes from three sources: First is the important paper by Dr. Shaughnessy on population statistics. I regret he can't be here, as I can barely do justice to his work. Second—"

The chairman interrupted her by waving a piece of pink paper, part of those three-part carbonless forms so popular in the twentieth century bureaucracy. Eager to return to the committee's good graces so they would be receptive to her story, she immediately shut up and waited.

The chairman continued, "The elusive Dr. Shaughnessy is here and ready to testify."

She couldn't believe her good luck. Maybe things were beginning to turn around for her and her cause. "That's good. I'd be happy to have him testify now."

In the gallery, observing the proceedings, Ani's head was spinning. Liam is here? She remembered that committee had requested to have him testify, but hadn't expected them to be able to locate him and get him here.

She felt guilty that her testimony had caused him to be dragged across the country. Surely he'd be disgusted to see that her family brought him another round of trouble. He's never going to want to see any Morenos ever again.

The chair announced, "Please escort Dr. Shaughnessy in."

Ani was even more surprised that he was accompanied by Ryan.

Her chest tightened looking at him. He looked like a lost boy. His head scanned back and forth, his mouth was open, his eyes blinking double time. She held her breath, feeling bad for the poor lost professor...until he spotted her, and positively grinned at her.

She smiled back, trying to radiate her feelings to him. Well. This might turn out OK. She felt a connection between them, a warmth.

"Dr. Shaughnessy, raise your right hand. Do you swear to tell the truth?"

Liam nodded.

"The committee wants to thank you for your excellent statistical work. Of course we don't understand all the details, but we do understand you were the first one to identify the dangerous drop in birth rates in American cities."

Liam didn't really listen. All he could think about was his discussion with Ryan in Dupont Circle. He replayed it in his head. *Did you see how she paid attention when you talked?*

Liam turned his head left to right facing each Representative in turn. He didn't really see any of them, but when he reached the right-most one, he paused and watched Ani out of the corner of his eye. Ryan was right! She's staring at me, with that crooked smile of hers.

"Dr. Shaughnessy?"

Liam recalled hearing something that sounded like thanks. He replied. "You're welcome. It's an honor to be here," leaving out *but I'd prefer different transportation next time.*

He spent the next fifteen, twenty minutes explaining big data, correlation, and his statistics, very happy to receive a better reception than at the tenure review meeting.

When Liam was done, the committee returned to Eleanor. *That was the longest I've seem a committee allow an academic to drone on and on about math or science.*

She took a deep breath and said, "The second source is from Angeline Moreno, who has already testified. I'd like to commend her for her excellent research which extends and corroborates Dr. Shaughnessy's. Her work reports the same effects in indigenous societies that he identified in leading information societies.

"Finally, the missing piece is from a mission I recently funded to Vietnam. That was the phone call I just received.

"The 'Pied Piper's Revenge' is quite real. In Vietnamese and Peruvian villages," she glanced at Ani Moreno and gave a single nod, "in major cities of the United States and Europe, in Africa, Asia—in every class and every race of people everywhere in the world, fecundity is declining." There was a rustling and murmuring, but that was not new. That was not *her news.*

"Your Honor, the decline in new births, the increase in miscarriages, and the aging of the overall population of the *entire world* is *not* a man-made problem. It is an attack from the only enemy capable of wiping out the human species. That enemy is the tiny, often deadly, life form known as the virus."

The audience rustled and murmured louder this time.

"Thanks to some fine work by two epidemiologists, Dr. Zaara Yessin from the Vietnam mission, and Dr. Shakhar Bhave from CDC, we now know that the virus outbreak began in Russian Georgia. As Ms. Moreno intuited, it appears likely that medical personnel associated with clinical trials exposed many indigenous groups to the virus.

"And if we are going to find a cure and prevent the extinction of the human race, we are going to have to have drug testing. For the sake of our species, sir, I beg you to recommend the United States NOT sign the United Nations resolution against drug testing. We are going to need every last person on the planet to help find the cure."

She stopped there to let that sink in.

Ryan and Liam and Ani and Connie and her boyfriend stopped in the middle of the Rotunda. Ryan stood close to the couple, so Liam had no choice but to stand next to Ani.

Ryan spoke up with a big smile, "You're all from out of town, do you want to come over to my place for a drink?"

Liam laughed. "I've seen his place. He's kidding." He glanced at Ani and she smiled at him. She reached out and took his hand.

Connie looked at Ani. "Ani has a great room—bigger than our apartment in San Francisco."

Ani held up her claim check from the cloak room. "Checked out already."

Just then Eleanor stepped close to the group. "Why don't you all come out to my place for a couple of days. I have lots of spare bedrooms. Of course," she smiled, "I'd expect you to earn your keep, exercising the horses or something."

She whispered to Ryan, "Claudia should be arriving there now, but I can't guarantee she'll stay. She's a pretty busy lady. I hear she's off to Camp David to advise the President on the possibility of a first cat or two."

Ryan blinked. He blurted out, "We're engaged!"

Instead of pyrotechnics, Eleanor just smiled.

Ani held Liam's hand tighter, "Am I just a dumb *rivereño* girl? Why is everyone so happy about a virus that is going to kill us all?"

Eleanor gasped and looked embarrassed. "Oh I forgot to tell them! This story has some good news. This virus seems to endow infected individuals with a more proficient immune system that protects them from other viruses, extending their life expectancy. We will live long healthy lives, which should give us more time to find a cure for this thing."

Ani released her held breath with a gasp and hugged Liam, hiding her tears against his chest. Here she was crying on him, again. But this time, with hope.

51 ≡ MIKE

Mike had such a big smile that he hadn't been able to say a word since they left the chapel. All his good things had happened at once. An Ly smiled at him and secretly held his hand under the table.

Zaara and Stenko entertained Thuy Qui's girls while Chi and Thuy organized the food.

Stenko and Zaara seemed pretty happy together. He loved his crazy happy family.

Waiters began to bring food. The table filled with a rainbow selection of small bowls.

"Okay," Zaara said. "I need someone to tell me what some of these are. I recognize the soup. What's this?" The younger of Thuy Qui's two girls giggled and explained in Vietnamese, and then tried to name the dishes in English, with a little help from Chi. They had egg rolls fried and not-fried, rolls wrapped in greens, steamed white and brown rice and an assortment of sauces and little pancakes with spicy filling, and of course Chi's favorite, *bánh xéo*. And the waiters were making another trip. It was, after all, a wedding feast, *and* a celebration of the discovery of the cause of the low birth rate.

Mike's smile faltered a bit. They were pretty sure they'd identified the

391

cause, but there was no cure in sight. Zaara had identified it. Not fancy Dr. Roseman with his fancy lab gear.

"You could be scientists, too," Zaara's voice carried. Mike looked their way. Thuy's daughters were sitting still, eyes wide. Not even a giggle escaped their lips.

"Scientist?" the younger one said. "Tell us the story how you find the virus again!"

Zaara laughed. "I was just eating dinner." She indicated their meal. "Not quite as nice as this, but there was lots of food. I lost count of what I had eaten, because my head was figuring things out. Not toxins; it's world-wide. The only thing we have world-wide is people. And the low birth rate in people. So it had to be an immune system thing, probably a virus." She waved her chopsticks, noticing the girls were still sitting like little statues. "Eat! Anyhow, it just took my brain awhile to sort it out. That's how scientists work, while they do stuff, any stuff—like eating dinner—their brains work. So my mind figured out that's what all those phone calls added up to. "

Chi laughed. "A keep-you-healthy virus."

Zaara nodded. "Thanks to this virus, you young ladies are going to live a long time." She leaned back and smiled at Chi. "And we will figure out how to side-step its effects on pregnancy. I know that's going to be Eleanor's top priority."

Mike's smile faded away. *Ellie*. He was going to have to leave his family soon and do her speaking engagements, as promised.

Zaara glanced his way. "They'll sort it out, Mike. You can count on it."

He nodded. "I believe Ellie can get just about anything done. But I was thinking how much I owe her. I gotta leave all this and go pay my dues."

Stenko's raspy voice carried from his end of the table. "Maybe you can make it a kind of honeymoon trip. I think Dr. Powell wouldn't mind at this point. You're a hero."

Mike felt An Ly stir beside him, sitting up straight and tilting her head to hear. Mike had never been sure how much English An Ly had picked up over the years, but she certainly seemed to understand "honeymoon trip."

Could he take her with him?

Chi jumped up. "And me too! I can go pick out my American wedding gown *in America!*"

"Oh, now she wants an American wedding gown," Mike said, laughing. Thuy Qui was nodding her head, and everyone was grinning.

"From America!" Chi insisted.

"Groovy," Mike said.

CODA

Pride and Prejudice (apologies to Jane) aka Lies, Damn Lies, and Statistics (apologies to whomever said it first)—A blog dedicated to odd stories about numbers

A departure from our usual

The prestigious Annals of Viral Genetics published an interesting paper this week in their online version. First, it was interesting because of the authors. These scholarly journals often list dozens of authors, usually the graduate students who did the work and a long list of MDs and PhDs to share in the glory. In addition to the usual, this article lists a Vietnam veteran, another veteran (both are retired Army Special Forces), and an anthropology student from Nanay Libre, Peru. If I understand the article—I didn't actually read it, but I saw a couple of reviews—it provides some insight into several statistical dilemmas previously discussed here.

AIPS

Evidently, something they're calling Acquired Immunoproficiency Syndrome (AIPS) has been lowering birthrates for decades. Scientists at WHO and CDC, who collaborated with the above-mentioned authors, confirmed this. The paper's acknowledgments went on for paragraphs. This is a global pandemic that has gone unnoticed for decades, silently causing miscarriages and infant deaths.

AIPS is caused by a lentivirus—Latin science-speak for slow virus, and the scientists' excuse for being slow themselves—which they inventively called Human Immunoproficiency Virus (HIpV).

HIpV infects B-cells.

This is where the fun begins. You have millions of different B-cells each waiting for a virus that matches its particular capabilities. It's like having millions of police officers each waiting for a criminal to appear with the DNA fingerprint they were issued when they joined the force. Most of them do nothing, because their target criminal/disease never attacks, or maybe doesn't even exist.

If their target shows up, they arm themselves to catch the criminal and post clones on every street corner prepared for the possible return of the fiend.

This is how vaccines work. They wake up one of these B-cells and then the clones are armed and dangerous when the disease shows up. Pretty cool?

Large numbers of cops hang out eating donuts, just in case, while a few active duty defenders patrol to attack known criminals.

Back to HIpV: I'm sure this is an over-simplification, but here goes: HIpV convinces the B-cells (donut eating reservists) that its target is around and the B-cell gets ready to attack. The result is lots more active cops.

One reviewer characterized HIpV as a "universal vaccine." For most people, their HIpV infection works just like that and they experience fewer diseases and, in fact, live longer, healthier lives. Fewer donut eaters, more active cops, longer, healthier lives, right?

Unfortunately, in many cases when a pregnant mother transfers her antibodies, *lots, lots more than usual*, to protect the fetus, *some* of these armed guards get confused and attack the fetus, resulting in miscarriage or infant mortality.

So good news and bad news: Longer healthier lives, smaller population.

That explains things, doesn't it? Or maybe not.

AFTERWORD: SCIENCE BEHIND THE FICTION

In this novel, we suppose Acquired Immunoproficiency Syndrome (AIPS) lowers fecundity and increases fetal mortality, while extending general life expectancy. Here is the imagined disease agent behind AIPS and its mechanism of action.

The authors are saying, "What if AIPS existed and was caused by a lentivirus called Human Immunoproficiency Virus (HIpV)." HIpV targets B-cells. Once inside, HIpV hijacks the B-cell by signaling antigen presence. The B-cell responds with the creation of antibodies and memory cells. During the replication of antibodies, the B-cell unknowingly replicates many mutated versions of HIpV and releases them into the lymphatic and circulatory systems. The mutated HIpV agents infect virgin B-cells, activated B-cells and memory B-cells. In all cases, HIpV imitates the internal signaling for antigen presence and reproduces along with antibody production.

The key is that HIpV is mostly conserved. Only the part that simulates the antigen mutates. Thus HIpV would stimulate the production of many different antibodies.

In the case of virgin B-cells, as with the presence of an actual antigen, both activated and memory B-cells are generated. When they are subsequently infected, secondary immune responses are generated.

This is an immune response without the presence of the target pathogen, a naturally occurring vaccine. Is such a process plausible? Well, consider rabies with its 100% mortality. Rabies antibodies should only be present in corpses (that's what 100% mortality means). However, the Texas wild child case found rabies antibodies in a living person, and there are several other similar cases (Google it). Could the antibodies have been created by a random process similar to the one described here? Maybe. Why not?

On the negative side, what might have caused the sudden death of Mai Linh's baby in chapter 5. Without getting too technical here, α_1-antitrypsin (A1AT) is required for effective lung function. For example, A1AT deficiency contributes to emphysema. There are over 100 variants of A1AT, so Mai Linh might have transferred antibodies against the paternal variant of A1AT to her baby, who subsequently died of pulmonary failure due to acute A1AT deficiency.

From the point-of-view of the host, HIpV is a something like a universal vaccine. HIpV induces the immune responses for antigens the host has never experienced. Since HIpV sets the record for uncontrolled mutations, as AIPS progresses, antibody diversity increases at the rate of a trillion new antibodies per year.

The circulating antibodies are dormant unless by some lucky (unlucky) chance the host is exposed to an actual pathogen. In this case, the host immediately mounts a strong, secondary response. For example, when a new strain of flu appears, some fraction of the HIpV-positive population is already immune. In this way HIpV is beneficial to the host.

HIpV theoretically employs a strategy of rampant mutation that arms infected individuals with a dynamic defense system, reversing the balance of power against most other viruses such as flu and HIV, which incidentally has a similar mutating mechanisms to gain their own biological advantage.

On the other hand, this increased diversity is unfortunately reflected in the immunoglobulin G (IgG) antibodies. These antibodies can pass from the mother to the fetus through the placenta (by transcytosis). These antibodies usually confer a baseline immunity from the mother, but in the case of AIPS, we suppose some of the trillions of different IgG antibodies target the fetus cells and cause a spontaneous abortion or miscarriage through secondary effects of an overactive, indiscriminate immune system.

Of course AIPS only exists in this fantasy world between science and fiction.

However, we respectfully remind the skeptics, that every parasite from a lowly virus to the exalted homo sapiens sapiens views its relationship with its host as symbiotic, an eternal plague of equals. Every parasite faces the paradox of its existence: too much success kills the host *and* the parasite. For billions of years, Nature has found new ways for successful parasites to cleverly tread this line between life and death...or die trying. After all this time, nothing should be surprising or considered impossible.

ACKNOWLEDGMENTS

Gratitude to Eugeni Vaisberg and Cindy Hazuka, two real scientists, for allowing me (D.R.) to visit their world of cell biology and drug discovery. If any of the biology contained herein makes sense, they deserve the credit, while the fabrications and inaccuracies belong to the authors alone.

Heartfelt gratitude to our early readers: Dani, Jennie, Lenny, and Samantha.

The first draft of this novel was written for National Novel Writing Month.

ABOUT THE AUTHORS

They live in Southern California, where they enjoy their cats and international travel.